William E. Norris

Billy Bellew

A novel

William E. Norris

Billy Bellew
A novel

ISBN/EAN: 9783337393816

Printed in Europe, USA, Canada, Australia, Japan

Cover: Foto ©Andreas Hilbeck / pixelio.de

More available books at **www.hansebooks.com**

BILLY BELLEW

A NOVEL

BY

W. E. NORRIS

AUTHOR OF 'THE ROGUE,' 'SAINT ANN'S,' ETC.

A NEW EDITION

LONDON
CHATTO & WINDUS
1899

CONTENTS

CONTENTS

BILLY BELLEW

CHAPTER I.

FOREIGN SERVICE.

ONE bitter January afternoon Billy Bellew, striding along at his accustomed high rate of speed through the fog and darkness of St. James's Street, reached the door of his club, which he had no sooner flung open than he was greeted by a little knot of friends, who had encountered one another a few minutes previously in the hall of that establishment.

'Hullo, Billy,' called out one of them, 'frozen out, like the rest of us, eh?'

'Rather!' answered the young man addressed, unbuttoning his fur-lined coat and rubbing his hands as he approached the group. 'I've been rapping that beastly old barometer for four days; but he said he didn't mean going down yet awhile, so I thought I had better come up. Do the theatres and give one's horses a rest, you know. After all, we've had a pretty good time of it, so far. I always think one gets the best of the hunting before Christmas.'

'Well, that's a cheerful view to take of the subject,' remarked the first speaker; 'but I can't say I agree with you. Personally, I don't care about riding over a blind country, and I'm a bit too old now to appreciate the pleasure of getting up in the dark. I haven't had a dozen days with the hounds yet, and Lord knows whether I shall get a dozen before I have to send my horses up to Tattersall's. It don't look like it at present.'

'Oh, you'll be all right,' returned Billy confidently; 'don't you worry yourself. A week of frost, or even a fortnight, isn't such a bad thing, when it comes at the right time.'

'I like your easy-going way of calling January the right time,' ejaculated a melancholy-looking little man, whose hands were thrust deep into the pockets of his overcoat, and whose hat was rammed down over his eyes. 'It may be right enough for you lazy beggars; but I'll be hanged if it's right for a poor devil of an M.P. I've got to begin work early next month, or my constituents will want to know the reason why. And it isn't going to freeze for a week or a fortnight; it's going to freeze for six weeks straight on end: it always does. I'll tell you what it is: I'm a devilish patient fellow, and I can stand a lot; but really and truly this isn't good enough. I shall get influenza and be ordered off to the Riviera—that's what I shall do.'

'Oh, I wouldn't do *that!*' said Billy, in a tone of

shocked remonstrance. 'Of course it must be an abominable nuisance for you to have to sit and listen, day after day, to a lot of jabbering duffers, and I can't think why you go in for that sort of thing. But I suppose you have your reasons; and, after all, you ought to be able to manage a run down into the country once a week. It isn't much; still, it's better than nothing. Better than kicking your heels at Nice or Cannes, or some such beastly hole, anyhow.'

The disconsolate legislator shook his head and refused to be comforted. He said he might as well give up hunting at once, and he believed he would give it up. He added that, if there was one character more obnoxious to him than another, it was that of the prosperous, unsympathetic brute who insisted upon making the best of his neighbours' misfortunes. Finally he dug Billy viciously in the ribs with his umbrella and wandered off towards the smoking-room, whither he was presently followed by the other malcontents, each of whom had his own particular tale of woe to narrate before departing.

The prosperous and unsympathetic brute did not accompany them; he found, on glancing at the clock, that there would hardly be time. He made a sort of conditional promise to dine in company with two of them and 'go on somewhere afterwards,' but he was careful to impress upon them that they mustn't wait for him, because he couldn't be quite sure yet what his engagements might be:

whereat they exchanged meaning smiles. So he marched off into the darkness again, a tall, well-knit figure ; and as the feeble glimmer of the gas-lamps fell upon him, the passers-by were privileged to behold for an instant a face which in point of beauty could, perhaps, hardly have been matched in London or out of it. For Billy Bellew, with his black hair, his violet eyes and his perfectly moulded features, might almost have posed as a model for a somewhat robust Apollo. He was clean-shaven, after the modern fashion, but his mouth was so well shaped and his upper-lip was so short that the modern fashion was by no means as unbecoming to him as it is to most men of his complexion.

'Poor old Billy!' remarked one of the friends whom he left behind him ; 'it's easy to guess what has brought *him* up to London, and why he looks so confoundedly hilarious over it.'

'He always looks hilarious,' said the other; 'it's his little way—just as it's your little way to look sulky. Splendid digestion, I suppose. It's simply inconceivable that he can have remained in love all this time with that yellow-haired, underbred woman, who is ten years older than he is, if she's a day.'

Most of us believe in quite a large number of inconceivable things, such as eternity and unlimited space, so that we ought to find no difficulty what-soever in grasping the idea that a well-to-do, well-connected and strikingly handsome young man

may fall in love and remain in love with an underbred woman who dyes her hair and is his senior
by a decade or thereabouts. As a matter of fact,
poor Billy had fallen in love with a lady answering
to that description ; and if he had not remained
in love with her for two years, he honestly thought
that he had. He would, indeed, have been terribly
ashamed of himself had he admitted a doubt upon
the subject into his mind ; although, seeing that
the lady in question was a married lady, it may
be deemed by some that his constancy was no
legitimate matter for pride. But, then, the amazing
innocence of Billy Bellew would doubtless be a
more difficult conception to some people than
eternity or infinite space.

He walked for a short distance along Piccadilly,
and then hailed a passing hansom, which took him
to a house in Lowndes Street, where he ascertained,
on inquiry, that Mrs. Littlewood was at home.
Presently he was ushered into one of those drawing-
rooms, encumbered by screens and drapery and
flowering plants and little tables adorned with old
silver knick-knacks, which would be really pretty if
they had not of late years acquired a certain
vulgarity of association ; and he was greeted, on
his entrance, by a lady who would also have been
really pretty, if late years had not produced the
effect upon her which years inevitably produce and
which art is powerless to conceal. Mrs. Littlewood's hair had once been golden ; but it had
never been (because nobody's ever is) of the colour

which it now claimed as its own, nor had she
always exhibited to the disrespectful wonder of the
world her present impossible complexion. However, her china-blue eyes and her girlish figure
remained to her: besides which, she dressed ad-
mirably and had very small hands and feet. She
started up from her low chair by the fireside,
exclaiming :

'So here you are at last! I began to think that
your telegram was a humbug, and that you had
gone in for skating, now that the hunting is
stopped.'

'Am I late ?' asked the young man, consulting
his watch and the clock on the mantelpiece. 'I'm
awfully sorry if I am ; but I just looked in at the
club for a minute or two, and those fellows kept
me, jawing away about the weather and one thing
and another. Well, and how have you been getting
on all this long time ?'

He dropped into a chair and rubbed his hands,
gazing smilingly at his opposite neighbour, who
responded by a shrug of her shoulders and a
grimace.

'I have been getting on so badly,' she answered,
'that the doctor tells me I must be getting off. I
suppose, as you have never made a single allusion
to it in your letters, you paid no attention to what I
told you about my having had a horrid cold, which
has settled on my chest ; but the truth is that I
have been wretchedly seedy, and we are going to
spend the rest of the winter in Algiers. I am

thankful to say that we have let the house; so it is possible for us to obey the doctor's orders.'

Mr. Bellew endeavoured to say what was kind and sympathetic: it was not his fault if experience had taught him how little cause there was for alarm in Mrs. Littlewood's transient ailments. But he rather clumsily forgot to express the dismay which he ought to have felt at the news of her impending departure from England.

'Oh, *you* don't care!' she returned pettishly; 'it will be all the same to you if I leave my bones in that outlandish place. As far as that goes, *I* shan't much care either—there are many worse things than death. What I do dread is the prospect of four or five months' *téte-à-téte* life with Alfred. You know what my life with him is!'

'Oh yes,' murmured Billy, shaking his head sorrowfully.

Not that he did know; but he knew what she had told him, and he also knew that Colonel Littlewood was a singularly despicable person. After a pause, she resumed:

'I think you might come out, too, Billy. You can't say that I am ever selfish with you, and I haven't attempted to drag you away from your beloved hunting since it began; but now that the frost has set in, it wouldn't be such a very great sacrifice to you to come abroad with us, and it would make all the difference to me. You could take up your quarters in a hotel near us, you know; I won't even suggest that you should share our villa, because I am well aware of the tremendous importance that you attach to gossip.'

Billy tried hard not to look aghast, and failed signally. Not such a very great sacrifice to leave England in the middle of the hunting season, and dawdle through interminable weeks of enforced idleness upon the shores of North Africa? Good Lord! But he only thought this, he did not say it; for in his own way he was something of a hero; and that wretched little woman knew full well how much heroism was implied in his cheerful rejoinder of:

'All right: I'll manage it. Only I shall want a little time to make arrangements and get rid of the horses and all that, you see. I'll follow you out in a week or so. You're off at once, I suppose?'

Mrs. Littlewood's nature was too essentially feminine to be magnanimous, and she had had too lengthy an experience of the slippery ways of men to run unnecessary risks. She said:

'We don't start until next Monday. You can easily make all the arrangements that you want to make before then, and I do hope you will travel with us. Alfred never thinks of anybody but himself, and doesn't even know how to take care of himself when he is removed from his ordinary surroundings. I really don't feel strong enough just now to look after him.'

She was, however, strong enough, it appeared, to go to the theatre that night, and she had taken a ticket for Billy, whom she expected to escort her.

He therefore gave up all idea of dining at the club, and, having signified his willingness to accompany the travellers on the following Monday, went away to change his clothes. As he was leaving the house, he encountered a dapper little red-faced personage, with small, twinkling eyes and a grayish moustache, who said:

'Hullo, old man! Been arranging matters with the wife? Devil of a nuisance, this fancy of hers for going abroad, ain't it? But you're going to join the party, I hope? You are, are you? That's all right! And we shall see you at dinner, shall we? That's all right!'

From the very beginning of the business—which now seemed such a long, long time ago—Colonel Littlewood had thought, or had affected to think, that it was all right. He was perhaps a bad husband; he certainly was not an affectionate one; he was a confirmed tippler; he had on various occasions borrowed money from his wife's friend, whom he invariably treated as a personal friend of his own and welcomed to his house at all times and seasons. He had persistently ignored rumours which could scarcely have failed to reach his ears. It was difficult to speak civilly to the man, and impossible to help despising him; yet it did not seem quite so certain as it ought to have seemed that some of those who despised him were less contemptible than he.

This was the unwelcome reflection which thrust itself upon Billy Bellew as he strode, with bent

head, along the filthy, slippery London pavement.
It was true that he had done Colonel Littlewood no
injury of which the law can take cognisance ; but
he had unquestionably done Mrs. Littlewood the
injury of compromising her, and he had also
(though that was a minor consideration) done a
good deal of injury to himself. He had, in short,
behaved like a fool. There was no blinking the
matter ; and, as he no longer attempted to blink it
in his self-communings, it will be perceived that he
was no longer in love. Nevertheless, he had once
been in love with the woman who had first flirted
with him, then made him her confidant, and had
finally given him to understand that, had it been
possible for her to begin her life over again, she
would have chosen him out of all the world as her
husband. As he was still fond of her, he still
believed in her, and he still pitied her from the
bottom of his heart. Only he sometimes wished
that she could bring herself to face the necessity of
submission to hard facts ; he sometimes wished
that she were a little less reckless and indifferent
to public opinion ; and sometimes (but that was an
idea upon which he hastened to turn his back) he
half suspected her of being a trifle selfish. For the
rest, any man who had dared to breathe a word
against Mrs. Littlewood's fair fame in the presence
of Billy Bellew would have been a sadly battered
and disfigured man within a few minutes after the
utterance of his shameful calumny.

Unfortunately, one cannot blacken the eyes of

ladies or knock their teeth down their throats; so
calumnies had been uttered, and it had been impossible to take any notice of them. And now he
was going to Algiers with the Littlewoods; and
everybody would hear of it; and he would have to
sell his horses in a hurry; and he didn't know
what on earth to do with himself out there; and
he wished he had never been born!

The above irritated soliloquy might naturally
enough be taken as portending that the end of a
foolish entanglement was in sight; but anyone
who had been aware of that soliloquy and had
arrived at that natural conclusion would have been
imperfectly acquainted with the character of Billy
Bellew. Such, indeed, was Billy's own case; for
he had never thought his character worthy of close
inspection, and had never supposed that he differed
in any essential particular from the rest of the
world. He did differ from the great majority in
one particular, namely, that he was absolutely un-
selfish. There are a few people like that, but only
a few, and most of them are old maids. Everything pointed to the probability that Billy would
remain an old bachelor; because he would have
submitted to any personal inconvenience rather
than cause Blanche Littlewood one moment of
additional distress, and it was certain that Blanche
Littlewood would have been infinitely distressed by
the loss of his allegiance.

So it came to pass that, in the early morning of
one of those divine winter days which our Northern

summer can only at rare intervals contrive to rival, three passengers from Marseilles disembarked upon the modern quay beneath the white and glittering old city of pirates. Two of them had been sea-sick and were cross; the third, upon whom had devolved all previous trouble and responsibility during their joint journey, was in his accustomed condition of equanimity, and was able to derive such enjoyment from the novelty of the scene as an uneducated sense of form and colour brought within the range of his capacities. He dispersed the vociferous Arabs; he obtained possession of the luggage, after a delay of which Mrs. Littlewood complained querulously; he chartered a conveyance, and, as a matter of course, he drove up to the suburb of Mustapha Supérieur with his companions to see them comfortably established in their villa before securing a resting-place for himself.

'This is very jolly—awfully pretty, and unlike anything one has ever seen before, and—and that sort of thing, you know,' was the comment upon the scenery which suggested itself to him while the little horses toiled up the dusty road towards that quarter which wealthy and invalid Anglo-Saxons have marked for their own.

Colonel Littlewood said rather snappishly, 'Oh, I dare say it's all right;' and Mrs. Littlewood remarked that paradise itself would hardly be worth gaining at the cost of so horrible a voyage. She added that she was quite sure the servants, who had been despatched by a previous steamer, would not have taken the trouble to put anything straight.

This gloomy foreboding was, unhappily, verified. The villa which Colonel Littlewood had taken, in obedience to his wife's behests, was a very charming house, built in the pseudo-Moorish style by an enlightened architect, surrounded by a prettily laid-out garden and commanding a view of the bay and the snowy Djurdjura Mountains beyond, which in itself justified the high rent demanded by the proprietor ; but breakfast was not ready, and the baths had not been unpacked, and Mr. Bellew had to perform many menial offices before he was released, without a word of thanks.

' Upon my word, Blanche, you do make that poor devil work like a slave !' exclaimed the Colonel, with a touch of compunction, after Billy had departed for the Hôtel d'Orient.

' Oh, he likes it, and it's good for him,' returned Mrs. Littlewood lightly.

It may have been good for him ; but it was an exaggeration to affirm that he liked it. However, as has already been intimated, he was one of the most good-natured of men, and he was irresistibly impelled by his temperament to make the best of things, even when things did not look particularly bright. Youth and redundant health are scarcely compatible with melancholy. It had been a trial to give up the hunting ; but that trial was now over and done with ; and the blue sky, and the white houses, and the sunny slopes, and the palm-trees,

and the feathery bamboos, were pleasant to the
eye.

'I expect one will manage to pull through somehow,' said Billy to himself in cheerful accents when
he reached the suburban hostelry where a couple of
rooms had been engaged for him by telegraph.

CHAPTER II.

WINIFRED FORBES.

THE town of Algiers faces east, and the wooded
slopes which trend upwards around and above it
are thickly sprinkled with whitewashed villas,
looking for the most part towards the same quarter
or a point or two northwards thereof. In old days
the inhabitants of the town naturally wished to
keep their country houses as cool as possible, and
the winter visitors who have supplanted them must
needs make the best of narrow windows and an in-
sufficient supply of sunshine. The winter visitors,
however, are gradually straggling further and
further away from the district known as Mustapha
Supérieur; so that some of them have already
overtopped the ridge which used to be considered
its utmost limit, and, turning their backs upon the
town and the bay, gaze due south across the wide
Metidja Plain. If they thus deprive themselves of
a charming and varied prospect, they acquire what
is perhaps of more practical importance to them,

the privilege of basking in the sun's rays until the
Angelus-bell rings and the brief twilight gives place
to darkness.   Not that the view of the Metidja and
the Atlas Mountains is wanting in space or beauty
of outline or exquisite soft gradations of tint.   It
lacks the Mediterranean ; but if the Mediterranean
were not within reach, it would satisfy most
people.

It amply satisfied the soul of Miss Winifred
Forbes, who sat in the little arbour at the end of
the garden one morning, looking out upon a scene
with which she was becoming familiarized by
degrees, but which it seemed to her impossible that
she could ever learn to accept as an everyday background to existence, like the view from the library
windows at home in Shropshire.   From a point
almost directly beneath her feet the hillside fell
away in abrupt declivities of uncultivated ground,
where the palmetto and the asphodel grew and
flourished amongst the rocks ; immediately opposite
were slopes, clothed with vineyards—a comparatively recent and scarcely a satisfactory feature in
the landscape ; beyond stretched the vast plain,
with its orange-groves, its cornfields and its
scattered habitations, and in the distance rose
range after range of purple hills, fading into
shadowy outlines against a sky of unclouded blue.
She was not of a poetic or romantic temperament ;
at least, if she was, she had been too busy all her
life to cultivate any natural tendency in that
direction ; but scenery and sunlight made her

happy and appealed to her, as, indeed, they do and
must to nine out of every ten human beings; and,
since nothing is more becoming than happiness to
the average human being, it may be said without
flattery of Miss Forbes that, as she sat contentedly
there in her clean pink cotton gown, she was an
agreeable object for the eye to rest upon.

Her mother, a dispassionate judge, was wont to
say, ' Winnie isn't exactly pretty—of course, nothing
like as pretty as Daisy; but she always looks nice,
and she has a clear, healthy skin.' Strictly speaking, her complexion did no doubt constitute her
sole valid claim to beauty, although she had a pair
of soft brown eyes which were wonderfully expressive at times, and which never expressed ill-
will to man, woman, or child. But the rest of her
features were not much to boast of, and she was
too tall, too thin, too angular, to meet the requirements of any artistic standard. Nevertheless, it
was universally and quite justly admitted that she
' looked nice.' Probably she was such a good girl
that she could not have helped looking nice, even
though fewer physical advantages had been vouch-
safed to her.

One knows, from having seen so many examples
of it, what invariably happens to a good girl who
is the eldest of her family, who has a younger
sister better-looking than herself, and whose parents
do not happen to be energetic persons. Ever since
she had reached years of discretion Winifred had
been at once the providence and the maid-of-all-

work of the Forbes household. It was she who engaged and dismissed the servants, ordered the dinner, scolded the cook, took the railway tickets and looked after the luggage; it was she who copied out manuscripts and corrected proofs for her erudite and inefficient father, a country gentleman with an odd mania for scribbling upon historical and political topics; it was she who supervised Daisy's wardrobe and subsidised that extravagant young woman with occasional doles out of her own not very liberal allowance; above all, it was upon her shoulders that the responsibility of seeing that Micky did not get his feet wet or overtire himself, or otherwise endanger his health, had, by common consent, been placed. Now, as Micky was a boy of fourteen, as he held decided views with respect to the right of every freeborn Briton to personal liberty, and as it was on his account that the Forbeses had been packed off South for the winter by their medical adviser, it will be seen that the task of keeping her young brother in a state of discipline and submission was not the easiest of those which Winifred was expected to discharge.

Presently he sauntered out of the house behind her, with his hands in his pockets, and, making his way across a somewhat untidy garden, which, in spite of neglect, was gay with tea-roses and geraniums and giant cincrarias, threw himself down upon the bench by his sister's side. He was tall for his age, but not as broad across the chest as his relations would have liked him to be, and the colour on his cheeks was rather too vivid to be a sign of health. For the rest, he promised to develop into a tolerably good-looking man, notwithstanding his short, turned-up nose, and his reddish-brown hair and eyes were much admired in the family.

'Winnie, my love,' he began, 'it is with sincere regret that I have to inform you of my inability to pursue my ordinary course of study this morning.'

Winifred did not rebuke him for the above disrespectful imitation of his father's accustomed tone and phraseology, because she knew by experience that remonstrances upon such points were seldom of much avail; she only shook her head, and said quietly:

'I can't give you another holiday, Micky. If you don't do your lessons now, you will be sorry for it when you go back to school and find yourself placed among the infants. After all, you must admit that you haven't been very hard worked since we came here.'

'I cheerfully make that admission, my love, and I feel the full force of your remarks. At the same time, it will be obvious to you that I cannot do my lessons in the absence of my kind preceptress, and my kind preceptress will be unavoidably absent this morning. Shortly before twelve o'clock, my love, you will put on your Sunday clothes and go out into society with your papa and mamma. Lady Ottery—may her shadow never be less!—has sent to beg that they will bring one of their charming daughters with them to her breakfast-party, and the lot has fallen upon you. It seems that a stray man has turned up, and a stray woman is wanted to match him.'

'But why isn't Daisy going?' asked Winifred, raising her eyebrows a little.

'Daisy has been approached upon the subject, and has declined. She said she would see the whole lot of them jolly well blowed first—or words to that effect. I am afraid our dear Daisy got out of bed the wrong side to-day—though it is not for me to complain. And I must say I should think a breakfast-party was a rather ghastly sort of entertainment.'

Perhaps Miss Forbes may have thought so too; but it would never have occurred to her that personal disinclination to take part in an entertainment could be any excuse for shirking it; and, as a matter of fact, breakfast-parties are not quite so objectionable abroad as they would be in England. English sojourners in Algiers and other Southern watering-places have, at all events, assimilated the foreign custom in that respect, contenting themselves with a cup of coffee and a roll at nine o'clock, and being prepared for social intercourse at an hour when, if they were at home, they would very properly refuse to see anybody. Lord and Lady Ottery, who occupied a villa of imposing dimensions, had invited no less than twenty people to share their mid-day meal that morning, and were now destined to provide food for twenty-two, including Winifred Forbes and the stray man of whom mention has been made.

The former hastened to array herself in what her brother, with masculine ignorance, had described as her 'Sunday clothes'; but she had several small jobs to attend to before starting, so that she vexed her father by keeping him waiting nearly three minutes. When she had seated herself, with her back to the horses, in the little open carriage which had been hired for the winter, Mr. Forbes— a tall, spare, nervous-looking old man, whose long gray hair fell over his coat-collar, and whose convex spectacles nearly hid the weak eyes behind them—thought it right to utter a mild remonstrance.

'Winifred, my love,' said he, 'you would save me an immensity of worry if you would try to cultivate the virtue of punctuality. One may almost call punctuality a virtue, and it is scarcely saying too much to call unpunctuality a vice. May I hope that you have looked over those proofs and made the corrections which I indicated to you? They really ought to be despatched to the printers by to-morrow's mail, at the latest.'

'I corrected the proofs last night and sent them off this morning, papa,' answered Winifred cheerfully. 'I'm sorry I wasn't down in time; but I wanted to make sure that Micky had something to eat before he started for his ride.'

Mrs. Forbes, who was small, fragile, very prettily

dressed, and had the remains of considerable beauty, exclaimed :

' You don't mean that you have let that boy go out riding all by himself again ! I cannot think that it is safe, Winnie. These Arab horses are so extraordinary in their ways of going on ! You say they are not vicious ; but if they aren't vicious, why are they always squealing ?'

Mr. Forbes explained. He was not himself an equestrian, but his historical and ethnographical researches had made him acquainted with the methods of equine management adopted by the various races of mankind, and he imparted his acquired information to his hearers in the low, level accents habitual to him, much as though he had been delivering a scientific lecture.

' I am given to understand,' he concluded, ' that Michael has a secure seat, and I do not share your apprehensions with regard to his physical safety, my dear. On the other hand, I confess that I am not free from anxiety on the score of his mental growth. When he is riding he cannot be studying, and he certainly should be made to study at least five hours of every day. I presume I may take it for granted that he will not accomplish even that modest minimum to-day.'

He would not accomplish so much as a fifth part thereof, and Winifred's eyes dropped apologetically beneath the accusing gaze of her father's spectacles. To be sure, it had been no fault of hers that she had been called away from her educational duties ;

but it was a very common experience with her to
be blamed for mishaps which she was innocent of
having caused, and she had a fine stock of unconscious philosophy at command. She was also
fortunate in being able to take things as they came,
and enjoy to the full whatever happened to strike
her at the moment as beautiful or pleasant; so she
enjoyed the warm sun, and the pellucid air, and the
distant views of sea and shore, and the picturesque
Oriental-looking figures which had already lost all
the charm of novelty for her mother. As for enjoying Lady Ottery's overgrown assemblage of ex-
patriated Britons, and the too sumptuous repast to
which they would presently be compelled to sit
down, that was another affair. Still, she was
willing to try.

Happily, it turned out that no great effort would
be necessary, for as soon as she and her parents
had joined the throng, fat, good-natured Lady
Ottery took her by the arm, and whispered:

'I'm not going to victimize you with an old
fogey, my dear; I've got the nicest of young men
for you—a Mr. Bellew. I don't know whether you
have ever heard of him, but he is pretty well
known as a gentleman rider. Ottery was quite
delighted to come across him yesterday. He used
to see a great deal of him hunting last winter, and
we both liked him immensely. Such a good sportsman, and so simple and modest; besides being
superlatively handsome, which isn't a drawback,
you know.'

The first thought that entered Winnie's mind, after she had been introduced to this highly-praised gentleman, and had been conducted by him into the Moorish dining-room, which was profusely decorated with the roses which Algiers provides without stint to those who can afford to pay for them, was, 'What a pity poor Daisy didn't come instead of me! This is just the sort of man whom she would have been sure to like.'

However, in the unavoidable absence of Daisy, there was no reason at all why other people shouldn't like him; and Winnie, for her part, soon discovered that she liked him very much indeed. He was, as Lady Ottery had truly said, remarkably modest and simple; he gave himself no airs upon the strength of personal beauty; he did not grumble (as almost everybody else in the room did) at being out of England, and he seemed quite eager to make acquaintance with his fellow-exiles.

'Well, you see, Miss Forbes,' said he in answer to some observation of hers, 'the way I look at it is this: what can't be cured must be endured. And, after all, I think this is rather a jolly sort of place, don't you? Lots of funny things to be seen, I mean; and I dare say one might get up a few picnics and excursions, and so on. I suppose you ride and drive about a good deal?'

Winnie replied that she did when she had time, but that she was generally rather busy at home; and so he heard all about Daisy and Micky and Mr. Forbes's literary labours, and they became excellent friends. Probably it was the interest which the young man displayed in Micky that won Miss Forbes's heart.

'Poor little chap!' he exclaimed compassionately. 'What awful hard lines for him to be seedy at his age! Fond of riding, you say? I wonder whether he would care to come out for a ride with me some day. I might be able to give him a hint or two, and I assure you that nothing is more important than learning to ride in the right way. If you begin wrong, you let yourself in for no end of bother afterwards.'

This offer was unhesitatingly accepted, as was also Mr. Bellew's further diffident suggestion that perhaps he might be allowed to call on Mr. and Mrs. Forbes.

There is a sort of freemasonry between all classes of human beings which stands in need of no explanatory signs. Rogues recognise one another at a glance, and so do honest folks. Unhappily, honest folks may, and not unfrequently do, find themselves in equivocal situations, so that Winifred had to modify the good opinion which she had formed of her companion before the party dispersed. She was standing beside him after breakfast, when coffee and cigarettes had been carried out into the garden, and when Lady Ottery, in the innocence of her heart, came up to inquire what in the world had brought him to Algiers of all places.

'Oh, I've come out with the Littlewoods!' he answered. 'Mrs. Littlewood has had a nasty cough, and they've been ordered to winter abroad. I don't think you know them, do you?'

The smile faded from Lady Ottery's lips.

'No; I don't know them,' she replied, a little dryly.

'They are great friends of mine,' said that foolish Billy; and his tone of voice was nothing short of defiant—'especially Mrs. Littlewood. She is about the best friend I have.'

'Yes,' returned Lady Ottery, moving off at once to speak to somebody else.

Billy, who was not skilful at disguising his feelings, was obviously annoyed, and lost no time in taking his leave. After he had departed, Lady Ottery regretfully narrated what she knew of his recent history to Mrs. Forbes, who, having been struck by his engaging manners, asked a few questions about him.

'It is a thousand pities,' said she; 'but I suppose the poor young man is bent upon making himself impossible for the present. I had no idea that he was here in tow of that dreadful Littlewood woman. Of course, one isn't supposed to know, and if only he will refrain from parading her before our eyes we needn't see her; but I suspect, from the way in which he spoke to me just now, that he means to play the idiot. It really is too provoking of him! He would have been so useful in a place like this, where well-connected and nice-looking bachelors are worth even more than they are in London.'

Mrs. Forbes was less anxious than the generality

of mothers to scrape acquaintance with eligible bachelors, because one of her daughters was already engaged to be married, and the other, she hoped, would be so ere long; therefore, as she drove away, she felt free to express her abhorrence of the conduct of such men as Mr. Bellew.

'Without cutting him—which is quite unnecessary —you had better avoid him for the future, Winnie dear,' was her concluding remark. 'Under the circumstances, I am surprised that he should try to force himself upon the society of the place at all.'

'I am very sorry,' said Winifred. 'I thought him so nice, and he asked if he might call, and he spoke of giving Micky some instruction in riding, too. Don't you think Lady Ottery may be mistaken about him?'

'It is impossible to make mistakes in matters of that kind,' answered Mrs. Forbes decisively. 'If he chooses to call, it can't be helped, and your father can leave a card upon him after a week or two; but it will be out of the question for us to know him. At all events, we must wait until we see what other people mean to do.'

CHAPTER III.

BILLY DOES THE STRAIGHT THING.

To wait humbly for a lead before taking action of any kind is the habitual attitude of fully three-fourths of the human race. Such is our inherent modesty that the majority of us don't care, as Billy Bellew would have put it, to 'break our own fences'; we have no wish to thrust ourselves into undue prominence; we are quite content to do what other people do and say. Now, it so happened that, for some little time after Billy's arrival in Algiers, people—and highly influential people a few of them were—said nothing but good of him. Mrs. Littlewood was in bed with a bad cold, which may to some extent have accounted for his having abstained from outraging public decorum; but it was, in any case, evident that he was upon terms of intimacy with the aristocracy of his native land, and this discovery softened Mrs. Forbes's heart towards him. She said to her eldest daughter that she had perhaps been a little hasty, and that perhaps dear Lady Ottery had also been a little hasty. All sorts of ill-natured stories got about; and very often, when you came to inquire into them, there was no real foundation for them; poor Mr. Bellew could hardly be as black as he had been painted, or Lady This and Lady That would never have asked him to dine with them, as Mrs. Forbes understood that they had done. In short, if poor Mr. Bellew should call, he was not to be turned away from the door.

It appeared, however, that Mr. Bellew was in no great hurry to fulfil his promise; and thus considerable disappointment was caused to Miss Daisy Forbes, who, having cross-questioned her sister about him, had come to the conclusion that she would like very much to make his acquaintance.

'Naughty he may be,' was her comment upon the information imparted to her, 'but he is sure to be nice. Naughty people always are nice; and in this deadly-lively place nobody is either the one or the other. If he doesn't turn up soon, you must write him a note and ask him to breakfast, Winnie. Perhaps he is shy and wants a little encouragement.'

'From what I saw of him, I shouldn't say that he suffered in that way,' answered Winnie, laughing. 'At all events, I certainly shall not send him an invitation; and, after all, I am not sure that I want him to come. He is too good-looking. Besides, I suppose one must assume that his affections are already engaged—as yours are, or ought to be.'

'According to you and mamma, his affections are sadly misplaced, and it would be an act of charity to him to divert them,' returned the younger girl composedly. 'As for mine, I can't think why you should say that they ought to be engaged. To the best of my belief, they are at present concentrated chiefly upon myself, and I don't propose to offer them as a free gift to any Mr. Bellew.'

Daisy Forbes had a happy conviction that whenever, and upon whomsoever, it might please her to bestow her affections, they would be enthusiastically accepted. Experience had justified her in holding that conviction; for she was a very pretty girl, and she had the whole art of flirtation at her fingers' ends. The bachelors of Salop had been as wax under the touch of those taper fingers; the bachelors of London had not escaped ; and if Miss Daisy was still a spinster, it was no doubt only because, as she herself averred, she had hitherto remained comfortably heartwhole. Winifred sighed as she gazed at her sister's small, compact figure, at her golden-brown hair and her clear blue eyes, and her pink and white complexion. There was a certain softness and a certain hardness about Daisy ; one couldn't help feeling occasional misgivings as to her ultimate fate, and one couldn't help wishing that she would anticipate and annul possible perils by falling in love with some honest man. The unfortunate thing was that she had not, to all appearance, fallen in love with Harry Lysaght, who was honest and in every way suitable, and to whom (supposing that she did not intend to marry him) she had behaved rather badly. It was true that there had been no actual engagement, but the affair had been upon the very brink of conclusion, when Micky had fallen so ill with bronchitis that the family had been sent off abroad post-haste. Of course, this had been great fun to Daisy, who delighted in tantalizing her admirers; but Winifred quite hoped that all would be satisfactorily arranged on their return home in the spring. Meanwhile Daisy had to be amused, if that could be managed ; and, so far, that had not been managed. The girl was bored and out of spirits—a state of things which, as her elder sister knew full well, was very apt to render her mischievous.

Taking everything into consideration, therefore, it seemed to be just as well that Mr. Bellew had forgotten or repented of his intention of calling at Le Bocage, which was the name of the villa temporarily inhabited by the Forbes family.

Winifred, on her side, had almost forgotten him, and had quite ceased to expect him by the time that he tardily redeemed his promise. Supported by the inexhaustible stock of patience and perseverance which was her birthright, she was helping Micky to construe a Horatian ode that afternoon. At his request, she had transferred the scene of their joint labours to the arbour at the end of the garden; and there (not without occasional longings to dismiss her reluctant pupil and let the whole hopeless business slide) she was endeavouring to turn his preposterous rendering of the Roman poet into passable English. A warm wind was blowing across the plain from the distant Sahara. It was not yet one of those terrible, furious siroccos which fill the atmosphere with fine sand and convert the lofty blue sky into a low, copper-coloured vault; but waves of tepid air were rolling softly in and relaxing the energies of all living creatures.

'*Auditis, an me ludit amabilis Insania ?*—do you hear, or does an amiable insanity delude me ?' asks Micky sleepily; and his instructress has to rouse herself with an effort, in order to point out that 'amiable insanity' can hardly have been the precise condition of mind contemplated by the author of the lines.

'Oh, I don't know,' returned the boy, yawning; 'I expect he must have been a bit off his head, or he wouldn't have written such bosh. I say, Winnie, don't you think we might knock off for to-day? It *is* so beastly hot! and I think I'm going to have a headache. You know the doctor said most particularly that I wasn't to have headaches.'

'I can't let you go for another half-hour, Micky,' the inexorable Winifred declared. 'Perhaps you may escape in twenty minutes if only you will try to get on. Come! "*Audire et videor pios errare per lucos amœnæ Quos et aquæ subeunt et auræ.*"'

Micky had resumed despondently :

'I seem to hear pious people wandering through something or other which both agreeable waters and airs——' when he interrupted himself by exclaiming in much more lively accents : 'Hullo! I seem to hear the voices of people who ain't a bit pious, and who are advancing in this direction. Heaven be praised! it's Daisy, accompanied by a visitor. Daisy isn't always what I could wish her to be; but I owe her a good turn for this, and I won't forget it.'

It was not Daisy's habit to receive visitors; still less was it her habit to share the company of such rare visitors as chanced to interest her with her sister. But when Mr. Bellew had been conducted by her into the summer-house, and had shaken hands with Winifred, and when Micky had joyfully gathered up his books in preparation for a strategic movement of retreat, she explained this departure from established custom.

'Very sorry to interrupt you, Winnie,' said she; 'it isn't my fault. Mr. Bellew simply refused to quit the premises without having seen you, so I had to bring him out here.'

Billy laughed and coloured slightly; he was neither too old nor too wicked to blush.

'I really ain't so pushing as all that, Miss Forbes,' he protested. 'But I did rather want to ask you whether we couldn't make up a riding-party one of these days; and—and you promised to introduce me to your brother, you know.'

Well, it was no hard matter to make friends with Mr. Michael Forbes, who was a shrewd observer, and who was graciously pleased to approve of the stranger's aspect. Boys always took to Billy Bellew, and boys make fewer mistakes at first sight than men. As we grow old we learn to distrust appearances, and we also, unfortunately, learn to distrust our instincts; but the lessons of experience, as every honest middle-aged man will admit, are of singularly little practical service to us.

Winifred, who, being a woman, was in some respects as good a judge of her fellow-creatures as a boy, could not for the life of her help thinking well of this pleasant, handsome, unassuming young fellow. Perhaps he had been maligned. Even if the story told about him were true, he might not be wholly inexcusable. At least, he spoke and acted like a gentleman; and it was very kind of him to take such an interest in Micky, to whose views upon the subject of horsemanship he was listening with the polite patience which masters of a craft never fail to display in their dealings with neophytes.

But Daisy, it may be, regarded their guest in a somewhat different, though not in a less flattering, light. Young men, whether in England or in Algeria, did not, according to her belief, call on Mrs. Forbes in order to listen to the chatter of a brat of fourteen, and she soon took measures to release Mr. Bellew from an incubus of which she felt sure that he would be glad to get rid.

'If I were you, Micky,' said she, 'I should make a bolt for it. Winnie has her eye upon you, and she is quite capable of dragging you off somewhere to finish your lessons before tea.'

There seemed to be something in that. Micky, after considering the question for a moment or two, decided to adopt the safer course. He tucked his books under his arm and held out his hand to his new friend, saying:

'Well, I think I'll be off now. The stables are just beyond the house, and if you'll ride up the road outside and whistle any morning about eleven o'clock, I'll be with you in a brace of shakes. I can show you a place where there's rare good galloping ground, and a bit of a jump, too.'

'All right; you'll hear me whistling for you before you're much older,' answered Billy;

whereupon the boy nodded and promptly disappeared.

A little ordinary tact, Daisy thought, would have led Winnie to follow his example; but Winnie was sometimes provokingly obtuse. She showed no disposition to withdraw, but resumed her seat, and asked Mr. Bellew whether he wouldn't rather sit down than stand. Moreover, when a servant came across the garden presently to announce that Mrs. Nugent had called, and please would one of the young ladies come in, she had the stupidity to remark:

'Perhaps you had better go, Daisy; Mrs. Nugent may want to see you, and I am sure she can't want to see me.'

It was a stupid thing to say; still, the advice might be worth taking, because Mrs. Nugent was a lady who gave frequent small dances and was very particular about securing exactly the right number of couples for them. It would be rather vexatious to be cut out of an invitation by one's elder sister, while nothing could possibly be more safe than to leave a potential admirer in the temporary custody of that elder sister. Therefore Daisy sighed and exclaimed:

'Bother the woman! I suppose I must go and do the civil to her; but she won't stay long, and I shall be out again in ten minutes or so. I hope you won't let Winnie drive you away before I return, Mr. Bellew.'

Mr. Bellew was evidently not anxious to be

driven away, nor was Winnie eager to dismiss him.
On the contrary, she was glad to have this opportunity of conversing with him for a short time in
private, and arriving, if possible, at some clear
comprehension of the man. She felt convinced
that he was more sinned against than sinning;
perhaps he might become communicative, and
perhaps she might be able to give him some assistance, verbal or other. It was not unnatural that
she should entertain this expectation, for many
men and women, recognising in her a sympathetic
soul, had been communicative with her, and many
were the men and women whom she had been
instrumental in helping out of difficulties. It was
for some such purpose that Winifred Forbes conceived that she had been created : probably she
was not mistaken.

Billy, for his part, conceived, not less naturally,
that Miss Forbes had been created for a totally
different purpose; and this was what prompted
him to remark, after a pause :

' It's awfully good of you to undertake that young
beggar's education. From what Mrs. Forbes told
me just now, I presume that you *are* undertaking
it ; and I should think that you must find him
rather a handful, don't you ?'

' No,' answered Winifred ; ' Micky is really a
good boy—quite as good as I want him to be. If
he hadn't occasional fits of naughtiness, he might
grow up into a little prig, which would be dreadful.
Of course, it is a great disadvantage to him to be

taken away from school, and of course he has a
fine contempt for female authority; but that can't
be helped. He is delicate, though I dare say you
don't think he looks so; and for this winter, at all
events, he must be taken care of.'

'Well, if I were you, I shouldn't bother much
about lessons, and I should let him have plenty of
exercise and open air; you may depend upon it
that that's what all boys want,' said Billy sapiently.
'That and kicking—which perhaps he may get
later on. Dear me, if I hadn't been well kicked in
my boyhood, and if I hadn't been kept in pretty
hard condition all my life, a nice sort of ruffian I
should be at the present moment! I ain't much
to boast of, as it is. That's the worst of having
been one's own father from the outset. One don't
mean any particular harm; but one is almost bound
to make an ass of one's self. And the stupid part
of it is that, after one has learnt a thing or two
by experience, one isn't allowed to make a fresh
start.'

'It's never too late to mend,' said Winifred.
'Have you made a very great ass of yourself?'

'So I'm told. Oh yes, I have made a great ass
of myself, no doubt; perhaps I ought to be thankful
that I have done no worse. Anyhow, as I was
saying, what's done can't be undone. Only I
think, if I had a son, or a younger brother, as you
have, I might be able to give him a few valuable
hints.'

'He wouldn't take them,' answered Winifred,

smiling. 'Everybody has to earn his own experience, and everybody—every man, at least—
should know how to control his own destiny. It
doesn't follow that because you have been silly in
the past you must be silly in the future.'

'Oh! doesn't it, though?' ejaculated the young
man ruefully.

But as soon as the words were out of his mouth
he felt ashamed of them. After all, it was a shabby
proceeding to vilify Blanche Littlewood by implica-
tion; and if he repented of what had occurred in
days gone by, the least that he could do, as a
gentleman, was to keep his repentance to himself.
Moreover, this tall girl, with the soft brown eyes,
whose sympathies he was, for some reason or
other, so anxious to gain, would not be likely to
think any the better of him for putting forward
Adam's old, unworthy excuse. Therefore he rose,
thrust his hands into his pockets, gazed for a
moment or two towards the declining sun, and
then, facing about, proceeded, with the somewhat
disconcerting directness which was characteristic of
him, to the point which he had been intending all
this time to approach.

'Look here, Miss Forbes,' said he; 'I want to
ask you something. After I went away the other
day, did Lady Ottery speak to you about me and
Mrs. Littlewood?'

'Yes,' answered Winifred, who, though slightly
disconcerted, was less so than most people would

have been under the circumstances ; ‘ since you ask
me, she did.’

‘ I suspected as much. Well, it’s always best to
start fair and have a clear understanding from the
first, don’t you think so ? I mean, if you like
people, and want to be friends with them and all
that, you know. I shan’t grumble if you say that
you don’t care about being friends with me or seeing
much more of me ; but I want you to know that
Mrs. Littlewood has been abominably calumniated.
The long and the short of it is that she has been
rather imprudent, and that’s what these old cats
never forgive. As for me, I’m glad to say that I’m
a friend of hers ; and anybody who thinks fit to
cut me because I’m a friend of hers is heartily
welcome to do so.’

It was hardly possible to help laughing at this
defiant assertion. The poor fellow could not have
betrayed himself more completely if he had stated
in the plainest of terms what he would have died
rather than reveal. But Winifred did not laugh ;
she only said :

‘ Oh, I hope we shall be friends, Mr. Bellew. I
quite believe what you tell me ; and you certainly
won’t be cut by me, unless mamma orders me to
cut you, which doesn’t seem likely.’

Billy drew a long breath of relief.

‘ Thanks ; I’m glad that’s over !’ he exclaimed.
‘ I had to say it, because it was the straight thing
to do ; but it’s a horrid subject, and we needn’t
refer to it again, I hope.’

Winifred thought she knew enough of human nature to feel tolerably certain that he would recur to it; but for the moment she was content to discourse with him about Micky, and about riding, and about the chances of sport which might be obtainable within reach of Algiers, until Daisy emerged from the house, having duly obtained her invitation from Mrs. Nugent, and being likewise provided with a cut-and-dried programme, which she at once submitted to Mr. Bellew for approval.

Could he, she asked, manage to make a long day of it, and accompany them on an excursion to Cap Caxine? They could picnic in some woods that she knew of, and Mr. and Mrs. Forbes could drive, and the rest of the party could go on horseback. And would the day after to-morrow suit him?

Winifred noticed, though Daisy did not, a momentary hesitation on Mr. Bellew's part, the cause of which was not far to seek. Doubtless he would have to obtain Mrs. Littlewood's permission before absenting himself for a whole day. But there was no ring of hesitation in his voice when he replied that he should like it of all things. Only he couldn't be absolutely sure of being free until he reached home. Might he send up a note in the morning?

Daisy having graciously acquiesced in this arrangement, he presently took his leave; and almost before he was out of hearing, the younger of the two girls said emphatically to the elder:

'Charming—quite charming! The best-looking

man I have ever seen in my life, and one of the pleasantest. Winnie, my dear, I shall make it my business to save that young man from himself— and his friends. Why should you have a monopoly of performing good deeds ? I will take Mr. Bellew off your hands, and you shall see what I will make of him.'

CHAPTER IV.

A LITTLE HOLIDAY.

IT would be a happy thing for some of us if the post came in only once a day, and all of us can escape from our present state of constant bombardment by the comparatively simple process of betaking ourselves to North Africa. Even there, however, the mail-steamer arrives every twenty-four hours in these times, bringing with it the usual and inevitable load of worry. On the morning after Mr. Bellew's visit to Le Bocage it brought a pile of letters, packets and newspapers to that destination for Mr. Forbes, a supply almost equally large for his wife, and a single epistle addressed to Winifred, who, as soon as she recognised the handwriting, put it into her pocket and carried it out with her to her favourite retreat at the end of the garden. Considering that it was a love-letter, that was a very natural and ordinary course to adopt ; yet she was not in quite so great a hurry to open it as the recipients of love-letters are commonly supposed and expected to be. The truth was that she had been engaged to Edmund Kirby for such a long time, and the prospect of the engagement terminating in marriage was still so remote, that the advent of his weekly account of himself had ceased to be a particularly exciting episode in her life. Moreover, his epistolary style was apt to be a trifle dreary and diffuse, while it not unfrequently happened that two-thirds of his space was taken up with records of family bickerings and dissensions which distressed Winifred, and which she could do nothing to allay.

The present letter, when perused, proved to be very much like a number of its predecessors. John Kirby had been getting into trouble again. He had turned up at Quarter Sessions in a state of shameful intoxication; there had been great difficulty about getting him home; the county newspapers had said nasty things, and there was a talk about removing his name from the Commission of the Peace. Edmund had been summoned from London by his mother, had tried the effect of remonstrances, and had been as good as kicked out of doors, with a request, delivered in the presence of the servants, that he would betake himself to the devil at his earliest convenience.

'All this,' the writer continued, 'coming upon me in the midst of my work (which it has, of course, interrupted), has been terribly harassing to me, and I miss your constant and ready sympathy more than I can tell you. I cannot acquit my mother of all blame in the matter; nor can I understand why her affection for John should lead her to accuse me of undue harshness in my conduct towards him. I think that he disgraces his position, and I should be dishonest if I did not tell him so; but things have come to such a pass now that I am afraid I shall not be able to tell him that or anything else for the future. He has to all intents and purposes warned me off the premises, and, were it not for the hope of seeing you, I doubt whether I should ever care to revisit Shropshire.'

Winifred Forbes had been betrothed to this country neighbour of hers at a very early age. The proposed match was not a brilliant one; for Edmund Kirby was only a struggling barrister; and the family property, which was now in the possession of his elder brother, a hard-riding, hard-drinking squire, did not produce a sufficient annual rent-roll to leave much margin for the support of younger sons; but Mrs. Forbes had given her sanction—partly because Winnie was no beauty, and partly because she was so useful at home. Beggars mustn't be choosers, Mrs. Forbes may have thought; and she may also have been reluctant to part with one who took nearly all the small burdens of daily life off her hands. For the rest, Winnie did not contemplate or desire immediate matrimony. Her sister was wont to aver that she would never have accepted Edmund Kirby if he had not been so ugly and so unlucky; and her sister ought to have known, if anybody did, what constituted the most urgent claims upon Winnie's regard.

Perhaps it was because she herself possessed neither of the above-mentioned claims that she was received with a touch of unusual asperity when she came tripping lightheartedly across the garden to announce that it was all right, and that Mr. Bellew would join their party on the morrow.

'I am not so sure that that makes it all right,' Winnie said. 'It won't be all right if you set to work to make a fool of the man. And I am afraid that is the notion that you have in your mind.'

'The notion that I have in my mind,' returned Daisy composedly, 'is that some people, including your friend Mr. Bellew, do not require to be made into what they already are. Another humble notion of mine is that you have heard from Edmund Kirby, and that his letter has upset your little temper. Why be so easily upset? If I had an Edmund Kirby — but, Heaven be praised, I haven't!—he wouldn't contrive to upset me, so long as we were separated by all these miles of land and water. Let us enjoy ourselves while we can, and make the most of the few good things that come in our way. I propose to enjoy my ride to-morrow, and I don't see any reason at all why you shouldn't enjoy yours. It won't be wildly exciting for you, I admit; but surely it will be a shade better than sitting at home and teaching Micky.'

Different people have different ideas of enjoyment, and Winifred, with the light of past experience before her eyes, did not anticipate a particularly delightful day. Nevertheless, in view of existing complications, there seemed little fear that Mr. Bellew would prove a source of danger to her sister's happiness; and this, it subsequently appeared, was likewise the opinion entertained by Mrs. Forbes, who remarked:

'He is really a very gentlemanlike young man— besides having plenty of money, I am told. Of course, if he were what Lady Ottery led us to suppose that he was, it would never do to allow him to become intimate with Daisy; but, from all I hear, I should think he could easily shake off that disreputable woman if he wanted to do so; and, under all the circumstances, I can't see any imprudence in our making friends with him.'

It may, at all events, be truthfully asserted on Billy's behalf that he was innocent of the faintest wish or intention to flirt with Miss Daisy Forbes. He did not even wish to ride beside her all day, and he was rather disappointed when, after presenting himself punctually at the appointed hour on the ensuing morning, he found that that was what he would have to do. He would have preferred assuming charge of the boy, whose seat and hands required correction; and he would infinitely have preferred a quiet chat with Winifred, who chose to canter on ahead and take her brother with her. One can't, however, expect to get one's own way invariably, and Billy was nothing if not good-natured, and the day was still young, and there was no denying that Miss Daisy was both pretty and attractive. So the simple hero of this simple tale submitted without any great reluctance to his fate, while his companion employed, successfully enough, the arts of an expert to fascinate him.

She suggested that there was no occasion for them to hurry themselves. The dust raised by the carriage in which Mr. and Mrs. Forbes were seated, the former reading a newspaper, and the latter apparently dropping off to sleep beneath a huge white sunshade, might as well be allowed to settle down again before they followed in its track; cantering along the highroad was good neither for man nor beast, and if Micky would insist upon cantering, he must be left to canter alone.

'Only he isn't alone,' Billy observed. 'It's rather hard lines on your sister that she should be obliged to pound along at such a pace in this heat.'

'Oh, she likes it,' answered Daisy; 'some people take a positive pleasure in doing things which everybody else hates, and Winnie is one of them. Don't distress yourself about her; I will take it upon myself to assure you that she isn't pining for your society or for mine.'

It was after that vicariously administered snub that Billy accepted his destiny—which, as has been said, was not such a very objectionable one, after all. The weather was brilliant, the scene was lovely and summer-like (for Algeria is a green

country in winter, only turning brown and melancholy towards the end of the long hot season, when
all the land is thirsting for rain), he was out for a
holiday, he had purchased a good little horse, and
he would indeed have been hard to please if he had
quarrelled with his company.

As a matter of fact, he neither quarrelled with it
nor appreciated it quite as highly as many men
might have done. He thought Miss Daisy Forbes
a very nice little girl; but he was not conscious of
any inclination to fall in love with her; and her
well-directed shots failed, somehow or other, to hit
the bull's-eye. Billy, in short, was good-temperedly
resigned, without being in the least enthusiastic or
grateful—which showed that there must be something altogether abnormal about his condition of
mind. Daisy, piqued by an indifference to which
she was unaccustomed, did her very best to discover
what was the matter with him, but did not succeed.
He declined to be drawn by references to Mrs.
Littlewood; more than once he responded with
total irrelevance to the questions addressed to him;
he really seemed, or affected to be, more interested
in Micky's horsemanship, which he was watching
from afar, than in nearer and worthier subjects of
study. From this it resulted that a long *tête-à-tête*
ride over hill and dale, past the palm-crowned
headland of the Bouzaréah and across the stretches
of rough, uncultivated country, whence wide views
of sea and plain and mountain were obtainable,
conveyed an impression of lazy satisfaction to one

of the equestrians, while it afflicted the other with a sense of lively irritation. When at length the shade of the pine-forest, under which it had been decided to halt for refreshments, was reached, Mr. Bellew (if he had only known it) was being inwardly stigmatized by the lady whom he had escorted so far on her way as a downright donkey; and this unflattering opinion of hers was confirmed by the alacrity with which he hastened to help Winnie to unpack the luncheon-basket. As if Winnie and the picturesque nondescript Arab servant who had been engaged to perform the functions of butler, footman and valet could not have accomplished that between them, without assistance! Such conduct was equivalent to a direct challenge; and Daisy, little though she might covet the admiration of a downright donkey, felt bound in honour to subjugate him.

He had no sort of suspicion of her designs or of his own peril. Presently he seated himself upon the ground between Winnie and Micky, and, while he was eating chicken pie and drinking champagne, addressed his remarks chiefly to the boy, who listened to them with proper deference. Micky knew enough about riding to know that he was only a beginner and that Mr. Bellew was a finished artist; he saw the point of counsels which more advanced performers are only too apt to treat with contempt, and he expressed his willingness to take a day's schooling whenever his Mentor could spare time to bestow that favour upon him.

'Between you and me,' he said confidentially,
'you had better come up in the morning; because
then you'll get me fresh, don't you see? In the
afternoon I'm so stupefied by lessons that I ain't
fit to jump over a stick. You might just represent
that to Winnie when you get a chance.'

Winnie did not overhear this astute bid for a
whole holiday, because she was giving all her
attention to her father, who was holding forth
upon the ineptitude of the French nation as
colonists, and who was prone to attacks of irri-
tability when (as sometimes happened during the
absence of his elder daughter) nobody took the
slightest notice of his harangues.

'These people,' he was saying, 'have flung
millions into a country which used to be the
granary of Rome, and they will never see their
money, or the value of it, back. The Spaniards,
the Maltese and the Mahonnais are reaping the
reward of the blood and treasure that they have
expended, and they have nothing to show, except
a few laurel-wreaths, which might have been won
quite as well in a desert. Why maintain an army
and make roads and railways for the benefit of
aliens? The Romans did not go to work after
that fashion; nor should we if Algeria were one
of our possessions.'

So the good man prosed on; and it was all quite
true, and it didn't in the least signify; and the
wind sighed through the pine branches, and Mrs.
Forbes closed her eyes, and Daisy, growing im-

patient, remarked in a loud voice that, if they were to get to Cap Caxine and home before dark, they ought to be moving.

It was Winifred who managed the executive department of the Forbes household, and Daisy who ruled supreme over it. The banquet and the period of repose which might have been allowed to follow it were curtailed in obedience to the latter's command; the sober revellers rose to their feet, the horses were released from the trees to which they had been secured, and then it was that Billy found an opportunity of addressing Miss Forbes.

'You aren't fond of riding,' said he in an affirmative rather than in an interrogative tone, while he was tightening her girths for her.

'How do you know that?' she asked, with some surprise.

'Oh, one can generally tell. Of course I can see that you have been accustomed to ride a good deal; but you haven't done it because you liked it. Your sister informed me just now that you liked doing things which everybody else hated. I suppose what she meant was, that you like doing things which other people like, because you want to please them. Yes; I should say that that was you all over.'

The compliment was perhaps a trifle clumsy and commonplace, but she might have excused it in consideration of the speaker's evident sincerity. Probably she herself would have been puzzled to

explain why it had the effect of provoking her; but
provoked she was, and her rejoinder was barely
civil.

'Please don't try to make me out a saint and
martyr,' she said. 'I assure you I am not at all
that sort of person. It is true that I don't particularly care about riding; still, I always enjoy a
ride with Micky—that is, provided that other people
don't join in and interrupt us.'

'Well, that's straight enough, at all events,'
Billy observed, looking a little glum. 'I was
going to suggest a change of partners this afternoon; but I won't make such an unwelcome
suggestion now.'

He would have wasted his breath if he had made
it, and Winifred was well aware of that fact, though
he might possibly be ignorant thereof. To imagine
that Daisy would put up with her brother's com-
panionship when a more or less interesting young
man was within reach was indeed to display a
surprising lack of knowledge of the ways of girls in
general, and of Miss Daisy Forbes in particular.
Still, it was nice of him to be so innocent, and it
was satisfactory to note that he had so far escaped
unharmed from the shafts which had doubtless
been aimed at his heart. Winnie would have gone
the length of admitting that she had no personal
objection to a change of partners, if Daisy had not
stepped up to claim her prey before anything more
could be said. As it was, Mr. Bellew was dismissed
with a strong impression upon his mind that he

had been metaphorically kicked, which was really
rather a pity.

There are, of course, male as well as female
flirts; and although the former may be—as they
certainly are—infinitely less skilful and cool-headed
than the latter, they are not unfrequently actuated
in their behaviour by precisely similar motives. If
Billy Bellew was unacquainted with the art of
flirtation, and had never taken the slightest pains
to familiarise himself with it, he was none the less
capable of meeting an accommodating siren half-
way. Only he was honestly unaware that his
altered demeanour towards Miss Daisy, as they
rode at a foot's pace down the steep hillside
together, was due to any mortification on his part
at having been disdainfully treated by her sister.
He was not in love with either of them; if he was
in love at all, he was in love with Blanche Littlewood; and he had no thought of being false to that
absent lady when his eyes encountered those of his
neighbour, as they did more than once during the
course of that downward ride.

Yet Daisy, who was an adept, and who ought
not to have been easily deceived, congratulated
herself upon having practically won the little game
that she was playing long before she and her
attendant cavalier reached Cap Caxine. By the
time that they arrived at the wind-swept promon-
tory, with its slim white lighthouse, where the
carriage and the other two riders were waiting
for them, she had heard as much as she wanted

to hear about him, and had told him as much about herself as she deemed it advisable to tell. She was confident that she had in a certain sense fascinated him, and she perceived that some exercise of tact and diplomacy would be required in order to complete her conquest. That was entirely satisfactory, because facile victories are not exciting, and a little mild excitement was just what she wanted to keep her spirits up during the term of her compulsory exile.

'We have been here more than half an hour; we thought something must have happened to you,' said Mr. Forbes, rather crossly. 'Winnie, my dear, you had better ride on as fast as you can with Michael. He ought not to be exposed to the risk of catching a chill at sunset; and indeed I should have preferred to avoid that risk myself, had it been possible.'

Winnie obeyed orders without so much as glancing at the new-comers, and the carriage also was presently set in motion once more. But Daisy, not being afraid of chills, was in no such hurry to get home. She asked Mr. Bellew whether he was in a hurry, and he was obliged to answer that he was not; although he had reasons of his own for doubting the wisdom of turning up at Colonel Littlewood's villa too late for dinner. Accordingly, they proceeded at a leisurely pace along the road which skirts the coast, past the Pointe Pescade, through the suburb of Saint Eugène, and so to the Bab-el-Oued, or western gate of Algiers. It

was a distance of about six miles, and Arab horses
are not good walkers.   The sun had dipped beyond
the purple rim of the Mediterranean, the brief twilight had deepened into night and the stars were
shining overhead, before this belated couple emerged
upon the eastern side of the town and cantered
up the hill towards Mustapha Supérieur.   Naturally,
it was incumbent upon Mr. Bellew to see his fellow-
excursionist safely home ; and although, after
taking leave of her, he galloped down to the Hôtel
d'Orient with scant regard for his horse's legs or
his personal safety, he could not begin to dress
until twenty minutes after the hour at which Mrs.
Littlewood was wont to dine.

This was, to say the least of it, unfortunate.   So
much so, in fact, that the prospect of coming
trouble robbed him of any pleasure that he might
otherwise have derived from the memory of a
delightful conversation.   Daisy Forbes was charming beyond a doubt; but he could have forgiven
her if she had charmed him with a trifle less of
prolixity.

CHAPTER V.

MRS. LITTLEWOOD TAKES THE FIELD.

Mrs. Littlewood, unfortunately, was a somewhat
exacting lady.   She had, it is true, granted Billy a
whole day's leave of absence, upon the understanding that he should dine with her, on his return,

and give a full account of himself; but such con-
cessions were very seldom made by her, nor, it may
safely be assumed, would she have made this one
if she had not hoped to gain some personal profit
thereby.   As a matter of fact, she wanted to know
Mrs. Forbes, and counted upon obtaining, through
Billy, an introduction to that lady.   She wanted to
know everybody in Algiers who, as she herself
would have phrased it, was 'worth knowing.'   With
the inconsistency characteristic of her sex, she
delighted in snapping her fingers at Mrs. Grundy,
but grew uneasy the moment that Mrs. Grundy's
respectable back was turned upon her.   Her wish
was to run with the hare and hunt with the hounds,
and she was as angry as ladies always are whenever it was demonstrated to her that this cannot be
done.   Now, she had that very day been made
the recipient of a most unqualified and unmistakable snub from Lady Ottery; so that she had
returned from the garden-party where the snub
had been administered in a thoroughly bad temper,
which naturally had not been improved by Billy's
failure to put in an appearance at the dinner-hour.

Her breathless slave hurried into the dining-
room just as the sweets were being removed, and
was joyously greeted by Colonel Littlewood, who
up to that moment had been having rather a
rough time of it.

'Hullo, old man!' called out the genial Colonel;
'better late than never! I've told 'em to keep
everything hot for you, and you shall have some

soup in half a jiffy. Took you a bit longer to escort those young women round a twenty-mile radius than you bargained for, eh ?'

Mrs. Littlewood said nothing, but looked pained and resigned. How well he knew that look! and how he had learned to dread it! Probably it was a mistake on her part to employ that method so frequently; but her mistakes, like her successes, were those of her sex. Long use and wont had taught Billy that she would not and could not be pacified without a scene; so he ate his dinner as quickly as he could and talked to the Colonel, who drank while he was eating, and he did not make matters worse by excessive apologies. After dinner the Colonel lit a cigar and made himself comfortable in an armchair, while the younger man rose and followed Mrs. Littlewood. Such was the established custom in that household, where, to be sure, cigars were not forbidden in the drawing-room, and where every guest was requested to do just as he pleased.

Much as Billy Bellew hated his host, he would just then have been better pleased with his host's company than with that of his hostess; but it was useless to attempt shirking the inevitable, and the inevitable overtook him without loss of time. He listened, with bent and submissive head, to a recital of grievances, every one of which was only too familiar to him; he made no effort to defend himself against the absurd accusations and reproaches with which he was assailed; he admitted

that he had been enjoying himself, that the Misses
Forbes were pretty girls, and even that he hoped to
see more of them. That was the worst of Billy:
you couldn't exasperate him, nor could you by any
means induce him to return railing for railing.
Mrs. Littlewood, who was not devoid of a certain
intermittent sense of humour, ended by laughing
through her tears, and exclaiming:

'Oh, well, if you *won't* quarrel, I suppose there is
nothing for it but to make friends; although I do
think that you might have been a little more
considerate. You knew what horrors I should
have to go through at Mrs. Ryland's garden-party;
you knew I should come home in wretched spirits,
and the least you could have done would have been
to spare me the additional misery of a domestic
meal with Alfred, who, as you can see for yourself, is in his usual condition at this hour of the
day.'

'I made as much haste as I could,' Billy
declared. 'I'm awfully sorry I couldn't get back
sooner; but I really didn't know that you were
likely to meet with any—er—annoyance at Mrs.
Ryland's party. I thought you were rather looking
forward to it.'

'Looking forward to it! As if I ever looked
forward nowadays to meeting a heap of strangers,
who have heard all about me—and all about you!
Isn't it always the same old story? They are
ready to welcome you; but they take very good
care not to welcome me. Your friend Lady Ottery

was all but insulting when I was introduced to her
this afternoon.'

' I'm awfully sorry,' murmured Billy, not knowing what else to say.

' Oh, I don't suppose you are particularly sorry ;
it makes no difference to you whether I am received
or cut. But I am not going to give in. I have
done nothing wrong, and I won't submit to be
treated as if I had.'

' Oh no, I wouldn't,' assented Billy rather feebly.
' Why should you, you know ?'

Mrs. Littlewood laughed again. This long-legged
admirer of hers really was rather funny at times—
especially when he did not intend to be so. By
degrees she recovered her good humour and made
her wishes known to him. He was to speak well
of her to Mrs. Forbes ; he was to enlist Mrs.
Forbes's sympathies on her behalf and to pave the
way for an acquaintance ; he was to dine with Mrs.
Ryland, whom he did not know, but who had
known the speaker from childhood and had stood
by her through thick and thin ; furthermore, he
was to signify to all whom it might concern that
Mrs. Littlewood's friends were his friends, while
her enemies were his enemies.

' It isn't that I care two straws what these
people think about me,' Mrs. Littlewood explained ;
' only I don't choose to live in a desert, or to be
shunned like a leper.'

A very simple method of avoiding so undesirable
a state of things was open to her ; but it was not

for him to suggest its adoption.   Upon the whole,
he was only too thankful that indignation against
Lady Ottery had diverted her mind from the jealous
misgivings to which she had given expression at
the beginning of their interview.   He had half
expected to be forbidden to hold any further intercourse with the Forbes family, so that it was a
relief to find that, on the contrary, he was positively
ordered to cultivate friendly relations with them.
Whether his efforts would produce the result aimed
at was another question.   He could not feel very
sanguine, having met with many previous disappointments in similar enterprises.

The conversation drifted into other channels, and
was kept up, after a desultory fashion, for the best
part of an hour, during which time no interruption
was made by Colonel Littlewood, who, presumably,
was snoring in the adjoining room.   It was an
evening like a hundred others which had preceded
it, and because it was like them it was more than a
trifle wearisome.   Billy knew that he was looking
bored ; he was ashamed of himself for looking so,
and still more ashamed of feeling so, but he
couldn't help it.   He could not think of anything
new to say ; everything that could be said had
long ago been said and repeated again and again.
No wonder there were frequent pauses, and no
wonder Mrs. Littlewood rose at length, yawning
undisguisedly, with the remark :

'You are preternaturally dull to-night ; hadn't
you better go home to bed ?   If you are quick and

cautious you may make your escape before Alfred wakes and comes to remind you that it is whisky-and-soda time.'

He offered no protest. There had been a time when he would have protested, but he had forgotten it, although she had not. On the other hand, there had never been a time when he had not loathed the nocturnal confidences of Colonel Littlewood, who was apt to become even more offensive and expansive than usual between eleven o'clock and midnight. So he said good-night and stole softly out of the house into that scented darkness which belongs to the paradise of flowering shrubs. He ought to have been safe from pursuit, and he probably would have been safe, if he had not played this game once or twice before, and if Colonel Littlewood had not been rather particularly anxious to have a few words with him. As it was, that hospitable personage caught him up before he reached the garden-gate and begged him to come back and 'have a drink,' adding that it really wasn't anything like late enough to turn in yet.

Billy excused himself upon the plea of fatigue; whereupon Colonel Littlewood rejoined, with a sigh:

' Well, you're a lucky chap to be able to tire yourself—I wish *I* could get a good gallop, I know; but, dash it all! I can't afford a horse—can't even afford to hire one for the day. Between you and me, I don't see how I'm going to afford to live at all in a place like this. Devilish expensive all round, it seems to me—rent, servants, food, every blessed thing! Upon my life, it's too bad that one's income shouldn't go as far in Africa as it does in London!'

Billy felt very much inclined to expedite matters by asking bluntly, 'How much do you want?' But, as Billy could not find it in his heart to be downright brutal, even to the man whom he disliked more than any other human being, he resisted the inclination and listened as patiently as he could to a series of more or less relevant statements, the upshot of which was to increase Colonel Littlewood's indebtedness to him by the sum of two hundred pounds. He walked down the hill dispirited and dissatisfied, not because he had thrown away another couple of hundreds (for he never troubled himself much about money, and had no need to do so), but because he was beginning to feel that his present position was almost intolerable.

'When you come to think of it,' said he, addressing the stars, 'the old women aren't so very far wrong, after all. They may tell lies, and one may be in an infernal rage with them; but if they knew that that fellow was borrowing of me just as often as he chose—well, one couldn't exactly blame them for drawing their own conclusions. I wonder whether Blanche knows? But of course she can't —eh?'

The stars winked, but returned no audible answer; and about an hour later the deep sleep of youth and health had released Billy Bellew from half-formed misgivings.

Misgivings of another and a more definite nature awaited his awakening. It had been all very well to rejoice that his budding intimacy with the Forbes family had not been nipped by the frost of Mrs. Littlewood's disapproval; but what hope was there that people of that sort would ever consent to associate with a lady whose reputation was not wholly untarnished? Miss Forbes might perhaps be open to representations and above commonplace prejudices; but her father and mother evidently belonged to the most exclusive and respectable section of the entire community. In the highest circles leniency may be looked for with a certain degree of confidence, but not in the ranks of the country gentry. He knew this because he was pretty well acquainted with both classes.

However, he could but try; and during that day and the three or four which followed it he did try his best. His promise of giving some instruction to Micky afforded him an excuse for riding up to Le Bocage; and, as he was informed on the first day that the boy had caught a slight cold, nothing could be more proper or natural than that he should return on the morrow and the ensuing day to make inquiries. Each time he was received by Mrs. Forbes and Daisy, but was not privileged to see Winifred, who, he presumed, was engaged with her brother. This was something of a disappoint-ment to him; although, to be sure, his immediate

business was rather with Mrs. Forbes than with
her eldest daughter. The moment that he thought
he saw an opportunity, he broached the delicate
subject as skilfully as he could, and was immediately made to perceive that he had better drop
it. All Mrs. Forbes's urbanity and affability disappeared at the mention of Mrs. Littlewood's name,
and she said, with marked coldness :

'Oh yes, I have heard of her. We have not met
her, and there is no likelihood of our doing so,
because we don't go out much here — except, of
course, among our friends.'

'I think you will meet her at Mrs. Ryland's,'
observed Billy. 'You are going to dine with her,
aren't you ?'

'With Mrs. Ryland? Yes, I believe we are;
but I hope—— Perhaps we shall have the
pleasure of meeting *you* there? So glad! What
wonderfully beautiful weather we have been having
lately, have we not?'

There was nothing more to be said, and Mr.
Bellew said no more. Failure was certain, and
already he foresaw that Mrs. Forbes would soon
be added to the list of those enemies whom it had
been enjoined upon him that he must count as his
own. Meanwhile there was nothing inimical about
the demeanour of Miss Daisy, who, on the conclusion of his visit, picked up a sunshade and stepped
out into the garden with him to see him mount his
horse. She, at all events, did not contemplate any
severing of their friendly relations; for she had

several little schemes for passing away the time
to propose to him, and she actually had the
audacity to suggest that, if her mother could not
act as chaperon on all the excursions which she
had in mind, Mrs. Littlewood might do so.

'Personally,' observed the girl, laughing, 'I don't
feel so terribly alarmed at Mrs. Littlewood; and
mamma wouldn't have shied at her in that violent
way if you hadn't looked as if you anticipated it.
Don't do it again; you would only make a worse
mess of it. You had far better trust to Mrs. Ryland,
who is a woman, and who knows how to manage
other women.'

The advice was probably sound; but it was
hardly the sort of advice which one would have
expected to receive from a simple, country-bred
girl. Her sister, Billy felt convinced, would have
spoken differently. He was not quite sure that he
liked Miss Daisy, pretty and entertaining though
she was. 'She's a bit too much in the foreground,'
he soliloquized, 'and the other one is a bit too
much in the background. I wish the other one
would come to that Ryland woman's feed instead
of her.'

Mrs. Ryland must have intimated a similar wish,
or else Daisy, who was not fond of dinner-parties,
must have cried off at the last moment; for when
Billy, with as near an approach to trepidation as
his admirable nervous system was capable of,
arrived upon what seemed only too likely to prove
a field of battle, he found Winifred Forbes standing

beside his hostess near the doorway. The room—
a long, narrow Moorish apartment, dimly lighted
by hanging lamps—seemed to be tolerably well
filled with guests; in the background could be
discerned Lady Ottery, seated upon a divan; and
next to Lady Ottery sat Mrs. Forbes, who wore an
expression of armed neutrality; and beyond Mrs.
Forbes sat Blanche Littlewood, in her powder, her
paint and her diamonds. The introduction had
taken place, then! Yes, it must certainly have
taken place, for Blanche was talking volubly to
Mrs. Forbes, who was talking to Lady Ottery, who
seemed to be blandly unconscious that there was
anybody else in the immediate neighbourhood.
The little tableau thus formed by the three ladies
on the sofa was somewhat comic, and Billy, whom
it suddenly struck in that light, could not repress
an abrupt chuckle; but his feeling, upon the whole,
was much more one of relief than of amusement.

'It doesn't look over and above promising,' he
reflected; 'but at least there hasn't been an actual
row.'

Mrs. Ryland, a tall, dark-haired, determined-
looking woman, shook him by the hand, and said,
in a rather louder voice than seemed absolutely
necessary, that she was very glad to make his
acquaintance, having heard so much of him from
her old friend Mrs. Littlewood. Mrs. Ryland, who
was well born, who had married a rich manufacturer,
and who entertained a good deal both in London
and in the country, perhaps felt powerful enough

to champion her former school companion. She
had always tried to do what she could for Blanche,
not believing that there was any real harm in the
woman, and she was trying to do what she could
for her now—with mediocre success, it was to be
feared. At any rate, she knew better than to send
Mrs. Littlewood into the dining-room with Mr.
Bellew, who was requested to take charge of Miss
Forbes, and to whom this request did not appear to
be unwelcome.

'Well, and how is Micky?' he asked, as they took
their places.

'Ever so much better, thanks,' answered Winifred; 'and quite ready to take a riding lesson
whenever you can make it convenient to call for
him. He begged me to mention that to you, with
his respects.'

'I *have* called lots of times, without getting a
glimpse of either him or you,' remarked Billy
somewhat reproachfully.

'Yes, I know; I was sorry; but it couldn't be
helped. I didn't want him to tire himself before
he was quite well again, and if I hadn't kept guard
over him all the time that you were in the house,
he would have made his escape. He would have
managed to get leave from my father or from my
mother, and of course you wouldn't have seen any
reason why he shouldn't ride. He looks stronger
than he is, and feels stronger, too, which is unfortunate in some ways.'

'Oh, he'll be all right, don't you be afraid,' said

Billy encouragingly, responding rather to a ring of anxiety in his neighbour's voice than to her actual words.

'I hope he will; but he gave us all a terrible fright before we left England. However, there's no use in meeting trouble half-way. And you'll take him for his promised ride some day soon, will you?'

'Certainly I will,' answered Billy, adding, after a momentary pause, 'that is, if I'm allowed.'

His eyes wandered as he spoke towards the other end of the table, where Mrs. Littlewood was bringing the influence of her charms to bear upon a sprightly elderly gentleman. He thought it quite upon the cards that an edict of prohibition might be issued from that quarter; but not wishing to betray his fears, he made haste to offer another explanation of his remark.

'You know what I told you that afternoon,' he said hurriedly. 'Well, now that your mother and Mrs. Littlewood have met, don't you think your mother may decline the honour of my future acquaintance?'

The inference was not precisely flattering to Mrs. Littlewood, but Winifred forbore to smile. She understood what he had not said; she possessed, indeed, the gift of understanding people before they confided in her, and this, no doubt, it was which led so many of them to tell her all their secrets. Before dinner was over, Billy had as good as told her (though not in words) all his, and had been

greatly comforted by her friendly sympathy.
Naturally, there were some things with which he
could not expect her to sympathise ; but these
were passed over lightly, and she contrived to
convey to him the impression that she gave him
credit for being what in truth he was—a thoroughly
honest and chivalrous, if somewhat foolish, gentleman. Also she gave him to understand that he
had no need to feel alarmed lest the gates of
Le Bocage should be closed against him, and even
hinted at the possibility of their being thrown
open to admit Mrs. Littlewood. For gates are
not the same as doors, nor can moral contagion
be imparted through the medium of visiting-cards.
Mrs. Littlewood, Winifred presumed, would leave
cards, and in due season her civility would be returned, and she would probably be satisfied with
that measure of recognition.

In the meantime, Mrs. Littlewood appeared to be
very well pleased with such measure of recognition
as she was already receiving. Throughout the
evening she behaved wonderfully well, while the
Colonel behaved as well as he could. Billy, who
saw them into their carriage when they departed,
but who, for once, did not accompany them home,
had much ado to restrain himself from thanking
them both. That would have been a very clumsy
thing to do ; but he thought he might be permitted
to thank Miss Forbes, even though he did not
specify the precise cause of his gratitude.

CHAPTER VI.

MICKY RECEIVES AND GIVES INFORMATION.

AN innocent and inexperienced male creature might not unnaturally have expected that Mrs. Littlewood would be only half pleased with the results of Mrs. Ryland's efforts on her behalf; but the innocent and inexperienced Billy placed such slight reliance upon his own judgment in questions affecting the opposite sex that he was hardly surprised, although he was greatly relieved, when that lady expressed herself altogether pleased.

'I was prepared for nothing less than a slap in the face,' she remarked calmly; 'and, instead of that, I have received several shakes of the hand. In another week or two I shall be kissed. Not that I am particularly ambitious of being kissed by your friend Mrs. Forbes; but I mean her to be very nice and polite to me, and I'm sure she will now. By the way, what made you say that her daughters were pretty? Is the other a duplicate of that lanky girl?'

'Well, no; I suppose most people would call the younger daughter a good deal prettier,' answered Billy; 'but I like the one you saw much the best. She's awfully jolly to talk to — no humbug or nonsense about her, you know.'

A more diplomatic reply could not have been made; and it is just possible that, for all his guilelessness and truthfulness, Billy may have

been aware of that. Mrs. Littlewood really could
not feel afraid of the lanky girl, and she thought
she knew Billy well enough to know that, if he had
entertained any *penchant* for the second Miss Forbes,
he would have betrayed it. No serious impediment,
therefore, was placed in the way of his fulfilling his
engagement to Micky; and he rode up to Le
Bocage one fine morning, having given previous
notice of his intention by a note to Winifred, whom
he begged to excuse her pupil from lessons for an
hour or two.

He found his young friend waiting expectantly
at the door, booted and spurred, and holding the
long-tailed, ewe-necked barb which had been purchased for him on the strong recommendation of a
local horse-dealer. Mrs. Forbes came down the
steps, shading her eyes with her left hand and
extending her right, while she smiled upon the
new-comer with an amiability which showed that
the sight of Mrs. Littlewood had not deprived him
of her esteem.

'I won't ask you to come in,' she said. 'Daisy
has gone down to the town on a shopping expedition
with her friend Mrs. Nugent, and Winnie is very
busy, writing from her father's dictation. Mr.
Forbes has promised an article to the *Modern
Review*, which, he says, must be finished to-day
or to-morrow, and sometimes he suffers so much
from his eyes that he is obliged to employ an
amanuensis.'

'For which, and all His mercies, the Lord's

name be praised!' observed Micky, as he climbed into the saddle. 'You see, Mr. Bellew, there's only one amanuensis in this house, and when her services are requisitioned, other folks get a chance to go out riding for the benefit of their health.'

The shapely head of the amanuensis could be seen through one of the open windows, bending over a writing-table; from the background the voice of the learned author could be heard monotonously rising and falling: 'If we consider dispassionately the lessons which history has to teach us upon this all-important point; if we cast a backward glance upon the consequences of democratic government, as evidenced in—Stop a moment! stop a moment! Winnie, my love, you scribble at such a headlong pace that you cause me to lose the thread of my ideas, and thus much valuable time is wasted. Please start again. If we consider——'

'I don't think we'll consider any longer; I think we'll be off,' said Micky in an irreverent whisper. 'Don't let us be guilty of wasting valuable time.'

So Billy had to move off in the sunshine, without so much as a nod of greeting from the patient scribe; and it did seem to him uncommonly hard that the patient scribe should be debarred from enjoying the sunshine which ought to have been everybody's property. He could not help saying as much to Micky, who replied:

'Well, I dare say it is; but, you see, Winnie delights in doing odd jobs.'

'It appears to me,' observed Mr. Bellew, with

something less than his usual good-humour, 'that in your family you delight in giving her odd jobs to do.'

The boy smiled and glanced sharply at the handsome young giant by his side. He had a queer, shrewd, humorous little face, and his keen eyes took note of many things which escaped the observation of his elders. 'The same notion has sometimes made its way into my own great mind,' he remarked. 'All the same, I don't see how it's to be helped. Supposing you were driving a team of three slugs and one willing one, what would you do?'

'Why, thrash the slugs, of course,' answered Billy unhesitatingly. 'Only I should take jolly good care not to distress a willing horse in that way.'

Micky shook his head. 'You might distress a horse; you wouldn't distress Winnie,' said he. 'She'll always do all the work. Some day, I suppose, she'll be put into double harness, and she'll do all the work then, and our work won't be done at all.'

'Unless you do it yourselves. And why shouldn't you? What is your personal line of work going to be?—soldier, sailor, tinker or tailor?'

'Soldier, I hope,' answered the boy; 'only it don't do to say much about it at present, because I'm an only son, you know, and I ain't warranted sound. What I should like would be a cavalry regiment; men in good cavalry regiments always have a fine time of it, don't they?'

' I've known some fellows who liked the life, and others who didn't,' said Billy. ' It depends very much upon where you may happen to be stationed, I expect. So long as you're in England it ought to be right enough ; I'm not so sure about India.'

' India would do me very well,' Micky declared ; ' I'd go there without being ordered, if I were grown up and had lots of money. You have lots of money, haven't you ?' he added, with a matter-of-fact curiosity which was not in the least impertinent.

' Oh dear no !—only just enough to be idle upon,' answered the other. ' And that's a doubtful blessing.'

' Well,' said Micky, ' if the governor will allow me enough to be idle upon, I shall take a look round the world, and the first place I shall make for will be India. I want to see some pig-sticking.'

' You'll have to learn how to ride before you can play that game,' observed Billy ; ' and you'll never ride while you hold your hands as high as you're holding them now. Try to get into the habit of keeping your elbows well pressed into your sides.'

Micky, who was neither conceited nor a fool, took in excellent part the admonitions which Mr. Bellew addressed to him from time to time while they were making their way down the steep descent towards Mustapha Inférieur. Boys will submit to anything from one whom they have once recognised as their master, and Michael Forbes knew a fine horseman when he saw him. Besides, Billy himself, so far

as manners and conversation went, was nothing
more than a big boy, which, as most of us can
remember, used once upon a time to mean a far
more important personage than a man.

So this couple proceeded, upon the best of terms,
on their downward course, making, through rock-
strewn lanes and byways, for the great brown
Champ de Manœuvre, where military evolutions
are sometimes carried out, and where, once or
twice in the course of the year, race meetings are
held.   It was Micky who had suggested this as
the most suitable place for a bit of schooling, alleg-
ing that there was no other safe galloping ground
within a day's journey.

'So this is what they call a racecourse out here,
is it?' was Billy's pensive remark on reaching
the bare, sun-baked expanse, across which clouds
of dust from the neighbouring high road were
drifting lazily.   A charming prospect revealed itself to right and to left of him—the tall, feathery
palms of the Jardin d'Essai, the wide blue expanse
of the sea, the white town rising abruptly, like a
great marble pyramid, from the waves.   But he
was not looking at these things; his gaze was concentrated on the ground, and he murmured, 'I
don't know what you call *safe;* but if I had a horse
worth anything at all, I'd as soon race him over
paving stones as over that!'

'Oh, well, I mean there ain't any holes or
boulders or scrub here, that's all,' Micky explained.
'Of course the racing is all skittles.   They stick

up a few mignonette boxes when they have their
meetings, and play at steeplechasing. I wish they
had left a few of them up now!' he added regretfully.

Even without those aids to instruction, Billy was
able to form a pretty accurate estimate of his pupil's
proficiency. After a preliminary gallop, he put
him through various manœuvres, and ended by
telling him frankly that he had a good deal to learn
and not a little to forget. 'And you must sit in
the right place. If a man doesn't sit in the right
place, he *can't* have good hands—mind that!'

He went on to formulate numerous other axioms
which, however, interesting to his limited audience,
might not prove equally so to the larger and more
mixed one addressed by his humble biographer,
and concluded his lecture by saying suddenly:
'Now you get on to my horse and try what you
can do with him.'

Micky was out of the saddle in a moment; but
Mr. Bellew only laughed and sat still.

'Get up again, my boy,' said he; 'I knew you
had seen this brute kicking and bucking just now,
and I wondered whether you would have the nerve
to ride him, that was all.'

Micky coloured. 'Did you think I was a funk,
then?' he asked resentfully.

'How should I know? Now, don't be angry,
Micky; I shan't think so any more; and if you
had been a bit short of nerve, you would only have
been what nine men out of every ten are, and what

I dare say we shall both of us be before we die. Pluck isn't quite the finest quality in the world— though I won't deny that I'm glad you've got it.'

The alliance was cemented by this episode; and Mentor and Telemachus turned their horses' heads towards the town, meaning to reach home by a more circuitous and less precipitous route than that which they had selected for their descent. Now, it came to pass that, after they had hit off the broad high road to Mustapha Supérieur, and were jogging along it, they were overtaken by a light victoria in which were seated two ladies, one of whom hailed them.

'So there you are!' she cried. 'And have you really been giving up a whole morning to pounding along in the dust with that pertinacious boy? How awfully good of you!'

Billy took off his hat to Miss Daisy Forbes and to Mrs. Nugent, with whom he had a slight acquaintance. He said: 'Not good a bit! We've been enjoying ourselves, in spite of the dust, haven't we, Micky?'

Then, as Mrs. Nugent's coachman did not receive orders to quicken his pace, the two equestrians moved on with the carriage, one on either side of it, and it so chanced that Billy found himself on Miss Daisy's side. It has already been said that Billy was anything but a lady-killer, and it might have been added that he was in a fair way towards becoming a woman-hater; yet it cannot be pretended that Daisy's method of treatment was

altogether disagreeable to him. She had certain
tricks of look and voice which, well worn though
they be, are always effective ; and when she told
him that she wouldn't have missed Mrs. Ryland's
dinner-party for the world, if only she had known
that he was to be there, she really seemed to be
speaking the truth. Then, too, there was something very innocent and engaging about the eager
manner in which she exhibited her purchases to
him, asking him whether he was a judge of Syrian
embroidery or Kabyle pottery, and making him
promise to accompany them on their next expedition to the bazaars. She was in the act of expressing
a hope that he meant to join the family mid-day
repast at Le Bocage, when her brother's high-
pitched voice interrupted their colloquy.

'I say, Mr. Bellew,' called out Micky across the
carriage, 'you don't want to go back by the road,
do you ? If we turn off to the right here, we can
take one of the Arab lanes, which will be ever so
much jollier.'

As the lane in question was a mere track, as steep
as a staircase in places, and overgrown with trees
and shrubs, and as, moreover, the choice of it in
preference to the highway would involve a considerable détour, Daisy was fully justified in scouting her
brother's suggestion. But the good-natured Billy
assented to it at once, remarking half apologetically
that he was out for the boy's amusement. He said
good-bye to the ladies and followed Micky, who
had lost no time in taking him at his word, up the

narrow path, between high banks of red earth and beneath the shade of interlacing boughs and creepers. It was not until they had advanced some little distance, their horses clambering up the rocks as only Arab horses can, that his young friend turned round, with a mischievous twinkle in his eye, to say :

'Sorry to drag you away, you know.'

'Oh, I didn't mind !' answered Billy placidly.

'Well, if you didn't mind, it's all right; only thought perhaps you did ; and—look here, Mr. Bellew, you're a friend of mine, and I want to give you a friendly tip about our beloved Daisy. I saw what she was after the other day at the picnic, and I may tell you, between ourselves, that she's a horrid little flirt. Besides which, she's half engaged, if she isn't quite engaged, to Harry Lysaght.'

'Oh, indeed !' said Billy, much amused. 'Well, really, this is very thoughtful of you, Micky, and I'm much indebted to you. And who is Harry Lysaght, if I may ask? Not a little curly-headed chap who used to hunt with the Quorn two seasons ago ? Now I come to think of it, I believe he did hail from your part of the world.'

Micky nodded. 'That's the man. He isn't at all a bad sort; only he makes a perfect idiot of himself about Daisy, and I suppose that's why she won't marry him and have done with it. She's sure to take him in the long run, though, because I believe she likes him about as well as anybody,

and he's got no end of a jolly place, with lots of
shooting, near us. I thought I'd just warn you;
but you needn't mention it, you know.'

Billy promised to keep his own counsel, and
asked no more questions. So far as he was concerned, Miss Daisy was heartily welcome to marry
Mr. Lysaght or any other man whom she might
fancy; still, he had reasons of his own for concur-
ring in Micky's description of her. 'Her sister's
little finger is worth her whole body,' was his
mental verdict upon a lady who was at that
moment driving homewards in the serene conviction that Mr. Bellew's name would shortly be added,
if indeed it might not already be added, to the list
of her victims.

CHAPTER VII.

A LITTLE DISAPPOINTMENT.

'I do not see Michael,' said Mr. Forbes fretfully, as
he took his place at the head of the breakfast-table,
after having terminated what he was pleased to call
a morning's hard work. 'Where's Michael?'

Mr. Forbes was one of those mild, querulous
tyrants whose tyranny is perhaps more hard to
bear than that of the loud-voiced, blustering variety.
He was not in the least conscious of being exacting;
but, as a matter of fact, he expected all the members of his family to subordinate their convenience
to his, and unpunctuality he resented as a personal
injury. Naturally, therefore, he could not accept

Winifred's statement that Micky had not returned from his ride yet, but would be sure to be back in a few minutes, as any sort of excuse.

'Winnie, my love,' said he, 'you are far too ready to make assertions without pausing to ask yourself whether they are accurate or not. How can it be possible for you to tell that Michael will reach the house in a few minutes? What we do know for certain is that he is well aware of the usual breakfast-hour; and if he cannot be here at the proper time, he should not be allowed to go out riding.'

'I only hope nothing has happened to the boy!' exclaimed Mrs. Forbes nervously. 'Are you sure that that horse is safe for him to ride, Winnie?'

'Don't be agitated, mamma,' said Daisy: 'nothing has happened to him. At least, nothing had happened to him about half an hour ago, when we overtook him and Mr. Bellew riding up from the town. They chose to turn up one of the Arab lanes towards El-Biar, instead of coming straight back with us, which is quite sufficient to account for their being late. 'I am sorry,' continued Daisy meditatively, 'that I didn't think at the time of mentioning our breakfast-hour; for I wanted to make a definite engagement with Mr. Bellew, and that little wretch Micky whisked him off before I could manage it.'

'My dear child!' ejaculated Mrs. Forbes, in accents of remonstrance—'a definite engagement with Mr. Bellew!'

'Why not? I don't mean a matrimonial engagement, *bien entendu*—only an engagement to come with us the next time that we go down to buy carpets and cushions and things; the time when *you're* coming, you know, mamma; so that nothing could be more proper. As it is, I must write him a note. Or perhaps it would be better if you were to write the note. That would be propriety raised to its highest expression.'

It was by this sort of quiet audacity that Daisy was accustomed to achieve her ends and carry her modest schemes into effect. Mrs. Forbes only protested feebly that she didn't understand why Mr. Bellew should be invited to go shopping.

'Oh, because he wants to go!' answered Daisy, without hesitation. 'Of course he wants to buy presents and some stuff to make up into a smoking suit, like everybody else, and he wouldn't know where to go unless somebody told him. He will be useful to us, too; men are always useful when it comes to bargaining. They don't say much; but they look cross and disgusted, and as the money is supposed to belong to them, that produces a good effect.'

Mrs. Forbes yielded to these arguments. She generally did yield to the arguments of her younger daughter, and very seldom to those of her elder, who, indeed, was about to offer some remarks in opposition to the project, when her attention was drawn off by the entrance of Micky, hot, dusty and jubilant.

'First class, thanks !' said he, thoughtfully forestalling an inquiry which nobody had as yet addressed to him; 'haven't enjoyed anything so much since I left my happy home. No, my dear Winnie, I have *not* washed my hands, and what's more, I ain't going to, until I've appeased the pangs of hunger. I say, I hope you people haven't eaten everything up !'

A formal and deliberate rebuke from Mr. Forbes was listened to in respectful silence, Micky only raising his head from his plate on the conclusion of it to wink solemnly at the company. Conversation was then resumed. The head of the family had left the room, and the others were preparing to follow his example, when a telegram was brought to Mrs. Forbes, who, on perusing it, gave utterance to a little pleased cry.

'Dear me !' she exclaimed, 'how nice ! Harry Lysaght is coming over here for a few weeks. He telegraphs from Marseilles, and I suppose he will arrive by to-morrow's boat. I wonder which hotel he means to go to ?'

Winnie looked almost as pleased as her mother; Micky stuck his hands into his pockets, threw himself back in his chair, stared up at the ceiling and whistled a tune ; as for Daisy, she was unable to conceal her discomfiture.

'Oh, *what* a bore !' she exclaimed. 'Won't even the whole length of France and the whole breadth of the Mediterranean save us from our friends ?'

But she speedily recovered herself, and, disdain-

ing to notice Micky's rude hilarity, remarked:
'After all, I don't care ; let him come if he likes.
He won't be our guest, so we shall be under no
obligation to entertain him.'

'But, my dear,' expostulated Mrs. Forbes, 'you
must remember that he has come all this distance
simply for the sake of seeing us.'

'Did he say that in his telegram? If he did, it
was pretty cool cheek on his part. One doesn't
travel long or short distances to see people without
having been asked.'

Mrs. Forbes thought she would say no more for
the present. She had never been able to manage
Daisy, and she was conscious of having hitherto
impeded, rather than promoted, Mr. Lysaght's suit
by injudicious partisanship. But Winifred was
less cautious. She went out into the garden with
her sister presently, and when they had seated
themselves beneath the shade of a spreading ilex,
said :

'I hope you are not going to be a goose, Daisy.'

'I hope,' answered Daisy, 'that I am not, and
I shouldn't think that I was. Still, one never
knows. One thing may be looked upon as beyond
dispute, and that is that Harry Lysaght is a goose.
Even he might have known better than to chase
me about in this exasperating way !'

'It doesn't seem like good policy, certainly,'
Winifred admitted. 'Nevertheless, it is the most
straightforward thing to do, and perhaps he may
think that the time for policy has gone by. And,

you know, Daisy, men—even the most patient of them—won't wait for ever.'

'I shouldn't have thought,' remarked Daisy, 'that your experience would have led you to that conclusion. Edmund Kirby has waited long enough, in all conscience, and he appears to be prepared to wait contentedly for the rest of his natural life.'

'That is quite different. I didn't mean to say that all men are in a hurry to get married—though I expect Harry Lysaght will be—but they all want to know whether they are going to be accepted or refused.'

'Of course they do, and no sooner are they accepted than they cease to be devoted slaves and begin to put on the airs of lords and masters. I haven't the slightest intention of putting Harry Lysaght out of his pain yet awhile, unless a point-blank refusal would do it; I don't mind telling you that much.'

'It is very silly of you, Daisy; because he isn't coming here for nothing : he is sure to insist upon an answer. And you do really care for him ?'

'Honour bright, I don't,' answered Daisy, yawning. 'I can see that he is a highly desirable sort of husband, and personally I like him very well—about as well as Mr. Bellew, for instance. Only of course he isn't quite as interesting as Mr. Bellew, because he hasn't yet provided himself with a Mrs. Littlewood.'

'I really think you had better leave Mr. Bellew to Mrs. Littlewood,' said Winifred.

'How immoral of you! On the contrary, it shall be my righteous mission to rescue him from that wicked enchantress—which reminds me that I ought to be setting about it at once. I must get mamma to write her note and despatch it. We'll all go and buy rubbish to-morrow afternoon.'

It was evident that nothing could prevent that somewhat uncalled-for invitation from being despatched; but it was by no means unlikely, Winifred thought, that Mr. Bellew might be prevented from accepting it. She forgot to take into account that her mother's messenger would be despatched to the Hôtel d'Orient, with instructions to await a reply, and that, should Mr. Bellew be found at home, he would have no opportunity of consulting other interested persons before deciding whether to say yes or no.

As luck would have it, he was found at home, and, judging from the tone of his reply, he experienced no indecision whatsoever about saying yes. He would, as requested, be at Le Bocage by three o'clock the next afternoon, he wrote, and he should like nothing better than to be initiated into the art of dealing with native vendors of curiosities.

So far, so good, Daisy thought; it now only remained for her to ascertain whether her father meant to form one of the party or not, because, for obvious reasons, it was desirable that the party should consist of four, not of three persons. Mr. Forbes having somewhat emphatically disclaimed any intention of wasting his time in the foolish and unprofitable manner suggested, it naturally devolved upon Winnie to fill the vacant place, and this she consented to do, after the old gentleman had accorded her a rather grudging leave of absence.

Among the minor disappointments of life, few are more irritating than the failure of a promising little plan upon which we have expended some pains, and it stands to reason that such a failure is rendered doubly irritating if it be brought about by the very person for whose benefit the plan has been designed. This was the trial which fate had in store for Miss Daisy Forbes, whose equanimity proved wholly inadequate to the strain placed upon it thereby. It was already bad enough that Mr. Bellew should keep her mother and her sister and her—especially her—waiting for a quarter of an hour; it was pretty cool (and she meant to tell him so) to expect three ladies to sit, with their hats and gloves on, and do nothing until it should suit him to keep his appointment. But these offences sank into insignificance by comparison with the enormity of that which was to follow. The carriage had been waiting at the door for the time above-mentioned, and Mrs. Forbes had just remarked, 'Really, my dear Daisy, if Mr. Bellew doesn't come presently, I think we must start without him,' when a breathless Arab messenger arrived, bearing a visiting card, upon which were scribbled these words: 'So sorry to find I can't come, after all. Many apologies.

'Rather unceremonious, I must say!' was the observation of the recipient.

Daisy remained speechless for a minute or two; but that was only because she was so much taken aback that she could not just at first think of anything strong enough to say. As soon as she recovered command of her vocabulary, which was a rich one, she proceeded to apply a string of epithets to Mr. Bellew which ought to have made that gentleman's ears tingle. Daisy was the only hot-tempered member of the Forbes family; which was doubtless the reason why she did pretty much as she pleased with the other members of the family. When she had flown into a rage in the days of her childhood, nobody had ever thought of throwing cold water over her; on the contrary, it had been everybody's business to soothe and comfort her, and much the same practice had continued to prevail in later years. So, during the drive down the hill, her mother, who sat beside her, and Winnie, who sat opposite with her back to the horses, vied with one another in well-meant but ineffectual efforts to allay her wrath. But it was useless to tell her that Mr. Bellew could not have intended to be guilty of a studied insult, and that he would probably be able to give some perfectly satisfactory explanation of his conduct.

'He will never get the chance of making any explanation to me!' she declared. 'You may receive him again, if you choose; I *won't*.'

Nevertheless, she derived some secret gratification from one suggestion which her sister, perhaps a little indiscreetly, put forward.

'I dare say he would have been only too glad to come,' said Winnie, 'if Mrs. Littlewood had given him leave. I shouldn't be at all surprised if she had forbidden him at the last moment.'

This, it need scarcely be said, was precisely what had occurred. Billy had presumed too far upon the rather unusual length to which his tether of late had been permitted to run, and he had received a sharp reminder that he was not a free agent. It would have been all right if he could have got off breakfasting with the Littlewoods that day; but he tried to get off and failed; then, most unfortunately it transpired that Mrs. Littlewood wanted him to go out driving with her; then he had to confess that he had a previous engagement, and then there was a terrible disturbance. Contrary to his usual custom, Billy did not at once submit to do as he was told. He pointed out that to throw Mrs. Forbes over without the shadow of an excuse for so doing would be abominably rude; he protested his willingness and anxiety to drive with Blanche on the morrow, and the day after, and any number of days after; only he did hope that she wouldn't insist upon making both him and herself disagreeably conspicuous by detaining him that afternoon.

'Because,' he added sapiently, 'if I don't turn up, and can't give a reason for not turning up,

they'll be perfectly certain to guess what has become of me.'

But Mrs. Littlewood was in one of her stubborn
and perverse moods. She said that if he was
ashamed of her company, he certainly could not do
better than forsake it; she observed that she had
for a long time past seen that he was tired of her;
she advised him to lose no time in hurrying up to
Le Bocage, lest his new friends should be growing
impatient; only, if he did go, she hoped he would
not trouble to come back again; because, humble
though she was, she was not quite humble enough
to care about sharing with Miss Forbes a friendship which had once been exclusively her own.
After which she burst into tears.

This was conclusive; but by the time that Mrs.
Littlewood's tears had been dried (from considerations of precaution which will readily be understood,
the greater proportion of these was heroically gulped
down), and Billy had surrendered at discretion, he
discovered, to his horror, that it was already three
o'clock. Hence the scribbled card and the breathless messenger.

Now, Billy was not the man to do things by
halves, and, having made up his mind to please
Blanche rather than himself, he put a pleasant
face upon it. Still, it must be confessed that his
face became considerably longer when he heard
what the object of their drive was to be. Mrs.
Littlewood may not have originally intended to
ransack the curiosity shops that afternoon; but

such was her declared intention now, and he dared not remonstrate, for fear of making her cry again. He could but hope that the curiosity shops of Algiers might be very numerous, and that Fortune, who had already treated him so cruelly, would spare him the additional misery of encountering the party which he had been compelled to desert.

The curiosity shops of Algiers are numerous enough; but that Billy should have hoped to avoid meeting Mrs. Forbes and her daughters in one or other of them only shows how imperfectly acquainted he was with the character of his fair companion. Mrs. Littlewood's victories, as he might have remembered, were seldom followed up by any display of magnanimity on her part, nor was she very prone to deny herself the gratification of her immediate wishes through any regard for ordinary prudence. Her present feeling was that Billy deserved some punishment, and that the Forbes family needed a reminder that Mr. Bellew was not at their beck and call. She therefore drove in rapid succession to the Rue Bab-Azoun, to the Place du Gouvernement and to several of the narrow streets that fringe the old town, making a few purchases (for which Billy paid), but taking little heed of the wares exhibited for her approval, until she reached a certain establishment in the Rue de la Lyre, at the door of which an open carriage was waiting.

Only too well did Billy know that carriage; from afar he had recognised the short silk jacket, the gaudy sash and the scarlet fez of the Arab coachman ; and he made a feeble, despairing attempt to avert the imminent catastrophe.

'I—I don't think this is much of a place,' he stammered ; 'there's another chap over the way who looks as if he'd be a great deal more likely to have the sort of things that you want.'

'What sort of things do I want?' inquired Mrs. Littlewood. 'If you know, you're better informed than I am.'

She had already alighted, and, without waiting for a reply, plunged into the dark recesses of the shop, whither Billy, after resisting an ignoble inclination to take to his heels, was fain to follow her. His eyes had not yet become accustomed to the obscurity when he heard her exclaim, in her most urbane and amiable voice—that voice which was always associated in his mind with moments of public humiliation :

'Oh, Mrs. Forbes, how do you do? I didn't recognise you at first. I suppose you are going the round of the shops, as we are. Do take pity on a poor stranger, and give me some advice. I really don't know what's good and what isn't, and I haven't the most distant idea of what one ought to pay. As for Mr. Bellew, I am sorry to say that he is utterly useless.'

CHAPTER VIII.

HARRY LYSAGHT.

AUDACITY was Mrs. Littlewood's favourite weapon; but it cannot be said for her that she always wielded it with skill or judgment. Sometimes, however, it served her purpose by depriving others of their presence of mind; and this was the effect which her altogether unexpected greeting produced upon Mrs. Forbes, who found herself shaking hands with the woman before she knew what she was about.

There are situations which are saved by their own excessive awkwardness. Everybody, except Mrs. Littlewood, felt so thoroughly apprehensive and uncomfortable that nobody was disposed to make things worse than they already were; and Mrs. Forbes, for one, instead of sticking her chin in the air and effecting a dignified retreat, began to explain, in a quite friendly, if somewhat hurried tone, that all the prettiest things were upstairs, that she herself was just going away, that she only wanted to conclude a bargain upon which she was engaged over a Kabyle rug, and so forth.

Billy, meanwhile, was standing in the background, looking the picture of misery. What could he do or say? To apologise for his defection would be a mere mockery, to jauntily ignore the whole business would require more impudence than he could summon up: there was nothing for

it but to wait patiently and allow them all to see
—as surely they must—that at least he was not
by his own choice in his present predicament.

Well, they could hardly help seeing that much;
and after a minute or two, during which the conversation between Mrs. Forbes and Mrs. Littlewood
had actually resolved itself into an amicable discussion about carpets and embroidered hangings,
he ventured to glance furtively at Winifred, whose
brown eyes were resting upon him with an expression of mingled amusement and compassion.
Thinking that he could read in them a permission
to advance, he did so, and said in a low voice:

'I'm awfully ashamed of myself; I'm afraid
you'll hardly believe that I haven't done this on
purpose; but the real truth is that I was just
starting to join you when I found that Mrs. Littlewood had counted upon my driving with her; and
so——'

'I don't see why you should be ashamed of yourself,' answered Winifred, smiling, and laying ever
so slight a stress upon the word 'you.' 'It isn't
your fault that you are in such universal request,
and you couldn't be in two places at one and the
same time. Anyhow, you owe no apology to
me, because it wasn't I who asked you to come
with us.'

She turned her head, as she spoke, towards her
sister, who was standing close by, and who, she
hoped, would take this opportunity of pardoning
the repentant offender. One cannot think of

everything, and in her anxiety to improve Daisy's spirits and temper she quite forgot that it would perhaps be no great misfortune were that young woman to carry out her threat of never speaking to Mr. Bellew again. Before anything more could be said, she was summoned by her mother to give assistance in the matter of the Kabyle rug, which the turbaned individual who was displaying it swore that he would rather give away as a present than part with for the price offered; and thus Billy was left face to face with the lady whom he had so deeply affronted.

By this time she had made up her mind to forgive him, for she understood very well what the state of the case was, and it was impossible to doubt that he was more sinned against than sinning. Still, as justice demanded that some rebuke should be administered, she remarked:

'I can't compliment you on your courage.'

Somehow or other, he looked a good deal less meek than he had done when speaking to Winnie a moment before. 'I haven't the courage to disappoint people, if that's what you mean,' he answered a little curtly. 'Mrs. Littlewood would have been disappointed if I had left her to take her drive all alone this afternoon, and of course I don't flatter myself that my presence or absence could make much difference to you. Still, I know it was bad manners not to keep my appointment, and I beg your pardon.'

'You must be an old hand at making excuses,'

remarked Daisy, laughing; ' it is clever of you to drive me into such a corner that I can only assure you that it doesn't in the least matter, or else confess that you did disappoint me by playing truant. Well, at the risk of increasing your vanity, I make you welcome to the information that I was disappointed. So much so, indeed, that I had almost resolved to decline your acquaintance for the future.'

' I'm glad you thought better of that,' said Billy. ' I suppose, if you had turned your back upon me, the rest of your family would have followed suit; and I should have been very sorry to be cut by my friend Micky and your sister.'

It was by this unlooked-for exhibition of severity that Mr. Bellew gave evidence of the abhorrence in which he held all flirts. It was true that his heart had not been touched by the tactics of Miss Daisy Forbes; still, as he very reasonably argued, it might have been, and it was anything but creditable to her to have behaved as she had done, considering that she was as good as engaged to another man. Unfortunately, the moral lesson which he desired to inculcate was completely thrown away upon its subject, who had not the most remote idea of what he was driving at, and for whom a recalcitrant wooer had all the attraction that a game fish possesses for the experienced angler. So far from taking offence, she set to work to dispel his imaginary ill-humour, and by the time that the Kabyle rug had at length passed into Mrs. Forbes's possession, her own ill-humour had completely vanished.

'*A tout péché miséricorde*,' she remarked complacently, after she had resumed her seat in the carriage and the horses' heads had been turned homewards. 'The poor man wasn't a willing sinner, at all events; one couldn't look at his face and think that of him.'

'I never noticed his face,' Mrs. Forbes confessed, with a sigh; 'I couldn't get beyond the face of that woman, which was outrageously powdered and painted. She took my breath away so by rushing at me in that way that I hardly know what I said, and I am afraid I was almost gushing. Winnie dear, I do think you might have tried to help me a little! The next thing will be that we shall have her dropping in at all hours of the day.'

Mrs. Littlewood, however, had no intention of doing that, and was well satisfied to rest upon her laurels for the present. She did not even allude to the little scene which has been described above until the time came for her to dismiss her patient escort, when she observed:

'I was determined that, if those good folks wanted to know you, they should know me; but I shall not quarrel with you over their favours. They are worthy sort of people, and the little one who made eyes at you is quite pretty; but I don't see how one could spend an hour in their company without yawning one's head off.'

Now, it came to pass on the following day that,

just as Billy was about to mount his horse at the door of the Hôtel d'Orient, he was accosted by a fresh-coloured, curly-headed young man, who said :

'I think I must claim acquaintance with you, though I dare say you don't remember me. My name is Lysaght; we used to meet out hunting the year before last.'

'Of course I remember you as well as possible,' answered Billy, shaking hands. 'Very glad to see you again; though this is about the last place in the world where I should have expected to see a sportsman. What has brought you here? Not health, I hope?' Then, suddenly remembering Micky's revelation, 'Oh, by the way, though—of course!—I forgot.'

Harry Lysaght did not ask him what he meant, but laughed in a half-gratified, half-sheepish manner, and said : 'I suppose you know the Forbeses?'

'Yes, a little; not very well. I've seen more of the boy than of any of the others. He's a good little chap, and ought to make a fine rider one of these days.'

'Perhaps—if he lives; but I'm afraid, from what I hear, that his lungs aren't sound. It's to be hoped that he'll come all right; for I'm sure I don't know what poor Winnie would do if anything happened to him.'

After this, the Forbes family were dismissed from the conversation in favour of certain hunting reminiscences, and presently the two men parted,

promising one another to meet again soon. They
had been scarcely more than acquaintances in
England ; but there was every probability of their
becoming friends in exile.

Harry Lysaght, indeed, not only liked, but profoundly admired Billy Bellew, whose prowess in
the hunting-field and as a gentleman-rider he had
often witnessed. Of Billy's private life he did not
know much ; but he did know what was supposed
to be pretty generally known about Mrs. Littlewood, and he was sorry to hear, later in the day,
from Daisy Forbes, that that lady was spending
the winter in Algiers.

'It's an awful pity, you know,' he said regretfully.

'So I think,' observed Daisy, 'and I'm doing
my little best to save him. Let us form a rescue
party, and unite in the good work. Bring him up
here with you as often as you can ; I shall always
be delighted to see him.'

If her object was to arouse her hearer's jealousy,
she failed ; for, although Harry Lysaght could be
and often was ridiculously jealous, it did not occur
to him to regard Mr. Bellew in the light of a possible rival. He himself had met with a much more
gracious reception than he had dared to hope for.
He had been very well aware that Daisy would not
like being pursued, and that was why he had given
no notice of his impending visit before arriving at
Marseilles. He had come because he had been
unable any longer to endure the pangs of separa-
tion ; but he had come fully prepared to be teased

and baffled and held at arm's length. He was rich, he had a fine estate, he was young and by no means bad-looking; he had a perfect right to demand an answer, and every excuse for anticipating a favourable one. But, being desperately in love, he feared his fate too much; so that Daisy was accustomed to amuse herself by toying with her prey. She had welcomed him, in fact, for no other reason than that she was glad to see him, and she was only glad to see him because she thought she could see her way to getting some additional amusement out of him. To make Harry jealous of Mr. Bellew would not be much fun; but to make Mr. Bellew jealous of Harry would be sport of a high order, and she hoped to enjoy it.

Her unsuspecting victim promised readily to do as he was asked. 'I suppose you are more or less joking,' he remarked; 'but, really and seriously, I believe what Bellew wants is a little more of ladies' society. Of course he has any number of friends, and I dare say he dines out a good bit during the season, and all that; but I never heard of his having a single intimate lady friend—unless you call Mrs. Littlewood a lady.'

Whether Mrs. Littlewood was a lady or not, her intimacy with Mr. Bellew was close enough and exacting enough to keep that unfortunate man pretty constantly on duty during the next two or three days. Harry Lysaght, with whom he had several chats, and who refreshed his soul with the latest intelligence from the shires, proposed in vain to him that they should pay a joint visit to Le Bocage. He had to decline, and he made no secret of his reason for doing so.

'Mrs. Littlewood asked me to look in,' he would say. 'She has been seedy, and she doesn't know many people here. I'm afraid I couldn't very well leave her in the lurch this afternoon.'

Harry, who had met Mrs. Littlewood in England, had, as in duty bound, left a card upon her. He had not been admitted, but he had encountered her husband in the town, and—finding, after a few tentative remarks, that he might do this with impunity—he had spoken his mind with some freedom to Billy upon the subject of the Colonel. Anybody was at liberty to revile Colonel Littlewood in Billy's presence; in fact, such revilings were rather agreeable to him, as partaking of the nature of a tacit admission that great allowances ought to be made for Colonel Littlewood's wife.

Meanwhile, Colonel Littlewood's wife kept him upon an uncommonly short allowance of freedom, and, although she had declared that she would not dispute with him for the favours of the Forbes family, took very good care that he should not receive an overdose of them. Fruitless, therefore, were the expectant lingerings of Micky at the stable gate, and fruitless all the efforts of Miss Daisy to initiate a well-conceived plan of campaign. The former was a good deal discouraged; the latter was only stimulated by preliminary rebuffs to fresh exertions. And success came to her at last, as indeed it almost always does to those who are not weary in ill-doing.

One afternoon Harry Lysaght intercepted Billy, who was, as usual, plodding along the dusty road on his way to Mrs. Littlewood's villa, and said :

'Are you doing anything on Thursday evening, Bellew ?'

'Thursday ?' repeated Billy meditatively. 'No, I don't think so. In fact, I'm sure I shall be free on Thursday, because the Littlewoods leave on that day. They're going up to Hammam R'irha for a week or so. Littlewood has a touch of the gout, or thinks he has.'

'Serve him right,' said Harry. 'I hope the waters will bring it out, and keep him squealing on his back for a month. *You* won't have to go with them, then ?'

'Well, no ; I'm not going with them. Perhaps I may follow—I'm not sure. Anyhow I shall be here on Thursday evening.'

'Then you'll come with us and see the Arab town by moonlight, won't you ? Mrs. Forbes told me particularly to ask you. There's a full moon and every prospect of fine weather, and it's quite one of the things to do. You drive to the Kasbah, you know, and then walk down. And I thought it would be rather jolly to have supper at one of the restaurants afterwards. You and I might treat the company if you felt inclined.'

Billy, it is needless to say, felt quite inclined

to take part in this little jaunt, and signified his assent, which was duly reported at Le Bocage immediately afterwards.

'That makes it all right, you see,' Harry Lysaght explained to Winnie, whom he already treated as a sister-in-law, and to whose counsel and assistance he had frequently had recourse in moments of perplexity; 'now we shall have an even number. You can walk with Bellew, and Mrs. Forbes can support your father's steps and keep him from running his head up against a wall.'

'Yes; that will be very nice,' answered Winnie with a demure smile.

It would have been cruel to mar the young man's sanguine anticipations by telling him what her own were; but it was, as she well knew, highly probable that Mr. Bellew would be appropriated by Daisy, and that upon her would devolve the task of administering balm to the wounded spirit of a gentleman who did not always receive such ministrations gratefully.

It is, however, impossible for any human being to foretell the course of events; even experience is no infallible guide, and a margin should always be allowed for the many disconcerting contingencies which do not throw their shadows before them. Amongst these latter was one which Harry Lysaght had assuredly never dreamt of taking into account, and which was revealed to him when he returned to the hotel to dress for dinner. Immediately after he had reached his room there came a knock at the door, and in strode Billy Bellew, who looked troubled and a little shamefaced.

'Look here, Lysaght,' said he, 'I don't know about this moonlight expedition; I think perhaps I'd better cry off. And yet, I don't quite see how I'm to do that, either. Well, the fact of the matter is that I told the Littlewoods I was going, and they said at once they would put off their start till Friday and come with us. Of course I couldn't say that it was Mrs. Forbes's party and that they must get an invitation from her. I couldn't say such a thing as that, could I? But at the same time, you know——'

'Oh, it's rather a bore; but it can't be helped,' interrupted Harry, trying not to look too much disgusted. 'After all, Mrs. Forbes does know Mrs. Littlewood; it's only that terrible Colonel who alarms me. But I suppose he won't—eh?'

Billy shook his head gloomily.

'I should think very likely he would; I wouldn't answer for him. He was making zigzags all over the Place du Gouvernement yesterday at three o'clock in the afternoon. I had to take him home in a fiacre and leave my horse with a boy, who jumped on to his back and of course got chucked. Luckily the horse knew his way to the stables. No, my dear fellow; the only plan is to change my mind, and go off to Hammam R'irha on Thursday.'

No doubt Harry was chiefly anxious that his party should not be spoiled by the retirement of that member of it whose presence was essential to its symmetry ; but he was also honestly desirous of freeing his friend from the clutches of the enchantress, and he perceived that the departure of the Littlewoods for Hammam R'irha, leaving Billy behind them, would afford opportunities which no true friend of the latter's would be justified in neglecting. Therefore he said cheerily :

'Nonsense ! we aren't going to let you off on any pretext. It will be all right, you'll see. You can take charge of Mrs. Littlewood, and the Colonel, if he isn't *too* drunk—and I don't suppose he will be —can walk with Winnie. Winnie is the best girl in the world; she won't mind walking with anybody. And I think, you know, we won't say anything about it at Le Bocage ; it would only make a fuss and a discussion and do no good.'

'I think Mrs. Forbes ought to be told,' said Billy. 'It isn't only about the Colonel ; for I dare say I shall be able to bring him up to the scratch pretty sober; but I am not at all sure that Mrs. Forbes cares about being intimate with Mrs. Littlewood. For the matter of that, I may say I'm quite sure she doesn't. And it isn't fair to spring a surprise upon her.'

Harry Lysaght was not so scrupulous. He said Mrs. Forbes wasn't a royalty ; you weren't bound to submit a list of your guests to her before inviting her to a supper-party. Moreover, supposing that a chance of objecting were given to her, and that she did object, where would they be then ?

'Well, not in Algiers,' answered Billy, with a

laugh. 'At least, one of us wouldn't. Upon my word, Lysaght, you had much better let me retire.'

But this Mr. Lysaght declared and swore that he would not do; so, after some further argument, Billy (who, to tell the truth, had no wish at all to visit Hammam R'irha) allowed his misgivings to be overruled.

CHAPTER IX.

MOONLIGHT.

WINIFRED FORBES stood in the moonlight on a little bare plateau near the old Moorish citadel, or Kasbah, which crowns the apex of the pyramid formed by the town of Algiers. The scene at which she was gazing with wondering eyes and parted lips seemed to her almost too lovely to be real; for, indeed, the Algerian moon has little affinity with the cold, hard luminary whose beams irradiate our Northern landscape on fine nights. There was nothing hard or cold about the wondrous panorama which Winifred beheld from her lofty standpoint. The snow-white houses of the Arab town, the domes and minarets of the mosques, the dark olive and ilex woods, the palms, swaying before the breath of a light wind, the great bay, with here and there a shimmering sail upon its surface, Cap Matifou beyond, and the mountains of Kabylia in the far distance—all these lay bathed in

a marvellously brilliant, yet soft, light, which trans-
figured and glorified them, but did not—or, at all
events, did not appear to—rob them of their colour.

Winifred had stolen a short distance away from
the others to regale her eyes with this exquisite
prospect, and for the moment she had forgotten
their existence—had forgotten the rather absurd
scene which had taken place a few minutes before,
when, on reaching the appointed trysting-spot, the
Forbes family had met, not only the two friends
whom they had expected to see, but a very lively
lady and a still more lively gentleman, who
cheerfully signified their intention of joining the
party. Her mother's undisguised annoyance, Mr.
Bellew's mournful, deprecating mien, Harry's
singularly ill-advised apologies, the affability of
Mrs. Littlewood, the noisy joviality of the Colonel,
her own desperate inclination to burst out laughing
—it had all passed away from her memory, and no
doubt she would have stood stock-still where she
was for another quarter of an hour, if somebody
had not come to rouse her out of her trance.

Somebody said, in a very gentle and apologetic
voice : 'They think we ought to be starting, Miss
Forbes. Old Hamoud, the guide, says we must
keep together, or we shall get lost in those narrow
streets.'

Winifred turned away obediently, but paused
after she had taken a few steps to throw one last,
lingering glance at the view. 'Isn't it beautiful!'
she exclaimed.

'Yes,' answered Billy, 'it is indeed; I don't think I have ever seen anything so beautiful before. But I can't enjoy it. I'm too much ashamed of myself. I ought not to have come, and I ought not to have let the Littlewoods come. It was a great mistake. I should have seen that at once from your mother's face—if I hadn't known it already.'

'What nonsense! The only person who made a mistake was Harry; he really ought to have known better than to apologise. As for mamma, she was surprised, and she naturally looked so, that was all. Pray don't distress yourself; you aren't in the least to blame.'

'Well, if *you* don't blame me, I don't so much mind,' said Billy, with a relieved sigh. 'The truth is that the Littlewoods offered to come; and when people offer to come anywhere with you, you can't very well tell them that you don't want them.'

'Especially not when you do want them. Ought you not to be escorting Mrs. Littlewood now? You needn't mind about me; I am quite accustomed to taking care of myself.'

The party, under the leadership of the turbaned Hamoud, had by this time been set in motion, and was progressing down the hill in irregular forma-tion. Mrs. Forbes, who had taken her husband by the arm, was evidently determined to avoid com-mitting herself and to devote her whole attention to her wifely duties. Behind her walked Mrs. Littlewood, offering occasional remarks, which apparently were not heard; then came Harry Lysaght, all by himself, and then Colonel Littlewood, who, judging by his loud and continuous laughter, was relating some humorous anecdote for Daisy's benefit. It certainly did look as if Billy ought to intervene and effect a redistribution of partners; but he could not help a strong feeling of reluctance to disturb the existing arrangement. Should he do what he was told to do, and what represented itself to him in the light of a duty towards several of his neighbours, or should he for once be selfish, and consult his own inclinations? It was unnecessary for him to vex his conscience with such questions; for one of his neighbours had no intention whatsoever of allowing him any choice in the matter. Daisy unceremoniously forsook the loquacious Colonel, and, stepping back to meet her sister, said:

'Winnie, I wish you would go and catch up Mrs. Littlewood. She has nobody to talk to, and mamma is in such terror of repeating the tragedy of Jack and Jill that she can't spare a thought for anything else.'

'Very well,' answered Winifred hesitatingly; 'but I think Mr. Bellew——'

'Oh, I am going to retain possession of Mr. Bellew,' interrupted Daisy briskly. 'I have a crow to pluck with him—several crows, indeed!'

Both Winifred Forbes and Mr. Bellew were addicted by nature to doing as they were bid. Neither of them protested, and so the former

presently found herself picking her way down the
steep and tortuous streets of the old town, side by
side with a lady against whom she had conceived a
strong prejudice. It is not easy to talk to people
against whom you are strongly prejudiced, and for
some little time Winnie's efforts met with no encouragement from her partner, who seemed to have
enough to do to keep her footing, even with the
support of Billy's walking-stick, which she had
borrowed. The so-called streets of the Arab
quarter are, for the most part, mere flights of
steps, paved with rough and slippery stones. Mrs.
Littlewood wore very high-heeled boots, and the
constant abrupt transitions from bright moonlight
to deep shadow might well have rendered advance
uncertain to a less absurdly-shod pedestrian. She
never raised her eyes to the low arched doorways,
the plaster arabesques and the overhanging upper
stories, sustained by groups of round, whitewashed
rafters, which delighted Winnie, but plodded onwards and downwards as best she could until she
reached a gateway with a porch, on either side of
which was a tiled seat. Here she flung herself
down, and took her companion's breath away by
asking, without a word of preface :

'What would you do if you had a husband like
mine ?'

'But—but I don't know what your husband is
like,' was the best reply that Winifred could hit
upon at such short notice.

'Well, at least, you know what he *looks* like ;

and that is what he is—that and more. I did think that just for this once—and after my begging him so particularly—I did think that he would have tried to refrain from disgracing me. But you see the state he is in; and it is always like that, and always will be. It seems as if he had sworn to prevent my ever knowing any nice people!'

Mrs. Littlewood took out her handkerchief. There were real tears in her eyes; for she was genuinely mortified and unhappy. As a matter of fact, her husband was not, and never had been, unkind to her; but his habits of intemperance had caused her to pass through some humiliating moments, and she quite believed that she was a deeply injured wife.

'Oh, but I think you must be mistaken,' said Winnie, who could not help being sorry for the woman. 'I really didn't notice anything about him—except, perhaps, that his voice was rather loud.'

'What is the use of saying that?' cried the other impatiently. 'If you didn't notice, I am sure everybody else did, that he is more than half tipsy; and unless I can get him away before the supper—which will be impossible—I shall have to take him home quite tipsy. Oh, that is nothing new, I assure you! And now let me ask you once more, what would you do if you had a husband like mine?'

'I suppose,' answered Winnie hesitatingly, 'I should try to make the best of him.'

She did not mean this as a rebuke, but it was accepted as such by Mrs. Littlewood, who continued to weep, and who remarked pathetically that it was easier to offer counsels of perfection than to follow them. She gave a moving account of her patience, her trials, her repeated disappointments. She said she was well aware that people called her fast and flighty, and a number of other bad names; but if these censorious persons only knew what her life at home was, surely even they would not blame her for escaping from it when she could and seeking such amusement as still remained within her reach. In short, she made out a case for herself which aroused the compassion and, to some extent, secured the sympathy of her hearer.

After a time they resumed their march. Mr. and Mrs. Forbes had long ago passed out of sight, and there was as yet no sign of the approach of the rear-guard; but when your only object is to reach the bottom of a steep hill, you cannot miss your way very badly. Mrs. Littlewood, thinking that she had gained an ally, had become more cheerful. She said :

'After all, we must hope for the best. A walk like this ought to sober him, and I dare say it will; for I am sure it must be agony to anyone with a threatening of gout to hobble down such places. To be sure, there remains the supper, but I shall trust to Billy to take care of him then.'

'Is Mr. Bellew any relation of yours?' asked Winifred, with just a touch of sharpness in her tone.

Mrs. Littlewood laughed.

'You know quite well that he isn't. Of course it's very shocking of me to call him by his Christian name, but I really couldn't get out of the habit at this time of day, and he would think I was dreadfully offended with him if I were to address him as Mr. Bellew.'

'Wouldn't it be rather a good thing if you were?' asked Winifred, wondering a little at her own temerity. 'A good thing for both of you, I mean.'

'It would be for *me*, no doubt,' answered Mrs. Littlewood. 'I am painfully conscious that poor Billy, without in the least intending it, has done me almost as much injury in the eyes of the world as my husband has. But, silly as you may think me, I couldn't find it in my heart to send him about his business. One can't be quite insensible to such devotion as his, though one may have done nothing at all to encourage it; and if it makes him happy to be near me, why should I grudge him that morsel of happiness?'

'Oh, if you are sure that it makes him happy— but he doesn't always look happy.'

'No, indeed, poor fellow! How could he? But I really believe that he suffers more on my account than on his own.'

Winifred, whose commiseration had by this time given place to contempt, was saying to herself: 'Well, you certainly are the most selfish, silly and vulgar woman I have ever met.' Mrs. Littlewood, on her side, was thinking: 'I perfectly understand

what you are driving at, my dear: I am to renounce Billy, and leave the field clear for Miss
Daisy, in return for which you will kindly lend
me your countenance, and introduce me to your
friends. Many thanks, but I do not feel tempted
to close with that offer; it is not quite good enough.'
She resumed aloud:

'If you knew Billy as well as I do, you would
understand the impossibility of my dismissing him.
He would be simply inconsolable! I suppose you
think he would fall in love with some girl or other
and marry her. I assure you he wouldn't; girls
are not attractive to him, and I doubt very much
whether marriage is, either. There is your sister,
for instance, who—you won't mind my saying so,
will you?—who is making innocent little efforts to
captivate him. Well, your sister is very pretty
and very charming, but she doesn't appeal to him
in any way. He told me the other day, when we
were talking about you both, that he liked you
much the best of the two. So you see!'

Winifred was very angry; but it was difficult
to make a crushing rejoinder, because there was no
denying that Daisy had made efforts to captivate
Mr. Bellew. Therefore she only quickened her
pace, and said:

'Perhaps you and he are the best judges of what
concerns yourselves; but I don't think you ought
to complain if disagreeable remarks are made
about you. Oh, there are papa and mamma and
Hamoud. I wonder what has become of the others.'

The arrival of the others was retarded by the circumstance that during the greater part of their walk they had been playing an absurd game of hide-and-seek. Harry, exasperated by the jocular familiarities of the Colonel, and determined to shake him off, had given chase as fast as his gouty companion, who had him by the arm, would let him to the couple in front; Daisy, well aware that she was being pursued, had dodged round corners with the docile Billy, had insisted upon exploring the most evil-smelling alleys, had twisted and turned and, upon the whole, had enjoyed herself very much, until at last she was caught in an open space by the breathless Harry and the still more breathless Colonel. Harry was a good deal ruffled. He scarcely troubled himself to lower his voice as he caught Billy by the elbow and said :

' Look here, Bellew, I didn't bargain for this sort of thing. You had better take charge of that brute and try if you can't get him to behave himself ; perhaps you understand his little ways better than I do. He's as drunk as a fly, you know.'

Thus for a second time was a charge of inebriety brought against poor Colonel Littlewood, who really was not intoxicated, only genial, and desirous of spending a merry evening. He had dined, though not any better than usual, and it is true that he had thoughtfully provided himself with a flask of cherry-brandy; but Harry had not allowed him time to put his lips to it, and he was only able to take a little refreshment when that impetuous young man had moved on, in company with the reluctant Daisy. Billy did not attempt to interfere with him. He was, indeed, sufficiently well acquainted with the Colonel's 'little ways' to know how futile any such attempt would be, and he also knew that the man's behaviour would be rendered neither better nor worse by so moderate a potation.

'Excitable sort of chap, your friend Lysaght,' remarked the Colonel, wiping his mouth. 'Never was so hustled in my life! Thought he'd have had me down once or twice—I did indeed! Dare say he won't be in such a hurry now he has got hold of the young woman, eh? So you and I will take it easy, old man. That confounded foot of mine is beginning to wake me up like blazes, I can tell you! Shouldn't wonder a bit if I had to stop in bed to-morrow, and give up Hammam what's-its-name.'

'Oh, you *must* go to Hammam R'irha!' said Billy earnestly. 'Don't let anything prevent you from going—even if you have to be carried down to the station. I am sure your case is one for strong and immediate measures.'

For a man upon the verge of a fit of gout, the Colonel was wonderfully hilarious. He said it was a jolly night, and those girls were jolly girls, and he wished he was walking with one of them. Leaning heavily upon Billy's arm, he narrated anecdotes of bygone moonlight nights which, as they did not redound to his credit, and perhaps were not even true, there is no need to record here; and from time to time, by way of letting off his superfluous spirits, he woke the echoes with an extraordinary bellow, explaining that it was a slight improvement upon the well-known *jodel* of the merry mountaineer.

Meanwhile, Harry Lysaght was receiving the punishment which was his due for having so audaciously taken the control of affairs into his own hands. Daisy was very much displeased with him, and it was not her habit to conceal her displeasure. She contrived to say so many spiteful things to him before they had advanced a hundred yards that his already sorely-tried temper gave way altogether and a downright quarrel ensued. Such quarrels were no uncommon feature in their intercourse. Daisy rather liked them, knowing that they always ended just when it pleased her to end them by signifying her readiness to accept an abject apology; but Harry took them very seriously, and was as miserable as could be wished while they lasted.

He was miserable enough when Daisy and he (no longer on speaking terms) reached the square at the entrance to the Governor's palace, where the rest of the party, except Billy and Colonel Littlewood, were waiting. The rest of the party had been waiting some time, and were cross. Mrs. Forbes was for going straight home, and if Winnie, touched by the wobegone aspect of her sister's admirer, had not intervened, she would probably have done so. Mr. Forbes remarked plaintively:

' Of course, my dear Lysaght, since you and your
friend have been kind enough to invite us to supper,
we must keep our engagement—although I may
say that, personally, I never touch supper, but
surely we may proceed to the restaurant without
further delay. No doubt Mr. Bellew would prefer
our doing so.'

To the restaurant they accordingly adjourned,
and they had scarcely taken their places at a
table which Harry's forethought had made beautiful with floral decoration, when Billy and the
Colonel came in. The supper was excellent; the
dishes were well chosen and well served, and the
champagne was iced to the right point; but,
viewed in the light of a festive gathering, it was
not a success. Mrs. Forbes obstinately refused to
talk to Mrs. Littlewood; Harry Lysaght was silent
and gloomy; Daisy, with her offending and
offended suitor on her left hand and the Colonel
on her right, was obviously out of temper, while
Billy, perceiving the general discontent, remorsefully accused himself of being its sole cause. He
murmured something of the sort to his neighbour,
who was not quite so prompt or so hearty with her
consolatory assurance as she had been earlier in
the evening.

' Oh, I think we have all enjoyed ourselves very
much—upon the whole,' she answered a little hesitatingly. ' I shall never forget that view from the
Kasbah, and it is really most kind of you to have
prepared such a magnificent entertainment as this

for us. Only you mustn't mind if we go away presently; because it has been rather a tiring walk for my father, and he always keeps very early hours.'

Winifred, in truth, had not yet recovered from the effects of her conversation with Mrs. Littlewood, which had produced a most unpleasant impression upon her: she did not feel equal to the task of comforting Mrs. Littlewood's admirer, and she was not sorry when her mother broke up the party by rising.

'Well, at all events,' thought Billy, after he had helped the Forbeses into their carriage and had seen them drive away, 'we haven't had a disreputable scene, as we might have had if they had stayed later. That's something to be thankful for!'

In point of fact, there was a little scene before Colonel Littlewood could be persuaded to go home. Since his arrival he had been steadily imbibing all the champagne that he could lay his hands upon; but he did not yet feel that he had had nearly enough, and he expressed his firm intention of remaining where he was for another hour at least. Consequently, a certain amount of mild coercion had to be employed.

The two entertainers gazed somewhat ruefully at one another after their guests had departed, and one of them could not help laughing.

'Upon my word, Lysaght, I'm awfully sorry,' he said; 'but I told you how it would be.'

'Oh no, you didn't—you couldn't!' returned

Harry, with considerable acerbity; 'I defy any-body to tell how things are going to be with *some* people. As for that brute Littlewood, I sincerely hope the waters of Hammam R'irha will drive the gout to his stomach and kill him.'

But Billy did not hope that. He had no love for the Colonel; but he certainly did not hope that.

CHAPTER X.

MICKY'S PRESCRIPTION.

ONE hot, but breezy afternoon the hero of this narrative and Micky Forbes, who had been out for a long ride together, were jogging along the high-road which leads through the village of Birman-draïs to Algiers. The horses were over their fetlocks in dust, which rose in dense clouds and swirled away before the wind; for that winter had been a fine one (Algerian winters are not always fine), and although there had been a storm, with torrents of rain, a week before, all traces of it had now vanished, save in the increased vividness of the green woods.

It was more than a week, it was more than ten days, since Colonel and Mrs. Littlewood had taken their departure for Hammam R'irha; yet Billy Bellew was still in Algiers. That he was still in Algiers was something of a surprise to himself, and certainly it was not for the lack of urgent entreaty that he had failed to follow the lady whose letters from the interior had reached him every day. According to Mrs. Littlewood, Hammam R'irha was one of the most detestable places on the earth's surface. Her husband liked it; he was taking the baths, he played baccarat every evening with a circle of choice spirits, and he slept during the greater part of the day. She, on the other hand, had neither baths nor baccarat, nor even books, to console her, and what to do with herself from morning to night she did not know. Of course there were walks, and there was a forest where people went and sat; but who wants to sit in a forest all alone? Assuredly not Mrs. Littlewood, who pathetically implored Billy to come and sit there with her.

He wrote to say that he would obey her summons immediately, but he had put off his departure from day to day, upon one pretext or another, although he had not deemed it necessary or advisable to mention precisely what his engagements were. Not all of these had taken him to Le Bocage; but it must be confessed that about three-fourths of them had. Latterly, too, he had not felt quite so guilty; because Mrs. Littlewood had written in a more cheerful strain. She had picked up a Captain Patten, she said, 'a very nice man,' who amused her and took walks with her and helped her to get through the long weary hours. Billy smiled when he read that artless avowal. Similar avowals had reached him before, and he knew why they were made, and formerly they had not been without the desired effect. Alas! once upon a time he would have thirsted for the blood of Captain Patten; now he only blessed the name of that unknown warrior.

Still, he did quite mean to go to Hammam R'irha, and he felt that the time had now fully come for him to carry out his intention. He had made up his mind to start on the morrow, which was doubtless one reason why he became so silent and abstracted towards the close of what he thought would very likely be his last ride with Micky Forbes. His dejected aspect had not escaped the sharp eyes of his young companion, who presently began:

'I say, Mr. Bellew, you've got a fit of the blues, haven't you?'

Billy sighed and shook his shoulders.

'Well, I believe I have, Micky,' he answered; 'one's bound to have them every now and then.'

'I sometimes get them myself,' Micky observed. 'The best cure is riding; but that doesn't seem to have answered with you. The next best thing that I know of is to have a good long jaw with Winnie. Winnie always makes you feel better, even when she doesn't say much; it's a sort of way she has.'

'That's perfectly true!' cried Billy, brightening up: 'I've noticed it again and again.'

Micky nodded judicially.

'Winnie,' he resumed, 'may not be quite what you would call a beauty; but, for my part, I like her face better than Daisy's.'

'So do I,' interpolated Billy.

'Yes; and she's worth hundreds and thousands of Daisies. If I were grown up, and if I weren't her brother, I'd marry Winnie like a shot.'

'You would have to get her consent first,' observed Billy, laughing.

'Oh, she'd consent right enough, if she thought I wanted it very badly. Anything that Winnie can give to a fellow-creature who wants it badly that fellow-creature will get, you may be sure.'

Micky spoke with emphasis and intention. He had conceived for Mr. Bellew one of those ardent and admiring attachments which most of us were capable of feeling in our early youth, and which some of us have actually felt. In later life we learn that the race of heroes is extinct and that the best of good fellows has his little defects. But Micky would have punched the head of any boy of his own size who should have dared to assert that Mr. Bellew lacked a single heroic quality. Billy realized his ideal of what a man ought to be, and, that being so, it seemed both natural and desirable to mate him with the ideal of womanhood—especially as a close observer could detect signs that his own inclination tended in that direction. Winifred, it was true, was engaged to Edmund Kirby—a stiff, solemn fellow, who was no sportsman; but the prospect of her ever marrying Kirby was so remote that it was hardly worth taking into account, and Micky had been careful to avoid all allusion to the subject in his conversations with his friend. What he had noticed—and noticed with satisfaction—was that, although during the previous ten days his younger sister had employed all her customary manœuvres for the discomfiture of Harry Lysaght and the subjugation of Mr. Bellew, the latter had evinced a very decided preference for the society of Winnie. He had not, to be sure, had a great deal of it, while he had been a great deal with Daisy; but that had been due to the force of circumstances. On this particular afternoon the force of circumstanes would give him a chance, Micky thought; because Mr. and Mrs. Forbes, accompanied by Daisy and her legitimate admirer, had driven over to the Maison Carrée, and were not likely to be back for another hour or so.

Consequently, when the ride was at an end, this juvenile schemer said :

'You'll put your horse in the stable and come in, won't you ? Winnie's sure to be somewhere about, and the others will turn up by tea-time, I expect.'

'Well,' said Billy, with becoming hesitation, 'if you think I shan't bore your sister.'

'I don't think you will,' answered Micky demurely; 'but if you find that you are boring her, or that she is boring you, you can call me, and I'll take you to see a gin that the gardener has set half-way down the hill. He swears there's been a hyena prowling round the last two nights, and we mean catching the brute if we can.'

Winifred was neither in the house nor at her usual post in the arbour; but her brother, who knew where to look for her, led the way down the steep hillside, beyond the limits of the garden, to a point where she was discovered, sure enough, seated on a flat rock amidst the rank growth of asphodel and wormwood, a large white umbrella over her head, an ink-bottle by her side, and a sheaf of proofs upon her knees.

She looked round and smiled.

'Back already?' she said. 'Have you had a pleasant ride? It must have been frightfully hot. Micky, oughtn't you to go in and change? The sun will be setting soon, you know.'

'All right,' answered Micky; 'I ain't going to sit down. I just want to have a look at that gin, and then I shall put myself indoors for the night.'

Having thus skilfully accomplished his purpose, he trotted off down the hill; and Winifred, gazing fondly after him, exclaimed :

'He *is* a good boy, isn't he? I don't suppose we know what a bother it is to boys to be perpetually told to change their clothes and keep out of draughts and all that.'

Billy had stretched his long limbs upon the ground by Miss Forbes's side.

'Yes, he is a good little chap,' he answered rather absently. And then, 'Am I interrupting you ?'

'No; I have almost finished, and there aren't so many mistakes as usual this time, because these slips have been printed from a manuscript of my copying. When papa sends his own manuscripts, we get most startling results, for nobody can read his handwriting, and the printers make up whole paragraphs out of their own heads.'

Billy took one of the proof-sheets between his finger and thumb and examined it with respectful wonder.

'It's extraordinary that a man should be able to reel off page after page like that and have them printed,' he remarked reflectively. 'How on earth they manage to do it beats me. I couldn't put two sentences together if my life depended upon it. But then, of course, I'm an utter duffer.'

'I don't think it's so very difficult,' said Winnie, laughing. 'Some people can do it, and some can't. It's an art like another—like riding, for instance.'

'Yes; riding *is* an art,' agreed Billy, with some animation. 'It isn't generally admitted, because almost everybody can sit on a horse's back; but the art's wanted, all the same. And the extraordinary thing is that you'll meet lots of men who go racing all over England every year of their lives without ever twigging it.'

'Well, you have "twigged" it, at all events,' Winnie remarked.

'Yes, I can ride; I'm glad I can do something. Not that it's much, though, when you come to think of it.' Billy heaved a profound sigh, and added: 'I sometimes wish I had never been born at all.'

Winifred looked rather grave. She thought she could guess what he wanted to say, and she was doubtful whether to listen to him or to change the subject. For some days past she had been disquieted about Mr. Bellew and her sister. Harry Lysaght had been growing jealous and suspicious, and, to tell the truth, some cause had been given him for jealousy and suspicion. Winifred, watching the couple, had come to the conclusion that Mr. Bellew, in spite of an outward show of indifference, had virtually succumbed; worse than that, she was very much afraid that Daisy herself was now continuing in earnest what had been begun in sport. It was a great pity, and, even if she could do nothing to arrest the progress of events, she did not at least wish to have any hand in the overthrow of poor Harry.

Billy, who was far from divining what she was thinking about, was a little disappointed by her silence. Presently he sighed again, and remarked:

'Well, it's been very jolly this last week, and now there's an end of it all. I'm off to Hammam R'irha to-morrow.'

'Really?' said Winifred, raising her eyebrows slightly, but not looking quite as regretful as he had hoped that she would look. 'I suppose you are going to join—your friends,' she added, after a pause. 'Micky will be sorry. Have you told him?'

'No,' answered Billy, with a perceptible ring of bitterness in his voice, 'I haven't broken the sad intelligence to Micky yet. I thought I had better begin with you, as there was no danger of *your* feelings being harrowed.'

Winifred changed her position a little, and turned her eyes, with an expression of kindly concern, upon the handsome young recumbent giant by her side.

'I hope you don't think me ungrateful,' she said; 'you have been most kind to Micky, and I am sure you have done him a world of good! I shall always remember your kindness to him.'

'Oh, there hasn't been any kindness—it has been one word for him and two for myself, really; and you have nothing at all to thank me for. All the same, I wish Micky wasn't the only person who was going to be sorry at my departure.'

Doubtless Micky would not be alone in deploring that event; but it was rather too much to expect of Winifred that she should say so, and she remained silent. As, however, he continued to gaze at her expectantly, she ended by remarking:

'After all, you are not going to spend the rest of your days at Hammam R'irha! I suppose you will return here with your friends?'

'Yes, I shall return with my friends,' answered Billy gloomily. 'That makes a difference, doesn't it?'

Winifred's colour rose. She thought he was taking a rather unfair advantage of the friendliness with which she had always treated him, and she wished him to understand, once for all, that he must not count upon her alliance. Therefore she said:

'Since you ask me, I must confess that I think

it does make a difference. I don't mean as to our knowing you and your coming here sometimes; but——'

She paused, finding it a little difficult to conclude the sentence which she had begun; but he did not help her out; so she had to resume: 'What I mean is that perhaps, under the circumstances, it is best not to be *too* intimate. I think you must see that yourself.'

She became very red after she had made this unequivocal and very uncivil declaration; but Billy, whose eyes were fixed upon a prickly-pear bush, the thick leaves of which he was slashing and hacking viciously with the handle of his riding-whip, did not detect that sign of distress. He himself was not red; on the contrary he was, as she could not help noticing, curiously pale.

'Yes, I quite see it,' he answered quietly; 'and I won't try to be intimate any more.'

Winnie's soft heart was immediately touched. She felt that she had been cruelly harsh, and she felt also—not for the first time—a great indignation against the selfishness of Mrs. Littlewood.

'Mr. Bellew,' she said gently, 'don't you think you might summon up courage to do a rather disagreeable thing, and—and regain your liberty? Don't misunderstand me,' she went on hurriedly, 'I don't want you to do it at once; that is, so far as we are concerned, it is of no great importance. I was thinking of yourself.'

Billy shook his head.

'Thank you; it's awfully good of you to think about me,' he answered; 'but I'm afraid I couldn't be such a brute as to claim my liberty. If it were given to me, that would be another thing. Sometimes I wonder whether you don't think worse of me and poor Blanche Littlewood than we deserve. I should like to tell you the whole story, if you didn't mind?'

'Oh, you needn't!' returned Winifred with a touch of impatience. 'I heard it all from her that night when we went to the old town. I am sorry that she has a tipsy husband; but I can't see that that is any reason why she should ruin your life for you.'

Billy sighed. He was too loyal to breathe a disparaging word about the woman of whose exactions he had grown so desperately weary—too loyal even to listen to any disparagement of her. If he had been disloyal in losing his heart to Winifred Forbes—and it was now beyond a doubt that he had lost both his heart and been disloyal in so doing—his duty clearly was to keep the secret of his treachery to himself. Not feeling quite confident that he would have it in his power to accomplish that feat if he remained where he was much longer, he jumped up and said abruptly that he thought he had better be off.

Towards the hour of sunset the atmosphere of the whole country-side round about Algiers is heavy with penetrating aromatic odours which rise from the flowering shrubs, the rosemary hedges, the asphodels, and the eucalyptus woods. Until Billy Bellew turned his back upon Algeria for the last time, the recurrence of that hour and of those mingled scents never failed to give him a sharp twinge about the region of the heart; nor did these ever fail to bring back to him the image of Winifred as he saw her then, standing with her back to the sunset sky, against which two tall stone-pines rose black and clearly defined. But he could not afterwards recall exactly what she had said. She had made some sort of an apology, he thought; she had promised to make his adieux to the others, and she had looked very sorry.

Yes, she had certainly looked very sorry; if that was any comfort, he might take it to himself and make the most of it, because he was not likely to get any other. Of course she had understood; and of course—as she had been careful to mention—the recovery of his liberty would not, even if he had recovered it, have been ' of any great importance ' to her. Upon the whole, Micky's prescription could hardly be said to have proved a success.

CHAPTER XI.

A WESTERLY BREEZE.

After all, Billy was not destined to journey to Hammam R'irha, or to sit with Mrs. Littlewood in the forest which adjoins that somewhat melancholy health resort. A letter which he found on his table when he reached the hotel conveyed to him the pleasing intelligence that the writer's term of banishment was nearly at an end.

'Alfred can't tear himself away from the baths and the baccarat,' she wrote; 'but, as he doesn't insist upon my remaining with him, and as he really doesn't require me, I have decided to strike my tent. I have written to the servants to say that they may expect me the day after to-morrow; but perhaps you had better go up there and see that the fires are lighted and the rooms properly aired. One can't trust these people. Captain Patten has kindly promised to take charge of me as far as Algiers. He is going off to Tunis, which I am sorry for, as he has really been a great comfort to me in the solitude which you didn't think it worth while to come and relieve. I don't know whether I may venture to hope that you will meet me at the station; but if that is too much trouble, I dare say you will kindly send *somebody* to collect my luggage for me.'

Billy obediently betook himself to the railway-station on the following day, after having ascertained that Mrs. Littlewood's fires were lighted and her rooms properly aired. He was half glad that he was not going to Hammam R'irha, half sorry that he was not to leave Algiers. It is always a little ridiculous to say good-bye and then remain where you are; moreover, he felt that, after what Winnie had said, it would be out of the question for him to resume his daily visits to Le Bocage.

She had as good as asked him to discontinue them; added to which it had been only too sadly evident that she despised him. Certainly she had a right to despise him, and if he had been insane enough to tell her in so many words that he loved her, she would have had a right to disbelieve him. Yet he did love her, and had loved her, he thought, almost from the date of their first meeting. How extraordinary it seemed now that he should have ever imagined himself in love with Blanche Littlewood! How extraordinary, and how very unfortunate!

'I should be a thundering blackguard if I were to desert her at this time of day, though!' he said to himself, as he paced up and down the platform, where a few natives, wrapped in dirty burnouses, were squatting patiently, and where three or four loud-voiced colonists in broad-leaved hats were quarrelling over some question of politics. 'No, I must stick to her until she gives me a hint that she has had enough of me.'

The very last time when any woman is likely to give such a hint is when she has reason to believe that it will not be wholly unwelcome, and Mrs. Littlewood, unfortunately, had not as yet had at all enough of Billy Bellew, who was useful to her in a hundred ways.

The long train rumbled slowly into the station after a time, and delivered her to her expectant admirer, of whom she at once proceeded to make use.

'Have you got a carriage for us?' she asked.

'Please take my dressing-case and the umbrellas—
and there's a bundle of rugs somewhere. Oh, and
will you go and look after the luggage? Tell them
on no account to put great, heavy boxes on the top
of my dress-basket; it won't bear that sort of
treatment, and these people are so horribly rough.
Stop one moment! I want to introduce you to
Captain Patten, who has charitably looked after
me during this detestable journey. I mean,' she
added, correcting herself with a gracious little
smile, 'that it *would* have been a detestable
journey if Captain Patten hadn't been with me to
cheer me up.'

Captain Patten did not present the appearance
of being particularly well qualified by nature to
cheer up anybody. He was a very long man with
a very long moustache and a countenance which
expressed absolutely nothing at all. He took off
his hat, held out his hand, and mentioned that he
would not have much more than time to get on
board the steamer for Tunis. He had taken leave
of Mrs. Littlewood and had disappeared when
Billy returned from his quest in the baggage
department.

'He reminds me a good deal of you,' Mrs.
Littlewood was so kind as to say, after she had
taken her place in the open carriage (alas! why
was it an open carriage, and why had cruel Fate
decreed that Lady Ottery and Mrs. Nugent and
half a dozen others should be driving down the
hill while this couple ascended it?); 'he has

just your cool, impassive way of taking everything as it comes. I'm not like that; I can't
pretend to be so philosophical. No, not even for
the sake of keeping the peace will I pretend that
I didn't think it very unkind of you to leave me
quite alone in that desert all this time.'

'But you weren't quite alone, it seems,' pleaded
Billy; 'besides, I was on the point of starting for
Hammam R'irha when I got your letter.'

'Oh, I dare say!' returned the lady sceptically;
'by your own account, you have been upon the
point of starting for the last ten days.'

However, she was more easily pacified than he
had dared to anticipate that she would be. Of
course he had to confess that, during her absence,
the greater part of his time had been spent with
the Forbes family; but, by good luck, she did not
happen to be jealous of Daisy, and apparently it
had never entered into her head to regard Winifred
as a possible rival. She ended by saying:

'Well, I think I must forgive you. It wouldn't
do to quarrel, now that we are going for once to
have a really happy time together, would it?
Alfred doesn't mean to hurry back; he said, "Oh,
you'll be all right with Billy Bellew to look after
you!" So like him, wasn't it?'

It was indeed—just like him! Also it would be
just like Mrs. Littlewood to insist upon having a
really happy time with Mr. Bellew under circumstances which surely demanded some slight exercise
of prudence and caution. It may be hoped that

the ensuing week was a happy one for her, because it was quite the reverse of happy for her docile companion. Naturally, he was kept on duty all day long; but even if he had not been, he would have abstained from calling on his friends at Le Bocage. He thought that the best plan would be not to go to the house again unless he was asked. They must have heard from Lysaght that he was still in Algiers, and if they wanted to see him they would probably say so. The chances were that they didn't want to see him, and that they would be glad of an excuse for quietly dropping his acquaintance. Lysaght, for one, had been a good deal less friendly in his manner of late.

But there were two inhabitants of Le Bocage who neither desired nor intended to drop Mr. Bellew's acquaintance. One of them ran down to the Hôtel d'Orient, waited till he appeared, asked him a number of embarrassing questions, and could by no means be induced to depart until he had promised to come out for a ride early in the morning, Billy having explained that he was pretty sure to be busy from breakfast-time onwards. The other accosted him at a garden-party to which he had been invited (and to which Mrs. Littlewood had not been invited) by Lady Ottery.

'Well, Mr. Bellew,' she began; 'and what is the meaning of this, please?'

'The meaning of what?' inquired Billy feebly.

He did not much like Daisy Forbes, but latterly she had amused him; and, although he thought it too bad of her to affect to flirt with him in order to exasperate her wooer, he could not but acknowledge that the temptation must be rather strong to exasperate a fellow who made such a fool of himself as Lysaght often did.

'Why, of your turning your back upon us without rhyme or reason,' she answered. 'What have we done? One likes at least to be told what one's offence is.'

'There's no offence at all,' answered Billy; 'only I haven't had much time to myself these last few days. You see, Mrs. Littlewood is back from Hammam R'irha, and——'

'Quite so; we all understand that you prefer Mrs. Littlewood's society to ours,' interrupted Daisy, who would have spoken with less good-humour if she had not been convinced of the contrary; 'but don't you think the two might sometimes be combined?'

Billy smiled, and shook his head. 'Not again, thank you. Have you forgotten our visit to the old town by moonlight?'

'Well, that was not exactly a success, I admit, but then there were reasons. Colonel Littlewood was one reason, and papa and mamma were two more. If Mrs. Littlewood will come out sailing with us the day after to-morrow, as I hope she will, none of those drawbacks will be present. Mr. Lysaght knows of a capital boat, and he wants us all to sail across to Cap Matifou. Wouldn't you like to come? It will be something to do, you know.   And you'll ask Mrs. Littlewood, won't you?'

'Of course I should like it very much,' answered Billy; 'but I can't say whether Mrs. Littlewood would or not. Why are you so anxious that she should come?'

'Because we must have a chaperon, don't you see. Nothing would induce mamma to enter a vessel of any sort or kind unless it is absolutely necessary, and she has taken it into her head that it wouldn't be proper for us to make this little expedition without a matron to look after us. I should have thought Winnie was as good as any matron; but mamma doesn't see it in that light, and it would be quite ridiculous to ask Lady Ottery, or any of those old things. So if Mrs. Littlewood refuses, I'm afraid the expedition will fall through. Perhaps you had better not tell her that, though.'

He was careful to steer clear of any such gratuitous folly, for he did not at all want the expedition to fall through. He was not sure that it sounded in all respects promising; still, it would at least bring him near to Winifred for an hour or two, and to be near her was the only form of happiness that he could now expect to enjoy. What was a little unlucky was that Mrs. Littlewood was a very indifferent sailor, and this was, in fact, the objection which that lady put forward as soon as the project was broached to her:

'I am not going to be sick in public to please

anybody,' she declared. 'I don't mind acting
chaperon if it's agreed beforehand that I'm not to
be asked to quit terra firma unless the sea is
smooth.'

'Well, one can't sail in a flat calm, you know,'
observed Billy; 'but if this wind holds, there won't
be any sea to speak of. I don't suppose the others
would care to go if it was really rough.'

Thus reassured, Mrs. Littlewood accepted without further demur the functions which it was
sought to impose upon her. She still hankered
after intimacy, or at least the appearance of
intimacy, with the Forbes family—she perceived
that it would be impossible for Mrs. Forbes to
ignore her after she had taken charge of the two
girls for a whole day; finally, she was growing
very weary of seeing nobody but Billy Bellew from
morning to night. Since her return, Billy had
been so attentive and devoted that he had ceased
to be interesting, and, good fellow though he was,
he did not, it had to be confessed, shine as a con-
versationalist.

At the time of the above conversation the wind
was in the north, which all along the Algerian coast
is the very best quarter that it can blow from, for
in those latitudes northerly breezes not only bring
clear skies and fine weather, but are always steady
and seldom strong. Unfortunately, a shift of
several points towards the west took place during
the night, and that, as Billy knew, made a difference. Not that it was blowing hard in the morn-

ing, but gusts could be seen sweeping over the bay, the sky was streaked with mares' tails, and the distances had become hazy.

'We shan't get across to Matifou to-day; or, at least, if we do, we shan't get back again,' Billy remarked to Harry Lysaght before starting to fetch Mrs. Littlewood.

'Oh, bosh!' returned Harry, in the petulant accents which had recently become habitual to him; 'it's all right. For goodness' sake, don't go and spoil the whole thing by saying that. There's no reason why we shouldn't have a sail, any way, and it will be easy enough to keep in under the land if we find there's too much sea outside.'

Billy had no wish to spoil sport, and he accordingly refrained from mentioning his misgivings to Mrs. Littlewood, who remarked with satisfaction that the sea was 'beautifully smooth.' That portion of it which she could see from her garden was smooth enough, but while driving down towards the town she obtained a wider and a much less comforting view. The great blue expanse of the bay was dappled with white caps, the eastern extremity of it looked much further off than usual; a steamer which was about to enter the harbour was rolling scandalously.

'Good gracious!' exclaimed Mrs. Littlewood, 'I'm not going out in that; why, it's blowing a gale!'

'Oh no, not a gale,' said Billy, laughing: 'but the wind *has* freshened in the last half-hour, I must admit. Still, we may as well go on to the quay and find out what the others would like to do.'

'It may interest you to find out what they would like to do,' returned Mrs. Littlewood calmly; 'but perhaps it is rather more to the purpose that you should hear what I should not like to do, and don't intend to do. Sooner than be tossed about on those mountainous waves I would disappoint every Forbes that ever lived—and you into the bargain.'

The waves could hardly be described as mountainous, but Billy was quite willing to let Mrs. Littlewood call them anything she pleased, so long as she did not order the coachman to turn round and drive home. Personally, he did not much care whether he went out sailing that day or not; what he wanted was to see Winifred, and he presumed that when once the party had been assembled, it would not immediately disperse.

Harry Lysaght stepped forward to open the carriage-door when they reached the quay; Winifred, Daisy and Micky were standing close behind him; the little open boat, with its Arab boatman, was gently rising and falling beside the landing steps. Evidently no idea of abandoning the expedition had been entertained, and Harry's face fell when Mrs. Littlewood ejaculated :

'You don't mean to say that you really think of sailing in such weather !'

'Oh, it isn't at all bad weather—it isn't, I assure you !' he answered eagerly. 'I think we shall have to give up Cap Matifou, because it would be such a long job to beat back; but there's no earthly reason why we shouldn't have a very jolly sail, and by keeping under the land we shall avoid anything like rough water. You'll be astonished to find how smooth it is when you get out.'

'That pleasing surprise will not be for me,' returned Mrs. Littlewood firmly. 'Very sorry to put you to inconvenience, good people; but I stipulated from the first that I wasn't to be taken to sea in rough weather, and I won't be—nothing would induce me! All I can say is that if you like to go without me, I won't tell. And you needn't bother about me. Mr. Bellew shall go the round of the mosques with me; I haven't seen them yet.'

As may be supposed, this suggestion was not very favourably received. Winifred was decidedly of opinion that a chaperon was necessary, Daisy had no notion of relinquishing Mr. Bellew, and Harry Lysaght was obstinately determined upon carrying out his plan.

'A pretty set of funks these fellows will think us!' he exclaimed angrily. 'Other people must do as they choose, but I'll go out, if I have to go alone!'

The above heroic resolution was only announced after a prolonged discussion, in the course of which it had become painfully apparent that Daisy had gone over to the enemy. Winifred, actuated by feelings of compassion, had backed up Harry, had

consented to waive the chaperon question, and had
even, by his request, seated herself in the boat.
Micky, on hearing that cowardice might possibly be
imputed to those who declined the risk of sea-
sickness, at once decided to join her, but was
ordered ashore again.

'You mustn't get wet,' Winifred whispered;
'please go with the others and leave Harry to me
for a little : that will be much the best way. Most
likely we shall join you before you have gone very
far.'

It may be that Harry had not quite expected to
be taken at his word ; but as Daisy promptly
turned on her heel, waving him a smiling adieu,
and as Mrs. Littlewood and Billy followed suit,
there was nothing for it but to shove off. He took
the tiller, and, while the Arab was hoisting the
sail, threw an indignant and reproachful glance at
poor Winnie, who certainly was not in her present
position for her own pleasure. He did not speak
until they were clear of the harbour, when he remarked with an angry laugh :

'This is sufficiently ridiculous, isn't it ?'

'*Tu l'as voulu, Georges Dandin ?*' thought Winifred to herself ; but she was too kind-hearted and
too sorry for him to express her thoughts. Instead
of doing so, she answered apologetically : ' It really
was the only way out of the difficulty. You wouldn't
give in, and Mrs. Littlewood wouldn't give in ; so
we had no alternative but a compromise.'

'I don't know what you call a compromise,'

returned the irate Harry. 'I remember that, when I was a small boy, I used sometimes to be asked whether I would fight or take a licking. As a general rule, I said I would fight, and then, as a general rule, I got the licking. It seems to me that I have been put in pretty much the same position to-day. Of course the whole thing was arranged beforehand: your sister never had the slightest intention of coming out sailing. Well, I might have meekly taken a licking and tramped through the town with you or Mrs. Littlewood, while she and Bellew lost their way in one of the back-streets; but I didn't see the fun of that. I preferred to fight, and—here I am.'

'Oh, but that doesn't prove that you have been licked,' said Winifred, laughing.

'Doesn't it? Glad you take such a cheerful view of the situation. For my own part, I believe my wisest course would be to admit myself beaten at once and go home by the next steamer.'

It took some time and not a little patience to persuade this young man that there was still hope for him, that Daisy was not guilty of the Macchiavelian design ascribed to her, and that Mrs. Littlewood might be trusted to keep a watchful eye upon Mr. Bellew. But Winifred, who knew how to manage him, accomplished her purpose eventually; though she did not venture to suggest getting about until they were well out to sea and she had been pretty well drenched with spray. But at length she made so bold as to remark:

'I doubt whether Mrs. Littlewood would have liked this; and, to tell you the honest truth, I don't altogether like it myself.'

By this time a nasty lumpy sea had got up, and the wind was blowing in violent gusts which rendered sailing, if not actually dangerous, decidedly unpleasant. Harry turned his head towards his consoler, and for the first time noticed her dripping condition.

'What a brute I am!' he exclaimed compunctiously; 'why, you're wet through! Of course we'll put back at once. I was thinking about myself and I clean forgot you; that's what you make everybody do, and the consequence is that you never get any thanks. Nevertheless, I do thank you, and I dare say you're right about Daisy —I hope you are. Anyhow, one can but try. I promise you that I'll behave very prettily to her when we get on shore.'

This was satisfactory; but the return voyage proved a long and troublesome business, so that the afternoon was well advanced before Winifred, with a ruined hat and jacket and her eyes and her mouth full of salt, disembarked at the landing-steps. At that time of day there really did not seem to be much use in hunting for the seceding members of the party.

CHAPTER XII.

MISPLACED CONFIDENCE.

IF Heaven had not blessed Billy Bellew with a singularly sweet temper, and if his own efforts had not secured for him an unfailing power of self-control, he would no doubt have said something that he ought not to have said when he saw the boat in which Winifred was seated pushed off from the quay. Even as it was, he could not help looking rather disgusted, and Daisy lost no time in taking him to task.

'Are you regretting that you didn't cast in your lot with those two adventurous spirits?' she inquired. 'If you are, and if you think their company would be more amusing than ours, it isn't too late to hail them.'

Billy said he only regretted that they should have been shipped off in that unnecessary way. 'I don't see why Lysaght should have been so obstinate about it,' he added.

Daisy shrugged her shoulders. 'He is apt to be obstinate,' she remarked; 'and sometimes it isn't a bad plan to let obstinate people have their way. They don't always like it when they have got it, you see. A little lesson of this kind will do Mr. Lysaght no harm.'

'Perhaps not; but it doesn't follow that your sister ought to be punished with him.'

'How many times am I to tell you that Winnie

is an exception to all general rules? Punishment indeed!—why, you couldn't have asked her to do anything that she would have enjoyed more than what she is doing now. You may depend upon it that she has already begun to stroke Mr. Lysaght down, and pat him on the back, and tell him what a fine fellow he is, and how disappointed we all are because Mrs. Littlewood wouldn't let us go out in his boat. Don't make yourself uneasy about Winnie; she is as happy as possible, and it only remains for us to be as happy as we can without her. Have you seen the mosques? It's your duty to see them some time or other, you know.'

Mrs. Littlewood concurred in this view, and Micky at once volunteered to run on and look for the indispensable Hamoud, who during many years has conducted foreign visitors to the sights of Algiers, has got up Aïssaoua fêtes for their amusement, and has given them the benefit of calm, disinterested counsel in their transactions with native dealers. Hamoud was, as usual, pacing majestically up and down the Boulevard de la République. His embroidered turban, his white burnous, his blue spectacles and his voluminous breeches were speedily recognised by Micky, who said, in the peculiar dialect which he had found quite adequate to the requirements of daily life in a French dependency:

'Look here, Hamoud, nous voulons voir les mosques and toutes les autres choses of that sort, you know; so, si vous n'êtes pas engagé, come on!'

Hamoud was free, and was entirely at the disposition of these ladies and gentlemen. He said
they would go first to the mosque in the Rue de la
Marine, which is the most ancient in the town, and
is believed to date from the eleventh century. It
is not a particularly striking or interesting edifice,
the interior being, like that of all mosques, absolutely bare, and the whitewashed columns and
horseshoe arches possessing no special claims to
beauty; still, Hamoud, after having, as in duty
bound, shod his party in enormous slippers, had a
good many leisurely observations to make upon the
subject. The truth is that the sights of Algiers are
few in number, and when one is paid by time it
does not do to neglect details.

For the rest, these sight-seers were in no hurry,
nor did they care very much whether what they
were being shown was worth looking at or not.
They were taken next to the Grand Mosque on the
Place du Gouvernement, the exterior of which, with
its white dome and illuminated clock-tower, was
already a familiar object to them; and then they
were led to the fish-market, which their guide
assured them, truly enough, was *très-curieux*.
Nowhere else in the world, one would think (and
hope) can such extraordinary and repulsive sea-
monsters be exhibited for sale as in the fish-market
of Algiers. Every variety of improbable-looking
crustacean, hideous caricatures of fish which are
not too lovely even in more Northern waters,
mussels and snails and horrible spotted eels, lie

there in profusion upon the wet slabs, and, judging by the noisy chaffering which is always going on around them, find willing purchasers.

'Do you mean to tell me,' asked Billy solemnly, as he pointed with his stick to a writhing heap of eels, 'that anybody actually eats those filthy snakes?'

'Plait-il?' said Hamoud; and then, realizing the nature of the question put to him: 'Oui, oui, c'est pour manger—excellent—vary goot!'

He gathered his fingers into a bunch, raised them to his lips and nodded expressively.

'Talking of eating,' remarked Mrs. Littlewood, 'what are we going to do about luncheon? I don't know how the rest of you may feel, but I'm getting rather hungry!'

'So am I,' said Micky; 'and, by Jove! the luncheon-basket has gone off in the boat.'

'I dare say it will be back again presently,' Mrs. Littlewood observed; 'nobody could be insane enough to stay out at sea much longer in this hurricane, and certainly nobody could feel tempted to eat. However, I don't think we will wait for its return. The best way will be for us to go to one of the hotels, and we can see whatever else there is to be seen in the afternoon, if you like. In the meantime, Hamoud might keep an eye on the quay, so as to be able to let Miss Forbes and Mr. Lysaght know where we are when they come in.'

This proposition meeting with general approval, a move was made towards the Hôtel de la Régence,

where a substantial, if not highly *recherché*, repast
was obtained; but although the preparing and con-
sumption thereof occupied a considerable time, the
missing couple did not make their appearance to
claim a share in it, and Billy ended by becoming
fidgety. The feathery bamboos outside the hotel
were tossing wildly in the wind, shutters were
banging, awnings were flapping and cracking like
musketry; it was just the sort of weather in which
an accident might easily happen, and that boat of
Lysaght's did not look as if she had much hold on
the water.

'I think, if you don't mind, I'll just go and
have a look out over the bay,' he said at length
to Daisy, whose efforts to entertain him had not
so far met with any marked success. 'You
needn't be in the least alarmed, I am sure; only
one doesn't quite know what sort of weather these
little craft make of it in a head wind, and it's
possible that our friends out there may be in need
of assistance.'

'We'll all go,' answered Daisy, rising promptly.
'Micky, if you eat any more bananas and dates
you'll make yourself ill, and then you'll catch it
from Winnie.'

She was not much alarmed for her sister's safety,
but she was by no means desirous that Mr. Bellew
should start off on a quixotic and unnecessary
voyage of rescue, and the patient Hamoud, who
was found leaning over the parapet of the boulevard
and gazing out to sea, earned her gratitude by

laughing at Billy's anxious inquiries. He pointed to the white sail which was swaying and dipping in the offing, and remarked that those who were in the boat had made up their minds to return a quarter of an hour before.

'Ils ne risquent rien, allez!' he added. 'Le batelier il est bon marin—goot sailah, comme vous dites, vous autres. Seulement, c'est du temps qu'il faut pour revenir. Ils en ont encore pour une heure et demie—one hour, one haff. Venez voir l'archevêché.'

Hamoud threw the corner of his burnous over his shoulder and waddled off in the direction of the old town, beckoning after the imperious fashion which is common to guides and *valets de place* all the world over. Daisy and Billy followed him, the former cheerfully and the latter a little reluctantly, while Mrs. Littlewood and Micky brought up the rear. It was not very like Mrs. Littlewood to acquiesce in an arrangement of that kind ; but, as has been said before, she was not jealous of Daisy Forbes, and she was just the least bit in the world tired of talking to Billy. Moreover, Micky amused her, which was a very good reason for walking with him and drawing him out.

Now, Micky was undoubtedly a very clever boy, but at his age one does not know everything, and it certainly had never occurred to him that the relations between his friend Mr. Bellew and Mrs. Littlewood could be other than those of ordinary friendship. Mrs. Littlewood was a married woman

—it is to be feared that he would also have called
her an old woman; she could, therefore, have
nothing to do with Mr. Bellew's love affairs, beyond
taking a benevolent interest in them, which, indeed,
she seemed to feel. Thus it was that Micky allowed
himself to be drawn out after a fashion and by
methods which he would assuredly have detected
and baffled, had he been a little older or a little
better informed.

Not that Mrs. Littlewood, when she began ques-
tioning him, had the faintest suspicion of what she
was about to hear. She was actuated merely by a
languid and rather contemptuous curiosity as to
the state of Daisy's affections. She knew by experience that women of all ages were perpetually
falling in love with Billy Bellew, and she knew that
that fortunate or unfortunate man almost always
remained in ignorance of the flattering fact. The
little Forbes girl might have lost her heart to him or
might be only flirting with him; either way, it did
not much signify; still, one might as well ascertain
the truth. And so, to her utter amazement, she
did ascertain the truth, or something very like it.
At first she was incredulous, taking it for granted
that the boy had made a sort of hero of his big
friend, as boys will, that he had naturally thought
it would be very nice to have his friend for a
brother-in-law and that he had not less naturally
overlooked the comparatively unimportant circumstance that his elder sister was hardly the kind of
person of whom a young and handsome man, with

considerable means and sporting tastes, was likely
to become enamoured. But by degrees the conviction forced itself upon her that Micky's assertions,
preposterous as they appeared, were founded upon
something more than a germ of reality. Billy was
such a fool—such a hopeless, helpless fool! It
would not, when you came to think of it, have been
a bit unlike him to idealize that tall, thin, commonplace girl, or to attribute to her all those domestic
virtues which he so profoundly admired, and which,
for that matter, she probably possessed. Mrs.
Littlewood raged inwardly at the thought of such
treachery; but her outward aspect remained smiling
and unruffled.

'Between you and me,' said Micky, who had been
much encouraged by the sympathetic tone in which
she had responded to his previous remarks, 'I don't
feel any more doubt about him. From one or two
things that he has said to me and others that I've
noticed, I'm almost sure of what he wants. But
I ain't quite so certain about *her*. I believe she
likes him; but she might have reasons for not quite
seeing her way to marry him, don't you know?'

'Really? What reasons, for instance?' inquired
Mrs. Littlewood benevolently.

Micky was upon the point of mentioning
Edmund Kirby, but thought better of it. 'Oh,
well, she may think she is wanted at home, or
something of that sort,' he answered. 'Anyhow,
I know this: just before you came back, and when
Mr. Bellew thought he was going to Hammam

R'irha, he had a long talk with her—I left them together on purpose—and she cried afterwards. I know she did, because her eyes were red ; and it takes a lot to make Winnie cry, I can tell you ! Now, should you say that she had been refusing him ?'

Mrs. Littlewood opined that such a lamentable occurrence was not outside the bounds of possibility ; but within her heart she said, ' Catch her refusing him ! She wouldn't get a chance like that twice in her life ! It's a great deal more likely that she has accepted him—subject to a condition which it isn't difficult to guess. Well, my good woman, your condition will not be complied with ; I can promise you that much.'

The conversation of which a fragment has been recorded above was not continuous. It was interrupted by perfunctory admiration of the architecture and the tiles at the Archbishop's Palace, by a cursory examination of the objects exposed in the museum, by the monotonous dissertations of Hamoud, and by occasional observations exchanged with Billy and his fair companion ; but it was resumed as often as occasion permitted, and the upshot of it was that Mrs. Littlewood prepared to take the war-path, while Micky congratulated himself upon having gained a powerful and benign ally.

Daisy, meanwhile, had not been wasting her time. If she fancied—as in fact she did—that she had succeeded both in fascinating Mr. Bellew and in making him a little jealous of Harry Lysaght, her error was not wholly inexcusable. Billy, as has been said, hated flirts; he considered that they deserved nothing except to be paid back in their own coin; so that when Daisy made a dead set at him, he did not scruple to respond to her advances, nor did he hesitate to humour her by looking mournful when she intimated that Harry, after having been punished for his display of bad temper, would be received back into her good graces. But the game did not amuse him in the least, and he was heartily weary of it long before she was.

His reiterated suggestions that it was time for them to move down towards the harbour meeting with no attention, he lost patience at length and announced that he would proceed thither alone; whereupon Hamoud, who remembered perhaps that he was now entitled to a day's pay, and that another hour of work would not make him any richer, peremptorily assembled his party, saying: 'Allons, descendons! vous avez tout vu.'

It did not prove necessary for them to descend any farther than the Boulevard de la République; for at the top of one of the long flights of steps which lead down from that spacious promenade to the quays they encountered Harry Lysaght and Winifred, the latter of whom greeted them with a cry of pleased surprise.

'Still here! We thought you would have gone home long ago.'

'For the matter of that,' observed Daisy, 'we thought you would have come in long ago ; but I suppose you were enjoying yourselves so much that you took no note of time.'

Harry, who was looking penitent and shame-faced, hastened to repudiate, in an undertone, the accusation that he had enjoyed himself, and Daisy beckoned him apart to lecture and forgive him. It may be that this little manœuvre was designed to attract the attention of Mr. Bellew; if so, it might as well have been omitted, for Billy had no eyes at the moment except for Winifred, whose draggled plight filled him with concern.

'You're literally soaking !' he exclaimed ; 'you must have had an awful time of it !'

'Oh, it's only salt water, I shan't hurt !' answered Winifred ; 'we didn't really have such a bad time of it. And you — have you had a pleasant day ?'

'No ; horrid,' answered Billy, with more truth than politeness.

Winifred raised her eyebrows, but did not request him to explain himself. She presumed that he had been quarrelling with Daisy ; quarrels between Daisy and her admirers were not uncommon events. After a short pause, she said : 'We have seen nothing of you for a long time.'

'Well—you cautioned me against trying to be too intimate,' Billy remarked.

Winifred was a long-suffering creature ; but after all she was human, and rather heavy demands had already been made upon her stock of patience that day. So she returned, in accents of decided displeasure :

'You must have understood what I meant, but I am sorry I expressed myself so stupidly. Please forgive me and forget that I ever made that speech. Besides, the house isn't mine, and I have no right to dictate to you whether you shall come to it often or seldom. I suppose you know that you can't come too often to please some of us.'

Billy was too crushed to attempt any rejoinder. He fell back, and after a few minutes the Forbes party drove away, leaving him with Mrs. Littlewood, who remarked pleasantly :

'What an appalling effect wind and waves produce upon some women ! Of course one always knew that that eldest girl was plain, but I had no idea *how* plain she was until I saw her with those wisps of wet hair hanging over her ears and her cheeks all red and shiny.'

But Billy did not rise. He answered meekly that he could understand some people thinking Miss Forbes plain, although he did not think so himself : 'But I dare say,' he added, 'I ain't much of a judge of beauty.'

CHAPTER XIII.

DAISY ACTS FROM THE HIGHEST MOTIVES.

THE climate of Algiers seemed determined that year to justify all that has been said and written

in its praise by its warmest partisans, and to prove
that the grumblers, who are at least equally
numerous, have dwelt with too much severity upon
its occasional aberrations. A heavy bank of clouds
had been visible behind the Bouzaréah as the
excursionists drove up the hill towards home; but
this ominous sign, which usually means a steady
downpour of forty-eight hours, heralded nothing
worse in the present instance than a storm during
the night and a few showers which passed away
before morning, leaving the skies bluer and the
trees greener than ever.

Winifred strolled out to the summer-house after
her early breakfast, as her habit was, and filled
her lungs with the delicious crisp air. There are
days when and places in which the mere joy of
being alive and in perfect health is, or ought to be,
enough to satisfy anybody, and Winifred would
have been very well contented with existence, had
she not been rather worried by a few comparative
trifles. For one thing, she was sorry that she
had spoken so snappishly to poor Mr. Bellew on
the previous evening. It was not her custom to
speak snappishly, and, from what she had since
seen and heard, she did not now believe that he
had deserved to be so spoken to. Daisy had been
very nice and pleasant to Harry Lysaght on the
way home; it had transpired incidentally that
Mr. Bellew had been 'bothering and fussing' the
whole afternoon about the absentees in the boat;
after all, it was no fault of his that he had been

made to spend several hours with a lady to whom he had intimated that he no longer meant to pay his addresses.

'I wish I hadn't been so rude to him!' Winifred thought remorsefully; 'but he did rather seem to be fishing for an invitation, and he ought to have known that I couldn't give him one. Well, I suppose he won't come here any more now—which is all the better, perhaps.'

Nevertheless, she sighed, for she had become fond of Billy, and she was very sorry for him. It was a fact that she had cried after that interview in which he had so submissively accepted her virtual prohibition of his visits, and possibly her tears may have been caused by sheer pity for his lot, which, in truth, was pitiable enough; but it is not certain that personal regret had nothing to do with them. Why must Daisy needs get up a flirtation with every man who came in her way? Why, if she intended to marry the man whom she really seemed to like better than anybody else, couldn't she do so and leave the rest of the world in peace? Next to a long engagement, nothing is so tiresome and fruitful in vexations of all kinds as a long courtship!

Although there was nobody to see her, Winifred blushed after she had formulated this last sentiment and glanced penitently at the unopened letter which she held in her hand. Was she tired of being engaged to her faithful Edmund? Of course she was not; she would as soon have

thought of being tired of her father or her mother.
Still, one may be very fond of a person and yet
find his letters a little prosy. This one, which she
now proceeded to read, was, if anything, prosier
than usual. It was not enlivened by the record of
any more family rows. Edmund had been too busy
to go home again, and had heard no news from
Shropshire, which, he said, he trusted might be
taken as good news. He was getting on in his
profession, and, by way of proving that he was, he
favoured his correspondent with a brief synopsis
of a case in which he had recently been engaged.
This, though doubtless worded in the clearest
available phraseology, was wholly unintelligible
to her. Then came a page and a half of observations upon current politics, which were more
comprehensible, but, it is to be feared, not much
too interesting to the recipient. Mr. Kirby was a
moderate Liberal; he was the sort of man who
could not very well be anything else, and his
political views were not of a nature to arouse
enthusiasm. He wound up by saying that he had
perused Mr. Forbes's article in the *Modern Review*
with very great interest and pleasure, and that he
looked forward to meeting the talented writer again
before long—' and you too,' he considerately added,
as an afterthought.

Winifred knew that the man himself was a great
deal better than his letters, that he was not in
reality as formal and pedantic as they made him
appear, and that, although he abstained from the

use of ardent language, his affection for her was as strong and genuine as everything else about him ; still, the fact remained that his letters chilled her. She was idly wondering whether Edmund would like or would sternly condemn Mr. Bellew, when Micky came out with his lesson-books to give another turn to her thoughts.

Micky was not in one of his most docile moods that morning. There were three outrageous false quantities in the copy of Latin verses which he submitted to his instructress. He had brought a chameleon—his latest acquisition—out with him, and devoted a good deal more attention to the variation in the creature's hues than to the solution of the problem in Euclid with which he was invited to grapple. He said there was a volatility in the atmosphere which was distinctly hostile to the concentration of the faculties upon any one subject, and, on being asked what he meant by talking such nonsense, replied that it might be nonsense, and that he shouldn't wonder if it was, but that he had heard his revered father use those very words a quarter of an hour ago, anyhow.

Winifred refused to have her attention diverted from the matter in hand. She plodded patiently along, and her reluctant pupil plodded patiently after her, until they arrived triumphantly at Q.E.F., whereupon Micky closed the book with a bang.

' That's capital,' said he ; ' now we know all about it. I say, Winnie, I've got an idea in my head.'

'Nobody who had been trying to teach you for the last half-hour would have thought so!' remarked Winifred, laughing. 'Well, what is your idea?'

'Why, Harry Lysaght turned up just now, a good hour before his usual time, and he looked uncommonly like a man with a purpose. He asked for Daisy, and presently they're going out for a walk together. Winnie, my love, it strikes me forcibly that the decisive moment has come.'

'You don't mean that!' exclaimed Winifred involuntarily. 'It's no concern of yours or mine, though,' she added at once; 'and we really must get on with our lessons.'

'Yes, in half a minute. I'm glad he has made up his mind to drive her into a corner at last, aren't you? She'll have to take him or leave him this time, and I think my Daisy knows too well on which side her bread is buttered to leave him. I suppose he held a consultation with you when you were out in the boat with him yesterday, didn't he?'

'My dear Micky, do you think that, if he had consulted me, I should be likely to talk about it to little boys?'

'My dear Winnie, I am very old for my age, and you might rely upon my discretion. But I don't particularly care to be told whether he consulted you or not, because I'm sure he did. Quite right, too; and it's lucky for him that he spent the day at sea. He wouldn't have enjoyed himself if he had been with us, and seen the way that Daisy carried on with Mr. Bellew.'

'Micky, you shouldn't try to be clever. You are always fancying that you see things and letting your imagination run away with you.'

'I am, am I? Well, there was nothing imaginary about Daisy's behaviour yesterday afternoon, at all events. I quite blushed for her! And she was jolly well sold, after all; for Mr. Bellew was wishing her at Jericho, and wishing himself in Harry Lysaght's place the whole time. I'll allow,' added Micky impartially, 'that it takes a bit of imagination to discover that sort of thing; but I did discover it.'

His imagination was also equal to the surmise that the above statement would not be unwelcome to his elder sister, and he at once perceived from her face that it had pleased her. That, to be sure, did not exactly prove what he hoped that it proved; but he felt encouraged to expatiate further upon the subject, and was about to do so, when he was authoritatively ordered to stop chattering and resume his studies.

But not much more was accomplished in the way of study that morning. Winifred herself could not keep her mind from wandering, and she ended by dismissing her pupil somewhat earlier than the regulation hour. Long before that she had caught a glimpse of Daisy and her lover skirting the hillside together at a leisurely pace. Surely they must have returned by now, and surely, if there were any good news to be told, Daisy would hasten to impart it to her. As far as that went, she would probably be the first to hear of any bad news; for Daisy, like the rest of the family, instinctively turned to her in moments of difficulty or emergency.

However, it was not Daisy, but Harry Lysaght, who eventually crossed the garden with hurried steps in search of her, and as soon as she saw him, she understood that he was the bearer of evil tidings. Harry, who was rather red in the face, and seemed to be labouring under considerable agitation, said:

'I've come to bid you good-bye. I shall leave by to-morrow's steamer, if I can get a berth; if I can't, I shall have to go by train to Oran and sail from there. I must get out of this as soon as possible, anyhow.'

Winifred started to her feet in dismay. 'Oh, I'm so very sorry!' she exclaimed. 'Is it really all over, then?'

'It's all over with me, if that's what you mean,' answered the young man rather roughly. 'Perhaps I ought to have expected as much, and perhaps I had no right to expect what I did; but I must say that I don't think I have been fairly treated.'

'If Daisy has refused you, I don't think that you have,' assented Winifred sorrowfully; 'but I can't believe that she intended to refuse you finally. Most likely it is a misunderstanding. You said something that made her angry, didn't you? Sit down and tell me all about it.'

Harry did not sit down, but he said that, since she wanted to know, he could tell her all about it in a very few words. He had asked Daisy to marry him, and she had answered that she didn't care sufficiently for him to do so; he supposed that was straight enough, wasn't it?

Winifred had to admit that, in the case of most girls, it might be so considered; but she reminded her hearer that Daisy was a little bit wilful and capricious. It wasn't wise, and he should have known that it wouldn't be wise, to approach her with a peremptory demand.

Harry shrugged his shoulders. 'An end must come to everything some time or other,' he remarked; 'you will hardly accuse me of headlong precipitation, I should hope! There was no misunderstanding and no anger; she simply said that she was very sorry, but that she found she didn't care enough for me to be my wife—so after that there wasn't much more to be said.'

'And did you say nothing more?'

'Oh, I was ass enough to say a good deal more; but I should have done better to hold my tongue. Well, it can't be helped, and I shouldn't dream of complaining to anybody except you, but to you I don't mind saying that I think she has treated me very badly. Certainly, before you left England, she gave me every excuse for expecting a different answer. Oh, I know things have happened since then—although you don't, or won't confess that you do. Of course she has a perfect right to prefer

Bellew to me, and I have no doubt that nine women out of ten would; only—I *was* first in the field, you see.'

'But I think—I hope you are mistaken about Mr. Bellew,' said Winifred feebly.

'No, my dear Winnie, I am not mistaken,' answered Harry, with rather a dreary laugh. 'I know when she is flirting with a man—I ought to know, having seen her do it so often!—and I know when she is in earnest, because I never saw her in earnest before. In point of fact I taxed her with it, and she scarcely denied it. Pretty poor form on my part, you'll say; but, between ourselves, I don't think either he or she has shown quite the best of good form in this business. Now I must be off. We shall meet again in the course of the summer, I suppose, and I shall try to look as if I didn't mind. I couldn't quite manage that at present, so —good-bye.'

Winifred gave him her hand. She felt that it would be useless to detain him any longer, and in the face of the statements he had made, she could hardly advise him to renew his suit, but she said she would have a talk with Daisy, and perhaps she would send him down a note in the afternoon.

'Oh no, you won't do that,' returned Harry, shaking his head; 'if you send a note to the Hôtel d'Orient at all, it will be a note to Bellew asking him to come and dine. After all, why shouldn't you? It's impossible to make everybody happy, and you naturally think more of your sister's

happiness than of mine. You were a real friend
to me while you could be, though, and I'm not
ungrateful.'

After he had departed, Winnie went into the
house, where she found the mid-day meal in progress, and received her father's customary rebuke
for unpunctuality. Mrs. Forbes had evidently been
in tears, Daisy looked calm, cool and obstinate,
and Micky made expressive grimaces from the other
side of the table. Immediately upon the conclusion
of the repast, Winifred was summoned to write
letters for her father, so it was not until an hour
later that she was able to obtain speech of Daisy,
whom she found waiting for her in the garden, and
who began:

'For Heaven's sake, don't scold! I have had
such a scolding as never was from mamma, and I
really can't stand any more. You must smooth
her down, Winnie, and tell her it's all right; she
won't listen to me.'

'But I don't think it *is* all right,' objected
Winnie; 'it seems to me that it is all wrong. If
you really don't care for poor Harry Lysaght——'

'Have I ever pretended that I cared for poor
Harry Lysaght? Haven't I told you scores of
times that I liked him very well, and that was all?
You know as well as I do that mamma isn't weep-
ing over the loss of Harry Lysaght, it's the loss of
Harry Lysaght's property that goes to her heart.
But let her cheer up; there are other men in the
world who have property or money. And what-

ever mamma's views may be, I should have thought that *you* would wish me to marry a man whom I could love—even if he hadn't any landed property.'

Winifred remained silent for a few moments. Then she remarked :

' Harry thinks there is such a man.'

' So he was kind enough to inform me. He is very welcome to his opinion.'

' That is rather hard upon him, don't you think ?'

' Upon whom ? Harry, or the anonymous man ?'

' Well, upon both, perhaps,' answered Winifred, laughing a little; ' but of course I meant Harry. By the way, you didn't allow the other man to remain anonymous, according to his account.'

' It was he who mentioned Mr. Bellew's name, not I. He said he was certain that I liked Mr. Bellew better than him, and I really couldn't contradict him without telling a fib.'

Winifred looked grave.

' Of course,' she began, ' I don't know how far matters have gone——'

' Oh, they haven't gone very far yet,' interrupted Daisy ; ' but I tell you frankly that I mean them to go a good deal farther before I have done with him. Now, Winnie, you needn't put on a scandalised face, because you were warned from the first that it was my pious intention to rescue him from the clutches of Mrs. Littlewood. If you call that being hard upon him, you must be blind to his true interests. Whether I shall marry him or not is another question.'

'I suppose,' remarked Winifred, 'it is just possible that he may not ask you?'

'Perfectly possible,' answered Daisy with a quiet smile, which implied that she did not deem such an omission on his part probable. 'As for Harry Lysaght,' she continued, 'I don't see that he has anything to grumble at; and I ought to be applauded, instead of abused, for having refused an indulgent husband and a charming house and lots of pin-money, from the highest motives. I say that for your benefit; you needn't pass it on to mamma; it wouldn't appeal to her. The way to comfort her is to dwell upon Mr. Bellew's wealth, which I hear is considerable.'

At this moment Mrs. Forbes's voice was heard plaintively calling Winnie from the window, and thus the colloquy came to an end.

Harry Lysaght received no note from Winnie that evening, but, on the other hand, Billy Bellew did receive an invitation to dinner from Mrs. Forbes, who, like a wise, constitutional sovereign, had decided to submit with as good a grace as she could to the vagaries of one over whom her authority was but nominal.

CHAPTER XIV.

THE CHEMIN DES AQUEDUCS.

OWING to a previous engagement, Mr. Bellew was unable to accept Mrs. Forbes's kind invitation to dinner; and he might have added that it would be a waste of time to send him any more such invitations, because he was sure to be previously engaged during the remainder of his sojourn in Algiers. Fortunately, however, for his peace of mind, he did not know this, nor did Mrs. Littlewood upbraid him for his faithlessness. On the contrary, she took more pains than she had for a long time past done to make herself pleasant to him; only she never missed an opportunity of saying something contemptuous about the elder Miss Forbes, and for about ten days she held him very tight indeed. These, it must be acknowledged, were not clever tactics; but Mrs. Littlewood was not a clever woman. She thought (but even clever women often fall into that error) that the ashes of a dead love may be fanned into life again; she thought that Billy was a goose, and that the only way to deal with him was to keep him out of temptation's way; furthermore, she was under the impression that she possessed sufficient influence over him to imbue him with her own views respecting other people.

For ten days, therefore, Billy was not allowed to see much of the Forbes family, although he had some rides with Micky in the early mornings; but at the expiration of that time Mrs. Littlewood's vigilance began to relax. She had satisfied herself that her devoted attendant had at least not been guilty of the atrocity of proposing to Miss Forbes; the meekness with which he listened to her hostile criticisms upon that lady helped to disarm suspicion; she reflected that the notions which find their way into the head of a small boy should not be taken too seriously; moreover, she really had great difficulty in believing that any man with eyes in his head could have been fascinated by one so immeasurably her inferior in the matter of looks. Consequently she let him have a little more rope, thereby unconsciously rendering a service to Daisy, whose patience and forbearance had been subjected to a severe strain all this time.

Daisy, in default of other facilities for cultivating amicable relations with Mr. Bellew, had been driven to join occasionally in those matutinal rides. Much as she hated early rising, and little as she relished the company of an intrusive and obstinate third person, she felt that she had no alternative. So she asked in a very humble manner whether she might sometimes be permitted to go out with her brother and his friend, and the request was of course granted. Her manner had, for some reason or other, become humble; she no longer attempted to domineer over Mr. Bellew, or to treat him as she was wont to treat her admirers; she would ride beside him for long distances without once opening her lips, and she accepted certain reprimands which he thought it right to administer to her upon her style of equitation with curious submissiveness. Billy thought her greatly improved, and began to like her much better than he had done. He had heard from Micky that she had rejected Harry Lysaght, and he suspected that she was already repenting of what she had done. But not for one moment did he suspect that he himself had had anything to do with that hasty and foolish rejection.

Of Winnie he obtained a glimpse, but only a glimpse, every now and then. It sometimes happened that she was in the garden or at the front door when he and his companions returned from their ride, and then she would say good-morning, or perhaps address a few words to him. Once he ventured to suggest that it would do her good to accompany them the next time they went out, but his proposal met with no encouragement.

'Don't you remember telling me,' she asked, 'that I was not fond of riding? You were quite right; I am not fond of it. Besides, I have so many other things to do.'

But although she would not ride with him, she did not seem to mind talking to him ; and he had more frequent occasions of exchanging ideas with her, after the reassured Mrs. Littlewood took to driving with her friend Mrs. Ryland, and leaving his afternoons free. What puzzled him a little was the half-compassionate, half-regretful look which he surprised every now and again in her brown eyes. Was she sorry for him because he was still in bondage, and because he refused to break his bonds ? He hoped it might be that, but he hardly thought it could be, for she never alluded even remotely to the subject. How, indeed, should he have guessed what she herself could not have explained ? According to her view of the situation,

Mr. Bellew was not at all to be pitied. He was going to break with Mrs. Littlewood; he had fallen in love with Daisy, who had obviously fallen in love (and for the very first time in her life) with him; no difficulties would be raised by Mr. and Mrs. Forbes, the latter of whom had made inquiries, and was prepared to give him a maternal welcome, now that Harry Lysaght was past praying for—no; Mr. Bellew could scarcely be called a fit subject for pity. Yet, somehow or other, she did pity him, and she regretted Daisy's perversity almost as much on his account as on Harry's. There may have been some dim, unformulated notion in her mind that he was too good for Daisy.

Meanwhile, the spring was advancing rapidly. The blossoms had fallen from the almond-trees; such of the aloes as proposed flowering prior to their demise were sending up long spikes ; the sun was growing more powerful every day, the winter visitants were becoming restless. Amongst the other gifts bestowed by the bounteous season came Colonel Littlewood, back from Hammam R'irha with a clean bill of health, but an empty pocket. Baccarat had of late treated him most unkindly, he explained to Billy, and his bad luck at that seductive game rendered the negotiation of a fresh loan imperative. Of course he got his money, and of course, in expressing his thanks, he gave utterance to the customary formula respecting ultimate repayment. Repayment was what Billy had never asked for and never anticipated; still, as he was not what in these days is accounted a rich man, it would have been convenient to him to see some of his money back. He more than suspected, too, that a further advance would be required in order to defray the expense of his friends' homeward journey. When would they go, he wondered ; and would he be expected to go with them when they went? He put some tentative queries upon the subject to the Colonel, who answered, with his habitual complaisance :

'Oh, *I* don't know, my dear fellow; you must ask the wife. You and she had better settle it between you.'

No necessity for consulting Mrs. Littlewood arose, for that lady had already settled what she meant to do, and in the course of the same evening she made her intentions known to the somewhat dismayed Billy.

'I think we have had about enough of this,' she told him. 'The people here haven't been so civil to us that we need break our hearts at leaving them ; and although I am sorry to tear you away from Le Bocage, I am afraid the time has come for me to issue marching-orders. It's rather too soon to go straight back to London, though—how would Tunis and Sicily, and then a leisurely trip through Italy, suit you ?'

Billy could not imagine anything much less likely to suit him than the above programme, but it was impossible to say so. What he did say, in hasty and guilty accents, was :

' That would be very nice—very nice indeed!
Only I'm not sure whether I oughtn't to get home
rather sooner than you will. I half promised to
ride for a man at Sandown, and—and there are a
lot of other things that I must see about. I was
thinking that I might perhaps stay on here for a
few days after you leave, and then travel straight
through to England.'

The scene which he had as good as invited
promptly followed, and an unconditional surrender
on his part followed the scene with equal prompti-
tude. It is all very well to sneer at his weakness,
but, under the circumstances, no amount of strength
would have availed him much. He had to choose
between surrender and quarrelling with Blanche,
and he could not quarrel with Blanche ; he would
have considered himself a downright brute if he
had done that. She gave him to understand that
his behaviour in proposing to desert her amounted
to something not very far short of downright
brutality ; she did not forgive him until she had
made him beg repeatedly for forgiveness ; and, by
way of guarding against any possible relapse into
insubordination, she despatched him to the town
the next day to find out about steamers and to
secure a passage to Tunis for himself, as well as
for her and her husband.

A sorrowful man was he when he set forth on
foot to obey her orders. It was true that the day
of his departure would have had to come sooner or
later, and that a prolongation of his sojourn in

Algiers would not have altered the fact that an insurmountable barrier existed between him and Winifred Forbes; but most people prefer to take a necessary dose of pain later rather than sooner, while no man of Billy Bellew's age believes, at the bottom of his heart, in insurmountable barriers.

The office of the Compagnie Transatlantique was crowded, and he had an absurd sort of hope that cabins might not be obtainable that week; but the short-mannered clerk behind the grating took his money and his order without hesitation, and presently pushed the tickets towards him. There is sometimes a difficulty about getting cabins for Marseilles at short notice; but the coasting service is less largely patronized. Billy turned away with a heavy heart, and, making for the door, almost ran into the arms of Winifred Forbes.

'I have come to take our passage,' she said. 'We are such a large party that we have to make our arrangements a week or two in advance. Are you here on the same errand?'

Billy nodded gloomily. 'Only I'm not taking time so very much by the forelock,' he said. 'We're bound for Tunis, and we sail in three days, I'm sorry to say.'

No one could have misinterpreted the expression which Winifred's face assumed when she heard this announcement. She not only looked startled; she looked almost horrified.

'In three days?' she echoed. 'But surely this is a very sudden resolution, is it not?'

'Yes, I suppose it is rather sudden ; but Mrs. Littlewood often does make up her mind in a hurry.'

'Ah—Mrs. Littlewood! You are going with her, then ?'

Well, if he was, that was hardly a reason for her addressing him in accents of seeming reproach ; she knew very well that he was compelled to do as Mrs. Littlewood told him. He made no reply, beyond a grunt, and then asked whether he could be of any use in taking her tickets for her, as a lady might have some trouble in elbowing her way through the throng. His offer was accepted, and thus he ascertained that the Forbes were not going to leave Algiers for another month. Another month ! Ah, if only some thrice-blessed Captain Patten could have been discovered to replace him, and if he could have remained quietly where he was for that length of time ! But what is the good of sighing for impossibilities ?

Winifred had recovered her equanimity when he rejoined her. She thanked him, and remarked : 'I suppose you are riding or driving ? I am going to walk up the hill.'

How like that selfish old father of hers to have sent her all that distance on foot, and to have made her do his troublesome jobs for him ! But Billy was glad that she meant to walk home, all the same.

'I am doing a constitutional, too,' he said. 'Perhaps—if you didn't mind—we might keep each other company.'

She assented at once. He gathered from her manner that she had rather expected his proposition, and that she had a reason for agreeing to it. Perhaps, in the kindness of her heart, she wanted to try the effect of some further remonstrances upon him. That, to be sure, would be a waste of breath; still, it would be happiness to be alone with her and to hear her voice, whatever she might think fit to say to him.

They did not return by the dusty highroad. Miss Forbes said that, if he wasn't in a hurry, she would prefer the Chemin des Aqueducs, a shady, winding road which follows the contour of the hills to the westward of Algiers, and which is certainly not adapted to meet the requirements of persons in a hurry. But Billy was very far from being such a person just then, and, after a steep climb through the white village of Isly, he gazed forward with satisfaction upon a long succession of clefts and ravines, into every one of which, as he knew, the sinuous way that lay before them plunged deeply. The vegetation on those hillsides is something marvellous to Northern eyes. The woods of ilex and silvery olives, with here and there a tall palm among them, the ragged bananas stooping over the garden-walls; above all, the profusion of creepers and the giant ivy which hangs in festoons from tree to tree—these, bathed in the intense yet mellow light of an Algerian sun, must needs move even an exiled fox-hunter and a disconsolate lover to appreciative wonder. Billy paid his tribute to the exquisite designs of Nature in characteristic terms.

'This fairly takes the cake!' he ejaculated. 'I ain't much of a judge of scenery, but I'd back Algiers to romp in from any other place within a thousand miles of England.'

'Yet you are going to leave it,' remarked Winifred.

'Well—I must, you know.'

'No, I don't know that at all. I don't understand your leaving like this. I wish you would explain.'

She spoke with an impatience which astonished him; if she did not understand, neither did he. But of course he could explain, and he proceeded to do so.

Even after listening to a perfectly explicit statement, Winifred did not appear to be satisfied. 'I suppose you must be speaking the truth,' she said; 'but I did not expect you to talk like that. A month ago I should have expected it—I shouldn't have wondered; but—but I thought you had changed some of your ideas of late. Certainly you have behaved as if you had.'

He heard her with increasing amazement. There could be no doubt now that she was reproaching him—but with what? It seemed sheer insanity to hope; and yet every word that she said seemed to be uttered with the deliberate intention of giving him hope. As they paced along from sunlight to shade, and out into the sunlight again, she begged him to be straightforward with her, and to tell her candidly whether anything had occurred to give him offence. If so, she believed she would be able to set it right. 'It is so much better to speak out while there is still time. Unless you speak out now, you will be sorry afterwards, I think.'

Mortal man could not resist that. Billy stopped short and threw out his hands.

'God knows I would have spoken long ago if I had thought—if I had dared to think—that there was the ghost of a chance for me!' he exclaimed. 'Even now I can hardly believe that there isn't some mistake, and I don't know what to say. But there is nothing really to say, because you have heard everything. You know how I love you, you know all about Blanche Littlewood—all that there is against me. I don't think it's so very bad—at least, not according to my lights. If it's bad of me to throw her over, I can't help it; nobody could help it! One thing I can tell you truly: I have never loved any woman on earth but you, and never so long as I live——'

'Stop! stop!' interrupted Winifred in a strangled voice. She had dropped in a sitting posture upon the parapet by the wayside; her cheeks were pale and her eyes dilated. 'You were right,' she went on presently; 'there has been a mistake—a horrible mistake! I don't think it can have been my fault; I hope you will believe that I never had the most distant suspicion of this! I was thinking of—of something quite different.'

Billy's heart sank.

'But you did know that I loved you,' he murmured; 'you must surely have known that!'

'Oh no!—how could I? It is the last thing that I should ever have dreamt of!' She got up, and continued in a calmer and more constrained voice: 'Perhaps I had better tell you that I am engaged to be married. I have been engaged for some years to a Mr. Kirby, a neighbour of ours at home.'

Billy groaned.

'Then, it would have been hopeless, anyhow,' he remarked.

'Yes, of course it would. I am very, very sorry; I wish I hadn't spoken as I did just now! You must have thought,' exclaimed Winifred, the pallor of her cheeks becoming replaced by a vivid blush as she recalled her indiscreet utterances—'you must have thought I was proposing to you! But you understand now, or, rather, you don't understand, and I don't want you to understand. Mr. Bellew, will you please try to forget what I said?'

'Yes, I'll try, if you wish it,' answered Billy dismally.

He was still quite in the dark as to her original meaning; but that was of small consequence.

Her present meaning was clear enough to force itself upon the most obtuse comprehension. After an interval of silence, during which they had resumed their walk, he asked:

'If this man Kirby had never existed, do you

think—would it have been possible for you ever to have cared for me?'

'As if anybody could answer such a question!' she returned irritably. But then she caught sight of his woebegone countenance and was moved to compassion. 'What might have been if everything had been different isn't much to the purpose, is it?' she resumed in a gentler tone. 'But I can't believe that we should ever have been suited to one another, you and I. We are so very unlike in all our habits and tastes. You, I suppose, live chiefly for sport, and sport has no attractions for me. My mission in life is to keep house and nurse people when they are ill, and make myself generally useful in a humdrum sort of way. You would be bored to death if you were condemned to spend the rest of your days with a person of that description; and if you will only try to realise what I am and what you are, I am sure you will see, after a time, that you have had a lucky escape.'

Billy smiled, but made no rejoinder. After they had walked about a hundred yards farther in silence, he said:

'Perhaps I had better leave you now, hadn't I? I can't talk, and I believe there's a short cut to the hotel from here. To-morrow I shall come and say good-bye to you all. By that time I shall be able to behave properly, I hope, and to look as if nothing had happened.'

She did not attempt to detain him, but she gave him her hand and repeated that she was very sorry,

whereupon they parted. Winifred walked steadily
on, but Billy remained standing still, with his
hands clasped behind his back and his head bowed.
When, five minutes later, a bend of the road
brought her once more in sight of the spot where
she had left him, he had not yet stirred.

CHAPTER XV

BILLY TAKES LEAVE.

UNSELFISHNESS is probably a virtue which, like
other virtues, admits of adoption and cultivation ;
but we may safely assume that in nine cases out of
every ten in which it is displayed the quality is
inborn. Winifred Forbes was scarcely conscious of
the fact that the welfare of others was more important to her than her own ; so that psychologists
may, if they please, deny her any credit for being
what she was. Nevertheless, she was, to say the
least of it, a little unusual, and the manner in
which she was affected by Mr. Bellew's unforeseen
declaration of love was scarcely that which it would
have produced upon the majority of young women.

What in the world was to become of Daisy ? and
how was she to be comforted ? This was what
Winnie kept asking herself, as she tramped along
the Chemin des Aqueducs, looking neither to right
nor left, and advancing more quickly than was
necessary towards the goal that she dreaded. She
had now no doubt, nor had she had any for some

time past, that her sister was in earnest. A
hundred trivial incidents had betrayed the girl's
secret; she was not flirting this time; she had not
refused Harry Lysaght out of mere perversity; she
had confidently anticipated what could never come;
and Daisy, alas! was not one who knew how to
bear disappointment or humiliation. It would be
terrible to have to tell her the truth; yet of course
she must be told.

'She is sure to blame me,' thought Winifred
disconsolately, 'and it does look as if I had been to
blame. Everybody would say so; everybody agrees
that men don't propose without some sort of encouragement. And the worst of it is, that I did
seem to encourage him this afternoon, though I
never did before—never, I am certain, before! Oh,
what a dolt I was, and how thankful I am that he
was too stupid to see what I was driving at! Only
I suppose he will see when he comes to think it
over; even he can hardly be so simple as to imagine
that I meant nothing at all.'

She laughed a little, as she recalled their conversation at cross-purposes, for all the world knows
that grief and vexation are not incompatible with
laughter. Then, being somewhat out of breath,
as well as conscious of a certain trembling in the
lower limbs, she sat down on the bank by the roadside, and tried to remember exactly what she had
said to him and what he had said to her. No
great effort of memory was required to bring it all
back to her with dreadful distinctness. He had

been reluctant to speak out; she had insisted upon his doing so; she had told him as plainly as possible that he was behaving badly by leaving the place; she had offered to explain away any misunderstanding which might have arisen—in short, it must be absolutely obvious to him that, since she had not been pleading her own cause, she had been pleading that of her sister. Then, in the natural sequence of things, she came to his amazing avowal, to her reception of it, to that last query of his which she impatiently stigmatized at the time as not being to the purpose. Assuredly it had not been to the purpose,—and perhaps, strictly speaking, he had had no business to ask such a question; yet she lingered for some minutes over the recollection of it, and wondered dreamily what would or might have happened if there had been no Edmund Kirby, no Daisy, and no Mrs. Littlewood to create complications.

Speculations of that kind are apt to be dangerous, and Winifred, after pursuing them for a short space, found herself upon the very brink of a discovery which she had no desire to make. She sprang back just in time to save herself from making it—in time, at least, to save herself from admitting that she had made it—and turned resolutely to the consideration of how she might best communicate the bad news to her family. She concluded at length that she was not bound to say anything about Mr. Bellew's proposal to herself; it would be sufficient to state the bare fact that he was going away; and if his departure should be attributed to Mrs. Littlewood's influence, that, after all, would be the cause to which he himself had assigned it. The only thing was that Daisy must, by some means or other, be preserved from humbling herself before him ; and that could be managed, Winifred thought. His leave-taking must of necessity be brief and formal, and Daisy should certainly not be left alone with him for a moment.

Having decided upon her line of action, she walked home, and, as it happened, saw nobody until the dinner-hour. Then, of course, she had to speak. She opened her mouth to do so several times without succeeding in getting out a word, but at length she forced herself to begin, in what, as she was painfully aware, sounded quite unlike her ordinary voice :

' By the way, I met Mr. Bellew at the ticket office ; he was engaging passages for Tunis. He is going there with Colonel and Mrs. Littlewood in a few days. They are not coming back again.'

After firing off these abrupt sentences, she attacked her soup with great vigour, and went near to choking herself over it. She did not dare to look up, and for a few seconds the silence was unbroken. At length Micky ejaculated in accents of consternation :

' Oh, I say !'

The clock had ticked off another dozen or so of interminable seconds before Mrs. Forbes remarked severely, but rather tremulously :

'I am very sorry to hear that that—that disgraceful intrigue has not come to an end; and I am very sorry, too, that we have allowed Mr. Bellew to be so much about the house. I think, Winnie dear, you have been scarcely prudent in throwing —er—er—Micky at his head, as you have done of late.'

But Daisy said nothing at all. When Winifred ventured to raise her eyes, she saw that the girl had fallen back in her chair and that her face was as white as the tablecloth. There was no concealment nor any attempt at concealment on her part; Daisy never did — perhaps could not — disguise her emotions. Winifred at once began to talk, and continued to talk incessantly for a matter of ten minutes. It was the only thing to be done, but it was not the easiest thing in the world to do, because nobody helped her. At last even Mr. Forbes, short-sighted and self-absorbed as he was, ended by suspecting that something was the matter. He peered over his spectacles at his younger daughter, and said:

' Daisy, my love, are you feeling unwell? If so, had you not better retire to your room and lie down? You appear to me to be upon the verge of one of those attacks of syncope to which young persons of your sex are frequently liable. Cold water and smelling-salts are, I believe, generally found to be efficient remedies.'

Daisy pushed back her chair, got up, and left the room without a word. Winifred rose with the intention of following her, but was detained by her father, who wanted to have the leg of a chicken divided for him. When he tried to accomplish such operations for himself the result generally was that his neighbour received the chicken bone, while everybody else within range of him was splashed all over with gravy. Having fulfilled the filial duty required of her, Winifred made for the door, throwing an interrogative glance at her mother, who responded peevishly in an undertone:

'Oh yes, if you like! But she isn't going to faint, and she doesn't want you.'

Mrs. Forbes was mistaken; for Daisy, who, like the rest of the family, instinctively turned to Winnie in times of tribulation, did want her sister. That, however, did not prevent her from according her sister an extremely discourteous reception. She had thrown herself down upon the bed, and when the intruder entered, she started up, saying:

'What do you want? Have you come to exult over me and to tell me that you knew all along how it would be? Perhaps you would like to telegraph for Harry Lysaght. I dare say he will come if you do; he isn't proud.'

Perhaps Daisy was not very proud, either. That thought did present itself to Winifred's mind; but she was too sorry and too full of sympathy for the poor little spoilt child to dwell upon it. She set to work to discharge a mission for the accomplishment of which she possessed exceptional facilities, and in a few minutes Daisy, who had thrown her arms round the consoler's neck, was sobbing out broken-heartedly : 'Oh, Winnie, what shall I do? what shall I do?'

Well, there really was not very much to be done, except to put a brave face upon disaster and to trust to the healing influences of time ; but neither of these courses could be recommended without an appearance of cruelty. Unfortunately, too, Winifred was debarred from holding out any of those fallacious hopes which it may have been expected of her that she should suggest. In honesty, as well as in kindness, she was bound to make it clear that, in her opinion, Mr. Bellew had no intentions, and it was some slight comfort to find that that was Daisy's own conviction.

'I have been caught in my own trap,' the girl said forlornly. 'He thought I was only flirting with him—oh, I saw plainly enough that that was what he thought at first!—and he determined to pay me out. He needn't have been so cruel, though; he needn't have tried in every possible way to make me believe that he loved me. I don't think it was quite fair and honourable to do that, do you, Winnie?'

'No,' answered Winifred hesitatingly, 'I don't think it was—if you are sure that he did.'

'Sure that he did! Am I likely to make a mistake about matters of that sort? Over and over again he has said things to me which could only have one meaning.'

She repeated some of his speeches. Perhaps he had really made them ; perhaps she only thought that he had made them; in either case she had read her own meaning into them, as the ineradicable habit of her sex is. Happily, it did not occur to her to blame her sister; the vials of her wrath, when these took the place of despondency, were poured forth upon Mrs. Littlewood, only a small portion of the overflowing measure being reserved for Billy. If she had shown a little more indignation against the latter, Winifred would have been better pleased and less apprehensive. By hook or by crook she must be kept from seeing Mr. Bellew and betraying herself, as she almost certainly would, in the event of her being brought face to face with him. When Daisy was happy or unhappy, pleased or angry, she never cared who knew it. She had practised no sort of deceit in her life, save such as she was wont to exercise in dealing with her admirers, and even that could hardly be called deceit of a very subtle character. It turned out, however, that Daisy did not wish to see Mr. Bellew again.

'If he asks for me you can tell him that I have gone out,' she said; 'I don't want him to know how miserable he has made me, though I suppose he does know. I shall never care for anybody else as long as I live—never! And to think that he cares for that hideous, painted old creature, whom he pretended to find such a bore!'

It would have made matters no better to suggest that perhaps he didn't care for the hideous, painted old creature, and Winifred maintained a guilty silence. It was at least some relief to know that Mr. Bellew's farewell visit, to which she looked forward with no little personal dread, would now in all probability prove a very brief and formal affair.

Mr. Bellew's visit did not disappoint expectation in that respect. He arrived shortly after three o'clock on the following afternoon, and brevity, even if his own inclinations had not tended that way, would have been urged upon him by the excessive formality of Mrs. Forbes, who was inwardly furious. It must be confessed that most mothers would have been furious in her place. To have lost a son-in-law of such rare excellence and desirability as Harry Lysaght was bad enough; but to have been made a positive fool of by the man whom, against her better judgment, she had consented to accept as a *pis-aller* was more than mortal woman could bear with equanimity. Still, prudence always counsels the concealment of our wounds, and a lucky thing it was for Mrs. Forbes that she had to deal with so unsuspicious and so preoccupied a personage as Billy Bellew.

He noticed, indeed, what he could hardly help noticing, that her manner was unusually cold; but he thought it very likely that she had been told of his offer to her elder daughter, and had been annoyed by it. For the rest, he said scarcely anything to her, beyond thanking her for her hospitality, and it was Winifred who preserved the short conversation from dying of inanition.

Winifred was very nervous, and so was he; but, all things considered, they performed their respective parts creditably enough. When he rose to go, he cast an imploring glance at her, the meaning of which she understood, though she was doubtful about the wisdom of complying with his mute request. But pity or good nature, or perhaps an unacknowledged desire to say a last kind word to him, got the better of her hesitation, and she followed him out to the front-door.

'Thank you for coming,' he said gratefully, as he stood, with bared head, in the full blaze of the sunshine. 'I wanted just to tell you how sorry I am if I distressed or vexed you yesterday. Of course I shouldn't have spoken as I did if I had known about that—about the other man.'

'Of course not; and of course you could not know,' answered Winifred. 'Perhaps I ought to have told you before; but I never thought for a moment—it seemed so utterly unlikely——'

'I don't see why it should have seemed unlikely,' said poor Billy.

'Oh, I think you must, if you will consider! But there is no help for it now, and you haven't distressed me—at least, not for myself. We must try to forget it, and—and part friends.'

'And am I never to see you again?'

Winifred looked down. 'I don't want to be disagreeable,' she answered; 'but I think, if we were to meet by chance in London or anywhere, it would be better for us to do no more than bow or shake hands. For many reasons, I would rather you didn't come and call.'

'Yes; I understand what you mean by "many reasons," and I dare say you are quite right. The only thing is that supposing—such a thing might happen, and sometimes I think it will—supposing I were no longer—in fact, that I were no longer upon quite such intimate terms with Mrs. Littlewood as I am now, might I call then?'

It was impossible for Winifred to explain that Mrs. Littlewood was not the obstacle. She fenced the question by replying: 'I don't know why you should wish for anything of the kind. Your calling upon us would only be embarrassing, and——'

'And it would not make you change your mind?'

'Of course it would not do that.'

'Well, nothing will ever make me change my mind, either. You are the only woman in the world for me, now and always. I hope you'll forgive my saying so, and remember that I said so. All sorts of strange things come to pass, and so long as you are unmarried there must be just a chance for me, however poor it may be. Such as it is, I'm going to take that chance.'

Winifred entreated him not to cherish any illusions of that description. She reminded him of what she had told him on the preceding day. It was not only that she was engaged to Edmund Kirby, who was getting on very well in his profession and would probably be in a position to marry before long, but that she felt sure she was utterly unfitted to be the wife of a sporting man. He must look out for some nice girl who was fond of hunting and knew a little about racing. 'And when you have found her, I will come to your wedding, if I am asked,' she added re-assuringly.

'You will never come to my wedding unless you come as the bride, Miss Forbes,' answered Billy. 'Please believe that, because it's the truth.'

He was going to add something more; but at that moment Mrs. Forbes, who doubtless thought that her unwelcome visitor had taken himself off by this time, was heard impatiently calling her daughter from the drawing-room; so their leave-taking was curtailed. Billy was halfway down the avenue before it occurred to him that he had omitted to send a message of farewell either to Miss Daisy or to Micky.

As regarded the latter, however, an opportunity of making amends for his forgetfulness was granted to him. He had not proceeded many yards along the lane which leads to Le Bocage, when a small figure jumped down from the high bank on his left hand, and, barring his passage, asked breathlessly: 'Oh, Mr. Bellew, are you really going away?'

'Yes, Micky, I'm off,' he replied, with an assumption of brisk cheerfulness. 'The best of friends must part, you know.'

'And ain't I ever to see you again?' the boy

asked, putting the same question that Billy himself had put a few minutes before, but looking even more dolorous over it. The truth was that Micky's tears were not very far off; though he would never have forgiven himself if he had allowed them to fall in the presence of one who would naturally despise such a girlish exhibition of weakness.

'Oh, you'll see me again right enough,' answered Billy. 'In another year or two we shall have you out hunting in Leicestershire, and then you'll be pretty safe to come across me, unless I break my neck in the meantime. Remember what I told you about sitting in the right place and keeping your hands low.'

The boy nodded, not being quite sure enough of his voice to make any articulate reply.

'And look here,' Billy went on, 'we've been capital friends, you and I, haven't we? I should like to give you some little thing just to put you in mind of me now and then.' He detached a small gold compass from his watch-chain. 'It isn't worth an awful lot of money,' he remarked; 'but I've found it useful more than once when I've lost my way in a fog or been overtaken by the darkness a dozen miles or so away from home.'

Micky's small brown fingers closed over the gift. 'I'll never lose it,' he said. And then, after a short pause: 'Mr. Bellew, I want to say something to you. I know well enough what has happened; I know why you're going away; the others didn't notice Winnie's face last night, but I did. And it isn't all up yet—it isn't really!'

Billy did not resent this plain speaking on the part of his young friend, nor did he affect to mis-understand it. He only smiled, and answered: 'I'm afraid it is all up, Micky; anyhow, she says it is.'

'That's only because she thinks she is bound to Edmund Kirby; and I don't believe she cares a brass farthing for him really. He's an awful stick!'

'Oh, he's an awful stick, is he? Still, she may be fond of him. She told me she didn't like sporting men very much.'

'Don't you believe it! She likes *you*, at all events; and if you'll only stick to it, and look us up in England, it will all come right at last, I'm sure. It's quite on the cards that Kirby may throw her over. He can't be in any desperate hurry to marry her, because they've been engaged since the flood, and it's all bosh about his not having money enough. I've heard mamma say so lots of times.'

This was good hearing, and Billy was so much in want of a little encouragement that he may be excused for having clutched at the straw extended to him. However, as he reflected, after taking leave of his juvenile counsellor, to whom he gave a solemn promise that he would write sometimes, there was another little difficulty of which the astute Micky knew nothing. That Winnie should

be set free by Edmund Kirby would not be enough;
it would still remain for him to obtain his release
from Blanche Littlewood, who was just about as
likely to let him go of her own free will as an Arab
slave-trader is to liberate his captives in an access
of philanthropy.

CHAPTER XVI.

BILLY HANDS IN HIS RESIGNATION.

THE town of Tunis, notwithstanding the French
occupation, has not yet lost its Oriental character.
The majestic Moors who stalk through its narrow,
ill-paved streets, or sit gravely smoking at the
doors of their shops in the covered bazaars, still
retain the eye for colour of which close contact
with civilization seems fated to deprive their race,
and wear clothes that delight the gaze of the
wandering artist. The long strings of camels, the
fat Jewesses in their amazing costume of short
jackets and closely-fitting tights, the scowling
fanatics who guard the approaches to the mosques
—these and a hundred other everyday sights give
evidence of a more primitive and more picturesque
phase of Eastern life than can be looked for now in
Algiers.

But the novelty and picturesqueness of the Bey's
capital left Billy Bellew cold and indifferent. To
him it was nothing more than a yellow primrose
was to the insensible Peter Bell. It was a dirty
town in North Africa where there was an uncom-

fortable hotel, a varied assortment of bad smells and nothing particular to do, except to visit the bazaars with Mrs. Littlewood and purchase innumerable things that he didn't want. Mrs. Littlewood wanted them, and got them; which was, perhaps, fortunate, inasmuch as the acquisition of marvellous shot silks and pieces of embroidery and carpets kept her in a tolerably good humour. Billy paid without bargaining. After all, that was what he was there for. It was a pity nature had made him such a very poor dissembler; because, if he could have contrived to look only ordinarily cheerful, he would have spared himself some unpleasant moments. As it was, Mrs. Littlewood's good humour was intermittent, and when she became provoked with him, she did not spare him.

'Don't you think you had better return to Algiers?' she asked him one afternoon. 'You have evidently left your heart there, and by going back you might possibly find it again. I should recommend you to stay three or four weeks and to make a point of seeing Miss Forbes every day. If that won't cure you, your case must indeed be hopeless!'

'I don't see the good of talking like that,' returned Billy. 'You know very well that I have taken my passage for Palermo, according to your instructions. As for Miss Forbes, it may interest you to hear that she is engaged to be married to some man who lives near them in Shropshire.'

Mrs. Littlewood raised her artistically-pencilled eyebrows and pursed up her lips. 'Oh, that's it, is it?' said she. 'Now we know why you have been looking as if you meditated self-destruction all this time! So she told you that she was engaged, did she? What could you have been saying to her to draw forth that confidential information? Well, I condole with you; though it is a comfort to think that you will soon be yourself again. Nobody has better reason than I have to be aware of the ease with which you recover from these little attacks.'

Sometimes she made his life a burden to him after that fashion; sometimes she had recourse to tears and reproaches. Neither method was agreeable; but of the two he preferred the former, and this, contrary to precedent, was the more frequently employed. He suspected, and could not help hoping, that Blanche had grown rather weary of him. Of course it was no longer possible for him to deceive himself as to the fact that he had grown terribly weary of her.

Better times—comparatively better times—were, however, in store for this unhappy lingerer in a false position. The resources of Tunis having been exhausted, the party took ship at La Goletta for Sicily; and when they reached Palermo, after a rough passage, which one of them bore very badly, were received on disembarking by a tall man with a heavy moustache who did not seem in the least surprised to see them.

'Don't look at me!' cried Mrs. Littlewood, waving him off with her sunshade. 'How could you be so cruel as to come and meet sea-sick people! Alfred, please take Captain Patten away and engage him in conversation. No words can describe what I have suffered on board that horrible steamer, and I know I must be of a livid green colour.'

She really was not; her cheeks had the usual lilac tint which, in these days, is considered such a vast improvement upon natural hues, and Captain Patten gallantly, but laboriously, rose to the level of the occasion.

'Not at all, Mrs. Littlewood, I assure you,' he declared. 'You're looking as fresh as a—as a—as I don't know what. You are, upon my word!'

Captain Patten was a man of few words; but what he lacked in eloquence he doubtless made up in power of appreciation. Billy was very pleased indeed to see him, and had not the common-sense to affect annoyance at having been kept in the dark as to what was obviously a preconcerted arrangement. Yet, stupid and provoking though he was, Mrs. Littlewood abstained for some days from avenging herself upon him. Perhaps she thought that she was avenging herself upon him by leaving him severely alone while she explored the town and its vicinity under the guidance of his long-legged substitute; perhaps she honestly enjoyed a change. Either way, he obtained a period of leisure, which Colonel Littlewood kindly strove to enliven for him.

Colonel Littlewood, it may be, was becoming a
trifle nervous. For many good reasons he did not
want to offend Billy Bellew, and, although he
reposed an admiring confidence in Blanche's knowledge of what she was about, it did, perhaps, occur
to him that there is such a thing as slipping
between two stools.

'Patten's a rare good fellow. Not much in
Blanche's style, you know,' he was careful to
explain ; ' but she took pity upon him at Hammam
R'irha, because he didn't seem to know what to do
with himself, poor beggar ! He talks of coming on
to Italy with us. I hope you won't mind him,
Bellew. Quiet sort of chap ; won't bother you in
any way. Was in some cavalry regiment, I
forget which ; but had enough of the service, and
is wandering about now, trying to amuse himself.
Seems to have plenty of the needful.'

In accents which had the unmistakable ring of
veracity, Billy expressed his willingness to welcome
this addition to their party. As a matter of fact,
Captain Patten did not bother him ; Captain Patten
bothered nobody. He was very solemn, very silent,
and apparently very devoted to the sprightly little
lady who had flung her net over him. When a
move was made to Naples, he gravely accepted the
post assigned to him, and was privileged to discharge some of the duties which had hitherto fallen
to Mr. Bellew's share. If he was jealous of the
man whom he had superseded, he kept his jealousy,
like his other emotions, discreetly veiled from the

eyes of the world, while that dull-witted Billy never made the slightest pretence of being jealous of him.

It was from Naples that our hero despatched the first of a series of letters which Micky Forbes carried about in his pocket until they reached a grimy and crumpled old age. They are still extant; but perhaps it is as well not to quote them at length, because the truth is that Billy's epistolary style was not quite on a level with that of Lord Chesterfield or Madame de Sévigné. As, however, they elicited replies in due course, they may be considered to have served their purpose. The one which bears the Naples postmark contains more questions than information ; but Captain Patten is alluded to in the course of it, and mention is made of the circumstance that Mrs. Littlewood and that gentleman are absent on an excursion to Pompeii.

' As for me,' the writer continues, ' I haven't got anything to do, except to sit here at the window and wish to heaven I was on board the steamer that sails for England to-night. It's jolly hot, and the water is about as blue as they make it; but I'm dead sick of foreign parts.'

It is a fact that Mr. Bellew spent a whole week at Naples without visiting Pompeii, Herculaneum, the Museo Borbonico or Vesuvius. The same may be said of Colonel Littlewood, who, however, acquired an exhaustive knowledge of all the principal *cafés* in the place and the various liquors obtainable there. Florence was treated with equal contempt by these unworthy travellers. To be sure, there chanced to be a race-meeting at the Cascine, to which Billy was permitted to conduct his friends in a carriage of his hiring, and at which he duly lost as many pairs of gloves as Mrs. Littlewood required him to lose; but churches and picture-galleries he left to Captain Patten, to whom nothing seemed to come amiss.

'It would be interesting,' remarked Mrs. Littlewood one evening, 'to hear how you pass your time. Is your own company so fascinating that you *never* tire of it?'

'Two's company, three's none,' answered Billy good-humouredly. 'Don't you trouble about me; *I'm* all right. When I've nothing else to do I study the time-tables and calculate how long it will take us to get home.'

'I don't know how you can expect the time-tables to tell you that,' returned Mrs. Littlewood with a frown. 'We are going to Venice and a great many other places before we make for home, I hope.'

Billy made no rejoinder. He could not share in Mrs. Littlewood's hope; but he was aware that he would, at all events, have to go to Venice. When he should have tarried for a decent length of time upon the shores of the Adriatic, it would surely be permissible for him to mention that a good many people were anxiously awaiting his return to his native land.

Probably the whole world can show no more lovely or charming city than Venice in fine spring weather; but in order to enjoy Venice or any other place it is, of course, desirable that you should not be eager and impatient to be somewhere else, and this may account for Billy Bellew's lack of enthusiasm in gazing upon a scene which called forth some guarded expressions of approval from Colonel Littlewood himself. Nevertheless, Billy's first morning in Venice was satisfactory to him; for it brought him, amongst a heap of English letters, one with an Algerian stamp and an address written in legible, though somewhat unformed, characters. This, when opened, proved to be a truly delightful epistle. Very few people know how to write letters —Billy himself, as has been mentioned, was far from having attained proficiency in that art—but there are just a few who seem to know by instinct exactly what to say to their correspondents, and Micky Forbes was of the number.

'Upon my word, that's a wonderful boy!' exclaimed Billy aloud, after he had perused the two closely written sheets forwarded to him by his young friend. 'He'll be a great man one of these days, you see if he won't! Grammar and spelling be hanged! He can describe things in a way that makes you see them, and that's more than I could do if my life depended on it.'

A more dispassionate critic might have pronounced a less flattering verdict, but it was certainly true that Micky's composition betrayed a clear comprehension of what Mr. Bellew would like to hear. The doings of the Forbes family were faithfully reported therein, but only one of the family

was dealt with in detail, and what was said about
her was of a nature to give comfort to a friend
whose absence she was represented as deploring.
Winnie, it appeared, had not been a bit like herself
since Mr. Bellew's departure. She had been dull
and out of spirits, she was always wishing that the
time had come for them to leave Algiers, she had
even gone so far as to confide to the writer that she
did not feel particularly well or happy.

'She's not really seedy, though,' Micky thoughtfully added ; 'it isn't that. Thank goodness, I'm not
seedy either ! The doctor says I'm as fit as a flea
now, and we are to cross to Marseilles the day after
to-morrow. I don't know whether I'm to go back
to school this summer or not, but I expect not, and
we are pretty sure to be in London next month.
Do look out for us. I shall look out for you every-
where. And please write again soon.'

How, after that, was Billy to help resolving that,
come what might of it, he would be in London
during the course of the ensuing month? After
all, there would probably be no difficulty, for it
was reasonable to anticipate that the Littlewoods
also would arrange to return before then. Great,
therefore, was his consternation when he met Mrs.
Littlewood at dinner—she had been out in a gondola
with Captain Patten nearly all day—when she informed him, as a piece of news which he would be
rejoiced to hear, that they had let their house in
Lowndes Street for the season.

'Now,' she remarked, 'we can dawdle about as

long as we like. When we are tired of this, we
will go on to Milan and the lakes; afterwards, if
the weather keeps fine, we might cross the Alps
and wander through Switzerland. Switzerland is
delightful before the tourist season sets in, and
Captain Patten has never been there. So he won't
mind Lucerne and Interlaken and all the other
hackneyed old places.'

Captain Patten, perceiving that he was expected
to say something, departed from his usual taci-
turnity so far as to declare :

'Always charmed, I'm sure, to be anywhere
where you are, Mrs. Littlewood.'

Billy had neither the good manners nor the
hypocrisy to follow this brilliant lead. He said
nothing at the time, and it was not until late in the
evening that the opportunity came to him of making
an announcement which he had determined to make.
In the meantime he had been privileged to share
a gondola with the Colonel, and in the company of
that charming associate had been propelled up and
down the Grand Canal in the wake of the bark
which bore Mrs. Littlewood and her silent slave.
The inevitable songsters, in their illuminated barges,
had been bawling out ' Santa Lucia !' and 'Funicoli
Funicolà !' beneath the Rialto ; the night air had
been balmy, and the starlight effects exquisite, no
doubt, for those who cared about such things ; but the
Colonel had been, if possible, rather more offensive
than usual, and Billy had more than once longed to
take him by the neck and heels and heave him over-

board. But now the Colonel had gone off some-where to quench his thirst, and Captain Patten had said good-night, and the time had evidently come for Billy to face whatever might be in store for him.

'I'm afraid,' he began rather abruptly, 'I can't manage the lakes and Switzerland; I must be getting back home. I'm sorry to be obliged to leave you, but it isn't as though you would have nobody. Your friend Patten seems game to stay with you as long as you want him.'

Mrs. Littlewood was indolently fanning herself. She smiled, and her smile was not precisely amiable.

'Just for the sake of curiosity,' she remarked, 'may I ask if you really think that Captain Patten is capable of filling your place?'

Billy looked down and fidgeted.

'Well, he seems to have shown himself pretty well able to fill it for some time past,' was the best reply that he could think of.

'Oh no, he hasn't; and I think you know that he hasn't. A year ago you would have been furious if I had even pretended that he had, as I have been doing lately. Come, let us be frank. You want a pretext for washing your hands of me, and I have given you one. You must admit that that was rather generous of me. Go, if you want to go, I have no power to prevent you; but please don't come back again and ask to be forgiven after you have got over your infatuation for that long, lanky girl.

You have been most successful in deceiving me once ; you will hardly deceive me a second time.'

Without being in the least clever or discerning, Mrs. Littlewood knew her man. Billy had always tried to behave fairly and honourably ; he could not but feel that it was neither fair nor honourable to desert a woman who had avowed that she loved him and whom he had once loved ; and this appeal of hers, which was not couched in the form of an appeal, would have induced him to renounce all hope of ever winning Winifred Forbes, if anything could have induced him to do that. But nothing could. All that Mrs. Littlewood could accomplish now was to make him thoroughly ashamed of himself—as it was, perhaps, only right that he should be. He made several attempts to speak, but checked himself each time, and finally broke off in despair with :

'It's no use, Blanche! I can't soften things down, much less plead excuses. You're quite right about Miss Forbes: I do love her, though it's true that she is engaged, as I told you, to another man. There! now you may abuse me to your heart's content ; I deserve anything that you may like to say of me.'

Mrs. Littlewood did not take advantage of the permission accorded to her ; she merely said, in a low voice : ' Thank you ; at least I can't complain of any dissimulation on your part this time. So it is all over at last ! I am not surprised ; I have seen for a long time what was coming ; and if it hadn't been Miss Forbes, it would have been somebody else, I suppose. I am well rewarded for all the sacrifices that I have made! If only I had known what you were! But, funny as you may think it, I really did believe in you.'

Poor Billy did not think it funny at all. Probably he had never before in his life—not even when Winifred had refused him—felt more utterly wretched than he did at that moment. Yet he could not unsay what he had said, nor could he remind Blanche that such sacrifices as she had made on his account had been made entirely against his wish and approval. He had simply wanted to pass as her friend; he still wanted to be her friend, and he was actually foolish enough to say so, instead of getting up and going away, which would have been a much better plan.

The consequence was that he had a terribly bad quarter of an hour. His feelings were not spared, his vows of days gone by were minutely recalled to his memory, his friendship was disdainfully rejected, and his presents were flung back with scorn in his teeth—though, to be sure, this latter form of chastisement proved in the sequel to be purely metaphorical. Mrs. Littlewood would not give him her hand at parting; she said the only request she had to make of him was that he would forget her.

' And that won't cost you a great effort,' she added bitterly.

The conduct of such women as Mrs. Littlewood is often perplexing. She was absolutely selfish,

she had a keen eye to the main chance; in all
probability she only cared for Billy Bellew because
it flattered her vanity to have a docile admirer
and suited her convenience to possess a liberal one.
Yet she may, for the time being, have fancied that
she was sincere in renouncing him and that she
meant her renunciation to be final. It not unfrequently happened to her to say and do things
overnight of which she repented in the morning.

But if she repented on the following morning, her
repentance came too late, for Billy was up and away
soon after sunrise; and sad was the soul and deep
were the curses of Colonel Littlewood when he
realized that his benevolent banker had absconded.

CHAPTER XVII.

EDMUND KIRBY'S HOLIDAY.

'THIS is a thousand times worse than Algiers!'
exclaimed Daisy Forbes despondently. 'Goodness
knows, Algiers was bad enough the last part of the
time; but for utter dulness and misery, home
beats it hollow. One had warmth and sunshine
out there, if one had nothing else.'

She had stationed herself beside one of the high
narrow windows in the library of the house where
she had been born, and was looking out upon a
landscape which on that bitter spring afternoon
looked very wintry. Winifred, who was seated at

a writing-table near her, and who had been busily engaged for two hours in setting her father's bills and other documents in order, glanced up and remarked as apologetically as if she had been answerable for the weather :

'It is too bad of the east wind to set in at this time of year; but perhaps it won't last. I only hope,' she added, with a troubled look, 'that we haven't come back too soon.'

It was not of her sister that Winifred was thinking when the latter uneasy aspiration escaped her; but Daisy appropriated it to herself as a matter of course.

'Oh, it isn't the having come back to England that I mind so much,' she returned discontentedly; but why couldn't we have stayed in London instead of rushing down here, where there's nothing to do and nobody to talk to? We all wanted to stay in London, except you.'

Nothing can be more certain than that, if the above assertion had been true, the Forbes family would have remained in London. They would have remained there even if Daisy had been alone in desiring it; for Daisy's wishes, which had always been more or less paramount with her relatives, had been yielded to without thought of controversy since she had become so pale and listless and dispirited. But, as a matter of fact, the girl had declared that she hated the bare idea of theatres and society, and had begged to be removed as soon as possible to the peace and solitude of Shropshire.

14

Winifred did not remind her of this; she only
said :

'Well, we shall be going up later, you know,
when everything will be looking more cheerful.
Even London isn't very pleasant in a black
east wind.'

'A row of houses and a yellow fog would be
more cheerful to look at than that!' groaned Daisy,
with a wave of her hand towards the prospect
outside the windows.

Stratton Park could not be called a pretty place,
although it would pass muster among a hundred
other English country houses of its class. The
plain white structure, built at a period when
domestic architecture was little considered, stood
rather low and rather too near to a sheet of
ornamental water, upon which Micky was at that
moment seated in a boat, fishing for perch and
tench. The garden was not much of a garden,
and the park was not much of a park; but the
former was bright with old-fashioned flowers
during the summer season, and the latter could
boast of some fine trees. Winifred rose and
walked to the window.

'I wish Micky would come in,' she said. 'It
seems a shame to send for him; but he must be
perished with cold.'

'Oh, I should think so,' answered Daisy, shrug-
ging her shoulders; 'but you would insist upon
bringing him here.'

Winifred had, it must be owned, given her vote

in favour of quitting the metropolis for Shropshire. She had not been left in ignorance of Micky's correspondence with Mr. Bellew; she had been informed that Mr. Bellew had left Venice on his way back to England, and it had seemed to her that, for Daisy's sake, a meeting ought, if possible, to be avoided. There was no trusting Daisy in her present mood; she was capable of doing and saying things which she might regret for the rest of her life. The girl appeared to have absolutely no self-respect; she either was or thought she was broken-hearted, and she did not care who knew it. Profoundly sorry as Winifred was for her, she could not but find her very trying at times. Before they had left Algiers she had worn her willow in so ostentatious a fashion that everybody—Lady Ottery, Mrs. Nugent and all the rest of them—had discovered what was the matter. If she were to be brought into contact again with Mr. Bellew, the chances were that even his phenomenal blindness would no longer remain proof against what could be seen with half an eye. Moreover, Winifred herself did not at all want to renew acquaintance with the disturber of their peace. He had disturbed her peace as well as Daisy's: she knew that now, having almost as little aptitude or inclination for deceiving herself as she had for deceiving others. It was not a thought to be dwelt upon; it was a thought to be resolutely thrust away. But we know what invariably happens when Nature is driven out with a pitchfork, and Winifred had long

ere this been forced to acknowledge in the secrecy
of her own heart that Billy Bellew might have
been more to her than he was, or ever could be
now, if she had not already plighted her troth to
Edmund Kirby. And Edmund, who had only
found time to spend half an hour with them during
their passage through London, was coming down
to Stratton that very afternoon for a week's holiday. Winifred felt it to be both a melancholy
and a shameful fact that she was not looking
forward to his visit with any great anticipation of
pleasure.

After a time Daisy consulted her watch, yawned
and rose. 'That ardent lover of yours will be here
presently, I suppose,' she remarked. 'I had better
make myself scarce. Why he doesn't go to his own
people, instead of quartering himself upon us, I
can't think.'

'It isn't very comfortable for him at home; he
doesn't hit it off with his brother, you know,' said
Winifred; 'but I don't think you will find him
much in your way, and there isn't the slightest
necessity for your leaving the room. Please don't
go.'

But Daisy laughed rather ill-naturedly and
replied that she hoped she knew better than to
play gooseberry; added to which, she experienced
no sort of yearning for Edmund Kirby's company.
So she went her way; and soon afterwards the
sound of carriage-wheels upon the gravel announced
the arrival of the guest.

Edmund Kirby entered the library, without having even waited to remove his overcoat. He held out both his hands, which were large and strong, and his grave, uncomely countenance was illumined by a smile which rendered it at least agreeable to look upon.

'They told me I should find you here,' he said. He was a big, broad-shouldered man, who looked a good many years older than he actually was. His hair was beginning to fall off and was turning gray at the temples; his face, which was clean-shaven, save for a slight whisker, already exhibited permanent lines, and in the matter of features could not be described otherwise than as decidedly plain. Nevertheless, it was an honest face and by no means a stupid one. Winifred rang for tea, and ministered to his needs while he talked. His speech was much less tiresome and pedantic than his letters.

'This is an unfortunate business about Daisy,' he remarked after a time. 'What made her refuse young Lysaght, do you suppose? You never gave me any distinct explanation of the affair; and I thought her looking very dull and out of sorts when I saw her in London. She hasn't been losing her heart to an Arab chief in Algeria, I hope?'

Winifred told him the whole story. He was sure to hear it sooner or later, and she seldom kept any secrets from Edmund, who, indeed, was both a trustworthy and a sensible confidant. Only she did not mention the offer of marriage which she had received, because that was hardly her own secret.

'I never met Mr. Bellew,' said he, when she had finished; 'but I have often heard of him. He goes by the name of Billy, and is said to be one of the best gentlemen-riders living. Not my style of man, of course; but a good fellow, I should imagine, from what people say of him. There's nothing against him to my knowledge, and he must be well off. I really see no reason why Daisy's romance shouldn't end happily. It would be more satisfactory, perhaps, if she would take young Lysaght; but if she won't, she won't.'

'But, unluckily, it is Mr. Bellew who won't take Daisy.'

'That remains to be seen. I have great faith in Daisy's powers of persuasion; and as for that Mrs. Littlewood whom you speak of, her powers can only be temporary. We lawyers hear a good deal about entanglements of that kind; they are always temporary. Mr. Bellew will be in London when you arrive; gay people like you will have no difficulty in meeting him; and then it will be all plain sailing, you'll see. Hullo! here's Micky, with a basket full of fish. Well, Micky, how are you? All right again?'

Micky had reasons of his own for deploring the existence and objecting to the presence of Mr. Kirby. He said:

'Oh, how do you do? Yes, I'm all right, thanks. Winnie, you shall have fish for breakfast

to-morrow morning. Look at this big fellow; I
must put him in the scales presently; and I've
caught lots of little ones.'

'You may catch anything you like, except a
chill,' said Winifred. 'Your nose is blue, and—oh,
Micky, I do believe you have been wading!'

'Couldn't help it, my dear,' answered Micky;
'but don't excite yourself. I ain't a bit cold, and
I'm going off to change as soon as I've taken this
basket to the kitchen.'

He departed at once on his errand, making a
grimace as he went at the back of the unconscious Kirby, who resumed his conversation with
Winifred.

But Winifred had ceased to be an attentive
listener. She was in constant alarm lest her
brother should fall ill again, and every time that
he came in with wet feet could think of nothing
else until she had satisfied herself that all the
precautions enjoined by the doctor had been taken.
After returning several totally irrelevant replies to
the observations of her betrothed, she begged to be
excused. 'I must just see that Micky is putting
on dry clothes,' she pleaded.

Edmund Kirby had been engaged for too long a
time, and was too sensible a man, to be exacting.
'Don't mind me,' he answered; 'I'll go and look
up Mr. Forbes; I want to have a talk with him
about that last article of his. But you should
beware of coddling the boy, Winnie; he'll be
delicate all his life long if you adopt that system.'

Unfortunately, there are cases in which no other system can be adopted ; unfortunately, also, there are people who are doomed to be delicate all their lives long, and whose lives are not likely to be long unless they are coddled. This is what strong men, who have never known a day's serious illness, are naturally reluctant to believe ; and Edmund Kirby only smiled when Winifred came into the drawing-room before dinner with a grave face, saying that she had been obliged to send Micky to bed. She wanted to send for a doctor into the bargain, but neither her father nor her mother considered that necessary. The latter remarked :

'He seemed to be quite comfortable when I saw him just now, only a little feverish. Of course he has caught cold ; but really, Winnie dear, I don't know what else you can expect if you allow him to stand about in wet boots with the thermometer almost at freezing-point.'

Winifred said no more, and the subject was dropped. She went straight upstairs after dinner, though, and did not reappear, so that Edmund Kirby went to bed with a slight sense of injury upon him. He could discuss politics, theology or philosophy with Mr. Forbes contentedly enough, but with the ladies of the family he did not get on very well in Winifred's absence. The ladies of the family thought him a bore, and were upon suffi-ciently intimate terms with him to make little secret of their sentiments. They tolerated him, they acquiesced in his engagement to Winnie ; but they were in no haste to welcome him as one of themselves, nor did they anticipate being called upon to do so for some time to come. Meanwhile, they had nothing particular to say to him, and when Winnie was out of the room they were very apt to ignore the circumstance that he was in it.

He was up early the next morning, as over-worked London men who are out for a country holiday always are, and at the front-door he found Dr. Hale, the local practitioner, mounting his horse.

'Hullo, doctor!' said he, 'have they sent for you to see the boy? Not much amiss, I hope?'

The doctor jerked up his bushy eyebrows, drew down the corners of his mouth, and replied: 'So do I, but one never knows how these things may end, and he's a bad subject for inflammation of the lungs, poor little chap! Don't tell them I said that, please; there's no use in frightening people, and he may be quite well again in a week. By the way, have you seen your brother?'

'Not yet,' answered Edmund; 'I only came down last night.'

'Well, see him as soon as you can, and frighten him if you can. He is one of the people whom there may be some use in frightening.'

'Do you mean that he is ill?' asked Edmund.

'My dear sir, he isn't ill—he is dying! You'll find him walking and riding about, much as usual; but he is simply killing himself. I've told him so scores of times, and he won't believe a word of it. You had better try if you can't make him believe you. Well, I must be off now; I shall look in again this evening.'

This warning with regard to his brother gave Edmund matter for serious reflection, and perhaps caused him to think less about Micky's illness than he might otherwise have done. Neither Winifred nor her mother came down to breakfast; but Mr. Forbes and Daisy did not appear to be much alarmed. The former soon betook himself to his study, while the latter evidently did not deem it any part of her duty to entertain Mr. Kirby; so he presently took his hat and stick, and, leaving a message with the butler to the effect that he would not be back until after luncheon, set off to walk to the home of his boyhood. It was rather a long walk, but he did not mind that; what he did mind a good deal was the prospect of the reception which awaited him at the end of it.

Some people know how to perform unpleasant duties and most people know how to shirk them; but it was Edmund Kirby's misfortune that he belonged to neither category. He had got to tell his brother sternly and forcibly that he was drinking himself to death, and in the course of that day he did so—with results which might have been foreseen. There was a terrible scene when he began to talk about hydropathic establishments and the necessity of submission to restraint; even poor old Mrs. Kirby, who had at first tried to mediate between the two brothers, ranged herself decisively upon the side of the elder after that, and the end of it was that Edmund had to depart with more celerity than dignity in order to avoid the scandal of a stand-up fight.

Bad news greeted him on his return to Stratton Park. Micky was worse—much worse. The doctor had again been summoned, and had made no secret of his misgivings; the whole household was in disorder and dismay, and it obviously behoved a visitor to pack his portmanteau. But Edmund was begged not to do that. He saw Winifred for a few minutes, and she assured him that there was no necessity for such a step.

'He is very ill,' she said, 'and he cannot be out of danger for some days; but I am sure we shall save him—we *must!* He has youth on his side, you know; and that is the main thing. Everybody says that is the main thing. Don't you think so yourself?'

'While there is life there is hope,' answered Edmund, who certainly was not skilful in hitting upon the right thing to say. He added, somewhat more happily: 'I only wish I could be of some help to you.'

Well, he could not be of much help; nor, for the next few days, did it look as if anybody could be of help to poor Micky, who lay fighting with such vitality as his small body contained against a malady which slays hundreds of strong men every year. But the weak sometimes win a battle in which the strong succumb; and on the day before that which must of necessity bring Edmund Kirby's holiday to a close, the invalid was pronounced to be all but safe.

'He only wants careful nursing now,' said Winifred, who had come downstairs to announce this joyful intelligence to her betrothed. 'We have had a dreadful fright; but we needn't be frightened any longer, thank God! I am so sorry that your visit has been such a dismal one. Perhaps you will be able to come again later on, though. And before you go, Micky wants very much to see you for a few minutes. He made such a point of it that Dr. Hale consented; but I am sure you will remember how weak he is and that he mustn't talk much.'

Edmund was rather surprised; for Micky and he had never been close allies, and he could not imagine what the boy could have to say to him. On the following morning, however, he of course obeyed the summons conveyed to him, and greatly shocked he was to see what a change had been wrought in the appearance of one who, to his somewhat careless scrutiny, had looked very much like other boys only a week before. Micky's cheeks had fallen in, there was not a particle of colour in his face, and his eyes had become large and brilliant. But he articulated without apparent difficulty. After sending away his nurse, he said:

'Come and sit down, Edmund; I want to talk to you. I believe I ain't going off the hooks this time, but it has been touch and go, I can tell you, and old Hale won't say I'm out of the wood yet. So, as there's something that I think you ought to know, I won't keep it to myself upon the chance of my ever seeing you again. It's about Winnie. I want you to let her off from her engagement to you.'

Edmund stared.

'To let her off from her engagement!' he repeated. 'Why should I do that, Micky? Does she wish for a release?'

'Oh, she wishes for it right enough, only she'll never ask for it. She isn't that sort. But it's as plain as a pikestaff that you and she weren't built for one another; and it isn't asking an awful lot of you to break the thing off.'

'My dear boy,' answered Edmund, smiling, 'I don't think you can know much about that; and surely your sister and I are the best judges of our suitability to one another. I need hardly say that, if she had ceased to care for me, or—or if she had begun to care for somebody else——'

'But that's just it,' interrupted Micky. 'She *does* care for somebody else, and I'm perfectly certain that her only reason for refusing him was that she thought herself bound to you. You may have heard her speak of Mr. Bellew. Well, he's the man.'

Edmund shook his head, still smiling.

'Oh no,' said he, 'you have made a little mistake, my boy; you forget, perhaps, that you have two sisters.'

But Micky was able, in a very few words, to demonstrate that he was under no misapprehension. If, in the course of the disclosures which he proceeded to make, he was not very tender to the feelings of his auditor, it must be remembered, in justice to him, that he did not believe his auditor's feelings to be in any great danger of laceration. For the rest, Edmund Kirby was a barrister by profession, and a man of strong will and steady nerves by nature. His face betrayed little emotion when Micky had made an end of speaking, and he said quietly, as he rose:

'Well, my boy, I'm obliged to you for what you have told me, and I will give the matter full and careful consideration. I shall not say anything to your sister before I leave—it will be better not to disturb her at present—but I will promise you not to force myself upon her in any way, and if she ever marries me it will be of her own free will. More than that I do not feel justified in saying for the moment; but you may rely upon that, and I hope it will satisfy you.'

Micky knitted his brows. He would have preferred a promise of immediate retirement; but one cannot expect to get everything, and he knew that Edmund Kirby was, as he mentally phrased it, 'a straight fellow, though he was such a solemn old stick.' He therefore nodded acquiescence and fell back upon his pillows, for in truth he was not equal to more words.

Half an hour later Edmund had bidden a cheer-full farewell to his entertainers and had driven away to the railway-station. He obtained a compartment in the train to himself, and greatly astonished Micky would have been if he could have seen the 'solemn old stick' seated there motionless, with his head buried in his hands, the whole way up to London.

CHAPTER XVIII.

BILLY GETS HIS COMPASS BACK.

FOR some days after Edmund Kirby's departure Micky continued, as Winifred asserted and believed, to make steady progress towards recovery ; but Dr. Hale would not say that his patient was out of danger yet, nor did he appear to be thoroughly satisfied with the results of his daily examination. One morning he betook himself to Mr. Forbes's study, instead of leaving the house as usual, and stated plainly that he would like to have a second opinion.

'Oh, certainly, Dr. Hale, if you wish it,' said Mr. Forbes, looking up from the volumes which he was consulting with the air of one who has been rather unwarrantably disturbed. 'My daughter gave me to understand that there was no further cause for anxiety ; still, if you wish it, I will of course write or telegraph to any London physician whom you may think proper to name.'

'I do wish it, and there is great cause for anxiety,

and it will be better to telegraph than to write,'
answered Dr. Hale bluntly, for he was not best
pleased with what he considered to be the old
gentleman's selfish apathy. 'Unfortunately, the
symptoms which have shown themselves are not
such as to admit of doubt or discussion, but you
will probably be glad afterwards to think that you
had the best advice obtainable.'

He named a celebrated authority on pulmonary
diseases, undertook to despatch the telegram himself, so as to save time, and marched off, leaving
Mr. Forbes a little alarmed and a good deal put
out. Winifred was immediately summoned to her
father's presence, and was asked to be so kind as
to explain what the meaning of all this was.

'Dr. Hale is a well-intentioned man, I have no
doubt,' Mr. Forbes said; 'but his manner is almost
offensively brusque, and he really shows very little
consideration either for my peace of mind or for my
pocket. I do not grudge necessary expenditure—I
have in fact sanctioned it; but at the same time
I do not think that the cost of bringing a London
physician down to Shropshire ought to be lightly
incurred.'

It was not very easy to explain that the expenditure was necessary, although the danger was
imaginary; but Winifred, who was accustomed to
managing her father, contrived, somehow or other,
to reassure him upon both points. She did not
want him to be frightened, she declared that she
herself was not frightened; and perhaps it was not

exactly fear, at least, not fear of the very worst, that kept knocking for admittance at the door of her heart. If it was, she kept the door tightly barred. She could not believe, she would not allow herself to believe, that Micky's life was in peril. From the first she had been certain that he would get well, and she clung obstinately to the conviction even after the great man had come and gone without uttering a single word of encouragement, even after it had become manifest to everybody in the sick-room, except herself, that the boy's strength was fast ebbing away.

What did distress her terribly, but more because of its pathos than because she realized the significance of the symptom, was that his mind had begun to wander. He was always fancying himself back in Algiers, always talking about riding, always eagerly appealing to somebody who was absent to say whether he was not sitting better, or whether he was not holding his hands right. And Mr. Bellew's name was for ever upon his lips. The little compass which Billy had given him, and the letters that he had received from Naples, Venice and other places, had been put under his pillow at his request. He constantly felt for them, and seemed to be more easy when he had clutched those treasures. One day, during an interval when he had all his wits about him, he implored Winnie to send for his beloved instructor and friend.

'He must be in London now, and if you write to his club, he'll get your letter. Tell him I'm very bad, and I know he'll come. I do so want to see him, Winnie.'

How could she refuse a plea which was repeated again and again with increasing urgency ? It would be awkward, perhaps even painful to have Mr. Bellew in the house, but such considerations seemed of little importance under such circumstances. She consulted her mother—who had sunk into a state of helpless, tearful ineptitude—and who said : ' Oh, send for him if you like—send for anybody you like. All I ask of you is to save my boy. That is the least you can do after having brought him to death's door by your carelessness.'

Thus it came to pass that Billy, on entering his club one morning, found an envelope marked ' Immediate,' the contents of which caused him to turn on his heel, without waiting for breakfast, and hail a passing hansom.

' Poor little chap !' he exclaimed aloud, as he clambered into the vehicle ; ' what a bad job! She doesn't say he's dying, though. Oh no, he can't be dying, you know; that would be too monstrous.

Like Winifred, and like a great many other people—like most of us, perhaps—he had a vague impression that terrible calamities only fall upon those who have done something to deserve them. Nevertheless, every day brings us abundant proof that Job's comforters did not get to the root of the mystery, and the sun continues to shine and the rain to fall upon the just as upon the unjust. It may, too, surely be maintained that we none of us know what are calamities and what are not.

If Billy Bellew could not regard his enforced journey down to Shropshire as an unmixed calamity, he must be pardoned. He was going to see Winifred, and he had been hungering and thirsting for the sight of her all these long weeks; he had not known how much he loved her until he had been separated from her; nor, in spite of all that had passed, had he given up hope. More than once, while he was sitting in the railway-carriage, he raised her letter to his lips. At least, he was going to see her, perhaps to spend several days in the house with her; and surely the very fact of her having sent for him might be taken as a sign that she was relenting, if only ever so little. But whatever may have been Billy's faults, selfishness was not one of them; and, notwithstanding a subdued exhilaration of which he was more than half ashamed, he did not forget the purpose of his journey. It would be an exaggeration, perhaps, to say that he was as deeply attached to Micky Forbes as Micky was to him; yet he had become very fond of the boy. He had an immense number of friends, but no near relations—nobody in whose affections he occupied the first or even the second place; assuredly nobody, except Micky, who would have thought of sending for him when overtaken by dangerous illness. Micky and he had always got on so well together, too, and had so thoroughly understood one another. One doesn't invariably get on well with one's nearest relations, nor is mutual comprehension the commonest thing in the world even between friends. Friendship and love often have to get on as best they can without it.

But Micky was not going to die—such a thing couldn't be! A boy so clever, so plucky and (since he was an only son) so necessary, could never have been created merely that he might be extinguished before he had time to do more than just show what he was made of. Thus Billy quieted the misgivings which he could not stifle altogether. He turned impatiently away from the coachman who had been sent to meet him at the station on his arrival, and who, in answer to his inquiry, said sorrowfully: 'Sinking fast, sir; nothing can't save him now, they tell me.' People of that class always insist upon making the worst of things, he thought.

The worst had, however, already happened. Already the blinds were drawn down at Stratton Park. Dr. Hale, who rode away from the house while Mr. Bellew was approaching it, was frowning and biting his lips, as even doctors sometimes find themselves compelled to do; the old butler, who held the door open, was sobbing without shame or disguise; never again would Micky's cheery, high-pitched voice be heard within those silent walls.

'The end come very sudden, sir,' the butler said. 'We didn't none of us have much hope—not these two days; but—but—oh dear, oh dear! I don't hardly know how to bear it, sir. Seems only yesterday that he used to come running into my pantry, when 'twas as much as he could do to walk alone, and his nurse she'd scold me for giving of him biscuits. And him so full of life—and a useless old fellow like me to be left here !'

Billy scarcely heard these incoherent utterances. He was dazed and confused ; he could only keep on repeating to himself stupidly, 'It is all over. The boy is dead—he is dead. I must go away ; I mustn't trouble them.'

He had recovered his senses sufficiently to ask that the carriage, which had been driven round to the stables, might be brought back, when someone came swiftly down the staircase and advanced towards him across the darkened hall. Was this Winifred ?—this tall, pale, haggard woman, who said :

' They will have told you that you have come too late. But he would not have known you if you had come earlier ; he was quite unconscious since the middle of last night.'

She was not crying, like the butler, nor did she falter in her speech ; but an indescribable change had come over both her voice and her face. Perhaps it was not only Micky who was dead ; perhaps the old Winnie had died with him, and would return no more. For, in truth, it is a mistake to suppose that we only die once.

She went on in the same composed, level tone : 'You were speaking of going away again ; I hope you will not do that, unless you are obliged. We should like you to stay until after the funeral; Micky would have wished it. And you will not be in anybody's way ; you will only be one of several people who must be asked.'

Billy said something ; he hardly knew what. It was impossible to express what he felt while she maintained that attitude of stony reserve, and he was sure that she did not wish him to utter commonplaces. She turned away, after giving some directions to the butler, who conducted him to his bedroom. He did not see her again until the day when poor little Micky's coffin was laid in the grave, nor did he see Mrs. Forbes, who had taken to her bed ; but Mr. Forbes and Daisy appeared at dinner the same evening, and he had several long talks with them before the uncles and cousins who had journeyed from various parts of England to attend the funeral arrived. They were both very unhappy, as was only natural, and allowances must be made for people who are very unhappy ; still, their grief occasionally took a form which was almost too much for Billy's forbearance. Mr. Forbes openly and querulously blamed Winifred for the blow which had fallen upon him and his house. She had been in charge of the boy, and she had allowed him to incur a risk which no sane person would have permitted.

'Of course I should on no account say this to her ; although it does seem to me that some slight acknowledgment, some few words of remorse, would not have been unbecoming on her part.'

Daisy did not go quite so far as that. What she complained of was the stubborn way in which Winnie kept them all at arm's length.

'She doesn't make the least effort to comfort any of us; she seems to think that poor dear Micky was her exclusive property, and that nobody else has a right to be miserable, now that he is gone.'

'I am sure you do her an injustice there,' Billy declared. 'Most likely she is afraid of breaking down, and no wonder.'

'Oh, it isn't that; it wouldn't matter if she did break down, since she won't stir beyond mamma's room or her own. We have to go about as usual and see to things.'

'But, from what the servants tell me, it is she who is making all the arrangements.'

'Yes, she is giving the orders that have to be given; but one can't feel grateful to people who relieve one of miseries and horrors in that hard-hearted way. She does her duty, she would always do that, only duty doesn't quite take the place of affection, does it? I don't believe Winnie has ever really cared for anyone except Micky. Certainly not for Edmund Kirby, whom she says she is going to marry.'

'You think she doesn't care for him?'

'I'm quite sure she doesn't. But I dare say she will marry him, all the same, because she will think it her duty to marry him. I can't understand that sort of self-sacrifice, can you? I see nothing

admirable in it; it seems to me horrid and unnatural to marry anyone whom you don't love.'

Daisy wept pretty constantly during this and
other conversations with the man whom she did love,
and his heart became much softened towards her
by reason of her words and her tears. He had not
given her credit for so much feeling. He thought
it very pardonable that she should long for her
sister's sympathy. He was a hundred miles from
suspecting that her sorrow (which was genuine
enough so far as it went) was beginning to be
lightened by a nascent hope of brighter days to
come. Otherwise he would hardly have fallen into
the extraordinary blunder of confiding his own
hopes, such as they were, to her.

It was on a warm, still afternoon, when he had
strolled out into the shrubberies with her, that he
innocently narrated the whole story of his love and
his rejection, which was listened to with the silence
of profound amazement. That avowal of Billy's
was probably the bitterest pill that had ever been
administered to Daisy in her life; but she was not
so much angry with him—though she had a confused impression that he had behaved rather
deceitfully—as startled, mortified and thrown off
her balance. A horse who has won every race in
which he has been engaged only to be beaten at
last by a rank outsider may, for anything that one
knows, experience similar sensations; at all events,
many horses, as Billy Bellew was aware, never run
so well again after sustaining such a defeat. It

was simply incomprehensible! To have been distanced by Mrs. Littlewood would have been sufficiently humiliating; still, Mrs. Littlewood, in spite of her age and her paint, was the sort of woman by whom men are frequently attracted. But Winnie, of all people in the world! Winnie, who had always been accounted the plain one of the family, who had seemed cut out for spinsterhood, and to whom the youths of the vicinity were wont to pay the doubtful compliment of treating her like a mother or an elder sister. It was fortunate for Daisy that she was not called upon to say much, and that Billy had become accustomed to hearing her speak in tremulous, tearful accents. What she did say was not particularly encouraging.

'If you ask me, I must confess that I don't think Winnie is at all likely to change her mind. You know what she is—a martyr to duty, and she is engaged to Edmund Kirby. Besides, with her straight-laced ideas—you see, people did talk a good deal about you and Mrs. Littlewood in Algiers.'

'Oh yes; I know there's that,' answered Billy sorrowfully.

'I should think that would be almost enough in itself; but of course one can never tell. I think, if you don't mind, I will go indoors again now. I feel so wretchedly ill, and it seems too heartless to be talking of engagements and marriages at a time like this.'

Billy had no more private interviews with Miss

Daisy Forbes after that. The uncles and cousins descended like a flight of crows in their black habiliments. On the morning of the funeral Edmund Kirby also arrived, so that the rivals were able to scrutinize one another, and even to exchange a few words. Both of them were fair-minded men, and the judgment of neither was prejudiced ; but it was scarcely within the limits of possibility that they should make friends. For the rest, the occasion did not admit of that, and one of them was so overcome by the sadness of the ceremony in which they presently had to take part that he had enough to do to abstain from making a fool of himself.

When all was over, and when the mourners had returned to the house, Winifred, who had stood with unfaltering composure beside the grave which her mother and sister had not felt equal to approaching, sent a message to Mr. Bellew that she would like to see him for a few minutes before he left. He found her waiting for him in the library, a slim black figure against the gray sky; for she had stationed herself close to one of the windows, with her back turned towards it. Not being a poetical or imaginative person, he could not have said what it was in her appearance or attitude that conveyed to him an impression of utter loneliness ; but he received that impression, and it gave him a sharp twinge at his heart. As he drew near she said :

‘I wanted to thank you for having come ; and I have something to give you. It’s only the little compass that you gave to Micky.   I thought perhaps you would like to have it again ; he was holding it in his hand when he died, and—and——'

She could not finish her sentence. The tears which she had restrained so long brimmed over her eyelids at last; one of them fell upon Billy's big, sinewy hand, which had gone forth instinctively to clasp hers.

'Oh, my poor dear !' he exclaimed, ' I'm so sorry —so dreadfully sorry !   And I can't do anything for you ; I can't even say anything !'

She drew her hand away and dried her eyes.

'Nobody can do anything,' she answered gently, ' and there is nothing to be said ; but I understand quite well how sorry you are, and I shall never forget you or your kindness to Micky.   Perhaps some time or other we shall meet again, and then if you haven't forgotten him—and I don't think you will —we can talk about him together.   Just now I couldn't speak of him even to you.   Good-bye. The kindest thing you can do for me at present is to leave me alone ; and I know you want to be kind.'

He took her at her word ; he could not possibly have intruded upon her grief at such a moment with a renewal of vows to which she had refused to listen in brighter days.   But, although his heart ached for her as he left the room, his spirits were lighter on his own account than they had been when he entered it.   She had promised that she would never forget him, and she had spoken of

meeting him again ; surely it was as permissible
to assume that her words meant a good deal as
that they meant next to nothing.

CHAPTER XIX.

DAISY'S RECOVERY.

EDMUND KIRBY remained at Stratton Park for
twenty-four hours longer than the other relations
and friends of the family who had attended the
funeral ; but he only saw Winifred for a few
minutes during that time, and she shed no tears
in his presence, as she had done in Billy Bellew's.
Edmund had never been Micky's friend, nor was
there anything disturbing to the composure in his
formally expressed, though doubtless sincere, con-
dolences. It was a result of Edmund's natural
temperament that he always expressed himself
formally when he was most moved, and there
were, besides, reasons of which Winifred knew
nothing for his being even less demonstrative than
usual on that occasion.

He had not forgotten his promise to the dead
boy, and he was fully purposed to keep it ; but he
had come to the conclusion that things must be
allowed to remain as they were for the present.
Apart from Winifred's manifest unfitness to enter
upon a prolonged explanation and discussion, he
was not yet certain that he would render her any
service by setting her free. He was not certain

that she loved that man Bellew; he was quite
certain that she was not the girl to fall in love with
mere physical beauty, and from all that he had
heard of his rival he doubted very much whether,
even if she did love him, she would consult her
own future happiness by marrying one whose
habits of life were totally opposed to hers. Moreover, he himself loved her—loved her with all the
strength of his calm, concentrated character; and
he was at least entitled to pause before relinquishing all that had hitherto lent brightness to a somewhat sunless existence. So, after saying what
seemed to be requisite and appropriate, he went
away; and it cannot be truthfully asserted that
anybody in the house missed him.

To say that Micky was missed in that sorrow-
stricken household is to give a very faint idea of
the blank left by the disappearance of its youngest
and liveliest inmate. Winifred, whose loss was in
reality far greater, and whose grief was likely to
prove far more permanent, than that of either of
her parents, was the only one who made any effort
to pick up the dropped thread of their common
life, to resume occupations which must eventually
be resumed, and even to affect a cheerfulness
which she could not feel. She was rewarded by
reproaches, by accusations of heartlessness, by
frequent hints that she was herself responsible for
the bereavement which had fallen upon the family;
but these things scarcely hurt her. When one has
broken an arm or leg, one does not grumble about

a few additional scratches, and by degrees she attained her object, which was to rouse the old people from their apathy and force them gently back into their respective grooves. With her sister she had more trouble. Daisy not only refused to be comforted, but refused in an extremely disagreeable manner.

'Please, don't let us have any more humbug!' the girl exclaimed irritably one day; 'I can stand anything but that. If you don't know why I should be more miserable than you are, you must be rather dull of comprehension; but of course you do know, and we had better not talk about it! The only thing that would do me the slightest good would be a change; and I suppose there is no chance of our leaving this dreadful, dreary place for months and months to come.'

Personally, Winifred had no desire to leave home, and the usual six or eight weeks' visit to London during the season was, under the sad circumstances, naturally abandoned; but as the summer went on, her father began to speak of running up for a few days by himself to transact some matters of business and to confer with his political and literary friends, while Mrs. Forbes, who had fallen into a chronic state of low spirits, evidently stood in need of deliverance from solitude, which was always to her one of the most intolerable of earthly ills. Winifred, therefore, ended by suggesting that the whole family should move to the metropolis; and in the nick of time came the offer, at a nominal rent, of a house in Hans Place from some old friends who had been ordered off to Kissingen, in consequence of having eaten too many dinners.

The offer was accepted, and the Forbeses took possession of their temporary residence towards the fag-end of the season, when every brick and paving-stone in the city was baked through and through, when weary Parliament men were pining for release, and when jaded maids and matrons were beginning to ask themselves whether, after all, the game had been worth the candle. The general stampede had not, however, yet set in; so that Mrs. Forbes was able to see her friends in a quiet way, and her husband could count upon a daily meeting with kindred spirits at the Athenæum.

As for Winifred, she found the loneliness of London a good deal more trying than the loneliness of home. She had nothing to do; she did not care to see people, nor, it appeared, did anybody particularly care to see her—not even Edmund Kirby, who wrote a short note (all his notes had been short of late, which was quite a new departure) to say that he would call as soon as he could, but that he was very full of work for the moment. Nevertheless, London contained one person who wanted to see her very much indeed, and whose unexpected good fortune it was to encounter her, one afternoon, in Kensington Gardens, where she had been sitting for more than an hour, idly watching the children and the nursemaids.

She greeted him with a faint semblance of her
old welcoming smile, and without any of the
emotion which caused him to stammer and stutter
absurdly.

'Oh yes ; I am quite well, thank you,' she said,
in response to his first intelligible inquiry. 'We
have come up to London for a few weeks, and I
think both my father and my mother are the better
for the change already.'

'But *you*,' Billy insisted — 'are you really
better ?'

'Yes,' she answered a little doubtfully, 'I
suppose I am better in one way. I don't mind
talking about Micky now, though we hardly ever
do talk about him at home. That is the most
terrible part of death, isn't it?—that one can't talk
naturally or easily about those who are dead, if
one has loved them. Nobody can.'

Billy could. Perhaps it was out of his power to
speak otherwise than naturally and easily upon
any subject; perhaps the intuitive sympathy of
love emboldened him to speak of his former pupil
in a way which he knew that Winnie would like,
although everybody might not have liked it. Be
that as it may, he persuaded her without difficulty
to sit down on a bench beneath one of the smoke-
blackened elm-trees, and for a quarter of an hour
she listened to him, and talked to him in an
unreserved fashion which certainly did her good.
To no one else had she confided her great trouble
—the trouble which beset her day and night—that

if she had not allowed her brother to go out fishing that day, he would not have caught the cold which had killed him. Billy, of course, said what every reasonable being would have said in his place; but he was not successful in comforting her.

'Oh, I quite understand that I am entitled to plead not guilty,' she replied; 'but nothing can alter the dreadful fact—nothing! If you had accidentally killed your brother out shooting, you would feel as I do, even though you might know that you had taken all the ordinary precautions.'

After this they sat silent for some minutes, and then she rose, saying that it was time for her to go home. 'I am so very glad to have seen you,' she added, 'and I can't tell you what a comfort it has been to me to talk about those dear old days that will never come back. I almost always think of you now when I think of my poor Micky.'

She seemed to have so completely put away from her the memory of the last of those old days that he hardly dared to remind her of it; but he could not let her go without ascertaining her address and repeating a request which she had not then seen fit to grant.

She was not very much inclined to grant it now; yet she hardly knew how to refuse. She did not wish to hurt his feelings; besides which, it would seem a little inconsistent to deny him the privilege of calling in Hans Place after he had stayed several days at Stratton. The sight of her hesitation decided him to mention something which he would

have mentioned before, had an opportunity of so
doing been accorded to him.

'I—I'm not quite as good friends with Mrs.
Littlewood as I used to be,' he blurted out, conscious of an uncomfortable increase of colour on
his sunburnt cheeks. 'I left them at Venice, and
we didn't part on the best of terms, and I've heard
nothing of them since. I—I thought you might
like to know,' he added apologetically.

'I am very glad, for your sake,' Winifred said;
'I always hoped, you know, that something of this
sort would happen sooner or later.'

'Well, I'm very glad too; it would be ridiculous
to pretend that I'm not. And—and now, I suppose,
Mrs. Forbes won't object to my coming to her
house?'

'No,' answered Winifred slowly, 'I don't think
my mother will object; only I can't quite promise
that she will see you. She has hardly begun to
receive visitors yet.'

Billy was upon the point of saying that, if he
called in Hans Place, it would not be for the
pleasure of seeing Mrs. Forbes; but he checked
himself in time, and he was likewise successful in
repressing other injudicious remarks which rose to
his lips during the few minutes that elapsed before
his companion requested him to call a hansom for
her.

Winifred, for her part, could only hope that she
had not acted injudiciously. The mischief, after
all, had been done, and was irremediable. Daisy

would not be any worse off than she already was for seeing Mr. Bellew again; nay, she might even be better off, since men do change their minds sometimes. Had he not, as a matter of fact, changed his mind about Mrs. Littlewood? It cannot be said that this line of thought, and the speculations arising out of it, were altogether agreeable to Winifred; but she resolutely persevered with them, because she felt that she ought to be ashamed of finding them disagreeable. Why should she grudge her sister an allegiance which had once been offered to herself, but which it had been, and must always be, out of the question for her to accept? There was, of course, no reason why she should thus play the dog-in-the-manger's part, and she determined that she would endeavour henceforth, so far as in her lay, to bring about what was requisite in order to make poor Daisy happy once more. Daisy had been really unhappy for a long time past; latterly, too, she had repelled all attempts at sympathy, and had become extremely reserved in her demeanour towards her sister. 'Reserved' was the charitable term that Winifred employed, but 'sulky' would have been nearer the truth.

Well, at all events, there was no sulky sound about the ringing laugh which greeted Winifred's startled ear, after she had reached home and was mounting the stairs towards the drawing-room. There are people—Winifred herself was one of them—who can laugh quite well when they are

unhappy; but there are others—and to this class
Daisy belonged—whose emotions admit of no
variety, and who must needs be either merry or
melancholy. These last do not sorrow long; but
while they do, their sorrow is very apparent indeed.
Now, Daisy had been sorrowing for several months
without intermission; if, then, she could laugh
like that again, it was certain that the tide must
have definitely turned. So much the better! The
turn of the tide must have come some day, and no
sensible person could have wished the girl to mope
and mourn longer than she had done. Winifred
was not in the least shocked; only she was rather
puzzled, because she could not imagine who had
succeeded in effecting so sudden a transformation.

She paused for a moment on the landing. She
could hear Daisy's voice in the drawing-room,
followed by a deeper and more masculine one;
after which there was a second outburst of hilarity.
Then she opened the door, and, not a little to her
amazement, beheld her sister in the act of tossing
lumps of sugar at Harry Lysaght, who, with his
right hand behind his back, was catching, or
attempting to catch, them in his left. He made a
very bad failure with the lump which was thrown
towards him when that tall, black figure entered
the room; he stood stock-still, smiling feebly,
looking extremely red and foolish, and not knowing
what to say. But Daisy came to his aid.

'Will you have some tea, Winnie?' she asked
calmly. 'I thought you had gone out driving with

mamma. Harry made his appearance a short time ago, and he has been teaching me a new game, by way of cheering me up; it isn't a very amusing game, but it's just a shade better than nothing at all. Our conversation had reached the vanishing-point, you see, when we started it.'

At any rate, it appeared to have answered its purpose. The old Daisy had returned; and what was even more surprising was that Harry also seemed to have returned, upon much the old terms —Harry, who all this time had been absent from home, whose absence had almost avowedly been due to reluctance to meet his former love, and who had not even gone down to Shropshire to attend Micky's funeral. He had written to Winifred at the time, and had said that he hoped she would understand why he felt unable to pay that last tribute of affection and respect in person. It was impossible to suppose that he would have been where he was, or would have conducted himself as he had just been conducting himself, unless advances of a very encouraging kind had been made to him. If such advances had indeed been made again, so much the better. Still, the situation was necessarily embarrassing, and he escaped from it as soon as he decently could.

Winifred did her best to set him at his ease; but he made her task so difficult for her that she was not at all sorry to see the last of him. He insisted upon pulling a long face and speaking in a subdued voice; although he did not allude in so

many words to the family affliction, he implied that
he had not really been forgetful of it, that Daisy's
merriment was merely assumed, and that he had
only recommended the throwing of lumps of sugar
about the room as a measure of temporary allevia-
tion.   In short, he was quite as maladroit as it was
at all possible to be.   When he had departed,
Daisy made his excuses and her own, and did so
with a better grace than she had shown in her
dealings with her sister for some months past.

'I know you must think me a brute, Winnie,'
she said; 'but I can't help it!   I'm not like you; I
can't just sit still and go on bearing things.   And
time does make a difference.   Not to you, perhaps;
but to commonplace wretches like me it does.'

'Of course it makes a difference to anybody,'
Winifred answered; 'the world goes round, and if
we wished ever so much to stand still, we couldn't.
I didn't think you a brute at all, and I was only too
glad to see Harry Lysaght here, though he was
about the last person whom I expected to see.   Did
you send for him, Daisy?'

'Well, I wrote him a note and told him he might
call if he liked; I did so want to see somebody
young again!   But I didn't send to him in the
way that you mean; please don't jump to headlong
conclusions.   I told him all along that I had no
quarrel with him.'

This artless confession on Daisy's part of her
inability to exist without an admirer of some sort
or kind was a reassuring symptom; but it threw

additional doubt upon the wisdom of bringing her once more into intimate relations with Billy Bellew. It was, however, indispensable that Winifred should make some mention of her late encounter, so she said :

'Somebody else is coming to see us soon, I believe. I met Mr. Bellew in the Park just now, and he asked whether he might call.'

It was not without trepidation that she spoke; but the effect of her announcement upon her sister was very far from being what she had anticipated.

'I was wondering whether he would turn up now or wait a little longer,' Daisy remarked, with a short laugh. 'Is it too soon to congratulate you? Anyhow, I beg to offer my congratulations in advance. Don't roll your eyes at me; I assure you they are quite sincere.'

'I don't know what you are talking about,' faltered Winifred ; for, indeed, there are occasions when even the most truthful people feel bound to make use of that formula.

'My dear Winnie, isn't it about time to drop pretence? You see, I happen to have heard upon the best authority—his own, in fact—that Mr. Bellew proposed to you before he left Algiers. He told me all about it when he was at Stratton, and I believe he rather hoped that I should intercede for him. But intercession is hardly necessary, I presume.'

'I wish you had not heard of it in that way !' exclaimed Winifred, much distressed. 'I would

have told you at the time, only it seemed best to
say nothing. And I am sure you can't really think
that I ever had any idea of marrying Mr. Bellew.
You know very well that I am engaged to Edmund
Kirby.'

'Oh yes; you are engaged to Edmund Kirby—
c'est entendu! But Edmund Kirby will be very
gently and considerately dismissed, and the blow
won't kill him; even if he were desperately in love
—which he isn't—the blow wouldn't kill him. I
ought to be something of an authority upon such
subjects, oughtn't I? Well, you see before you a
case of complete recovery. I don't know how I
came to make such an idiot of myself; most likely
I should never have wasted a second thought upon
him if he had not begun by snubbing me. Anyhow,
he ended as he began, and the last dose was
tolerably effectual.'

Winifred gazed earnestly at her sister.

'I hope you are speaking the truth!' she exclaimed half involuntarily.

'Oh, you may make your mind easy; I am
speaking the truth. You'll admit that I generally
do. I haven't the power of keeping things dark
that some people have, though I think I have kept
your secret pretty well all this time. Here comes
mamma back from her drive. I'll promise not to
let her into your secret until you give me leave, if
you'll promise in return not to reveal my little
secret to Mr. Bellew.'

CHAPTER XX.

THE UNWELCOME GUEST.

Busy as Edmund Kirby was, he might very well
have spared an hour of his valuable time for a visit
to Hans Place; still, he had no great difficulty in
persuading himself that circumstances had compelled him to postpone that duty and pleasure from
day to day. But when he felt that it could be
postponed no longer, he did find very great difficulty
in making up his mind what to do or say. The
case, to be sure (supposing that it had not been his
own case) was one of elementary simplicity. He
had only to go straight to Winifred, tell her what
he had heard from her brother, and assure her
that, if she indeed loved another man, he would
never think of holding her to an engagement which
she had entered into at a time when she had had
few opportunities of judging what other men were
like. Since, however, the case was his own,
Edmund could not help allowing weight to reasonable doubts and hesitations. He loved Winifred
with all his heart, which, to do him justice, was a
warm and steadfast one; he had never loved, or
dreamt of loving, anybody else; if he had been
undemonstrative, that was partly because it was
his nature to be so and partly because he had
felt so certain of her affection. Owing to their
long betrothal, they had grown to be more like
married people than lovers; it was natural that their

mutual relations should have become established upon that footing; and it was also natural—so, at least, those who had greater knowledge of such subjects than Edmund Kirby could pretend to affirm—for women to be affected by passing caprices. Does a man surrender his wife when he suspects that she has permitted her fancy to wander from its allegiance for a moment? And would he consult her happiness if he did, or could?

Such self-communings were scarcely consistent with the strict integrity which had hitherto governed all Edmund Kirby's actions, and they failed to bring him any nearer to a decision. His strong inclination was to wait and trust to time; but his conscience told him that he ought, at all events, to give Winifred a chance of claiming her liberty. That might, perhaps, be managed without any mention being made of Mr. Bellew's name; the mere fact that he was not yet in a position to fix any date for their marriage would afford her a fair pretext, if she wanted one. Finally, he set forth, without a definite programme, to pay his long-deferred call; he resolved to be guided by whatever kind of reception might be accorded to him. He was received, as it chanced, by Mrs. Forbes, who soon took occasion to mention that she did not feel up to much talking that day. It had always been Edmund's privilege to bore his prospective mother-in-law intolerably, and she knew him too well to stand upon ceremony with him.

'Winifred is with her father, writing from

dictation,' she said. 'I dare say you can see her for a few minutes, if you don't mind going down to the dining-room and ringing the bell.'

He had a craven desire to reply that he would not interrupt Mr. Forbes's literary occupations; but he stifled it, and shortly afterwards the meeting which he had so greatly dreaded had become an accomplished fact. The first thing that struck him, after he had taken note, with concern, of Winifred's pallor, and the dark semicircles beneath her eyes, was that she was really and unmistakably glad to see him again. She held his hand while she sat beside him; she led him on to talk about his work, about his never-ending domestic worries, and about his plans for the approaching holiday season; she was as kind, as sympathetic, as comforting as ever, and perhaps—yes, certainly she was more openly affectionate.

These omens, which some very sagacious persons might not have considered wholly favourable, had a reassuring effect upon Edmund Kirby; still, he could not allow them to divert him from his purpose. It took him rather a long time to explain how, after anxious thought, he had arrived at the conclusion that he ought to release her from her engagement; but he got through his appointed task at last, and, all things considered, he did not perform it so badly. A man who does not deem his actual income sufficient to marry upon, and who can only look forward to a narrow increase in his earnings, ought, no doubt, to say the sort of

things that he said : probably also the general run
of men who say such things expect the sort of
answer that he obtained.

But Edmund, who had not quite ventured to
expect it, was overjoyed when it came. Winifred
had no thought of deserting him; she was willing
to wait for him as long as it might be necessary
(possibly, if she had spoken her whole thought,
she might have said the longer the better); she
declared, with a smile, that she should continue
to look upon him as her affianced husband, unless
he wished to throw her over, and she begged him
never to doubt her again.

But she did not ask him whether he had any
special reason for doubting her; she did not tell
him that she had met Mr. Bellew; nor, during an
interview which her duty to her father obliged her
to curtail, did she make a single reference to Micky.
The above omissions were somewhat significant, and
it was perhaps fortunate that ignorance and pre-
occupation prevented Edmund from noticing them.
He went away, promising to come again as soon as
he could, and telling himself that he had now
faithfully obeyed the voice of conscience.

It was on the following afternoon that Harry
Lysaght, dropping in about tea-time, found the
three ladies at home, and was greeted in a very
friendly manner by them all. Mrs. Forbes's
welcome in particular was so warm as to be
almost enthusiastic. She had, of course, heard
of his previous visit, she had drawn natural

conclusions from that circumstance and from Daisy's recovered cheerfulness; her own cheerfulness had in a great measure been restored, and she had said to her elder daughter:

'One can't be thankful enough that Harry Lysaght has such a forgiving disposition. The whole thing will come on again now, you will see, and I hope and trust we shall hear no more of that wretched Bellew creature.'

One consequence of this speech was that Winifred abstained from distressing her mother by mentioning her encounter with Mr. Bellew in Kensington Gardens, and another was that she gave private instructions to the butler not to admit that gentleman if he should call. It was the best plan, she thought—the only plan. He would be hurt, perhaps, and she herself would be sorry to miss seeing him again; but there was no help for it. Some day, when Daisy should be safely married, or perhaps when her own marriage should be a thing of the past, they might meet once more and talk over old days without harm or danger; but for the present such talks could not safely be indulged in. She had to admit that they could not safely be indulged in, although she avoided a too close scrutiny of reasons.

But we are all of us at the mercy of accidents, and Mr. Forbes's butler happened just then to be very much at the mercy of a neighbouring housekeeper to whom he was paying his addresses. Thus it came to pass that, after having carried the tea up to the drawing-room, he deserted the post of duty in order to slip round the corner for a few minutes, and thus the uninformed footman, answering the door-bell in his absence, solemnly announced Mr. Bellew to a dismayed coterie. Winifred caught her breath; Mrs. Forbes gave utterance to a subdued but perfectly audible exclamation of annoyance; Harry Lysaght glared savagely at the intruder; only Daisy retained her self-command and smiled with mingled amiability and amusement.

As for Billy, who could not but perceive that his entrance was inopportune, he behaved quite irreproachably. He did not seem to notice anything; he shook hands with everybody, including Harry Lysaght, whose salutation was scarcely that of a friend; he sat down, took the cup of tea which Daisy offered him and at once set to work to make polite conversation. The truth was that he did not care in the least whether any of them, except Winnie, were glad to see him or not; and Winnie had given him leave to call. Nevertheless, it was obviously expedient that he should cut short his present visit. The freezing civility of Mrs. Forbes and Lysaght's undisguised irritation were hardly atoned for by the gracious vivacity with which Daisy responded to his remarks, and, although Winifred tried to make the best of an awkward business, she said little and was visibly disconcerted.

Mrs. Forbes took advantage of the inevitable pause which soon supervened, to say, without addressing herself to anybody in particular : 'It is extraordinary that such a number of people should be still left in London.   One thought, and rather hoped, that everybody, except members of Parliament and business men, would have gone away by this time. Not that it matters very much to us ; for of course we are only seeing a few very old friends—unless the servants make a mistake, as they sometimes do.'

After that, it only remained for a visitor who had been admitted by mistake to retreat as speedily and gracefully as might be. This Billy did soon after he had swallowed his tea and had declined a second cup, comforting himself with the reflection that it would not, in any case, have been worth his while to protract a dialogue which included so many participants. He was, however, conscious of a feeling of discouragement and disappointment as he walked away. It was now quite clear that Mrs. Forbes would have nothing to say to him if she could help it ; there had been a disquieting suggestion of sarcasm about Daisy's amenities ; he could not help doubting whether Winnie herself had really wished or intended him to take advantage of the permission that he had obtained from her. And why in the world had Lysaght been so abominably uncivil ? One could understand the fellow having been silly enough to be jealous out in Algiers ; but he must know very well by this time that there had never been the slightest ground for such jealousy.

Mr. Lysaght appeared, as if in answer to these musings, to speak for himself. He must have been tolerably expeditious about taking his leave, and he must have run from Hans Place to Piccadilly; for he was a short-legged man, and Billy Bellew habitually covered nearly as much ground in one stride as he did in two. As a matter of fact, he seemed to be a little out of breath.

'I thought I would catch you up if I could, Bellew,' he explained; 'I want to have a word or two with you. It's rather unpleasant, of course; but it would be still more unpleasant, I think, if we didn't come to some sort of an understanding.'

'About what?' inquired Billy somewhat shortly.

'Well, about your visiting the Forbeses. To speak candidly, I don't like it, and I don't call it quite fair. If they wanted you, nobody would have a right to complain; but, since they don't want you—and you yourself must have seen this afternoon that they did not want you—is it very good form to thrust yourself upon them? They can't very well slam the door in your face, you see.'

'I should have thought they could; but I certainly don't wish to thrust myself upon anybody. Are you commissioned to tell me that I'm not wanted?'

'Oh, no; I'm speaking entirely on my own hook; but there can't be much doubt of the fact. That is, as regards three of the family. Unfortunately, I can't be so positive about the fourth.'

'H'm! And what business is it of yours, if one

may ask ?' inquired Billy, who quite mistook his interlocutor's drift.

'I suppose you know what took me to Algiers,' returned Harry, with an embarrassed laugh; 'I dare say you know, too, why I left in such a hurry, and you can probably guess what my—my hopes still are. All that doesn't entitle me to interfere with you or dictate to you, you may say. Perhaps it doesn't; but I may venture to call myself a friend of the family, and, for the matter of that, I thought a few months ago that I might venture to call myself a friend of yours.'

'My dear fellow,' said Billy, in something more like his customary good-humoured accents, 'I'm sure I never wished to be anything except a friend to you. It was no fault of mine if you chose to take it into your head that I was your enemy.'

'Well, that's just what I thought, and that's why I followed you just now. It can't trouble or inconvenience you much to leave London at this time of year, and if you would only go away, you would do a real service to more persons than one. I'll speak more plainly, if you insist upon it; but it is not over and above pleasant even to speak as plainly as this, and I take it that you understand what I mean.'

Billy stroked his chin reflectively. 'Yes, I understand,' he answered; 'and it so happens that I have arranged to start on a yachting cruise with another fellow in a few days. I was rather thinking of crying off; but after what you've said,

I don't know that I will. Perhaps, after all, I oughtn't to intrude upon them while they are in such deep mourning. Of course it's different for you.'

'Exactly so,' agreed Harry eagerly; 'it really is different—I stand upon quite another footing.'

'Yes. But mind you, Lysaght, I'm not promising to drop their acquaintance. That I will never do until she—until they tell me in so many words that they don't want to know me any more. I shall certainly try to see them again in the autumn.'

'Oh, it will be all right by then; there won't be the slightest objection to your seeing them in the autumn,' returned Harry, with an alacrity which rather surprised the other; 'it's only just for the present that they'd rather you left them alone. Well, I'm awfully obliged to you, Bellew, and I'm sorry I was so beastly rude while you were sitting there at tea; I hope you'll overlook it. And I say, Bellew, my place isn't far from Stratton, you know; so if you cared to come down for a few days' covert-shooting towards the end of the year, I should be only too glad to put you up.'

It was difficult to reconcile this sudden outburst of cordiality with the speaker's previous assertions and implications; but the effect of it was to send Billy off to his club in greatly improved spirits. 'I've been in too great a hurry, that's what it is,' he mused. 'And, when you come to think of it, that's pretty much what the old lady gave me to understand. I don't suppose she's particularly fond of me, anyhow, though she used to be amiable enough at one time. So I must sail for the Hebrides or the Orkneys, or wherever it is. I wonder whether that beggar will tell them where I've gone, and why I've gone.'

This seemed, upon further reflection, to be so uncertain that Billy at length resolved to take the liberty of inditing a few lines to Winifred. The subjoined composition, notwithstanding its brevity, was the outcome of much thought, and a profligate expenditure of club notepaper:

'MY DEAR MISS FORBES,

'I dare say you may have heard from Lysaght that I am starting in a day or two on a yachting cruise, and I suppose there is no hope of my seeing you again before I sail. From what Lysaght said, and from your mother's manner this afternoon, I am afraid she was not best pleased with me for forcing my way into your house at a time when you are not receiving visitors; but *you* know, though she doesn't, that all your troubles are my troubles, and that I am not heartless and forgetful; so I am sure I need not apologise to you.

'There are other things which I should like to say if I dared; but perhaps it is better not. Only I want you to believe that, whatever happens, and wherever I may be, I shall be

'Always and only yours,
'W. BELLEW.'

Billy, after reading over the final copy of this missive, thought that it was not so bad; and in truth it might have been worse. It elicited a prompt and very kindly reply, in which Winifred contrived to show that she appreciated his delicacy and forbearance, while abstaining from any allusion to the things which he had left unsaid. She herself left a good deal unsaid; for she did not wish to give him pain, and it seemed unnecessary to repeat what he already knew, or to rebuke him for subscribing himself after a fashion which only Edmund Kirby had the right to use.

With her letter in his pocket, and some unjustifiable hopes in his heart, Billy set out for Southampton to join his friend's yacht. Mrs. Forbes is now kind enough to say that he behaved very like a gentleman in taking himself off at what might have proved to be a critical moment. Mrs. Forbes it is true, does not know, and never will know, what were the real motives of his gentlemanlike conduct on that occasion; but even if she were informed of them, she would probably continue to speak well of Billy Bellew, who has, indeed, given her the best of all reasons for speaking well of him.

CHAPTER XXI.

CHANGES.

BILLY BELLEW's abrupt disappearance from the scene was the solution of a difficulty, and, as such, was doubtless a subject for thankfulness; yet one may deplore many events which one would not cancel, if one had the power ; and Winifred permitted herself some occasional moments of self-pity in that she was now severed from the only human being to whom she could speak openly of her great sorrow. Every day that sorrow was becoming less keen and less present to those about her, more and more did they show a disposition to relegate it to the background, to treat it as the friends of a man who is afflicted with some mortal disease are wont to treat his malady. Such things cannot be forgotten, but it is considered to be both cruel and in bad taste to make mention of them. This is the common fate of the dead ; at first they are not talked about, because it is too painful to talk about them ; as time goes on they are forgotten, because their names have ceased to be familiar.

Moreover, other and more cheerful topics of conversation inevitably arise : such as, for instance, the immense and unlooked-for consolation which had been granted to Mrs. Forbes by Harry Lysaght's return and Daisy's welcome of him. There was never any counting upon Daisy ; still, it did not seem unreasonable to believe that she had at last made up her mind to accept her long-suffering wooer, and now that Mr. Bellew had, by the mercy of Heaven, been removed, a fond mother might fairly hope that no further complications would present themselves. Harry Lysaght himself entertained the same hope, basing it upon the same ground, of which he made no secret in talking matters over with Winifred. As soon as he found out that she was not too engrossed by her personal grief to listen to him, he reinstated her in her old position as his confidant, and frankly confessed to her that it was he who had persuaded Billy to vanish into space.

' The fact was,' said he, ' that I couldn't feel safe —not that I do feel safe yet, but I mean that I couldn't feel anything like safe while he was hanging about. We might have had all the old trouble over again. Out of sight is out of mind. It isn't that she cares for him, but that she can't resist trying to make him care for her, don't you see. And I suppose she rather enjoys torturing me too. However, I'm almost sure it will be all right now.'

Winifred remembered that her sister had once described Harry Lysaght as not being proud, and certainly he seemed to deserve that character. Humility is a virtue ; but there is such a thing as carrying it to outrageous lengths.

' I do hope,' she exclaimed apprehensively, ' that you didn't tell Mr. Bellew what you were afraid of ! Even if you didn't mind his knowing for your own sake, you ought to have remembered that you had no right to betray Daisy.'

' My dear Winifred, there wasn't anything to betray ; you don't suppose that Daisy was ever in love with the man, do you? Well, you needn't laugh ; I know I did suppose so for a time ; but it was natural enough for me to make a mistake. However, all I said to Bellew was that you none of you wanted to see him just now, and that I didn't think it very good form on his part to force himself upon you. I put it upon your being in mourning, you know—and all that. He quite saw it, and he gave in almost immediately. Bellew is really an awfully good fellow, though perhaps he's a bit dense.'

Happily, Billy Bellew was not the only person treated of in the present narrative who possessed that thrice-blessed quality of density. From the moment that his potential rival was removed from his path Harry Lysaght ceased to be jealous of him, and it may be doubted whether, up to the present time of writing, he has ever divined that he once had most legitimate cause for jealousy. His second courtship progressed smoothly and swiftly in the seclusion of the house in Hans Place, whither no other male visitor of less than sixty years of age ever penetrated; he was secure from those anxieties which Daisy might have amused herself by inflicting upon him, had she had the chance; and before London was quite empty that city contained at least one perfectly happy man.

It was all very satisfactory, of course, and Winifred was glad that her sister had at last chosen the man whom she ought to have chosen at first; but it was difficult to share Mrs. Forbes's exultation or to stifle certain misgivings. These, however, Daisy, as soon as she perceived their existence, kindly made haste to allay.

'I know what you're thinking about,' said she to

her sister; 'but you really needn't distress yourself any longer on that score. Everybody has these little attacks, though everybody doesn't own to them, as I did; and everybody is cured who gets such a douche of cold water as I have had thrown over me. Truly and honestly, I like Harry much better than Mr. Bellew. Besides, I doubt whether it is a good plan to start by being passionately in love with your husband.'

'I don't know of any better plan,' observed Winifred doubtfully.

'Yet you propose to marry Edmund Kirby! At least, you say you do, and you have cheerfully sent off Mr. Bellew on a yachting cruise, without so much as inquiring who his shipmates are to be. Well, I suppose you know your own business best; but I should have thought that was rather a dangerous experiment to try. People who go off yachting in unknown company sometimes forget to come back again.'

Daisy only laughed, and was avowedly incredulous, when she was assured that, if Winnie ever married at all, it would be Edmund Kirby, not Mr. Bellew, who would stand beside her at the altar; but she promised to keep her convictions on that subject to herself, and to respect a secret which could hardly be said to belong to her. Probably she was not very anxious to proclaim how completely she had mistaken the meaning of Billy's attentions in Algiers; probably, also, she had little attention to spare from matters of more urgent

and personal importance to her than her sister's
ultimate destiny. For she had yielded to Harry's
earnest entreaties, and had consented to fix an
early date for their wedding. The ceremony must,
of necessity, be a very quiet affair; but she was
determined that her trousseau should be in all
respects worthy of a rich man's wife, and there was
not too much time in which to provide it.

It was not until the middle of August that the
dressmakers and milliners released their open-
handed customer, and the wreaths which had been
left upon Micky's grave were withered and brown
long before Winifred could return to replace them
with fresh ones. Then, after a few weeks, during
which Harry rode or drove over to Stratton every
day, and helped by his cheerful presence to dispel
the gloom which still clung to the house, the
wedding was solemnised in the same little church
which, not so long before, had witnessed a more
mournful rite, attended by very nearly the same
people. Mrs. Forbes and Winifred laid aside their
black dresses for the day, but resumed them on the
morrow; resuming also, as was indeed inevitable,
their interrupted melancholy. Mrs. Forbes was
rejoiced to think that Daisy was well and happily
married; but as soon as the excitement was over,
she relapsed into a state of depression and fretful-
ness from which it was no easy task to rouse her.

Winifred had to undertake that task, and accomplished it with more or less of success. She had
plenty of leisure to devote to it in those days; for

her father was allowing contemporary literature a brief respite, and Edmund Kirby was, by her advice, and in compliance with her request, spending a well-earned holiday in the Alps. Edmund had at first been reluctant to leave England, but had ended by agreeing with her that, since his brother would not receive him, and since he had not been invited to take up his quarters at Stratton Park, the best thing he could do was to recruit exhausted nature by a change of air and scene. He had been sorry to part from her; but he had not been afraid. The confidence which he reposed in her was unbounded; she had told him that he must never doubt her again, and he did not doubt her; even after he heard that Mr. Bellew had called in Hans Place he felt no uneasiness. He had distinctly offered her her freedom, and she had as distinctly refused to listen to his offer; it followed, as a matter of course, that poor little Micky had been entirely misled as to her supposed change of sentiments.

Winifred was all the more touched by his faith in her loyalty because, do what she would, she could not always keep herself from doubting whether she wholly deserved it, and because she suspected that some rumour about her and Mr. Bellew must have reached his ears. In answering his letters, which were now as numerous and as prolix as of yore, she was careful not to vex him by reporting rumours which had reached not only her ears, but those of everybody else in the county.

John Kirby's excesses had arrived at such a pitch that it was becoming a serious question with the county magnates whether some public notice would not have to be taken of them. If the man would have been satisfied with being carried to bed drunk every night, an infirmity which, after all, chiefly concerned himself might have been ignored ; but the mischief of it was that he must needs stagger scandalously through the streets of the market-town in broad daylight, that he insisted upon taking his place on the bench beside brother magistrates who did not care to be seen speaking to him, and that, when there, he was apt to conduct himself in a manner calculated to bring contempt upon the whole class of the great unpaid. For the time being he was ill with what was believed to be his third attack of *delirium tremens;* but he had such an iron constitution that he was pretty sure to be as well as ever again ere long.

Such, at least, was the despondent expectation of the neighbouring county gentlemen ; but Dr. Hale, who was of a different opinion, rode over to Stratton Park one day to ask for Edmund Kirby's exact address.

'Mrs. Kirby doesn't seem to know where he is,' the doctor explained to Winifred, when she had been sent for in order that she might supply the required information ; 'and they ought to telegraph for him. His brother may die at any moment.'

'Is it so bad as that?' asked Winifred, a good deal shocked and startled.

'Well, it's like that; I don't know whether you can call it bad. One is sorry that any man should die in such a way; but one can't feel sorry to think that the world will soon be rid of him, and that he will be replaced by a steady, respectable fellow. Edmund has worked hard, and he has good abilities; but luck hasn't favoured him so far. When he succeeds to the property we may hope to see him distinguish himself; he ought to have no difficulty about getting into Parliament, I should say.'

So decisive an opinion, coming from so competent an authority, gave Winifred food for reflection. If John Kirby was really going to die and Edmund was about to become a comparatively rich man, it followed that certain contingencies which had hitherto appeared to be remote must now be regarded as imminent; and she was not quite prepared to face them. During the next few days she searched her heart and conscience more closely than she had ever done before, with results which were not, upon the whole, satisfactory to her. She was very much afraid that she would have to tell Edmund something which she did not at all want to tell him, and which she had not, until that moment, plainly admitted to herself. It was not, perhaps, very important—she felt almost sure that it was not important—still, there it was, and as matters stood she was bound in honour to make her statement. Later on there might not be the same necessity; if only John Kirby would get well

again, and live for a few more years, bygones
might very well be treated as bygones. Probably
she was the only human being, with the exception
of poor old Mrs. Kirby, who prayed fervently for
the recovery of that reprobate.

But prayer, as all divines are agreed, is of
doubtful utility when the motives which prompt it
are purely selfish, and that may have been one
reason why no miracle was wrought in John
Kirby's case. By the time that his brother had
returned post-haste from the Continent, he was
suffering from a complication of maladies against
which medical skill was powerless ; so that Edmund,
who found his way to Stratton Park on the day
succeeding that of his arrival, could only report
that there was nothing more to be done. Edmund
was distressed and worried, and even a little
remorseful (for, indeed, he had never been too
tender in his treatment of the dying man) ; but he
expressed in somewhat warmer language than
usual the joy that it gave him to be once more
within sight and hearing of Winifred, and although,
of course, he said nothing about it, she perceived
that the idea which had occurred to her had
likewise suggested itself to him. He had spent a
great many years in the wilderness ; it was but
natural that he should be eager to cross the frontier
of the Promised Land.

According to him, John was not in immediate
danger, though recovery was impossible ; the doctor
had spoken of a week or ten days ; but the struggle

might be still further protracted. 'In any case,' he said, 'I hope to run over and see you again to-morrow, for I can be of no use at home, unfortunately, and my mother seems to prefer being left to herself.'

However, he did not return on the morrow, because John Kirby died that night, and the news of what had occurred reached Stratton Park soon after breakfast the next morning. Mrs. Forbes, who conveyed it to her daughter, was not restrained by any false feeling of delicacy from congratulating her upon the vast improvement thus brought about in Edmund's fortunes.

'He really will be quite well off,' she said. 'One can't expect that he will inherit any ready money, but I fancy that he must have laid by something. Naturally, he will give up his profession now, and I should think he would wish to be married as soon as possible. I am so glad for your sake, Winnie dear. It was becoming quite a Jacob and Rachel business.'

'Oh, but we haven't in the least minded waiting,' answered Winifred quickly; 'and I am sure we are neither of us in a hurry now. He will have a great many arrangements to make before he can settle down to his new life, and—and I think I am of some little use at home, am I not?'

This plea for delay would have been recognised as very cogent a twelvemonth before; in fact, it was just because her eldest daughter was in the habit of taking housekeeping and all other small daily worries off her hands that Mrs. Forbes had acquiesced in that interminable engagement. But times were changed now, and she proceeded amiably and relentlessly to cut the ground from beneath the supplicant's feet.

'My dear,' said she, with a sigh, 'you have been most useful; I can't think how we should ever have got on without you—while there were four of us. The time has at last come, though, for you to think a little of yourself. I have been talking things over with your father, and he quite agrees with me that it would be too miserable for us to go on living here, deprived of all our children. We think of letting the place for a few years and travelling abroad. Perhaps when the cold weather sets in we may go back to Algiers for the winter. It suited your father very well last year, and we should find a few friends there, which is always an inducement. My own idea is that much the best plan would be for you and Edmund to be quietly married before we start—say in November.'

To go back to Algiers for the winter! Winifred started and shuddered at such a suggestion. How could her mother bear the thought of returning to a place where every familiar sight and sound and scent must revive the memory of what they had lost? For herself, she felt that she could not do it. Rather than that, she would marry Edmund Kirby the next day; rather—far rather—would she die. She merely remarked, by way of reply, that no doubt it would be good for them all to leave home for a time, and so fell to wondering why she should, even in thought, have bracketed her marriage and her death as two alternatives only comparatively preferable to the tortures of memory with which she had been threatened. Because she was really very fond of Edmund, and she knew that his wife would be fortunate among women. To be sure, there was that disagreeable confession which it would be her duty to make to him before the date of their wedding could be appointed.

Presently Mrs. Forbes, who was toasting her toes before the fire — for the autumn mornings were chilly—looked up from the weekly paper which she was perusing to say :

'Dear me! Mr. Bellew has been upon the point of death with typhoid fever. Now that he can't give us any more trouble, one feels free to be sorry for him, poor fellow! Not so much on account of his illness, since it seems that he is getting better, as because that dreadful Littlewood woman has been nursing him, they say. Of course she will have a double hold over him now. How shocking it is that these things should be talked about, and even commented upon in print, without a word of disapproval! Society has certainly changed very much for the worse since my young days, and I do think that one of the most discreditable signs of the times is the circulation of these so-called society papers.'

Mrs. Forbes held out the journal in question, of

which she was a constant and attentive reader, to her daughter, whose eye was at once caught by the following paragraph:

'The dangerous illness of the popular "Billy" Bellew has caused widespread regret and anxiety. He is still lying at the shooting-box of his friend Mr. Maxwell, in Aberdeenshire, where he was seized with the attack of typhoid fever which so nearly terminated his career. But the latest reports are very reassuring, and we may hope to see Billy winning fresh laurels in the pigskin when the great steeplechasing events of the coming season are decided. He himself, it is said, attributes his escape from the jaws of death solely to the un-wearying attentions of his old friend Mrs. Little-wood, who has been with him throughout his illness, and who has steadfastly refused to resign her post in the sick-room at the bidding of trained nurses.'

Winifred laid down the paper, remarking calmly:

'Yes; it is a pity that Mrs. Littlewood was in the house at the time; as you say, he can hardly hope to shake off her hold upon him now. And I should think his life would have been quite as safe in the hands of a trained nurse as in hers.'

Soon afterwards she rose and left the room. If she shed a few tears in private, that did not prove much; had she not wept once before in Algiers, on less provocation? Billy had not then sworn that he loved her, and her only; nor had he assured her that he had finally broken with Mrs. Littlewood. It was true that she did not wish him to remain faithful to his vows; still, it did seem very sad that he should have fallen back into his old servitude. Moreover, women always find something especially pathetic in the thought of a strong man being laid low. And Micky had been so fond of him; and she herself was very much attached to him, both for Micky's sake and for his own. Upon the whole, Winifred could have brought forward many excellent and convincing excuses for her tears.

CHAPTER XXII.

A FULL CONFESSION.

'The late John Kirby,' remarked Mr. Forbes, 'was not a man whom it was possible to regard with any of that respect or esteem which I might be wrongly supposed to have entertained for him, were I to attend his funeral in person. Of the dead it has long been agreed by common consent that nothing but good shall be spoken; yet even in the case of those who have passed, as it were, out of our jurisdiction, it is inexpedient to pay honour where no honour is due, and I fear that the fact of my presence in the churchyard to-morrow would be liable to misconstruction. However, we will send the carriage.'

These sentiments, when rendered into less beautiful language, simply meant that Mr. Forbes was not going to expose himself to the risk of catching cold for the sake of a disreputable ruffian, whose demise was a boon to the community in general and to the Forbes family in particular. Somewhat similar views must have been held by the neighbouring nobility and gentry; for although a long line of carriages followed the imposing hearse which bore John Kirby's body to the grave, they were all of them empty; and perhaps the tenantry only attended in such large numbers from a sense of duty to the new squire and a not unnatural wish to start well with him. The obsequies were conducted with much pomp and at considerable expense, Edmund being a great stickler for the due observance of use and wont in such matters. The same sense of respect for traditional customs led him to remain indoors, with all the blinds drawn down, until one more coffin had been added to the row in the family vault; but on the following day he thought there could be no harm in his betaking himself to Stratton Park, where his advent was fully expected.

It was partly because she felt quite certain of his putting in an appearance that afternoon that Winifred left the house soon after luncheon and wandered down through the garden towards the park. He would see her mother, and if he should wish to follow her, it would be easy enough for him to do so; but there was a chance—just the ghost of a chance—that he might be content to postpone their meeting to another day; and although Winifred was no coward, she was not exempt from that desire to stave off the inevitable as long as possible which is common to frail humanity. However, she did not think very much about Edmund Kirby after she had set out on her walk. It was one of those soft, still autumn days, the beauty and the melancholy of which are peculiarly English. Although the sun was shining, the prevailing tints of the landscape were a silvery grey; a thin haze blurred the outlines of the trees and hung over the fields and the low hills; the foliage was changing, a few dead leaves were already fluttering to the ground, and the grass was still wet with yesterday's dew. The annual death of Nature had not yet come; but forebodings of its approach were in the air. That death would of course be succeeded by the annual resurrection; but it seemed to Winifred that there could never be any more spring or summer for her. It was over—quite over and done with—that dear old life, which had had its little worries, but through which there had always run an undercurrent of youth and felicity. Never again would Micky play truant; never again would she pursue him breathlessly through the stable-yard, and away down to the muddy home-covert; never again would she ride with him to see the hounds meet; never again would the sound of his shrill young voice call her from her accounts or her copying work. The whole atmosphere was heavy with the weight of that eternal, pitiless silence. Oh, no! her mother was right; life at poor old Stratton had become impossible.

She visited a dozen familiar spots, every one of which spoke to her of Micky, telling herself that to her dying day she would not, if she could help it, visit them again: she wanted to see them to say good-bye, that was all. During the remainder of the time that must elapse before she quitted the home of her childhood for ever, she would only leave the house to go out driving with her mother or to walk down to the village. Finally, she reached the shore of the lake which had been the innocent cause of so much sorrow, and stood for a while beside the rotting boathouse, gazing at the smooth, gray surface of the water. The boat, which had only been secured by a chain from the stern, had floated out from the shelter and was in need of baling; there was a tin bait-box on one of the seats and a spare line lay near it. Probably nobody had approached the spot since that fatal day, so many months ago, when Mickey had left it, bearing his fish-basket with him in triumph. Winifred stooped down, grasped the chain, and was drawing the boat towards her, when a voice from behind her back said:

'Can I help you?'

She turned her sad, pale face towards the tall man in black clothes, whose appearance did not startle her, and answered:

'I wanted to get hold of that little bait-box. I think Micky must have forgotten it and left it there.'

Edmund soon secured that treasure, and handed

it to her without a word. He was full of sorrow
and sympathy for her ; but, not knowing what to
say, he held his peace, like the sensible man that
he was ; and so for a brief space there was silence.
He broke it at length by remarking :

'I have just had a long chat with your mother.
She tells me that Mr. Forbes thinks of letting the
place and going abroad for a time. It sounds like
a wise plan.'

'Oh yes; it is the only plan,' agreed Winifred.
'I didn't think of it until she mentioned it ; but I
see now that we couldn't have stayed on here. We
should have all learnt to hate it ; and that would
have been too dreadful.'

'It is natural that you should have such a feeling,' said Edmund ; 'but I hope you don't mean
that the whole neighbourhood has become distaste-
ful to you. For your parents to leave England is
all very well, but my home—our home—must be
in Shropshire now, and I am afraid it will be my
clear duty to inhabit it for eight or nine months of
the year.'

'Oh, of course.'

'And your mother thinks,' Edmund went on,
'that it would be better for you not to accompany
them when they start on their travels. She thinks
that if you and I were quietly married before then,
nobody could accuse us, under the circumstances,
of a want of proper feeling ; and she says, truly
enough, that, as your sister's wedding has taken
place since—since your trouble, there is no real

reason why yours should not. I do not think it at all likely that my own mother would raise any objection; she, too, speaks of going South for change and rest.' He added, after a short pause: 'I don't like the idea of hurrying you, and you shall not be hurried if you dislike it; but at least there is no harm, I hope, in my telling you what I should wish.'

He spoke in an apologetic tone, and was evidently prepared for opposition; but he met with none.

'I don't want to go abroad,' Winifred said, 'and I quite think, as you and mamma do, that if we are married without any fuss or rejoicings, we shall not be called heartless. Besides, I don't know that it would so very much matter if we were.'

She came to a full stop here; but as Edmund was beginning to speak, she interrupted him by adding:

'Only there is something that I must tell you before I marry you. It is a rather disagreeable thing to have to say, and perhaps—I don't know—perhaps, after you have heard it, you may not wish to marry me at all. Still, I am sure that it ought to be said.'

'I also have something to tell you,' Edmund observed; 'and it is so disagreeable to me to mention it that I have put off doing so longer than, perhaps, I ought to have done. But we shall both feel better when we have relieved our minds. Will you begin, or shall I?'

'Oh, I will speak first, please,' answered Winifred, with a faint smile. 'What I have to say will be soon said. You remember my telling you, after we came back from Algiers, about Daisy and Mr. Bellew? Well, I didn't tell you the whole truth then. If I had, I should have told you that Mr. Bellew made me an offer of marriage just before he left. I was utterly taken by surprise; I had never supposed that he was thinking of anything of the kind, and I honestly believe that I had never been anything more than friendly with him.'

Edmund nodded, and looked as if he expected her to continue. Evidently she had neither astonished nor angered him, so far.

'Did you know of this, then?' she asked.

'Yes; I knew that Bellew had proposed to you and had been refused; I will tell you presently how I came to hear of it. But that was not all you had to say, was it?'

Winifred sighed.

'No, not quite all,' she answered. 'Mr. Bellew was here for a few days in the spring, as you know, but I scarcely saw him or spoke to him, and it was only by the merest chance that I met him afterwards, one day, in London. Then we did talk for a long time about Micky—you know how fond Micky was of him?—but we didn't speak of—of other things. Only I understood that he had not changed. A day or two later he called in Hans Place, but mamma snubbed him and Harry Lysaght was jealous of him, so he went off yachting. I have not seen him since.'

'But you have wished to see him?'

'I don't think I have—not in the way that you mean. I suppose in one sense I shall always wish to see him, because there is nobody else in the world who seems to me like a sort of link with Micky. But in reality I shall go out of my way to avoid meeting him; for—oh, how shall I make you understand!'

'My dear,' said Edmund gently, 'it is not difficult to understand, though I dare say it is difficult for you to explain. I will try to make it a little easier. What I had to say to you—and perhaps I ought to have said it before now—was this: You remember that poor little Micky was very anxious to speak to me during his last illness. We thought then, you know, that he had taken a turn for the better and was getting well again; but he himself must have felt some doubts, for he told me that, in case of our never meeting again, he wished me to know what had occurred in Algiers. His impression was that you had only refused Mr. Bellew because you considered yourself bound by your engagement to me, and he asked me to promise that I would release you from that engagement. Of course I could not comply with such a request upon the spur of the moment, and without having satisfied myself that I ought to do so; but I did promise that you should never marry me against your will. Afterwards in London, as you will recollect, I offered to set you free, though I did not mention all the reasons that I had for thinking that freedom might be welcome to you. I should have gone on to mention them, I hope, if your reply had been less decided; but as it was, I believed what I wanted to believe, and took it for granted that Micky had made a mistake. I couldn't feel quite easy in my mind, though, and I meant to tell you to-day about that interview that I had with him. Now, my dear Winnie, I know as well as possible what your goodness and unselfishness have made you resolve to do; but it wouldn't really be a right thing, or even a kind thing, to marry me when your heart belongs to another man. You would be treating me badly if you did that; you aren't treating me badly by giving me pain which you can't help now, and I suppose you could no more help loving that other man than I could help loving you.'

'But I don't!—I don't!' exclaimed Winifred, who was not misled by the above unemotional speech, and who knew how great an effort it had cost Edmund Kirby to make it. 'What I thought you ought to be told—what I wanted you to understand—but I almost despair of making you or anybody else understand it!—was not that I care for Mr. Bellew more than I do for you, but only that, if everything had been different, I might perhaps have loved him.'

Her pale face flushed all over, and she lowered her eyelids.

'There!' she murmured, 'now I have told the truth and the whole truth. If, after that confes-

sion, you still wish me to be your wife, I will marry
you as willingly as I would have done at any time
during all these years.   More willingly, indeed, for
I have no home duties now.'

Edmund looked puzzled. He was not a man
who understood, or particularly wanted to understand, fine gradations of sentiment.   He wanted to
do what was right and straightforward, and it
appeared to him that there should be no splitting
of hairs upon so important a question as that of
marriage.

'I may be dull of comprehension,' he said, ' but
you don't convince me that you are not in reality
in love with Bellew. You say you will go out of
your way to avoid him ; you say that you might
have loved him if everything had been different ;
doesn't all that mean that you would have allowed
yourself to love him if you had not been engaged
to me ?'

'No, it doesn't mean that, Edmund. I wasn't
thinking only of my engagement when I spoke of
things being different ; I was thinking of him, too.
He would have to be different—very different
indeed from what he is—before I could love him.'

Edmund's brow cleared a little.

'Well,' he remarked, 'it is true that Bellew's
tastes are quite unlike yours, and I can hardly
imagine you leading the kind of life that he leads.
Not that there is any harm in it, and I don't wish
to sneer at racing and hunting men, who are
at least very superior to loafers; only you have

never been accustomed to think and talk about nothing but horses.'

Winifred smiled. 'I should certainly be a fish out of water at Melton or Newmarket,' said she; 'but that was not quite what I meant. I meant that Mr. Bellew, good and kind-hearted as he is, and thoroughly manly in some ways, is not manly in others. Perhaps it is just because he is so good and kind-hearted that he is so lamentably weak. You won't have forgotten what I told you about him and Mrs. Littlewood. She is not at all a nice woman: he wanted to shake himself free of her, and before I had any suspicion that he cared for me, I used to try and induce him to screw up his courage to the sticking-point. But he never could. She made him ridiculous in Algiers; it was she who dragged him ostentatiously away from the place, in spite of his reluctance. In London he assured me that he had broken with her finally; yet it seems that when he was taken ill in Scotland a short time ago, he made haste to send for her. Mamma showed me a paragraph in a newspaper, which said that he ascribed his recovery to her careful nursing. Do you understand any better now?'

If he did not, he at all events thought that he did. There was nothing incomprehensible to him in the disdain which a right-minded woman must naturally feel for a man who, while professing to love her, had not the moral courage to renounce a bygone entanglement of which he was weary. And

if he himself did not yet occupy quite so high a
place in her affections as that man might have
occupied, he had at least done nothing to forfeit
her respect. Nor was it unreasonable to hope that,
as years went on, she might learn to love him with
a love which he had hitherto, perhaps, exerted
himself too little to earn. Something of this kind
he said to her; and her reply was of a nature
to satisfy him and to relieve him of all his
doubts.

'I wouldn't marry you, Edmund,' she declared,
'if I didn't feel sure that I could do my duty and
be a good wife to you. We know each other so
well that we needn't be afraid of making any of
those dreadful discoveries which often cause un-
happiness amongst married people. Only you
mustn't expect me to be always cheerful or to be
the same as I was before I lost Micky. I feel as if
I had grown old before my time; you'll have to
make the best of an old woman.'

'My dear,' answered Edmund, ' whether you are
old or young, cheerful or sad, you will always be
yourself. You won't hear me complaining of you,
and any slightest wish of yours that I can gratify
I will gratify; that I promise you.'

She knew that he would keep his promise, and
she was neither unhappy nor ungrateful, as they
walked slowly back towards the house together in
the waning light. Gratitude is, indeed, due for
the love of any honest gentleman; and as for
happiness, how many people ever obtain it in its

supremest form, or, obtaining it, are able to keep their hold upon it ?   Winifred was more than reconciled to a destiny which, now that she had unbosomed herself of her secret, she could contemplate without dread or misgiving; she recognised, too, the chivalrous forbearance of her future husband, who had refrained from demanding more than she was able to give him.

Nevertheless, there must always be a touch of sadness in the certainty that supreme happiness is absolutely unobtainable.

CHAPTER XXIII.

THE MINISTERING ANGEL.

CRUISING is, in these days, a very common form of recreation amongst the well-to-do; but probably there are only two classes of persons who can be said to really enjoy it: the keen sailor, who usually contents himself with a small vessel and is seldom to be met with in the Solent or on the west coast of Scotland; and the overworked man, to whom the mere fact of having absolutely nothing to do and no letters to write or receive is in itself sufficient.   Billy Bellew belonged to neither category; so that, in spite of fine weather and pleasant company, he found the long summer days a good deal longer than they ought to have been after he had sailed from Southampton on board his friend's yacht.   And this was fortunate; because his one

wish was to get through the summer and early
autumn with all possible despatch. He had his
programme all ready mapped out, and under ordinary circumstances he would have admitted that
it was not one to grumble at. So many weeks
yachting ; so many weeks on the moors, with old
Maxwell and other friends from whom he had
received invitations ; perhaps a little stalking ;
then, if there should be time enough left, a week
or so of cub-hunting ; and then—well, then surely
it would be permissible to drop a line to Lysaght
and hint that Shropshire adjoins Cheshire, in
which latter county he had decided to take up his
hunting-quarters for the winter. He could not
help—for the matter of that, he did not wish to
help—being sanguine. He reasoned that, if
Winnie had had no idea of ultimately yield-
ing, she would not have been so anxious to
send him away; he thought it very natural that
in the first freshness of her sorrow she should
shrink from contemplating consolation, and he
bore no ill-will against Harry Lysaght for having
interfered in the matter. ‘ I’m such a duffer,’ he
reflected; ‘ I don’t make any allowance for women’s
sensibilities ; and I dare say, if I had stayed on in
London, I should only have succeeded in rubbing
them all the wrong way and making them hate
the sight of me. I expect I’m best where I am for
the present.’

Nevertheless, it was very tedious where he was.
The long swell of the lazy Atlantic, the tumbling

seas of St. George's Channel, the wild, melancholy beauty of the north Irish coast, the marvellous colouring of the Sound of Jura, and the noise and bustle of tourist-ridden Oban—all these were tedious to him. Not quite so bad, perhaps, as Naples and Florence and Venice; still, wearisome enough. Who cares to sit and look at an interminable succession of dissolving views, while waiting for the verdict which is to determine the whole course of his future life? There were several other men on board. They occupied themselves principally in playing poker, snoozing over the newspapers and devising ingenious practical jokes for the benefit of Billy, whose spirits, they remarked, required rousing. They were very good fellows in their way—certainly much better company than Colonel Littlewood — and Billy had always liked them. It was not their fault that they had bored him to death now. At Portree one of them, who had received a batch of letters, had a rather interesting piece of intelligence to impart.

'You know little Lysaght, don't you, Bellew?' said he. 'Going to be married in a few weeks to some girl who lives near him in Shropshire. A Miss Forbes whom he has been wanting to marry for ever so long, it seems; only she wasn't quite in such a hurry as he was. Looks as if she was rather in a hurry now that she has made up her mind, doesn't it? Well, she's a lucky young woman; for Lysaght ain't half a bad little chap, and he has more money than he can spend. Wedding to be quite private, owing to a recent bereavement in the bride's family. H'm! I trust that may be taken as a delicate and kindly intimation that no presents are expected.'

This ungenerous view of the case by no means commended itself to Billy, who forthwith despatched an order to a well-known firm of silversmiths and a letter of warm congratulation to Harry Lysaght, in which he made so bold as to send his kindest remembrances to Winnie, together with the expression of a hope that he might find himself within reach of Stratton Park before the year was out. His letter and his present were gratefully acknowledged in due course; but Harry quite forgot to deliver the kindest remembrances and the accompanying message. How could an excited bridegroom-elect be expected to carry such trivialities in his head?

The incident, however, was of service to Billy, inasmuch as it enabled him to feel himself, for a time, more or less in touch with the Forbes family. Moreover, Harry alluded to shooting prospects in his reply, and mentioned that he fully intended to be home again by the middle of November.

Whether Billy was destined to shoot pheasants in November or not was for some weeks after this a very doubtful question; but it was quite certain that he would shoot no grouse that year. It may have been at one of the ports in which the yacht lay before he quitted her, or it may have been in Edinburgh, where he spent a night, that he picked up the germs of the sickness which prostrated him immediately after his arrival at Mr. Maxwell's shooting lodge; either way, it soon became evident that he was in for typhoid fever, and sorely perplexed his host was to know what was to be done with him. The one thing which could assuredly not be done was to move him; so additional medical assistance and trained nurses were telegraphed for, and the disadvantages of a remote locality had to be contended against as best they might. Mr. Maxwell, a kindly, fussy old gentleman, at first proposed to send for his wife, but yielded to the representations of his other guests, who were convinced that Mrs. Maxwell's health would not stand the strain which it was sought to impose upon her. As Mrs. Maxwell was a smart lady, who affected to be something of an invalid, and who detested discomfort of any kind, it is more than likely that the other guests were right; but her husband continued to be very uneasy.

'It would be an awful thing if the poor fellow were to die here!' said he. 'I don't half like the responsibility of having a man dangerously ill in the house, with no lady to see whether he is being properly attended to or not.'

Billy, luckily for him, soon became unconscious of all the trouble that he was causing. He was conscious, indeed, of nothing but a prolonged and hideous nightmare, in which his personal identity seemed to have slipped away from him; so that he could not be sure whether it was he himself or somebody else who was burning and suffering on that narrow bed. But by degrees and at intervals his senses began to return to him, and he became dimly aware that there was somebody strangely resembling Blanche Littlewood who was always at his side. At first he was too weak to do more than wonder whether it really was Blanche, and, if so, how she came to be there. Sometimes she spoke to him and sometimes he made a faint monosyllabic reply, without having understood what she said; only one day, when there came a sound as of a heavy man approaching on tip-toe, and when presently the ruddy, sympathetic countenance of old Mr. Maxwell was bent over him, he made an effort and asked a few questions.

'Oh, *you're* all right, old man,' Mr. Maxwell said reassuringly, in answer to some of these; 'you aren't going up aloft just yet—don't you flatter yourself! Yes; you've had rather a long bout of it, and you've been about as bad as you could be; but the doctor pronounced you out of danger nearly a week ago. All you have to do now is to get well and take your time about it. Trouble? nonsense, my dear fellow! you've given no trouble to any of us, I can assure you. We've been going on shooting and everything, just as usual, ever since that excellent little woman came and insisted upon taking charge of you. Upon my word, I can't feel thankful enough to her and—and her husband.'

'Her husband!' repeated Billy feebly. And then, in a dismayed tone, 'Is *he* here, too?'

' Well, yes ; he's here. She couldn't very well have come without him, you see, could she? Oh, that's all right ; he has liked himself very well here, I think ; and of course we were only too glad to have another gun after you were laid on the shelf. Quite a boon to us, in fact.'

'He hasn't shot anybody yet, then ?'

' N—no, not exactly. That is, of course not! Why the deuce should he? Now, look here, Bellew ; I mustn't let you talk any more, or I shall catch it from Mrs. Littlewood. I'll come in and see you again as soon as she gives me leave, but I'm afraid I have exceeded my time already.'

It may have been because Mr. Maxwell was not desirous of being further interrogated as to Colonel Littlewood's exploits that he left the room so precipitately ; but Billy did not need to be told what a dangerous neighbour the Colonel (who had once been a crack shot) had become of late years, while he knew only too well how dreadfully offensive the Colonel was apt to be after dinner every evening. What a time poor old Maxwell and his friends must have been having of it with the man !

This thought disturbed and distressed him more than the unexplained fact that Mrs. Littlewood had established herself upon the premises, for his brain was not yet in working order, and could not deal with more than one subject at a time. But he was soon enlightened by Blanche herself, who told him how, by the happiest accident, she and Alfred had been staying with some people a few miles away

when the news of his illness had reached them;
how she had at once implored Mr. Maxwell to en-
trust the patient to her care, and how she had
occupied her present post of responsibility for more
than a month. She spoke of it all as a matter of
course; her voice was subdued and soothing; she
was arrayed in a garb appropriate to the circumstances, and she made arrangements and gave instructions as coolly as if she had been his wife or
his sister. She seemed to have clean forgotten
that they had not parted precisely on terms of
amity.

Billy himself had half forgotten what the actual
state of affairs was, and had only a confused impression that Fortune had, somehow or other,
played him a scurvy trick. By degrees, however,
he began to realise what that trick had been and
what its consequences were likely to be. Blanche
Littlewood, for reasons best known to herself, had
not only pardoned him, but had laid him under an
obligation which he could not, without the basest
ingratitude, ignore. If, in return, she should claim
once more the fealty which he had vowed to her in
years gone by, could he have the heart to meet her
with a renewed declaration of independence?
Would he, if she should demand it, be bound in
honour to renounce, at her bidding, the woman
whom he loved? These were hard questions, and
he debated them inwardly for many days, without saying a word about them. But when at
length he was able to leave his bed for a few hours

together, and when, one afternoon, he was half
sitting, half reclining, before the fire, with Blanche,
who had been reading a novel aloud, opposite to
him, the time seemed to have come for them to
arrive at some sort of an understanding. He
opened the proceedings by inquiring what had
become of Captain Patten.

'Captain Patten,' replied Blanche serenely, 'has
vanished into infinite space. He was a worthy
and useful creature in some ways; but I don't
think I ever met anyone who had a clearer conviction of the necessity of taking care of himself,
and I rather suspect that Alfred frightened him.
Alfred, as you may be aware, has a tiresome habit
of asking his friends to oblige him with small loans,
and the consequence is that some of them cease to
be his friends rather suddenly. Captain Patten
ceased quite suddenly, and I hadn't the curiosity to
inquire why he had departed or where he had
gone.' She added presently, in a tone of mild
reproach : 'I think you might have known better
than to be jealous of Captain Patten.'

'But I never was jealous of him,' Billy protested.
'I never thought of such a thing. It wasn't on
that account, you know, that we parted in Venice.'

'Wasn't it? Well, perhaps I was the jealous
one, then. At all events, we were both of us angry,
and we quarrelled, and now we must try to forget
that we ever quarrelled. That is always the best
plan, isn't it?'

'I dare say it is, as a general rule; only I wanted

to explain that I had no more intention of quarrelling with you then than I have now. And I think I ought to say, too, that I haven't changed in any way since then—not in *any* way.'

Mrs. Littlewood declined to understand him. 'Indeed, you have changed very much, my poor Billy !' she returned, laughing. 'Shall I fetch a looking-glass for you ? You will want one soon, when you shave off that black beard, which really must come off. I insist upon it !'

He gave in for the time being, promising himself that he would be more explicit upon some future occasion ; but that future occasion never came. She was wonderfully skilful in staving it off whenever it seemed to be at hand ; she made no allusion to the Forbeses, nor would she take any notice of his own tentative allusions. Her manner had also undergone a complete and perplexing alteration. Instead of being peevish and exacting, as of yore, she was always cheerful, always patient, always on the watch to supply those numberless small needs which an invalid experiences, but scarcely cares to mention. She treated him as if he belonged to her ; yet she said never a word of love, nor did she seem to expect that he should do so.

Thus day succeeded day until Mr. Maxwell's engagements compelled him to leave the Highlands. It was not yet thought expedient for Billy to travel, and the old gentleman entreated him to remain where he was until he should be quite convalescent, adding :

'I know I am leaving you in good hands; for Colonel and Mrs. Littlewood have most kindly promised to stay and take care of you. There really seem to be no limits to Mrs. Littlewood's kindness.'

There really seemed to be none; and the dreadful part of it was that her kindness was going to be rewarded, if not with ingratitude, with something which might only too probably represent itself to her under that aspect. The last week of Billy's sojourn in Aberdeenshire was less pleasant than those immediately preceding it had been. He was able to take his meals downstairs now, able to go out for drives and short walks, able also to renew intercourse with the Colonel, who welcomed him boisterously, borrowed a hundred pounds of him and waxed uproarious over Mr. Maxwell's whisky. It was quite clear that the Colonel must not be allowed to go on scandalising the servants any longer; it was quite clear, too, that Billy had no further excuse for trespassing upon the hospitality of the absent owner.

He said as much one fine, frosty October morning to Mrs. Littlewood, who at once agreed with him. They would all travel South together as far as York, she said; after which she and her husband would proceed to London, while Billy could carry out the intention which he had previously expressed of betaking himself to the Midlands, in order to inspect his hunters. She was so reasonable and, as he could not help feeling, so generous that he was quite unable to find any adequate words in which to thank her. For the rest, she declared that she desired no thanks; he had already conferred the greatest boon upon her that he had it in his power to confer by getting well.

'I haven't so many friends in the world that I can afford to lose the best of them,' she added.

Well, she should, at least, never lose his friendship; he was determined of that. Not even to please Winifred herself would he turn his back upon the woman who had tended him with such untiring devotion and had dealt with him in so merciful and magnanimous a spirit. But Winifred, he felt sure, would ask no such sacrifice of him. Winifred, who was herself merciful and magnanimous, would undoubtedly admit, when once the facts should have been related to her, that he could not possibly consent to it. She might not approve of everything in Mrs. Littlewood's past conduct; she might not, just at first, feel very amicably disposed towards her; but she would certainly acknowledge what everyone must needs acknowledge; and in time, perhaps, he would have the happiness of seeing Winifred and Blanche fast friends. The poor fellow actually believed that that was possible. It was, therefore, not in the least surprising that he should have believed, as he did, in the ultimate success of his suit. Apparently Blanche did not mean to oppose it, and he had regarded Edmund Kirby all along as a *quantité négligeable.*

In this fools' paradise he lived contentedly enough for some little time, while his strength slowly came back to him, and while he made arrangements for the transfer of his horses into Cheshire. Some friends of his who resided in the latter county (indeed, there was scarcely a county in England which did not contain some friends of Billy Bellew's) invited him to go to them for the opening meet of the season and stay until the modest mansion which he had hired in their neighbourhood should be quite ready for his reception. Having accepted their invitation, he betook himself to London to make some necessary purchases, and, of course, to pay his respects in Lowndes Street. But Mrs. Littlewood was not at home when he called, and he learnt from her husband, who greeted him with affectionate cordiality, that she had left town for a few weeks.

'Come and dine to-morrow evening, old chap,' the hospitable Colonel said, 'and meet one or two other fellows. The wife's off paying visits at country houses, and I'm *en garsong* for a bit. Fact of the matter is, I'm not so keen about staying in places where there's shooting as I once was. My eyesight isn't what it used to be, and people are apt to be beastly uncivil nowadays if you happen to be out of form. That old beggar Maxwell got into no end of a stew one day in Scotland because a man had his legs peppered. I don't believe I was the culprit at all, but he swore I was, and he was uncommon nasty about it, I can tell you. I don't care,' the Colonel added, drawing himself up with dignity and twirling his moustache, 'to expose myself to that kind of thing, you know.'

Billy declined the dinner, pleading that he was still obliged to be very careful in the matter of diet and early hours. He said he was extremely sorry to have missed Mrs. Littlewood, and he really was sorry. Yet it cannot be truthfully asserted that he was overjoyed when, on reaching his destination in Cheshire a few days later, he found her established in the house as one of his fellow-guests. He had not at all expected to meet her there, he would fain have avoided telling her that he meditated a speedy excursion into the adjoining county, and he was vexed to hear from his hostess that she had invited herself. That lady availed herself of the privilege of old acquaintanceship to speak with perfect candour upon the subject.

'For the last two years,' said she, 'I haven't asked Blanche Littlewood to stay with us, and I dare say you know why I haven't. Of course it was good of her to nurse you when you were ill; but I confess that I was sorry and disappointed when I was told of what she had done, for I quite hoped that there had been an amicable rupture between you. Unfortunately, I know you too well to have the faintest hope of your attempting to emancipate yourself now that, as you so absurdly affirm, she has saved your life, but I wish you would give her a gentle hint that I can't let her make use of me in this way a second time. To put things in brutally plain language, I don't wish the house to get a bad name.'

It was all very well for Billy to protest indignantly against language which he declared to be totally unjustifiable as well as brutal, but he could not deny that Mrs. Littlewood had probably come down to Cheshire for the express purpose of staying under the same roof with him ; nor did Mrs. Littlewood herself deny it when they met. The moment that he saw her his heart sank, for he perceived at once that she had reverted to her former self. The powder, the rouge, the darkened eyelids, the fashionably-cut but somewhat exaggerated costume —all those features which in far Aberdeenshire had been so delightfully conspicuous by their absence, were now to the fore again, as was also, alas ! the old air of triumphant proprietorship and defiant indifference to the world's opinion. After dinner, she beckoned him away from the rest of the company into the library, where she threw herself down upon a sofa, and, making him sit beside her, asked him whether he didn't think it very nice of her to have arranged this little surprise for him.

He was troubled and annoyed; his nerves, perhaps, had been rendered sensitive by his illness, and before he could check himself he answered sharply :

'No ; I don't think it nice at all. I wish to Heaven you wouldn't do such things !'

She raised her eyebrows.

'That means ?' said she interrogatively.

'It only means that I can't see the use of it. It does you a lot of harm, it makes people say things which aren't true, but which can't be contradicted, and—and it places me in a horribly false position.'

'Oh—a false position?'

'Yes; because it gives me the appearance of being something more than I want to be, and what I hope I always shall be—your friend.'

'You used to wish to be something more,' Mrs. Littlewood remarked.

Billy looked down. By the sound of her voice he knew that the interview was not going to be a pleasant one; but it was unavoidable, and the best plan was to clear away ambiguity once for all.

'I thought,' said he, 'that we had agreed in Venice to close that chapter. Can't we close it and be friends? After what I told you then—and when I was ill I told you again, you know, that I hadn't changed in any way—you must see that there is nothing else to be done. You must see that if I wished it ever so much, I couldn't go back and be what I was last year or the year before.'

But that was just what Mrs. Littlewood did not see. She said that love, if it were in any sense worthy of being called by that name, was eternal; she believed and was sure that Billy had once loved her; she would not and could not believe that he was really a traitor. For her own part, she could pardon anything and everything to one whom she loved. Certainly she had been angered and hurt by that fancy of his for Miss Forbes, but she had known all along that it was only a passing fancy and that he would return to her in the end. As matters had fallen out, it was she who had returned to him, and perhaps that had been foolish of her; but could she have left him to die? Warming with her theme, she became really eloquent. She pointed out, what was true enough, that it was she, and she alone, who had suffered in social esteem through their intimacy; that she had not hesitated to brave the comments of malicious tongues when she had flown to his sick-bed; and that, although she did not grudge one of the sacrifices which she had made for his sake, it was nothing short of an insult to talk to her of friendship now.

Billy groaned. He was very remorseful—a great deal more remorseful than he had any need to be— yet what could he do? As he had said, he could not go back and be what he had once been.

'It's best to tell you the truth, Blanche,' he burst out. 'God knows I'm not ungrateful to you, but you would only think me a humbug if I tried to explain how I feel about it all. The truth is that I am going to marry Winifred Forbes, if she will have me; and as soon as I can, I shall make my way into Shropshire and ask her again. That's why I came to this part of the world.'

Mrs. Littlewood stared at him for a moment, and then, to his amazement, broke out into a loud laugh.

'Do you mean to say that you haven't heard, then?' she ejaculated.

'Heard what?' asked Billy.

'Why, that the girl is upon the point of being married to her old flame? Indeed, I'm not at all sure that she isn't actually married now. The wedding was to be to-day or to-morrow, I know. Who but you would have waited tranquilly all this time until it quite suited your convenience to throw the handkerchief, never doubting that the young woman would likewise sit patiently in a corner awaiting your pleasure? I thought, of course, that you had given up all idea of espousing her, though you might still be cherishing some sentimental regrets.'

Never has such a thing been heard of as that a man of Billy Bellew's strength and stature should faint away on receiving a startling piece of intelligence; even delicate ladies have, in the latter part of the present century, wholly abandoned the practice. But Billy was hardly out of the convalescent stage yet, and so for a few seconds he felt that pause of the heart, that cold moisture of the brow and that deathly sickness which are the usual precursors of unconsciousness.

'Is this true? Do you *know* that it is true?' he gasped out hoarsely.

'Dear me, yes! I heard all about it from Mrs. Ryland weeks ago, and there are half a dozen people in the house now who can convince you, if you are sceptical. It seems that the man—Kirby, isn't his name?—succeeded to a property the other day, and the Forbeses certainly don't appear to have lost time in calling upon him to redeem his promise. Perhaps you will excuse me from condoling with you. All prejudice apart, I must say that I think you have had a lucky escape.'

Then all of a sudden she changed her tone, and, laying her hand upon his coat-sleeve, murmured: 'Don't be angry with me! I'm not angry with you, though some people might think I had a right to be. Haven't I told you that I can forgive until seventy times seven?'

But Billy could make no answer.

He rose abruptly and staggered towards the door, making uncertain clutches at the furniture as he went. It was soon known that he had been taken ill and had been obliged to go to bed; but his servant, who had received instructions to admit nobody into his room, assured Mrs. Littlewood and other anxious inquirers that the indisposition was merely temporary and that his master intended to hunt on the morrow, as had been arranged.

CHAPTER XXIV.

BILLY MAKES HIS ESCAPE.

It was not very much sleep that Billy Bellew obtained that night. When he reached his bedroom he felt quite sufficiently ill and exhausted to go to bed, and he did so; but he was far too broad awake to remain there; so, as soon as his man had left him, he rose, put on a smoking-suit, dropped into an armchair before the fire, and sat for a long time staring vacantly at the glowing coals.

At first he could not put any order into his thoughts; the one fact that Winifred was lost to him for ever was all that he could realise. But by degrees many things became clear to him, and he wondered at the fatuity which had hitherto blinded him to what was so patent. How had he ever been insane enough to believe that Winifred would consent to be his wife? He had misunder-stood her as completely as he had misunderstood Blanche Littlewood—only in an opposite sense. The woman whom he loved had offered him friend-ship; the woman whose friendship he would gladly have retained claimed love from him, and would take nothing less. It could not have been other-wise. They had obeyed their respective natures and had acted as they were quite certain to act, under given circumstances. It was easy to under-stand that Winifred, whether she loved Kirby or not, would never allow herself to play the man false to whom she had plighted her troth. And most likely she would be happy with Kirby, even though she might not be actually in love with him.

'She thinks so much more of other people's happiness than she does of her own,' sighed Billy, 'that, so long as he is contented, she won't ask for anything else. She is like that—one or two people in the world are like that, I suppose.'

He himself, little as he suspected it, was not so very unlike that, and it was chiefly his unselfishness that saved him from giving way to despair. Winifred had chosen her destiny, and would not be dissatisfied with it: that was something. It was something, too, that Blanche, to whom he owed so much, and from whom he could not desire to be permanently alienated, would now have things as she wished to have them. All would go on as heretofore, he supposed. He would continue to be more or less at her beck and call. He would continue to subsidize the accommodating Colonel, and she would continue to be ostracised by those who deemed it incumbent upon them to discountenance such irregularities. After all, what did it signify? Very little indeed to him, and presumably still less to her, since she had never winced at gossip as he had done. For the rest, he contemplated the present and the future from something of a fatalistic standpoint. Both were the logical and inevitable outcome of the past. To use language which is somewhat out of date, but which may be none the worse on that account, he had done wrong and had got to suffer for it. Because it cannot be right to make love to your neighbour's wife, even though your love-making be confined to verbal expressions, and even though, upon more mature consideration, you should discover that you have never been in love with her at all.

It was not until nearly two o'clock in the morning that a terrible idea suddenly presented itself to this belated seeker after truth and resignation. What if the Colonel were to die? The contingency was neither a fanciful nor a remote one. A middle-aged man, with a short neck and a red face, who had led a thoroughly unhealthy life for many years, might apply in vain to any insurance company, and, supposing that Mrs. Littlewood should be left a widow, would it not become Billy Bellew's bounden duty to make that reparation to her which she would unquestionably expect? Every argument that she had employed to show that his proffered friendship was an insult to her now would apply with double force then; there was no getting out of the fact that he had compromised her, and it was difficult to see how there could be any honourable getting out of his obligation to marry her, when and if she should be released from her present bondage. All the same, he could hardly bring himself to face the thought. Eventually he might have to face it; but not now—surely not now, while his wounds were still fresh and bleeding!

'I hope to God I may die first myself, that's all!' muttered poor Billy as he returned to his bed. 'It isn't so very unlikely, when you come to think of it. I've had plenty of narrow shaves before now, and I shall have plenty more—riding the animals that I do. And there's no better death than breaking your neck over a fence while hounds are running.'

He slept a little after this, and when he made his appearance at the breakfast-table some hours later, he was able to respond cheerily to the many queries showered upon him with respect to his health.

Now, if Billy had desired to break his neck that very day, he could not have made choice of a more promising and capable accomplice than his chestnut mare the Shrew, whom he had selected to carry him. His host shook his head when he saw her, and said:

'I wish you would sell that brute, Bellew; she isn't safe to ride—I don't care how good a man she has on her back.'

'Oh, she's all right with me,' answered Billy. 'As for selling her, I don't suppose I could get a ten-pound note for her. Besides which, I shouldn't like to be a murderer.'

He had bought her for a song, by reason of her evil reputation, and had won half a dozen steeple-chases with her, though he had seldom hunted her. She was a magnificently made mare, with marvellous speed, endurance and jumping power, but so violent and excitable that nine men out of ten would have pronounced her useless with hounds. Moreover, she was afflicted with a temper which was easily roused, and which, when roused, displayed itself in every form that equine ingenuity can compass. Billy had somehow or other contrived to get on terms with her. He always rode her in a plain snaffle, and was wont to affirm that, so long as she was not interfered with, she was the safest mare in England. Still, she was hardly the animal to take to an opening meet, when the whole countryside had turned out in force, and when every road and lane was blocked with vehicles. He had to keep clear of the throng; and, under the circumstances, he was not sorry to have so good an excuse for deserting the ladies.

The hounds were not long in finding, and, although Billy got away under considerable disadvantages, he was soon with them. The mare, of course, bolted. That was what she always did; and it would have been not only impossible to hold her, but very unwise to attempt it. Her rider sat down in his saddle and began to enjoy himself. He knew that she was no fool; he knew that she would steady down after the first burst; and meanwhile it was glorious to feel that, in spite of all, life still had its happy moments. The Shrew, too, was enjoying herself. The country was rather a stiff one; but nothing seemed to come amiss to her, and she sailed on, taking her fences in perfect style, and finally clearing, without an effort, a brook which reduced the field to a very select few.

But shortly after this a thing happened to her and to her rider which had never happened before since they had arrived at a mutual understanding. How it came to pass Billy could not have explaind. Certainly the hedge looked big, black and ragged, and the take-off was bad, and she was going at racing speed; yet it was madness to attempt to steady her, and he did so quite involuntarily. The moment that he realised his mistake he dropped his hands; but it was too late. The mare threw up her head, whipped round, and they were within an ace of parting company. The incident in itself was not

of very great importance, for he got her through a
gap presently, and was even able to make up his
lost ground, but to Billy it was pregnant with the
saddest significance.

'It has come at last,' he muttered to himself;
'my nerve is going. I'll never hunt again if I can't
go straight; and if I have to give up hunting, God
help me!'

This much was, at all events, certain, that he
had seen the best of his first day's hunting that
season. The mare's temper was upset; she could
not or would not forget that he had touched her
mouth once; she began to rush madly at her
fences; she made several bad blunders; and he
was glad enough when a brilliant but comparatively
brief run was terminated by a kill in the open.
For the first time in his life he found himself
almost wishing that the next covert might be drawn
blank.

Meanwhile, Mrs. Littlewood and her hostess had
been trying to see something of the run on wheels,
and had been quite unsuccessful. Indeed, a heavy
barouche is not a conveyance very well adapted for
that purpose, which was doubtless one reason why
they had been left in undisputed possession of it.
On the other hand, the opportunity thus afforded
of administering a well-meant and kindly lecture
was not to be neglected by a lady who had once
been on terms of greater intimacy with Mrs. Littlewood than she was now. So she talked at considerable length, and said some very sensible

things, not one of which produced the faintest impression upon her companion.

'If you were Mrs. Grundy in person you could not be more convincing,' Blanche wound up a protracted discussion by saying; 'but, you see, the truth is that Mrs. Grundy and I fell out some years ago, and I couldn't propitiate her now, if I tried. Therefore I am not going to try; nor is Billy. It may be very sad, but it is a fact that we don't care.'

'Well, I can say no more,' returned the other, out of patience. 'I think you are—— But perhaps I had better not tell you what I think you are, and perhaps we had better turn towards home. We have seen the last of the hunt for to-day, I expect.'

As a matter of fact, they were nearer than she supposed to the hounds, who by this time had started a second fox and had run him some distance; but it so chanced that, owing to the lie of the land and the set of the wind, the first intimation of their vicinity that reached her ears was the sound of a galloping horse's hoofs upon the road behind her. She turned round and recognised her husband, who at once signalled to her to stop the carriage.

'Good heavens, George!' she exclaimed when he drew near, 'what has happened? You are as pale as death. Has there been an accident?'

'Yes,' he answered hurriedly, 'Bellew has had a bad fall. I want the carriage, if you don't mind.

You won't have a very long walk home **if** you cut across the fields.'

He would not return any definite answer to the agitated questions with which the two ladies plied him, but he was very urgent that they should start on their walk immediately, and all the time that they were interrogating him, he kept glancing over his shoulder. At length he jumped off his horse, took his wife by the arm and drew her aside.

'For God's sake get that woman away!' he whispered. 'They are carrying him down the road, and she mustn't see him. She can do no good; nor can you.'

'Oh, George!—do you mean that he is dead?'

'He has broken his neck. He put that brute of a mare of his at a gate, and she breasted it—never tried to rise. I suppose he must have pitched on his chin. Oh, poor dear old Billy! to think that it should have ended like this!'

It was, at least, as we know, the end which he would have chosen; and nobody can know whether, if his life had been prolonged for a few more years, he would have been able to dispose of it according to his choice or not. While the husband and wife were still whispering together, Mrs. Littlewood joined them.

'You need not trouble to make any mystery about it,' she said quietly; 'I know he has been killed. If he had only been badly hurt, you would have told me so. Don't think about me, please; I shall not get in your way, and I have no title to be considered, you know.'

Then she sank down upon the bank by the roadside and sat—with her elbows on her knees, and her chin supported by her clasped hands—a pathetic picture of blank despair, in her fine clothes and the unaltered juvenile bloom of her drawn cheeks.

Soon a slowly-moving procession came in sight. Six members of the hunt were carrying the dead man, whose white face, upturned to the sky, had not been covered and bore no disfiguring marks. His colourless lips were curved into a faint smile. They lifted him, with some difficulty, into the carriage, and then fell back. One or two of them were completely and undisguisedly overcome; every one of them was deeply moved, for all Billy Bellew's acquaintances had been his friends. But Mrs. Littlewood watched them in silence and with dry eyes. There was no good in crying; there never would be any good in crying again. Tears had been of service to her on many and many a past occasion, but the man who had been distressed and moulded to her will by them had passed for ever beyond the reach of such influences. Her calamity was as irremediable as it was cruel. Vain had been her sacrifices; for she had made real and great sacrifices, though they had been unsolicited by him: she had lost caste permanently, and she had gained nothing—absolutely nothing, not even poor Billy's love. It does not seem likely that any-

one who has read this record of a part of Mrs.
Littlewood's life will feel much pity for her; yet it
may be acknowledged that she was punished in
proportion to her offences.

At that same hour the bells of the parish church
at Stratton were ringing merrily in honour of a
very unostentatious wedding which had just taken
place.   The bride and bridegroom had already
driven away, and had been followed by most of
those few near relations who had witnessed the
ceremony.   Mr. and Mrs. Lysaght, whose own
orange-blossoms had hardly faded as yet, were
about to step into their brougham when the former
said:

'Well, I'm glad that's over! Between you and
me, I was a little bit nervous, for I wasn't sure how
she would get through it. I knew she would have
to walk past poor little Micky's grave, you see.'

'You needn't have been alarmed,' Daisy answered,
'nothing would ever make Winnie break down.
Besides, I believe she is perfectly contented—
though *why* she should be contented, Heaven alone
knows!'

'That was a queer business about her and
Bellew,' Harry remarked musingly; 'I should
never have believed it if you hadn't told me. One
would have said they were the last couple in the
world to take a fancy to one another. And you
think she really did care for him?'

'I thought so; I am not sure that I think so.
Winnie has always been incomprehensible to me,

and always will be, I suppose. Most likely that is because I am too much of a sinner to enter into the sensations of a saint.'

'Such as you are, you are good enough for me,' said Harry complacently.

'I flatter myself that I am. But Edmund Kirby isn't good enough for Winnie, and if you are wasting sympathy upon her, as I can see that you are, you may take comfort from the thought that Mr. Bellew wouldn't have been good enough for her either.'

THE END.

(SEE NEXT PAGE.)

"Give sorrow word the grief that doth not speak
Whispers the o'erfraught heart and bids it break."—*Shakespere*.

AN ALPHABETICAL CATALOGUE
OF BOOKS IN FICTION AND
GENERAL LITERATURE
PUBLISHED BY
CHATTO & WINDUS
III ST. MARTIN'S LANE
CHARING CROSS
LONDON, W.C.
[MAR. 1899.]

About (Edmond).—The Fellah: An Egyptian Novel. Translated by Sir RANDAL ROBERTS. Post 8vo, illustrated boards, 2s.

Adams (W. Davenport), Works by.
A Dictionary of the Drama: being a comprehensive Guide to the Plays, Playwrights, Players, and Playhouses of the United Kingdom and America, from the Earliest Times to the Present Day. Crown 8vo, half-bound, 12s. 6d. [*Preparing.*
Quips and Quiddities. Selected by W. DAVENPORT ADAMS. Post 8vo, cloth limp, 2s. 6d.

Agony Column (The) of 'The Times,' from 1800 to 1870. Edited with an Introduction, by ALICE CLAY. Post 8vo, cloth limp, 2s. 6d.

Aidé (Hamilton), Novels by. Post 8vo, illustrated boards, 2s. each.
Carr of Carrlyon. | Confidences.

Alden (W. L.).—A Lost Soul: Being the Confession and Defence of Charles Lindsay. Fcap. 8vo, cloth boards, 1s. 6d.

Alexander (Mrs.), Novels by. Post 8vo, illustrated boards, 2s. each.
Maid, Wife, or Widow? | Valerie's Fate. | Blind Fate.

Crown 8vo, cloth, 3s. 6d. each; post 8vo, picture boards, 2s. each.
A Life Interest. | Mona's Choice. | By Woman's Wit.

Allen (F. M.).—Green as Grass. Crown 8vo, cloth, 3s. 6d.

Allen (Grant), Works by. Crown 8vo, cloth, 6s. each.
The Evolutionist at Large. | Moorland Idylls.
Post-Prandial Philosophy. Crown 8vo, art linen, 3s. 6d.

Crown 8vo, cloth extra, 3s. 6d. each; post 8vo, illustrated boards, 2s. each.

Babylon. 12 Illustrations.	The Devil's Die.	The Duchess of Powysland.
Strange Stories. Frontis.	This Mortal Coil.	Blood Royal.
The Beckoning Hand.	The Tents of Shem. Frontis.	Ivan Greet's Masterpiece.
For Maimie's Sake.	The Great Taboo.	The Scallywag. 24 Illusts.
Philistia.	Dumaresq's Daughter.	At Market Value.
In all Shades.	Under Sealed Orders.	

Dr. Palliser's Patient. Fcap. 8vo, cloth boards, 1s. 6d.

Anderson (Mary).—Othello's Occupation. Crown 8vo, cloth, 3s. 6d.

Antipodean (The): An Australasian Annual. Edited by A. B. PATERSON and G. ESSEX EVANS. Medium 8vo, with Illustrations, 1s.

Arnold (Edwin Lester), Stories by.
The Wonderful Adventures of Phra the Phœnician. Crown 8vo, cloth extra, with 12 Illustrations by H. M. PAGET, 3s. 6d.; post 8vo, illustrated boards, 2s.
The Constable of St. Nicholas. With Frontispiece by S. L. WOOD. Crown 8vo, cloth, 3s. 6d.

Artemus Ward's Works. With Portrait and Facsimile. Crown 8vo, cloth extra, 3s. 6d.—Also a POPULAR EDITION, post 8vo, picture boards, 2s.

Ashton (John), Works by. Crown 8vo, cloth extra, 7s. 6d. each
History of the Chap-Books of the 18th Century. With 334 Illustrations.
Humour, Wit, and Satire of the Seventeenth Century. With 82 Illustrations.
English Caricature and Satire on Napoleon the First. With 115 Illustrations.
Modern Street Ballads. With 57 Illustrations.
Social Life in the Reign of Queen Anne. With 85 Illustrations. Crown 8vo, cloth, 3s. 6d.

Bacteria, Yeast Fungi, and Allied Species, A Synopsis of. By
W. B. GROVE, B.A. With 87 Illustrations. Crown 8vo, cloth extra, 3s. 6d.

Bardsley (Rev. C. Wareing, M.A.), Works by.
English Surnames : Their Sources and Significations. Crown 8vo, cloth, 7s. 6d.
Curiosities of Puritan Nomenclature. Crown 8vo, cloth, 3s. 6d.

Baring Gould (Sabine, Author of 'John Herring,' &c.), Novels by.
Crown 8vo, cloth extra, 3s. 6d. each ; post 8vo, illustrated boards, 2s. each.
Red Spider. | Eve.

Barr (Robert: Luke Sharp), Stories by. Cr. 8vo, cl., 3s. 6d. each.
In a Steamer Chair. With Frontispiece and Vignette by DEMAIN HAMMOND.
From Whose Bourne, &c. With 47 Illustrations by HAL HURST and others.
Revenge ! With 12 Illustrations by LANCELOT SPEED and others.
A Woman Intervenes. Crown 8vo, cloth, with 8 Illustrations by HAL HURST, 3s. 6d.

Barrett (Frank), Novels by.
Post 8vo, illustrated boards, 2s. each ; cloth, 2s. 6d. each.
Fettered for Life. | A Prodigal's Progress.
The Sin of Olga Zassoulich. | John Ford ; and His Helpmate.
Between Life and Death. | A Recoiling Vengeance.
Folly Morrison. | Honest Davie. | Lieut. Barnabas. | Found Guilty.
Little Lady Linton. | For Love and Honour.
Crown 8vo, cloth, 3s. 6d. each ; post 8vo, picture boards, 2s each : cloth limp, 2s. 6d. each.
The Woman of the Iron Bracelets. | The Harding Scandal.
A Missing Witness. With 8 Illustrations by W. H. MARGETSON.
Was She Justified ? Crown 8vo, cloth, gilt top, 6s.
Under a Strange Mask. With 19 Illustrations by E. F. BREWTNALL. Crown 8vo, cloth, 3s. 6d.

Barrett (Joan).—Monte Carlo Stories. Fcap. 8vo, cloth, 1s. 6d.

Beaconsfield, Lord. By T. P. O'CONNOR, M.P. Cr. 8vo, cloth, 5s.

Beauchamp (Shelsley).—Grantley Grange. Post 8vo, boards, 2s.

Besant (Sir Walter) and James Rice, Novels by.
Crown 8vo, cloth extra, 3s. 6d. each ; post 8vo, illustrated boards, 2s. each ; cloth limp, 2s. 6d. each.
Ready-Money Mortiboy. | By Celia's Arbour.
My Little Girl. | The Chaplain of the Fleet.
With Harp and Crown. | The Seamy Side.
This Son of Vulcan. | The Case of Mr. Lucraft, &c.
The Golden Butterfly. | 'Twas in Trafalgar's Bay, &c.
The Monks of Thelema. | The Ten Years' Tenant, &c.
. There is also a LIBRARY EDITION of the above Twelve Volumes, handsomely set in new type on a
large crown 8vo page, and bound in cloth extra, 6s. each ; and a POPULAR EDITION of **The Golden
Butterfly**, medium 8vo, 6d. ; cloth, 1s.

Besant (Sir Walter), Novels by.
Crown 8vo, cloth extra, 3s. 6d. each ; post 8vo, illustrated boards, 2s. each : cloth limp, 2s. 6d. each.
All Sorts and Conditions of Men. With 12 Illustrations by FRED. BARNARD.
The Captains' Room, &c. With Frontispiece by E. J. WHEELER.
All in a Garden Fair. With 6 Illustrations by HARRY FURNISS.
Dorothy Forster. With Frontispiece by CHARLES GREEN.
Uncle Jack, and other Stories. | Children of Gibeon.
The World Went Very Well Then. With 12 Illustrations by A. FORESTIER.
Herr Paulus : His Rise, his Greatness, and his Fall. | The Bell of St. Paul's.
For Faith and Freedom. With Illustrations by A. FORESTIER and F. WADDY.
To Call Her Mine, &c. With 9 Illustrations by A. FORESTIER.
The Holy Rose, &c. With Frontispiece by F. BARNARD.
Armorel of Lyonesse : A Romance of To-day. With 12 Illustrations by F. BARNARD.
St. Katherine's by the Tower. With 12 Illustrations by C. GREEN.
Verbena Camellia Stephanotis, &c. With a Frontispiece by GORDON BROWNE.
The Ivory Gate. | The Rebel Queen.
Beyond the Dreams of Avarice. With 12 Illustrations by W. H. HYDE.
In Deacon's Orders, &c. With Frontispiece by A. FORESTIER. | The Revolt of L. . . . .
The Master Craftsman. | The City of Refuge.
A Fountain Sealed. With Frontispiece by H. G. BURGESS. Crown 8vo, cloth, 3s. 6d.
The Orange Girl. Crown 8vo, cloth, gilt top, 6s. [Preparing.
All Sorts and Conditions of Men. CHEAP POPULAR EDITION, medium 8vo, 6d. ; cloth, 1s. ;
or bound with the POPULAR EDITION of **The Golden Butterfly**, cloth, 2s.

The Charm, and other Drawing-room Plays. By Sir WALTER BESANT and WALTER H. POLLOCK.
With 50 Illustrations by CHRIS HAMMOND and JULE GOODMAN. Crown 8vo, cloth, gilt edges, 6s. ;
or blue cloth, to range with the Uniform Edition of Sir WALTER BESANT'S Novels, 3s. 6d.

Fifty Years Ago. With 144 Illustrations. Crown 8vo, cloth, 3s. 6d.
The Eulogy of Richard Jefferies. With Portrait. Crown 8vo, cloth, 6s.
London. With 125 Illustrations. Demy 8vo, cloth, 7s. 6d.
Westminster. With Etched Frontispiece by F. S. WALKER, R.E., and 130 Illustrations by
WILLIAM PATTEN and others. Demy 8vo, cloth, 7s. 6d.
South London. With Etched Frontispiece by F. S. WALKER, R.E., and 118 Illustrations.
Demy 8vo, cloth, gilt top, 18s.
Sir Richard Whittington. With Frontispiece. Crown 8vo, art linen, 3s. 6d.
Gaspard de Coligny. With a Portrait. Crown 8vo, art linen, 3s. 6d.

Bechstein (Ludwig).—As Pretty as Seven, and other German
Stories. With Additional Tales by the Brothers GRIMM, and 98 Illustrations by RICHTER. Square
8vo, cloth extra, 6s. 6d. gilt edges, 7s. 6d.

Bellew (Frank).—The Art of Amusing: A Collection of Graceful
Arts, Games, Tricks, Puzzles, and Charades. With 300 Illustrations. Crown 8vo, cloth extra, 4s. 6d.

Bennett (W. C., LL.D.).—Songs for Sailors. Post 8vo, cl. limp, 2s.

Bewick (Thomas) and his Pupils. By AUSTIN DOBSON. With 95
Illustrations. Square 8vo, cloth extra, 6s.

Bierce (Ambrose).—In the Midst of Life: Tales of Soldiers and
Civilians. Crown 8vo, cloth extra, 3s. 6d. ; post 8vo, illustrated boards, 2s.

Bill Nye's Comic History of the United States. With 146 Illustrations by F. OPPER. Crown 8vo, cloth extra, 3s. 6d.

Biré (Edmond). — Diary of a Citizen of Paris during 'The
Terror.' Translated and Edited by JOHN DE VILLIERS. With 2 Photogravure Portraits. Two Vols.,
demy 8vo, cloth, 21s.

Blackburn's (Henry) Art Handbooks.

Academy Notes, 1893.
Academy Notes, 1875-79. Complete in
One Vol., with 600 Illustrations. Cloth, 6s.
Academy Notes, 1880-84. Complete in
One Vol., with 700 Illustrations. Cloth, 6s.
Academy Notes, 1890-94. Complete in
One Vol., with 800 Illustrations. Cloth, 7s. 6d.
Grosvenor Notes, Vol. I., **1877-82.** With
300 Illustrations. Demy 8vo, cloth 6s.
Grosvenor Notes, Vol. II., **1883-87.** With
300 Illustrations. Demy 8vo, cloth, 6s.

Grosvenor Notes, Vol. III., **1888-90.** With
230 Illustrations. Demy 8vo cloth, 3s. 6d.
The New Gallery, 1888-1892. With 250
Illustrations. Demy 8vo, cloth, 6s.
English Pictures at the National Gallery.
With 114 Illustrations. 1s.
Old Masters at the National Gallery.
With 128 Illustrations. 1s. 6d.
**Illustrated Catalogue to the National
Gallery.** With 242 Illusts. Demy 8vo, cloth, 3s.

The Illustrated Catalogue of the Paris Salon, 1898. With 300 Sketches. 3s.

Blind (Mathilde), Poems by.
The Ascent of Man. Crown 8vo, cloth, 5s.
Dramas in Miniature. With a Frontispiece by F. MADOX BROWN. Crown 8vo, cloth, 5s.
Songs and Sonnets. Fcap. 8vo vellum and gold, 5s.
Birds of Passage: Songs of the Orient and Occident. Second Edition. Crown 8vo, linen, 6s. net.

Bourget (Paul).—A Living Lie. Translated by JOHN DE VILLIERS.
With special Preface for the English Edition. Crown 8vo, cloth, 3s. 6d.

Bourne (H. R. Fox), Books by.
English Merchants: Memoirs in Illustration of the Progress of British Commerce. With 32 Illus-
trations. Crown 8vo, cloth, 3s. 6d.
English Newspapers: Chapters in the History of Journalism. Two Vols., demy 8vo, cloth, 25s.
The Other Side of the Emin Pasha Relief Expedition. Crown 8vo, cloth, 6s.

Boyle (Frederick), Works by. Post 8vo, illustrated bds., 2s. each.
Chronicles of No-Man's Land. | Camp Notes. | Savage Life.

Brand (John).—Observations on Popular Antiquities; chiefly
illustrating the Origin of our Vulgar Customs, Ceremonies, and Superstitions. With the Additions of Sir
HENRY ELLIS, and numerous Illustrations. Crown 8vo, cloth extra, 7s. 6d.

Brayshaw (J. Dodsworth).—Slum Silhouettes: Stories of London
Life. Crown 8vo, cloth, 3s. 6d.

Brewer (Rev. Dr.), Works by.
**The Reader's Handbook of Famous Names in Fiction, Allusions, References,
Proverbs, Plots, Stories, and Poems.** Together with an ENGLISH AND AMERICAN
BIBLIOGRAPHY, and a LIST OF THE AUTHORS AND DATES OF DRAMAS AND OPERAS. A
New Edition, Revised and Enlarged. Crown 8vo, cloth, 7s. 6d.
A Dictionary of Miracles: Imitative, Realistic, and Dogmatic. Crown 8vo, cloth, 3s. 6d.

Brewster (Sir David), Works by. Post 8vo, cloth, 4s. 6d. each.
More Worlds than One: Creed of the Philosopher and Hope of the Christian. With Plates.
The Martyrs of Science: GALILEO, TYCHO BRAHE, and KEPLER. With Portraits.
Letters on Natural Magic. With numerous Illustrations.

Brillat-Savarin.— Gastronomy as a Fine Art. Translated by
R. E. ANDERSON, M.A. Post 8vo, half-bound, 2s.

Bryden (H. A.).—An Exiled Scot: A Romance. With a Frontispiece. Crown 8vo, cloth, 6s.

Brydges (Harold).—Uncle Sam at Home. With 91 Illustrations.
Post 8vo, illustrated boards, 2s. ; cloth limp, 2s. 6d.

Buchanan (Robert), Novels, &c., by.

Crown 8vo, cloth extra, 3s. 6d. each ; post 8vo, illustrated boards, 2s. each.

The Shadow of the Sword.
A Child of Nature. With Frontispiece.
God and the Man. With 11 Illustrations by
Lady Kilpatrick.   [FRED. BARNARD.
The Martyrdom of Madeline. With
Frontispiece by A. W. COOPER.

Love Me for Ever. With Frontispiece.
Annan Water. | Foxglove Manor.
The New Abelard. | Rachel Dene.
Matt : A Story of a Caravan. With Frontispiece.
The Master of the Mine. With Frontispiece.
The Heir of Linne. | Woman and the Man.

Red and White Heather. Crown 8vo, cloth extra, 3s. 6d.

The Wandering Jew : a Christmas Carol. Crown 8vo, cloth, 6s.

The Charlatan. By ROBERT BUCHANAN and HENRY MURRAY. Crown 8vo, cloth, with a
Frontispiece by T. H. ROBINSON, 3s. 6d. ; post 8vo, picture boards, 2s.

Burton (Robert).—The Anatomy of Melancholy. With Transla-
tions of the Quotations. Demy 8vo, cloth extra, 7s. 6d.

Melancholy Anatomised : An Abridgment of BURTON'S ANATOMY. Post 8vo, half-bd., 2s. 6d.

Caine (Hall), Novels by. Crown 8vo, cloth extra, 3s. 6d. each. ; post
8vo, illustrated boards, 2s. each ; cloth limp, 2s. 6d. each.

The Shadow of a Crime. | A Son of Hagar. | The Deemster.

Also LIBRARY EDITIONS of The Deemster and The Shadow of a Crime, set in new type,
crown 8vo, and bound uniform with The Christian, 6s. each ; and CHEAP POPULAR EDITIONS of
The Deemster and The Shadow of a Crime, medium 8vo, portrait-cover, 6d. each ; cloth, 1s.
each.

Cameron (Commander V. Lovett).—The Cruise of the 'Black
Prince' Privateer. Post 8vo, picture boards, 2s.

Captain Coignet, Soldier of the Empire : An Autobiography.
Edited by LOREDAN LARCHEY. Translated by Mrs. CAREY. With 100 Illustrations. Crown 8vo,
cloth, 3s. 6d.

Carlyle (Jane Welsh), Life of. By Mrs. ALEXANDER IRELAND. With
Portrait and Facsimile Letter. Small demy 8vo, cloth extra, 7s. 6d.

Carlyle (Thomas).—On the Choice of Books. Post 8vo, cl., 1s. 6d.

Correspondence of Thomas Carlyle and R. W. Emerson, 1834-1872. Edited by
C. E. NORTON. With Portraits. Two Vols., crown 8vo, cloth, 24s.

Carruth (Hayden).—The Adventures of Jones. With 17 Illustra-
tions. Fcap. 8vo, cloth, 2s.

Chambers (Robert W.), Stories of Paris Life by.

The King in Yellow. Crown 8vo, cloth, 3s. 6d. ; fcap. 8vo, cloth limp, 2s. 6d.
In the Quarter. Fcap. 8vo, cloth, 2s. 6d.

Chapman's (George), Works. Vol. I., Plays Complete, including the
Doubtful Ones.—Vol. II., Poems and Minor Translations, with Essay by A. C. SWINBURNE.—Vol.
III., Translations of the Iliad and Odyssey. Three Vols., crown 8vo, cloth, 3s. 6d. each.

Chapple (J. Mitchell).—The Minor Chord : The Story of a Prima
Donna. Crown 8vo, cloth, 3s. 6d.

Chatto (W. A.) and J. Jackson.—A Treatise on Wood Engraving,
Historical and Practical. With Chapter by H. G. BOHN, and 450 fine Illusts. Large 4to, half-leather, 28s.

Chaucer for Children : A Golden Key. By Mrs. H. R. HAWEIS. With
8 Coloured Plates and 30 Woodcuts. Crown 4to, cloth extra, 3s. 6d.

Chaucer for Schools. With the Story of his Times and his Work. By Mrs. H. R. HAWEIS.
A New Edition, revised. With a Frontispiece. Demy 8vo, cloth, 2s. 6d.

Chess, The Laws and Practice of. With an Analysis of the Open-
ings. By HOWARD STAUNTON. Edited by R. B. WORMALD. Crown 8vo, cloth, 5s.

The Minor Tactics of Chess : A Treatise on the Deployment of the Forces in obedience to Strategic Principle. By F. K. YOUNG and E. C. HOWELL. Long fcap. 8vo, cloth, 2s. 6d.

The Hastings Chess Tournament. Containing the Authorised Account of the 230 Games
played Aug.-Sept., 1895. With Annotations by PILLSBURY, LASKER, TARRASCH, STEINITZ,
SCHIFFERS, TEICHMANN, BARDELEBEN, BLACKBURNE, GUNSBERG, TINSLEY, MASON, and
ALBIN ; Biographical Sketches of the Chess Masters, and 22 Portraits. Edited by H. F. CHESHIRE.
Cheaper Edition. Crown 8vo, cloth, 5s.

Clare (Austin), Stories by.

For the Love of a Lass. Post 8vo, illustrated boards, 2s. ; cloth, 2s. 6d.
By the Rise of the River : Tales and Sketches in South Tynedale. Crown 8vo, cloth, 3s. 6d.

Clive (Mrs. Archer), Novels by. Post 8vo, illust. boards, 2s. each.
Paul Ferroll. | Why Paul Ferroll Killed his Wife.

Clodd (Edward, F.R.A.S.).—Myths and Dreams. Cr. 8vo, 3s. 6d.

Coates (Anne).—Rie's Diary. Crown 8vo, cloth, 3s. 6d.

Cobban (J. Maclaren), Novels by.
The Cure of Souls. Post 8vo, Illustrated boards, 2s.
The Red Sultan. Crown 8vo, cloth extra, 3s. 6d. ; post 8vo, illustrated boards, 2s.
The Burdon of Isabel. Crown 8vo, cloth extra, 3s. 6d.

Coleman (John).—Curly: An Actor's Story. With 21 Illustrations
by J. C. DOLLMAN. Crown 8vo, picture cover, 1s.

Coleridge (M. E.).—The Seven Sleepers of Ephesus. Fcap 8vo,
cloth, 1s. 6d. ; leatherette, 1s.

Collins (C. Allston).—The Bar Sinister. Post 8vo, boards, 2s.

Collins (John Churton, M.A.), Books by.
Illustrations of Tennyson. Crown 8vo, cloth extra, 6s.
Jonathan Swift. A Biographical and Critical Study. Crown 8vo, cloth extra, 8s.

Collins (Mortimer and Frances), Novels by.
Crown 8vo, cloth extra, 3s. 6d. each ; post 8vo, illustrated boards, 2s. each.
From Midnight to Midnight. | Blacksmith and Scholar.
Transmigration. | You Play me False. | The Village Comedy.
Post 8vo, illustrated boards, 2s. each.
Sweet Anne Page. | A Fight with Fortune. | Sweet and Twenty. | Frances.

Collins (Wilkie), Novels by.
Crown 8vo, cloth extra, many Illustrated, 3s. 6d. each ; post 8vo, picture boards, 2s. each ;
cloth limp, 2s. 6d. each.

Antonina.	My Miscellanies.	Jezebel's Daughter.
Basil.	Armadale.	The Black Robe.
Hide and Seek.	Poor Miss Finch.	Heart and Science.
The Woman in White.	Miss or Mrs.?	'I Say No.'
The Moonstone.	The New Magdalen.	A Rogue's Life.
Man and Wife.	The Frozen Deep.	The Evil Genius.
After Dark.	The Law and the Lady.	Little Novels.
The Dead Secret.	The Two Destinies.	The Legacy of Cain.
The Queen of Hearts.	The Haunted Hotel.	Blind Love.
No Name.	The Fallen Leaves.	

POPULAR EDITIONS. Medium 8vo, 6d. each ; cloth, 1s. each.
The Woman in White. | The Moonstone. | Antonina. | The Dead Secret.

The Woman in White and The Moonstone. POPULAR EDITION, in One Volume, medium
8vo, cloth, 2s.

Colman's (George) Humorous Works: 'Broad Grins,' 'My Night-
gown and Slippers,' &c. With Life and Frontispiece. Crown 8vo, cloth extra, 3s. 6d.

Colquhoun (M. J.).—Every Inch a Soldier. Crown 8vo, cloth,
3s. 6d. ; post 8vo, illustrated boards, 2s.

Colt-breaking, Hints on. By W. M. HUTCHISON. Cr. 8vo, cl., 3s. 6d.

Convalescent Cookery. By CATHERINE RYAN. Cr. 8vo, 1s. ; cl., 1s. 6d.

Conway (Moncure D.).—George Washington's Rules of Civility
Traced to their Sources and Restored. Fcap. 8vo, Japanese vellum, 2s. 6d.

Cook (Dutton), Novels by.
Post 8vo, illustrated boards, 2s. each.
Leo. | Paul Foster's Daughter.

Cooper (Edward H.).—Geoffory Hamilton. Cr. 8vo, cloth, 3s. 6d.

Cornwall.—Popular Romances of the West of England; or, The
Drolls, Traditions, and Superstitions of Old Cornwall. Collected by ROBERT HUNT, F.R.S. With
two Steel Plates by GEORGE CRUIKSHANK. Crown 8vo, cloth, 7s. 6d.

Cotes (V. Cecil).—Two Girls on a Barge. With 44 Illustrations by
F. H. TOWNSEND. Crown 8vo, cloth extra, 3s. 6d. ; post 8vo, cloth, 2s. 6d.

Craddock (C. Egbert), Stories by.
The Prophet of the Great Smoky Mountains. Post 8vo, illustrated boards, 2s.
His Vanished Star. Crown 8vo, cloth extra, 3s. 6d.

Cram (Ralph Adams).—Black Spirits and White. Fcap. 8vo,
cloth, 1s. 6d.

Crellin (H. N.), Books by.
Romances of the Old Seraglio. With 28 Illustrations by S. L. WOOD. Crown 8vo, cloth, 3s. 6d.
Tales of the Caliph. Crown 8vo, cloth, 2s.
The Nazarenes: A Drama. Crown 8vo, 1s.

Crim (Matt.).—Adventures of a Fair Rebel. Crown 8vo, cloth
extra, with a Frontispiece by DAN. BEARD, 3s. 6d.; post 8vo, illustrated boards, 2s.

Crockett (S. R.) and others. — Tales of Our Coast. By S. R.
CROCKETT, GILBERT PARKER, HAROLD FREDERIC, 'Q.,' and W. CLARK RUSSELL. With 2
Illustrations by FRANK BRANGWYN. Crown 8vo, cloth, 3s. 6d.

Croker (Mrs. B. M.), Novels by. Crown 8vo, cloth extra, 3s. 6d.
each; post 8vo, illustrated boards, 2s. each; cloth limp, 2s. 6d. each.

Pretty Miss Neville.	Interference.	Village Tales & Jungle
Proper Pride.	A Family Likeness.	Tragedies.
A Bird of Passage.	'To Let.'	The Real Lady Hilda.
Diana Barrington.	A Third Person.	Married or Single?
Two Masters.	Mr. Jervis.	

Crown 8vo, cloth extra, 3s. 6d. each.

In the Kingdom of Kerry. | Beyond the Pale.

Miss Balmaine's Past. Crown 8vo, buckram, gilt top, 6s.
Infatuation. (A 'TIMES NOVEL.') Crown 8vo, buckram, 6s.

Cruikshank's Comic Almanack. Complete in Two SERIES: The
FIRST, from 1835 to 1843; the SECOND, from 1844 to 1853. A Gathering of the Best Humour of
THACKERAY, HOOD, MAYHEW, ALBERT SMITH, A'BECKETT, ROBERT BROUGH, &c. With
numerous Steel Engravings and Woodcuts by GEORGE CRUIKSHANK, HINE, LANDELLS, &c.
Two Vols., crown 8vo, cloth gilt, 7s. 6d. each.
The Life of George Cruikshank. By BLANCHARD JERROLD. With 84 Illustrations and a
Bibliography. Crown 8vo, cloth extra, 3s. 6d.

Cumming (C. F. Gordon), Works by. Demy 8vo, cl. ex., 8s. 6d. ea.
In the Hebrides. With an Autotype Frontispiece and 23 Illustrations.
In the Himalayas and on the Indian Plains. With 42 Illustrations.
Two Happy Years in Ceylon. With 28 Illustrations.

Via Cornwall to Egypt. With a Photogravure Frontispiece. Demy 8vo, cloth, 7s. 6d.

Cussans (John E.).—A Handbook of Heraldry; with Instructions
for Tracing Pedigrees and Deciphering Ancient MSS., &c. Fourth Edition, revised, with 408 Woodcuts
and 2 Coloured Plates. Crown 8vo, cloth extra, 6s.

Cyples (W.).—Hearts of Gold. Cr. 8vo, cl., 3s. 6d.; post 8vo, bds., 2s.

Daudet (Alphonse).—The Evangelist; or, Port Salvation. Crown
8vo, cloth extra, 3s. 6d.; post 8vo, illustrated boards, 2s.

Davenant (Francis, M.A.).—Hints for Parents on the Choice of
a Profession for their Sons when Starting in Life. Crown 8vo, cloth, 1s. 6d.

Davidson (Hugh Coleman).—Mr. Sadler's Daughters. With a
Frontispiece by STANLEY WOOD. Crown 8vo, cloth extra, 3s. 6d.

Davies (Dr. N. E. Yorke-), Works by. Cr. 8vo, 1s. ea.; cl., 1s. 6d. e-
One Thousand Medical Maxims and Surgical Hints.
Nursery Hints: A Mother's Guide in Health and Disease.
Foods for the Fat: The Dietetic Cure of Corpulency and of Gout.

Aids to Long Life. Crown 8vo, 2s.; cloth limp, 2s. 6d.

Davies' (Sir John) Complete Poetical Works. Collected and Edited,
with Introduction and Notes, by Rev. A. B. GROSART, D.D. Two Vols., crown 8vo, cloth, 3s. 6d. each.

Dawson (Erasmus, M.B.).—The Fountain of Youth. Crown 8vo,
cloth extra, with Two Illustrations by HUME NISBET, 3s. 6d.; post 8vo, illustrated boards, 2s.

De Guerin (Maurice), The Journal of. Edited by G. S. TREBUTIEN.
With a Memoir by SAINTE-BEUVE. Translated from the 20th French Edition by JESSIE P. FROTH-
INGHAM. Fcap. 8vo, half-bound, 2s. 6d.

De Maistre (Xavier).—A Journey Round my Room. Translated
by HENRY ATTWELL. Post 8vo, cloth limp, 2s. 6d.

De Mille (James).—A Castle in Spain. Crown 8vo, cloth extra, with
a Frontispiece, 3s. 6d.; post 8vo, illustrated boards, 2s.

Derby (The): The Blue Ribbon of the Turf. With Brief Accounts
of THE OAKS. By LOUIS HENRY CURZON. Crown 8vo, cloth limp, 2s. 6d.

Derwent (Leith), Novels by. Cr. 8vo, cl., 3s. 6d. ea.; post 8vo, 2s. ea.
Our Lady of Tears. | Circe's Lovers.

Dewar (T. R.).—A Ramble Round the Globe. With 220 Illustrations. Crown 8vo, cloth extra, 7s. 6d.

De Windt (Harry), Books by.
Through the Gold-Fields of Alaska to Bering Straits. With Map and 33 full-page Illustrations. Demy 8vo, cloth extra. 16s.
Stories of Travel and Adventure. Crown 8vo, cloth, 3s. 6d. [Shortly.

Dickens (Charles), About England with. By ALFRED RIMMER. With 57 Illustrations by C. A. VANDERHOOF and the AUTHOR. Square 8vo, cloth, 3s. 6d.

Dictionaries.
The Reader's Handbook of Famous Names in Fiction, Allusions, References, Proverbs, Plots, Stories, and Poems. Together with an ENGLISH AND AMERICAN BIBLIOGRAPHY, and a LIST OF THE AUTHORS AND DATES OF DRAMAS AND OPERAS. By Rev. E. C. BREWER, LL.D. A New Edition, Revised and Enlarged. Crown 8vo, cloth, 7s. 6d.
A Dictionary of Miracles: Imitative, Realistic, and Dogmatic. By the Rev. E. C. BREWER, LL.D. Crown 8vo, cloth, 3s. 6d.
Familiar Short Sayings of Great Men. With Historical and Explanatory Notes by SAMUEL A. BENT, A.M. Crown 8vo, cloth extra, 7s. 6d.
The Slang Dictionary: Etymological, Historical, and Anecdotal. Crown 8vo, cloth, 6s. 6d.
Words, Facts, and Phrases: A Dictionary of Curious, Quaint, and Out-of-the-Way Matters. By ELIEZER EDWARDS. Crown 8vo, cloth extra, 3s. 6d.

Dilke (Rt. Hon. Sir Charles, Bart., M.P.).—The British Empire. Crown 8vo, buckram, 3s. 6d.

Dobson (Austin), Works by.
Thomas Bewick and his Pupils. With 95 Illustrations. Square 8vo, cloth, 6s.
Four Frenchwomen. With Four Portraits. Crown 8vo, buckram, gilt top, 6s.
Eighteenth Century Vignettes. IN THREE SERIES. Crown 8vo, buckram, 6s. each.
A Paladin of Philanthropy, and other Papers. With 2 Illustrations Crown 8vo, buckram, 6s. [April.

Dobson (W. T.).—Poetical Ingenuities and Eccentricities. Post 8vo, cloth limp, 2s. 6d.

Donovan (Dick), Detective Stories by.
Post 8vo, illustrated boards, 2s. each; cloth limp, 2s. 6d. each.

The Man-Hunter. **Wanted!**	**A Detective's Triumphs.**
Caught at Last.	**In the Grip of the Law.**
Tracked and Taken.	**From Information Received.**
Who Poisoned Hetty Duncan?	**Link by Link.** **Dark Deeds.**
Suspicion Aroused.	**Riddles Read.**

Crown 8vo, cloth extra, 3s. 6d. each; post 8vo, illustrated boards, 2s. each; cloth, 2s. 6d. each.
The Man from Manchester. With 23 Illustrations.
Tracked to Doom. With Six full-page Illustrations by GORDON BROWNE.
The Mystery of Jamaica Terrace. | **The Chronicles of Michael Danevitch.**
The Records of Vincent Trill, of the Detective Service. Crown 8vo, cloth, 3s. 6d.

Dowling (Richard).—Old Corcoran's Money. Crown 8vo, cl., 3s. 6d.

Doyle (A. Conan).—The Firm of Girdlestone. Cr. 8vo, cl., 3s. 6d.

Dramatists, The Old. Cr. 8vo, cl. ex., with Portraits, 3s. 6d. per Vol.
Ben Jonson's Works. With Notes, Critical and Explanatory, and a Biographical Memoir by WILLIAM GIFFORD. Edited by Colonel CUNNINGHAM. Three Vols.
Chapman's Works. Three Vols. Vol. I. contains the Plays complete; Vol. II., Poems and Minor Translations, with an Essay by A. C. SWINBURNE; Vol. III., Translations of the Iliad and Odyssey.
Marlowe's Works. Edited, with Notes, by Colonel CUNNINGHAM. One Vol.
Massinger's Plays. From GIFFORD'S Text. Edited by Colonel CUNNINGHAM. One Vol.

Duncan (Sara Jeannette: Mrs. EVERARD COTES), Works by.
Crown 8vo, cloth extra, 7s. 6d. each.
A Social Departure. With 111 Illustrations by F. H. TOWNSEND.
An American Girl in London. With 80 Illustrations by F. H. TOWNSEND.
The Simple Adventures of a Memsahib. With 37 Illustrations by F. H. TOWNSEND.
Crown 8vo, cloth extra, 3s. 6d. each.
A Daughter of To-Day. | **Vernon's Aunt.** With 47 Illustrations by HAL HURST.

Dutt (Romesh C.).—England and India: A Record of Progress during One Hundred Years. Crown 8vo, cloth, 2s.

Dyer (T. F. Thiselton).—The Folk-Lore of Plants. Cr. 8vo, cl., 6s.

Early English Poets. Edited, with Introductions and Annotations by Rev. A. B. GROSART, D.D. Crown 8vo, cloth boards, 3s. 6d. per Volume.
Fletcher's (Giles) Complete Poems. One Vol.
Davies' (Sir John) Complete Poetical Works. Two Vols.
Herrick's (Robert) Complete Collected Poems. Three Vols.
Sidney's (Sir Philip) Complete Poetical Works. Three Vols.

Edgcumbe (Sir E. R. Pearce).—Zephyrus: A Holiday in Brazil and on the River Plate. With 41 Illustrations Crown 8vo, cloth extra, 5s.

Edwardes (Mrs. Annie), Novels by. Post 8vo, illust. bds., 2s. each.
Archie Lovell. | **A Point of Honour.**
A Plaster Saint. Crown 8vo, cloth, 3s. 6d. [Shortly.

Edwards (Eliezer).—Words, Facts, and Phrases: A Dictionary of Curious, Quaint, and Out-of-the-Way Matters. Cheaper Edition. Crown 8vo, cloth, 3s. 6d.

Edwards (M. Betham-), Novels by.
Kitty. Post 8vo, boards, 2s.; cloth, 2s. 6d. | **Felicia.** Post 8vo, illustrated boards, 2s.

Egerton (Rev. J. C., M.A.).— Sussex Folk and Sussex Ways. With Introduction by Rev. Dr. H. WACE, and Four Illustrations. Crown 8vo, cloth extra, 5s.

Eggleston (Edward).--Roxy: A Novel. Post 8vo, illust. boards, 2s.

Englishman's House, The: A Practical Guide for Selecting or Building a House. By C. J. RICHARDSON. Coloured Frontispiece and 534 Illusts. Cr. 8vo, cloth, 7s. 6d.

Ewald (Alex. Charles, F.S.A.), Works by.
The Life and Times of Prince Charles Stuart, Count of Albany (THE YOUNG PRETENDER). With a Portrait. Crown 8vo, cloth extra, 7s. 6d.
Stories from the State Papers. With Autotype Frontispiece. Crown 8vo, cloth, 6s.

Eyes, Our: How to Preserve Them. By JOHN BROWNING. Cr. 8vo, 1s.

Familiar Short Sayings of Great Men. By SAMUEL ARTHUR BENT, A.M. Fifth Edition, Revised and Enlarged. Crown 8vo, cloth extra, 7s. 6d.

Faraday (Michael), Works by. Post 8vo, cloth extra, 4s. 6d. each.
The Chemical History of a Candle: Lectures delivered before a Juvenile Audience. Edited by WILLIAM CROOKES, F.C.S. With numerous Illustrations.
On the Various Forces of Nature, and their Relations to each other. Edited by WILLIAM CROOKES, F.C.S. With Illustrations.

Farrer (J. Anson), Works by.
Military Manners and Customs. Crown 8vo, cloth extra, 6s.
War: Three Essays, reprinted from 'Military Manners and Customs.' Crown 8vo, 1s.; cloth, 1s. 6d.

Fenn (G. Manville), Novels by.
Crown 8vo, cloth extra, 3s. 6d. each; post 8vo, illustrated boards, 2s. each.
The New Mistress. | **Witness to the Deed.** | **The Tiger Lily.** | **The White Virgin.**

A Woman Worth Winning. Crown 8vo, cloth, gilt top, 6s.
A Crimson Crime. Crown 8vo, cloth, gilt top, 6s. *[Preparing.*

In the press. NEW EDITIONS. Crown 8vo, cloth, 3s. 6d. each.

Commodore Junk.	**Eve at the Wheel; and The Chaplain's Craze.**
Black Blood.	
Double Cunning.	**The Man with a Shadow.**
A Bag of Diamonds; and The Dark House.	**One Maid's Mischief.**
	The Story of Antony Grace.
A Fluttered Dovecote.	**This Man's Wife.**
King of the Castle.	**In Jeopardy.**
The Master of the Ceremonies.	

Fin=Bec.—The Cupboard Papers: Observations on the Art of Living and Dining. Post 8vo, cloth limp, 2s. 6d.

Firework=Making, The Complete Art of; or, The Pyrotechnist's Treasury. By THOMAS KENTISH. With 267 Illustrations. Crown 8vo, cloth, 3s. 6d.

First Book, My. By WALTER BESANT, JAMES PAYN, W. CLARK RUSSELL, GRANT ALLEN, HALL CAINE, GEORGE R SIMS, RUDYARD KIPLING, A. CONAN DOYLE, M. E. BRADDON, F. W. ROBINSON, H. RIDER HAGGARD, R M. BALLANTYNE, I. ZANGWILL, MORLEY ROBERTS, D. CHRISTIE MURRAY, MARY CORELLI, J. K. JEROME, JOHN STRANGE WINTER, BRET HARTE, 'Q.,' ROBERT BUCHANAN, and R. L. STEVENSON. With a Prefatory Story by JEROME K. JEROME, and 185 Illustrations. A New Edition. Small demy 8vo, art linen, 3s. 6d.

Fitzgerald (Percy), Works by.
Little Essays: Passages from the Letters of CHARLES LAMB. Post 8vo, cloth, 2s. 6d.
Fatal Zero. Crown 8vo, cloth extra, 3s. 6d.; post 8vo, illustrated boards, 2s.

Post 8vo, illustrated boards, 2s. each.

Bella Donna.	**The Lady of Brantome.**	**The Second Mrs. Tillotson.**
Polly.	**Never Forgotten.**	**Seventy-five Brooke Street.**

Sir Henry Irving: Twenty Years at the Lyceum. With Portrait. Crown 8vo, 1s.; cloth, 1s. 6d.

Flammarion (Camille), Works by.
Popular Astronomy: A General Description of the Heavens. Translated by J. ELLARD GORE, F.R.A.S. With Three Plates and 288 Illustrations. Medium 8vo, cloth, 10s. 6d.
Urania: A Romance. With 87 Illustrations. Crown 8vo, cloth extra, 5s.

Fletcher's (Giles, B.D.) Complete Poems: Christ's Victorie in Heaven, Christ's Victorie on Earth, Christ's Triumph over Death, and Minor Poems. With Notes by Rev. A. B. GROSART, D.D. Crown 8vo, cloth boards, 3s. 6d.

Fonblanque (Albany).—Filthy Lucre. Post 8vo, illust. boards, 2s.

Forbes (Archibald).—The Life of Napoleon III. With Photogravure Frontispiece and Thirty-six full-page Illustrations. Demy 8vo, cloth, gilt top, 10s.

Fowler (J. Kersley).—Records of Old Times Historical, Social, Political, Sporting, and Agricultural. With Eight full-page Illustrations. Demy 8vo, cloth, 10s. 6d.

Francillon (R. E.), Novels by. Crown 8vo, cloth extra, 3s. 6d. each; post 8vo, illustrated boards, 2s. each.

One by One. | **A Real Queen.** | **A Dog and his Shadow.**
Ropes of Sand. Illustrated

Post 8vo, illustrated boards, 2s. each.

Queen Cophetua. | **Olympia.** | **Romances of the Law.** | **King or Knave?**
Jack Doyle's Daughter. Crown 8vo, cloth, 3s. 6d.

Frederic (Harold), Novels by. Post 8vo, cloth extra, 3s. 6d. each; illustrated boards 2s. each.
Seth's Brother's Wife. | **The Lawton Girl.**

French Literature, A History of. By HENRY VAN LAUN. Three Vols., demy 8vo, cloth boards, 7s. 6d. each.

Fry's (Herbert) Royal Guide to the London Charities. Edited by JOHN LANE. Published Annually. Crown 8vo, cloth, 1s. 6d.

Gardening Books. Post 8vo, 1s. each; cloth limp, 1s. 6d. each.
A Year's Work in Garden and Greenhouse. By GEORGE GLENNY.
Household Horticulture. By TOM and JANE JERROLD. Illustrated.
The Garden that Paid the Rent. By TOM JERROLD.

My Garden Wild. By FRANCIS G. HEATH. Crown 8vo, cloth, gilt edges, 6s.

Gardner (Mrs. Alan).—Rifle and Spear with the Rajpoots: Being the Narrative of a Winter's Travel and Sport in Northern India. With numerous Illustrations by the Author and F. H. TOWNSEND. Demy 4to, half-bound, 21s.

Garrett (Edward).—The Capel Girls: A Novel. Post 8vo, illustrated boards, 2s.

Gaulot (Paul).—The Red Shirts: A Story of the Revolution. Translated by JOHN DE VILLIERS. With a Frontispiece by STANLEY WOOD. Crown 8vo, cloth, 3s. 6d.

Gentleman's Magazine, The. 1s. Monthly. Contains Stories, Articles upon Literature, Science, Biography, and Art, and 'Table Talk' by SYLVANUS URBAN.
. *Bound Volumes for recent years kept in stock, 8s. 6d. each. Cases for binding, 2s. each.*

Gentleman's Annual, The. Published Annually in November. 1s.

German Popular Stories. Collected by the Brothers GRIMM and Translated by EDGAR TAYLOR. With Introduction by JOHN RUSKIN, and 22 Steel Plates after GEORGE CRUIKSHANK. Square 8vo, cloth, 6s. 6d.; gilt edges, 7s. 6d.

Gibbon (Chas.), Novels by. Cr. 8vo, cl., 3s. 6d. ea.; post 8vo, bds., 2s. ea.
Robin Gray. With Frontispiece. | **Loving a Dream.** | **The Braes of Yarrow.**
The Golden Shaft. With Frontispiece. | **Of High Degree.**

Post 8vo, illustrated boards, 2s. each.

The Flower of the Forest. | **In Love and War.**
The Dead Heart. | **A Heart's Problem.**
For Lack of Gold. | **By Mead and Stream.**
What Will the World Say? | **Fancy Free.**
For the King. | **A Hard Knot.** | **In Honour Bound.**
Queen of the Meadow. | **Heart's Delight.**
In Pastures Green. | **Blood Money.**

Gibney (Somerville). — Sentenced! Crown 8vo, cloth, 1s. 6d.

Gilbert (W. S.), Original Plays by. In Three Series, 2s. 6d. each.
The FIRST SERIES contains: The Wicked World—Pygmalion and Galatea—Charity—The Princess—The Palace of Truth—Trial by Jury.
The SECOND SERIES: Broken Hearts—Engaged—Sweethearts—Gretchen—Dan'l Druce—Tom Cobb—H.M.S. 'Pinafore'—The Sorcerer—The Pirates of Penzance.
The THIRD SERIES: Comedy and Tragedy—Foggerty's Fairy—Rosencrantz and Guildenstern—Patience—Princess Ida—The Mikado—Ruddigore—The Yeomen of the Guard—The Gondoliers—The Mountebanks—Utopia.

Eight Original Comic Operas written by W. S. GILBERT. In Two Series. Demy 8vo, cloth, 2s. 6d. each. The FIRST containing: The Sorcerer—H.M.S. 'Pinafore'—The Pirates of Penzance—Iolanthe—Patience—Princess Ida—The Mikado—Trial by Jury.
The SECOND SERIES containing: The Gondoliers—The Grand Duke—The Yeomen of the Guard—His Excellency—Utopia, Limited—Ruddigore—The Mountebanks—Haste to the Wedding.
The Gilbert and Sullivan Birthday Book: Quotations for Every Day in the Year, selected from Plays by W. S. GILBERT set to Music by Sir A. SULLIVAN. Compiled by ALEX. WATSON. Royal 16mo, Japanese leather, 2s. 6d.

Gilbert (William), Novels by. Post 8vo, illustrated bds., 2s. each.
Dr. Austin's Guests. | James Duke, Costermonger.
The Wizard of the Mountain.

Glanville (Ernest), Novels by.
Crown 8vo, cloth extra, 3s. 6d. each; post 8vo, illustrated boards, 2s. each.
The Lost Heiress: A Tale of Love, Battle, and Adventure. With Two Illustrations by H. NISBET.
The Fossicker: A Romance of Mashonaland. With Two Illustrations by HUME NISBET.
A Fair Colonist. With a Frontispiece by STANLEY WOOD.

The Golden Rock. With a Frontispiece by STANLEY WOOD. Crown 8vo, cloth extra, 3s. 6d.
Kloof Yarns. Crown 8vo, picture cover, 1s.; cloth, 1s. 6d.
Tales from the Veld. With Twelve Illustrations by M. NISBET. Crown 8vo, cloth, 3s. 6d.

Glenny (George).—A Year's Work in Garden and Greenhouse:
Practical Advice as to the Management of the Flower, Fruit, and Frame Garden. Post 8vo, 1s.; cloth, 1s. 6d.

Godwin (William).—Lives of the Necromancers. Post 8vo, cl., 2s.

Golden Treasury of Thought, The: An Encyclopædia of QUOTA-
TIONS. Edited by THEODORE TAYLOR. Crown 8vo, cloth gilt, 7s. 6d.

Gontaut, Memoirs of the Duchesse de (Gouvernante to the Chil-
dren of France), 1773-1836. With Two Photogravures. Two Vols., demy 8vo, cloth extra, 21s.

Goodman (E. J.).—The Fate of Herbert Wayne. Cr. 8vo, 3s. 6d.

Greeks and Romans, The Life of the, described from Antique
Monuments. By ERNST GUHL and W. KONER. Edited by Dr. F. HUEFFER. With 545 Illustrations. Large crown 8vo, cloth extra, 7s. 6d.

Greville (Henry), Novels by.
Post 8vo, illustrated boards, 2s. each.
Nikanor. Translated by ELIZA E. CHASE.
A Noble Woman. Translated by ALBERT D. VANDAM.

Grey (Sir George).—The Romance of a Proconsul: Being the
Personal Life and Memoirs of Sir GEORGE GREY, K.C.B. By JAMES MILNE. With Portrait. Crown
8vo, cloth, 5s.

Griffith (Cecil).—Corinthia Marazion: A Novel. Crown 8vo, cloth
extra, 3s. 6d.; post 8vo, illustrated boards, 2s.

Grundy (Sydney).—The Days of his Vanity: A Passage in the
Life of a Young Man. Crown 8vo, cloth extra, 3s. 6d.; post 8vo, illustrated boards, 2s.

Habberton (John, Author of ' Helen's Babies '), **Novels by.**
Post 8vo, illustrated boards, 2s. each; cloth limp, 2s. 6d. each.
Brueton's Bayou. | Country Luck.

Hair, The: Its Treatment in Health, Weakness, and Disease. Translated from the German of Dr. J. PINCUS. Crown 8vo, 1s.; cloth, 1s. 6d.

Hake (Dr. Thomas Gordon), Poems by. Cr. 8vo, cl. ex., 6s. each.
New Symbols. | Legends of the Morrow. | The Serpent Play.
Maiden Ecstasy. Small 4to, cloth extra, 8s.

Halifax (C.).—Dr. Rumsey's Patient. By Mrs. L. T. MEADE and
CLIFFORD HALIFAX, M.D. Crown 8vo, cloth, 2s. 6d.

Hall (Mrs. S. C.).—Sketches of Irish Character. With numerous
Illustrations on Steel and Wood by MACLISE, GILBERT, HARVEY, and GEORGE CRUIKSHANK.
Small demy 8vo, cloth extra, 7s. 6d.

Hall (Owen), Novels by.
The Track of a Storm. Cheaper Edition. Crown 8vo, cloth, 3s. 6d.
Jetsam. Crown 8vo, cloth, 3s. 6d.

Halliday (Andrew).—Every-day Papers. Post 8vo, boards, 2s.

Hamilton (Cosmo).—The Glamour of the Impossible: An Im-
probability. Crown 8vo, cloth gilt, 3s. 6d.

Handwriting, The Philosophy of. With over 100 Facsimiles and
Explanatory Text. By DON FELIX DE SALAMANCA. Post 8vo, cloth limp, 2s. 6d.

Hanky-Panky: Easy and Difficult Tricks, White Magic, Sleight of
Hand, &c. Edited by W. H. CREMER. With 200 Illustrations. Crown 8vo, cloth extra, 4s. 6d.

Hardy (Thomas).—Under the Greenwood Tree. Crown 8vo, cloth
extra, with Portrait and 15 Illustrations, 3s. 6d.; post 8vo, illustrated boards, 2s. cloth limp, 2s. 6d.

Harte's (Bret) Collected Works. Revised by the Author. LIBRARY EDITION, in Nine Volumes, crown 8vo, cloth extra, 6s. each.

Vol.   I. COMPLETE POETICAL AND DRAMATIC WORKS. With Steel-plate Portrait.
,,   II. THE LUCK OF ROARING CAMP—BOHEMIAN PAPERS—AMERICAN LEGEND
,,   III. TALES OF THE ARGONAUTS—EASTERN SKETCHES.
,,   IV. GABRIEL CONROY. | Vol. V. STORIES—CONDENSED NOVELS, &c.
,,   VI. TALES OF THE PACIFIC SLOPE.
,,   VII. TALES OF THE PACIFIC SLOPE—II. With Portrait by JOHN PETTIE, R.A.
,,   VIII. TALES OF THE PINE AND THE CYPRESS.
,,   IX. BUCKEYE AND CHAPPAREL.

Bret Harte's Choice Works, in Prose and Verse. With Portrait of the Author and 40 Illustrations. Crown 8vo, cloth, 3s. 6d.
Bret Harte's Poetical Works. Printed on hand-made paper. Crown 8vo, buckram, 4s. 6d.
Some Later Verses. Crown 8vo, linen gilt, 5s.
The Queen of the Pirate Isle. With 28 Original Drawings by KATE GREENAWAY, reproduced in Colours by EDMUND EVANS. Small 4to, cloth, 5s.

Crown 8vo, cloth extra, 3s. 6d. each ; post 8vo, picture boards, 2s. each.
A Waif of the Plains. With 60 Illustrations by STANLEY L. WOOD.
A Ward of the Golden Gate. With 59 Illustrations by STANLEY L. WOOD.

Crown 8vo, cloth extra, 3s. 6d. each.
A Sappho of Green Springs, &c. With Two Illustrations by HUME NISBET.
Colonel Starbottle's Client, and Some Other People. With a Frontispiece.
Susy: A Novel. With Frontispiece and Vignette by J. A. CHRISTIE.
Sally Dows, &c. With 47 Illustrations by W. D. ALMOND and others.
A Protegee of Jack Hamlin's, &c. With 26 Illustrations by W. SMALL and others.
The Bell-Ringer of Angel's, &c. With 39 Illustrations by DUDLEY HARDY and others.
Clarence: A Story of the American War. With Eight Illustrations by A. JULE GOODMAN.
Barker's Luck, &c. With 39 Illustrations by A. FORESTIER, PAUL HARDY, &c.
Devil's Ford, &c. With a Frontispiece by W. H. OVEREND.
The Crusade of the "Excelsior." With a Frontispiece by J. BERNARD PARTRIDGE.
Three Partners; or, The Big Strike on Heavy Tree Hill. With 8 Illustrations by J. GULICH.
Tales of Trail and Town. With Frontispiece by G. P. JACOMB-HOOD.

Post 8vo, illustrated boards, 2s. each.

Gabriel Conroy.	**The Luck of Roaring Camp, &c**
An Heiress of Red Dog, &c.	**Californian Stories.**

Post 8vo, illustrated boards, 2s. each ; cloth, 2s. 6d. each.

Flip.	**Maruja.**	**A Phyllis of the Sierras.**

Haweis (Mrs. H. R.), Books by.
The Art of Beauty. With Coloured Frontispiece and 91 Illustrations. Square 8vo, cloth bds., 6s.
The Art of Decoration. With Coloured Frontispiece and 74 Illustrations. Sq. 8vo, cloth bds., 6s.
The Art of Dress. With 32 Illustrations. Post 8vo, 1s. ; cloth, 1s. 6d.
Chaucer for Schools. With the Story of his Times and his Work. A New Edition, revised. With a Frontispiece. Demy 8vo, cloth, 2s. 6d.
Chaucer for Children. With 38 Illustrations (8 Coloured). Crown 4to, cloth extra, 3s. 6d.

Haweis (Rev. H. R., M.A.), Books by.
American Humorists: WASHINGTON IRVING, OLIVER WENDELL HOLMES, JAMES RUSSELL LOWELL, ARTEMUS WARD, MARK TWAIN, and BRET HARTE. Third Edition. Crown 8vo, cloth extra, 6s.
Travel and Talk, 1885-93-95: My Hundred Thousand Miles of Travel through America—Canada—New Zealand—Tasmania—Australia—Ceylon—The Paradises of the Pacific. With Photogravure Frontispieces. A New Edition. Two Vols., crown 8vo, cloth, 12s.

Hawthorne (Julian), Novels by.
Crown 8vo, cloth extra, 3s. 6d. each ; post 8vo, illustrated boards, 2s. each.

Garth.	**Ellice Quentin.**	**Beatrix Randolph.** With Four Illusts.
Sebastian Strome.		**David Poindexter's Disappearance.**
Fortune's Fool.	**Dust.** Four Illusts.	**The Spectre of the Camera.**

Post 8vo, illustrated boards, 2s. each.

Miss Cadogna.	**Love—or a Name.**

Helps (Sir Arthur), Books by. Post 8vo, cloth limp, 2s. 6d. each.

Animals and their Masters.	**Social Pressure.**

Ivan de Biron: A Novel. Crown 8vo, cloth extra, 3s. 6d. ; post 8vo, illustrated boards, 2s.

Henderson (Isaac).—Agatha Page: A Novel. Cr. 8vo, cl., 3s. 6d.

Henty (G. A.), Novels by.
Rujub, the Juggler. With Eight Illustrations by STANLEY L. WOOD, PRESENTATION EDITION, small demy 8vo, cloth, gilt edges, 5s. ; cr. 8vo, cloth, 3s. 6d. ; post 8vo, illust. boards, 2s.

Crown 8vo, cloth, 3s. 6d. each.

The Queen's Cup.	**Dorothy's Double.**

Colonel Thorndyke's Secret. Crown 8vo, cloth, gilt top, 6s. ; PRESENTATION EDITION, with a Frontispiece by STANLEY WOOD, small demy 8vo, cloth, gilt edges, 5s.

Herman (Henry).—A Leading Lady. Post 8vo, bds., 2s. ; cl., 2s. 6d.

Herrick's (Robert) Hesperides, Noble Numbers, and Complete
Collected Poems. With Memorial-Introduction and Notes by the Rev. A. B. GROSART, D.D., Steel Portrait, &c. Three Vols., crown 8vo, cloth boards, 3s. 6d. each.

Hertzka (Dr. Theodor).—Freeland: A Social Anticipation. Translated by ARTHUR RANSOM. Crown 8vo, cloth extra, 6s.

Hesse-Wartegg (Chevalier Ernst von).— Tunis: The Land and the People. With 22 Illustrations. Crown 8vo, cloth extra, 3s. 6d.

Hill (Headon).—Zambra the Detective. Crown 8vo, cloth, 3s. 6d. ; post 8vo, picture boards, 2s. : cloth, 2s. 6d.

Hill (John), Works by.
Treason-Felony. Post 8vo, boards, 2s. | The Common Ancestor. Cr. 8vo, cloth, 3s. 6d.

Hoey (Mrs. Cashel).—The Lover's Creed. Post 8vo, boards, 2s.

Holiday, Where to go for a. By E. P. SHOLL, Sir H. MAXWELL, Bart., M.P., JOHN WATSON, JANE BARLOW, MARY LOVETT CAMERON, JUSTIN H. McCARTHY, PAUL LANGE, J. W. GRAHAM, J. H. SALTER, PHŒBE ALLEN, S. J. BECKETT, L. RIVERS VINE, and C. F. GORDON CUMMING. Crown 8vo, 1s. : cloth, 1s. 6d.

Hollingshead (John).—Niagara Spray. Crown 8vo, 1s.

Holmes (Gordon, M.D.)—The Science of Voice Production and Voice Preservation. Crown 8vo, 1s. : cloth, 1s. 6d.

Holmes (Oliver Wendell), Works by.
The Autocrat of the Breakfast-Table. Illustrated by J. GORDON THOMSON. Post 8vo, cloth limp, 2s. 6d.— Another Edition, post 8vo, cloth, 2s.
The Autocrat of the Breakfast-Table and The Professor at the Breakfast-Table. In One Vol. Post 8vo, half-bound, 2s.

Hood's (Thomas) Choice Works in Prose and Verse. With Life of the Author, Portrait, and 200 Illustrations. Crown 8vo, cloth, 3s. 6d.
Hood's Whims and Oddities. With 85 Illustrations. Post 8vo, half-bound, 2s.

Hood (Tom).—From Nowhere to the North Pole: A Noah's Arkæological Narrative. With 25 Illustrations by W. BRUNTON and E. C. BARNES. Cr. 8vo, cloth, 6s.

Hook's (Theodore) Choice Humorous Works; including his Ludicrous Adventures, Bons Mots, Puns, and Hoaxes. With Life of the Author, Portraits, Facsimiles and Illustrations. Crown 8vo, cloth extra, 7s. 6d.

Hooper (Mrs. Geo.).—The House of Raby. Post 8vo, boards, 2s.

Hopkins (Tighe), Novels by.
Nell Haffenden. With 8 Illustrations by C. GREGORY. Crown 8vo, cloth, 6s.

Crown 8vo. cloth, 3s. 6d. each.
'Twixt Love and Duty. With a Frontispiece. | For Freedom.
The Nugents of Carriconna. | The Incomplete Adventurer.

Horne (R. Hengist). — Orion: An Epic Poem. With Photograph Portrait by SUMMERS. Tenth Edition. Crown 8vo, cloth extra, 7s.

Hungerford (Mrs., Author of ' Molly Bawn '), Novels by.
Post 8vo, illustrated boards, 2s. each : cloth limp, 2s. 6d. each.
A Maiden All Forlorn. | A Modern Circe. | An Unsatisfactory Lover.
Marvel. | A Mental Struggle. | Lady Patty.
In Durance Vile. |

Crown 8vo, cloth extra, 3s. 6d. each ; post 8vo, illustrated boards, 2s. each ; cloth limp, 2s. 6d. each.
April's Lady. | The Three Graces.
Peter's Wife. | The Professor's Experiment.
Lady Verner's Flight. | Nora Crelna.
The Red-House Mystery. |

Crown 8vo, cloth extra, 3s. 6d. each.
An Anxious Moment. | A Point of Conscience.
The Coming of Chloe. | Lovice.

Hunt's (Leigh) Essays: A Tale for a Chimney Corner, &c. Edited by EDMUND OLLIER. Post 8vo, half-bound, 2s.

Hunt (Mrs. Alfred), Novels by.
Crown 8vo, cloth extra, 3s. 6d. each ; post 8vo, illustrated boards, 2s. each.
The Leaden Casket. | Self-Condemned. | That Other Person.
Thornicroft's Model. Post 8vo, boards, 2s. | Mrs. Juliet. Crown 8vo, cloth extra, 3s. 6d.

Hutchison (W. M.).—Hints on Colt-breaking. With 25 Illustrations. Crown 8vo, cloth extra, 2s. 6d.

Hydrophobia: An Account of M. PASTEUR'S System ; The Technique of his Method, and Statistics. By RENAUD SUZOR. M.B. Crown 8vo, cloth extra, 6s.

Hyne (C. J. Cutcliffe).—Honour of Thieves. Cr. 8vo, cloth, 3s. 6d.

Impressions (The) of Aureole. Cheaper Edition, with a New Preface. Post 8vo, blush-rose paper and cloth. 2s. 6d.

Indoor Paupers. By ONE OF THEM. Crown 8vo, 1s. ; cloth, 1s. 6d.

Innkeeper's Handbook (The) and Licensed Victualler's Manual. By J. TREVOR-DAVIES. A New Edition. Crown 8vo, cloth, 2s. [Shortly.

Irish Wit and Humour, Songs of. Collected and Edited by A. PERCEVAL GRAVES. Post 8vo, cloth limp, 2s. 6d.

Irving (Sir Henry): A Record of over Twenty Years at the Lyceum. By PERCY FITZGERALD. With Portrait. Crown 8vo, 1s. ; cloth, 1s. 6d.

James (C. T. C.).—A Romance of the Queen's Hounds. Post 8vo, cloth limp, 1s. 6d.

Jameson (William).—My Dead Self. Post 8vo, bds., 2s. ; cl , 2s. 6d.

Japp (Alex. H., LL.D.).—Dramatic Pictures, &c. Cr. 8vo, cloth, 5s.

Jay (Harriett), Novels by. Post 8vo, illustrated boards. 2s. each.
The Dark Colleen. | The Queen of Connaught.

Jefferies (Richard), Books by. Post 8vo, cloth limp, 2s 6d. each.
Nature near London. | The Life of the Fields. | The Open Air.
₊ Also the HAND-MADE PAPER EDITION, crown 8vo, buckram, gilt top, 6s. each.

The Eulogy of Richard Jefferies. By Sir WALTER BESANT. With a Photograph Portrait. Crown 8vo, cloth extra, 6s.

Jennings (Henry J.), Works by.
Curiosities of Criticism. Post 8vo, cloth limp, 2s. 6d.
Lord Tennyson: A Biographical Sketch. With Portrait. Post 8vo, 1s. ; cloth, 1s. 6d.

Jerome (Jerome K.), Books by.
Stageland. With 64 Illustrations by J. BERNARD PARTRIDGE. Fcap. 4to, picture cover, 1s.
John Ingerfield, &c. With 9 Illusts. by A. S. BOYD and JOHN GULICH. Fcap. 8vo, pic. cov. 1s. 6d.
The Prude's Progress: A Comedy by J. K. JEROME and EDEN PHILLPOTTS. Cr. 8vo, 1s. 6d

Jerrold (Douglas).—The Barber's Chair; and The Hedgehog Letters. Post 8vo, printed on laid paper and half-bound, 2s.

Jerrold (Tom), Works by. Post 8vo, 1s. ea. ; cloth limp, 1s. 6d. each.
The Garden that Paid the Rent.
Household Horticulture: A Gossip about Flowers. Illustrated.

Jesse (Edward).—Scenes and Occupations of a Country Life. Post 8vo, cloth limp, 2s.

Jones (William, F.S.A.), Works by. Cr. 8vo, cl. extra, 3s. 6d. each.
Finger-Ring Lore: Historical, Legendary, and Anecdotal. With Hundreds of Illustrations.
Credulities, Past and Present. Including the Sea and Seamen, Miners, Talismans, Word and Letter Divination, Exorcising and Blessing of Animals, Birds, Eggs, Luck, &c. With Frontispiece.
Crowns and Coronations: A History of Regalia. With 91 Illustrations.

Jonson's (Ben) Works. With Notes Critical and Explanatory, and a Biographical Memoir by WILLIAM GIFFORD. Edited by Colonel CUNNINGHAM. Three Vols, crown 8vo, cloth extra, 3s. 6d. each.

Josephus, The Complete Works of. Translated by WHISTON. Containing 'The Antiquities of the Jews' and 'The Wars of the Jews.' With 52 Illustrations and Maps. Two Vols., demy 8vo, half-bound, 12s. 6d.

Kempt (Robert).—Pencil and Palette: Chapters on Art and Artists. Post 8vo, cloth limp, 2s. 6d.

Kershaw (Mark). — Colonial Facts and Fictions: Humorous Sketches. Post 8vo, illustrated boards, 2s. ; cloth, 2s. 6d.

King (R. Ashe), Novels by.
Post 8vo, illustrated boards, 2s. each.
'The Wearing of the Green.' | Passion's Slave. | Bell Barry.

A Drawn Game. Crown 8vo, cloth, 3s. 6d. ; post 8vo, illustrated boards, 2s.

Knight (William, M.R.C.S., and Edward, L.R.C.P.). — The Patient's Vade Mecum: How to Get Most Benefit from Medical Advice. Cr. 8vo, 1s.; cl., 1s. 6d.

Knights (The) of the Lion: A Romance of the Thirteenth Century. Edited, with an Introduction, by the MARQUESS OF LORNE, K.T. Crown 8vo, cloth extra, 6s.

Lamb's (Charles) Complete Works in Prose and Verse, including 'Poetry for Children' and 'Prince Dorus.' Edited, with Notes and Introduction, by R. H. SHEPHERD. With Two Portraits and Facsimile of the 'Essay on Roast Pig.' Crown 8vo, cloth, 3s. 6d.
The Essays of Elia. Post 8vo, printed on laid paper and half-bound, 2s.
Little Essays: Sketches and Characters by CHARLES LAMB, selected from his Letters by PERCY FITZGERALD. Post 8vo, cloth limp, 2s. 6d.
The Dramatic Essays of Charles Lamb. With Introduction and Notes by BRANDER MATTHEWS, and Steel-plate Portrait. Fcap. 8vo, half-bound, 2s. 6d.

Lambert (George). — The President of Boravia. Crown 8vo, cl., 3s. 6d.

Landor (Walter Savage). — Citation and Examination of William Shakspeare, &c., before Sir Thomas Lucy, touching Deer-stealing, 19th September, 1582. To which is added, **A Conference of Master Edmund Spenser** with the Earl of Essex, touching the State of Ireland, 1595. Fcap. 8vo, half-Roxburghe, 2s. 6d.

Lane (Edward William). — The Thousand and One Nights, commonly called in England **The Arabian Nights' Entertainments.** Translated from the Arabic, with Notes. Illustrated with many hundred Engravings from Designs by HARVEY. Edited by EDWARD STANLEY POOLE. With Preface by STANLEY LANE-POOLE. Three Vols., demy 8vo, cloth, 7s. 6d. ea.

Larwood (Jacob), Works by.
Anecdotes of the Clergy. Post 8vo, laid paper, half-bound, 2s.

Post 8vo, cloth limp, 2s. 6d. each.

| Forensic Anecdotes. | Theatrical Anecdotes. |

Lehmann (R. C.), Works by. Post 8vo, 1s. each; cloth, 1s. 6d. each.
Harry Fludyer at Cambridge.
Conversational Hints for Young Shooters: A Guide to Polite Talk.

Leigh (Henry S.). — Carols of Cockayne. Printed on hand-made paper, bound in buckram, 5s.

Leland (C. Godfrey). — A Manual of Mending and Repairing. With Diagrams. Crown 8vo, cloth, 5s.

Lepelletier (Edmond). — Madame Sans-Gène. Translated from the French by JOHN DE VILLIERS. Crown 8vo, cloth, 3s. 6d.; post 8vo, picture boards, 2s.

Leys (John). — The Lindsays: A Romance. Post 8vo, illust. bds., 2s.

Lilburn (Adam). — A Tragedy in Marble. Crown 8vo, cloth, 3s. 6d.

Lindsay (Harry, Author of 'Methodist Idylls'), Novels by.
Rhoda Roberts. Crown 8vo, cloth, 3s. 6d.
The Jacobite: A Romance of the Conspiracy of 'The Forty.' Crown 8vo, cloth, gilt top, 6s.

Linton (E. Lynn), Works by.

Crown 8vo, cloth extra, 3s. 6d. each; post 8vo, illustrated boards, 2s. each.

Patricia Kemball. Iono.	Under which Lord? With 12 Illustrations.
The Atonement of Leam Dundas.	'My Love!' Sowing the Wind.
The World Well Lost. With 12 Illusts.	Paston Carew, Millionaire and Miser.
The One Too Many.	Dulcie Everton. With a Silken Thread.

Post 8vo, cloth limp, 2s. 6d. each.

| Witch Stories. | Ourselves: Essays on Women. |

Freeshooting: Extracts from the Works of Mrs. LYNN LINTON.
The Rebel of the Family. Post 8vo, illustrated boards, 2s.

Lucy (Henry W.). — Gideon Fleyce: A Novel. Crown 8vo, cloth extra, 3s. 6d.; post 8vo, illustrated boards, 2s.

Macalpine (Avery), Novels by.
Teresa Itasca. Crown 8vo, cloth extra, 1s.
Broken Wings. With Six Illustrations by W. J. HENNESSY. Crown 8vo, cloth extra, 6s.

MacColl (Hugh), Novels by.
Mr. Stranger's Sealed Packet. Post 8vo, illustrated boards, 2s.
Ednor Whitlock. Crown 8vo, cloth extra, 6s.

Macdonell (Agnes). — Quaker Cousins. Post 8vo, boards, 2s.

MacGregor (Robert). — Pastimes and Players: Notes on Popular Games. Post 8vo, cloth limp, 2s. 6d.

Mackay (Charles, LL.D.). — Interludes and Undertones; or, Music at Twilight. Crown 8vo, cloth extra, 6s.

McCarthy (Justin, M.P.), Works by.

A History of Our Own Times, from the Accession of Queen Victoria to the General Election of 1880. LIBRARY EDITION. Four Vols., demy 8vo, cloth extra, 12s. each.—Also a POPULAR EDITION, in Four Vols., crown 8vo, cloth extra, 6s. each.—And the JUBILEE EDITION, with an Appendix of Events to the end of 1886, in Two Vols., large crown 8vo, cloth extra, 7s. 6d. each.

A History of Our Own Times, from 1880 to the Diamond Jubilee. Demy 8vo, cloth extra, 12s. Uniform with the LIBRARY EDITION of the first Four Volumes.

A Short History of Our Own Times. One Vol., crown 8vo, cloth extra, 6s.—Also a CHEAP POPULAR EDITION, post 8vo, cloth limp, 2s. 6d.

A History of the Four Georges. Four Vols., demy 8vo, cl. ex., 12s. each. [Vols. I. & II. ready.

Reminiscences. Two Vols., demy 8vo, cloth, 24s. [Shortly.

Crown 8vo, cloth extra, 3s. 6d. each; post 8vo, illustrated boards, 2s. each; cloth limp, 2s. 6d. each.

The Waterdale Neighbours.	**Donna Quixote.** With 12 Illustrations.
My Enemy's Daughter.	**The Comet of a Season.**
A Fair Saxon.	**Maid of Athens.** With 12 Illustrations.
Linley Rochford.	**Camiola:** A Girl with a Fortune.
Dear Lady Disdain.	**The Dictator.**
Miss Misanthrope. With 12 Illustrations.	**Red Diamonds.** **The Riddle Ring.**

The Three Disgraces, and other Stories. Crown 8vo, cloth, 3s. 6d.

'The Right Honourable.' By JUSTIN McCARTHY, M.P., and Mrs. CAMPBELL PRAED. Crown 8vo, cloth extra, 6s.

McCarthy (Justin Huntly), Works by.

The French Revolution. (Constituent Assembly, 1789-91.) Four Vols., demy 8vo, cloth, 12s. each.

An Outline of the History of Ireland. Crown 8vo, 1s.: cloth, 1s. 6d.

Ireland Since the Union: Sketches of Irish History, 1798-1886. Crown 8vo, cloth, 6s.

Hafiz in London: Poems. Small 8vo, gold cloth, 3s. 6d.

Our Sensation Novel. Crown 8vo, picture cover, 1s.; cloth limp, 1s. 6d.

Doom: An Atlantic Episode. Crown 8vo, picture cover, 1s.

Dolly: A Sketch. Crown 8vo, picture cover, 1s.; cloth limp, 1s. 6d.

Lily Lass: A Romance. Crown 8vo, picture cover, 1s.; cloth limp, 1s. 6d.

The Thousand and One Days. With Two Photogravures. Two Vols., crown 8vo, half-bd., 12s.

A London Legend. Crown 8vo, cloth, 3s. 6d.

The Royal Christopher. Crown 8vo, cloth, 3s. 6d.

MacDonald (George, LL.D.), Books by.

Works of Fancy and Imagination. Ten Vols., 16mo, cloth, gilt edges, in cloth case, 21s.; or the Volumes may be had separately, in Grolier cloth, at 2s. 6d. each.

Vol. I. WITHIN AND WITHOUT.—THE HIDDEN LIFE.

" II. THE DISCIPLE.—THE GOSPEL WOMEN.—BOOK OF SONNETS.—ORGAN SONGS.

" III. VIOLIN SONGS.—SONGS OF THE DAYS AND NIGHTS.—A BOOK OF DREAMS.—ROADSIDE POEMS.—POEMS FOR CHILDREN.

" IV. PARABLES.—BALLADS.—SCOTCH SONGS.

" V. & VI. PHANTASTES: A Faerie Romance. | Vol. VII. THE PORTENT.

" VIII. THE LIGHT PRINCESS.—THE GIANT'S HEART.—SHADOWS.

" IX. CROSS PURPOSES.—THE GOLDEN KEY.—THE CARASOYN.—LITTLE DAYLIGHT.

" X. THE CRUEL PAINTER.—THE WOW O' RIVVEN.—THE CASTLE.—THE BROKEN SWORDS. —THE GRAY WOLF.—UNCLE CORNELIUS.

Poetical Works of George MacDonald. Collected and Arranged by the Author. Two Vols., crown 8vo, buckram, 12s.

A Threefold Cord. Edited by GEORGE MACDONALD. Post 8vo, cloth, 5s.

Phantastes: A Faerie Romance. With 25 Illustrations by J. BELL. Crown 8vo, cloth extra, 3s. 6d.

Heather and Snow: A Novel. Crown 8vo, cloth extra, 3s. 6d.; post 8vo, illustrated boards, 2s.

Lilith: A Romance. SECOND EDITION. Crown 8vo, cloth extra, 6s.

Maclise Portrait Gallery (The) of Illustrious Literary Charac-

ters: 85 Portraits by DANIEL MACLISE; with Memoirs—Biographical, Critical, Bibliographical, and Anecdotal—illustrative of the Literature of the former half of the Present Century, by WILLIAM BATES, B.A. Crown 8vo, cloth extra, 3s. 6d.

Macquoid (Mrs.), Works by. Square 8vo, cloth extra, 6s. each.

In the Ardennes. With 50 Illustrations by THOMAS R. MACQUOID.

Pictures and Legends from Normandy and Brittany. 34 Illusts. by T. R. MACQUOID.

Through Normandy. With 92 Illustrations by T. R. MACQUOID, and a Map.

Through Brittany. With 35 Illustrations by T. R. MACQUOID, and a Map.

About Yorkshire. With 67 Illustrations by T. R. MACQUOID.

Post 8vo, illustrated boards, 2s. each.

The Evil Eye, and other Stories.	**Lost Rose,** and other Stories.

Magician's Own Book, The: Performances with Eggs, Hats, &c.

Edited by W. H. CREMER. With 200 Illustrations. Crown 8vo, cloth extra, 4s. 6d.

Magic Lantern, The, and its Management: Including full Practical

Directions. By T. C. HEPWORTH. With 10 Illustrations. Crown 8vo, 1s.; cloth, 1s. 6d.

Magna Charta: An Exact Facsimile of the Original in the British

Museum, 3 feet by 2 feet, with Arms and Seals emblazoned in Gold and Colours, 5s.

Mallory (Sir Thomas). — Mort d'Arthur: The Stories of King

Arthur and of the Knights of the Round Table. (A Selection.) Edited by B. MONTGOMERIE RAN-KING. Post 8vo, cloth limp, 2s.

Mallock (W. H.), Works by.
The New Republic. Post 8vo, picture cover, 2s. ; cloth limp, 2s. 6d.
The New Paul & Virginia : Positivism on an Island. Post 8vo, cloth, 2s. 6d.
A Romance of the Nineteenth Century. Crown 8vo, cloth 6s. ; post 8vo, illust. boards, 2s.

Poems. Small 4to, parchment, 8s.
Is Life Worth Living? Crown 8vo, cloth extra, 6s.

Margueritte (Paul and Victor).—The Disaster. Translated by
FREDERIC LEES. Crown 8vo, cloth, 3s. 6d.

Marlowe's Works. Including his Translations. Edited, with Notes
and Introductions, by Colonel CUNNINGHAM. Crown 8vo, cloth extra, 3s. 6d.

Massinger's Plays. From the Text of WILLIAM GIFFORD. Edited
by Col. CUNNINGHAM. Crown 8vo, cloth extra, 3s. 6d.

Masterman (J.).—Half-a-Dozen Daughters. Post 8vo, boards, 2s.

Mathams (Rev. Walter, F.R.G.S.).—Comrades All. Fcp. 8vo, cloth
limp, 1s. ; cloth gilt, 2s.

Matthews (Brander).—A Secret of the Sea, &c. Post 8vo, illus-
trated boards, 2s. ; cloth limp, 2s. 6d.

Meade (L. T.), Novels by.
A Soldier of Fortune. Crown 8vo, cloth, 3s. 6d. ; post 8vo, illustrated boards, 2s.

Crown 8vo, cloth, 3s. 6d. each.
The Voice of the Charmer. With 8 Illustrations.
In an Iron Grip.
Dr. Rumsey's Patient. By L. T. MEADE and CLIFFORD HALIFAX, M.D.

On the Brink of a Chasm. Crown 8vo, cloth, gilt top, 6s.

Merrick (Leonard), Novels by.
The Man who was Good. Post 8vo, picture boards, 2s.

Crown 8vo, cloth, 3s. 6d. each.
This Stage of Fools. | Cynthia : A Daughter of the Philistines.

Mexican Mustang (On a), through Texas to the Rio Grande. By
A. E. SWEET and J. ARMOY KNOX. With 265 Illustrations. Crown 8vo, cloth extra, 7s. 6d.

Middlemass (Jean), Novels by. Post 8vo, illust. boards, 2s. each.
Touch and Go. | Mr. Dorillion.

Miller (Mrs. F. Fenwick).—Physiology for the Young; or, The
House of Life. With numerous Illustrations. Post 8vo, cloth limp, 2s. 6d.

Milton (J. L.), Works by. Post 8vo, 1s. each ; cloth, 1s. 6d. each
The Hygiene of the Skin. With Directions for Diet, Soaps, Baths, Wines, &c.
The Bath in Diseases of the Skin.
The Laws of Life, and their Relation to Diseases of the Skin.

Minto (Wm.).—Was She Good or Bad? Cr. 8vo, 1s ; cloth, 1s. 6d.

Mitford (Bertram), Novels by. Crown 8vo, cloth extra, 3s. 6d. each.
The Gun-Runner: A Romance of Zululand. With a Frontispiece by STANLEY L. WOOD.
The Luck of Gerard Ridgeley. With a Frontispiece by STANLEY L. WOOD.
The King's Assegai. With Six full-page Illustrations by STANLEY L. WOOD.
Renshaw Fanning's Quest. With a Frontispiece by STANLEY L. WOOD.

Molesworth (Mrs.).—Hathercourt Rectory. Post 8vo, illustrated
boards, 2s.

Moncrieff (W. D. Scott-).—The Abdication: An Historical Drama.
With Seven Etchings by JOHN PETTIE, W. Q. ORCHARDSON, J. MACWHIRTER, COLIN HUNTER,
R. MACBETH and TOM GRAHAM. Imperial 4to, buckram, 21s.

Moore (Thomas), Works by.
The Epicurean ; and Alciphron. Post 8vo, half-bound, 2s.
Prose and Verse ; including Suppressed Passages from the MEMOIRS OF LORD BYRON. Edited
by R. H. SHEPHERD. With Portrait. Crown 8vo, cloth extra, 7s. 6d.

Muddock (J. E.) Stories by.
Crown 8vo, cloth extra, 3s. 6d. each.
Maid Marian and Robin Hood. With 12 Illustrations by STANLEY WOOD.
Basile the Jester. With Frontispiece by STANLEY WOOD.
Young Lochinvar.
Post 8vo, illustrated boards, 2s. each.
The Dead Man's Secret. | From the Bosom of the Deep.
Stories Weird and Wonderful. Post 8vo, illustrated boards, 2s. ; cloth, 2s. 6d.

Murray (D. Christie), Novels by.

Crown 8vo, cloth extra, 3s. 6d. each ; post 8vo, illustrated boards, 2s. each.

A Life's Atonement.	A Model Father.	Bob Martin's Little Girl.
Joseph's Coat. 12 Illusts.	Old Blazer's Hero.	Time's Revenges.
Coals of Fire. 3 Illusts.	Cynic Fortune. Frontisp.	A Wasted Crime.
Val Strange.	By the Gate of the Sea.	In Direst Peril.
Hearts.	A Bit of Human Nature.	Mount Despair.
The Way of the World.	First Person Singular.	A Capful o' Nails.

The Making of a Novelist: An Experiment in Autobiography. With a Collotype Portrait. Cr. 8vo, buckram, 3s. 6d.

My Contemporaries in Fiction. Crown 8vo, buckram, 3s. 6d.

Crown 8vo, cloth, 3s. 6d. each.

This Little World.
Tales in Prose and Verse. With Frontispiece by ARTHUR HOPKINS.
A Race for Millions.

Murray (D. Christie) and Henry Herman, Novels by.

Crown 8vo, cloth extra, 3s. 6d. each ; post 8vo, illustrated boards, 2s. each.

One Traveller Returns. | The Bishops' Bible.
Paul Jones's Alias, &c. With Illustrations by A. FORESTIER and G. NICOLET.

Murray (Henry), Novels by.

Post 8vo, illustrated boards, 2s. each ; cloth, 2s. 6d. each.

A Game of Bluff. | A Song of Sixpence.

Newbolt (Henry).—Taken from the Enemy. Fcp. 8vo, cloth, 1s. 6d.; leatherette, 1s.

Nisbet (Hume), Books by.

'Bail Up.' Crown 8vo, cloth extra, 3s. 6d.; post 8vo, illustrated boards, 2s.
Dr. Bernard St. Vincent. Post 8vo, illustrated boards, 2s.
Lessons in Art. With 21 Illustrations. Crown 8vo, cloth extra, 2s. 6d.

Norris (W. E.), Novels by. Crown 8vo, cloth, 3s. 6d. each ; post 8vo, picture boards, 2s. each.

Saint Ann's.
Billy Bellew. With a Frontispiece by F. H. TOWNSEND.
Miss Wentworth's Idea. Crown 8vo, cloth, 3s. 6d.

O'Hanlon (Alice), Novels by. Post 8vo, illustrated boards, 2s. each.

The Unforeseen. | Chance? or Fate?

Ohnet (Georges), Novels by. Post 8vo, illustrated boards, 2s. each.

Doctor Rameau. | A Last Love.
A Weird Gift. Crown 8vo, cloth, 3s. 6d.; post 8vo, picture boards, 2s.

Oliphant (Mrs.), Novels by. Post 8vo, illustrated boards, 2s. each.

The Primrose Path. | Whiteladies.
The Greatest Heiress in England.
The Sorceress. Crown 8vo, cloth, 3s. 6d.; post 8vo, picture boards, 2s.

O'Reilly (Mrs.).—Phœbe's Fortunes. Post 8vo, illust. boards, 2s.

O'Shaughnessy (Arthur), Poems by:

Fcap. 8vo, cloth extra, 7s. 6d. each.

Music and Moonlight. | Songs of a Worker.
Lays of France. Crown 8vo, cloth extra, 10s. 6d.

Ouida, Novels by. Cr. 8vo, cl., 3s. 6d. ea.; post 8vo, illust. bds., 2s. ea.

Held in Bondage.	A Dog of Flanders.	In Maremma.	Wanda.
Tricotrin.	Pascarel.	Signa.	Bimbi.	Syrlin.
Strathmore.	Chandos.	Two Wooden Shoes.	Frescoes.	Othmar.
Cecil Castlemaine's Gage	In a Winter City.	Princess Napraxine.
Under Two Flags.	Ariadne.	Friendship.	Guilderoy.	Ruffino.
Puck.	Idalia.	A Village Commune.	Two Offenders.
Folle-Farine.	Moths.	Pipistrello.	Santa Barbara.

POPULAR EDITIONS, Medium 8vo, 6d. each ; cloth, 1s. each.

Under Two Flags. | Moths.
Under Two Flags and Moths, POPULAR EDITIONS, in One Volume, medium 8vo, cloth, 2s.
Wisdom, Wit, and Pathos, selected from the Works of OUIDA by F. SYDNEY MORRIS. Post 8vo, cloth extra, 5s.—CHEAP EDITION, illustrated boards, 2s.

Page (H. A.).—Thoreau: His Life and Aims. With Portrait. Post 8vo, cloth, 2s. 6d.

Pandurang Hari; or, Memoirs of a Hindoo. With Preface by Sir BARTLE FRERE. Post 8vo, illustrated boards, 2s.

Parker (Rev. Joseph, D.D.).—Might Have Been: some Life Notes. Crown 8vo, cloth, 6s.

Pascal's Provincial Letters. A New Translation, with Historical Introduction and Notes by T. M'CRIE, D.D. Post 8vo, half-cloth, 2s.

Paul (Margaret A.).—Gentle and Simple. Crown 8vo, cloth, with Frontispiece by HELEN PATERSON, 3s. 6d.; post 8vo, illustrated boards, 2s.

Payn (James), Novels by.

Crown 8vo, cloth extra, 3s. 6d. each; post 8vo, illustrated boards, 2s. each.

Lost Sir Massingberd.
Walter's Word. | A County Family.
Less Black than We're Painted.
By Proxy. | For Cash Only.
High Spirits.
Under One Roof.
A Confidential Agent. With 12 Illusts.
A Grape from a Thorn. With 12 Illusts.

Holiday Tasks.
The Canon's Ward. With Portrait.
The Talk of the Town. With 12 Illusts.
Glow-Worm Tales.
The Mystery of Mirbridge.
The Word and the Will.
The Burnt Million.
Sunny Stories. | A Trying Patient.

Post 8vo, illustrated boards, 2s. each.

Humorous Stories. | From Exile.
The Foster Brothers.
The Family Scapegrace.
Married Beneath Him.
Bentinck's Tutor.
A Perfect Treasure.
Like Father, Like Son.
A Woman's Vengeance.
Carlyon's Year. | Cecil's Tryst.
Murphy's Master. | At Her Mercy.

The Clyffards of Clyffe.
Found Dead. | Gwendoline's Harvest.
Mirk Abbey. | A Marine Residence.
Some Private Views.
Not Wooed, But Won.
Two Hundred Pounds Reward.
The Best of Husbands.
Halves. | What He Cost Her.
Fallen Fortunes. | Kit: A Memory.
A Prince of the Blood.

A Modern Dick Whittington; or, A Patron of Letters. With a Portrait of the Author. Crown 8vo, cloth, 3s. 6d.
In Peril and Privation. With 17 Illustrations. Crown 8vo, cloth, 3s. 6d.
Notes from the 'News.' Crown 8vo, portrait cover, 1s.; cloth, 1s. 6d.
By Proxy. POPULAR EDITION, medium 8vo, 6d.; cloth, 1s.

Payne (Will).—Jerry the Dreamer. Crown 8vo, cloth, 3s. 6d.

Pennell (H. Cholmondeley), Works by. Post 8vo, cloth, 2s. 6d. ea.

Puck on Pegasus. With Illustrations.
Pegasus Re-Saddled. With Ten full-page Illustrations by G. DU MAURIER.
The Muses of Mayfair: Vers de Société. Selected by H. C. PENNELL.

Phelps (E. Stuart), Works by. Post 8vo, 1s. ea.; cloth, 1s. 6d. ea.

Beyond the Gates. | An Old Maid's Paradise. | Burglars in Paradise.
Jack the Fisherman. Illustrated by C. W. REED. Crown 8vo, cloth, 1s. 6d.

Phil May's Sketch-Book. Containing 54 Humorous Cartoons. A

New Edition. Crown folio, cloth, 2s. 6d.

Phipson (Dr. T. L.), Books by. Crown 8vo, art canvas, gilt top, 5s. ea.

Famous Violinists and Fine Violins.
Voice and Violin: Sketches, Anecdotes, and Reminiscences.

Planche (J. R.), Works by.

The Pursuivant of Arms. With Six Plates and 209 Illustrations. Crown 8vo, cloth, 7s. 6d.
Songs and Poems, 1819-1879. With Introduction by Mrs. MACKARNESS. Crown 8vo, cloth, 6s.

Plutarch's Lives of Illustrious Men. With Notes and a Life of

Plutarch by JOHN and WM. LANGHORNE, and Portraits. Two Vols., demy 8vo, half-bound 10s. 6d.

Poe's (Edgar Allan) Choice Works in Prose and Poetry. With Intro-

duction by CHARLES BAUDELAIRE. Portrait and Facsimiles. Crown 8vo, cloth, 7s. 6d.
The Mystery of Marie Roget, &c. Post 8vo, illustrated boards, 2s.

Pollock (W. H.).—The Charm, and other Drawing-room Plays. By

Sir WALTER BESANT and WALTER H. POLLOCK. With 50 Illustrations. Crown 8vo, cloth gilt, 6s.

Pollock (Wilfred).—War and a Wheel: The Græco-Turkish War as

Seen from a Bicycle. With a Map. Crown 8vo, picture cover, 1s.

Pope's Poetical Works. Post 8vo, cloth limp, 2s.

Porter (John).—Kingsclere. Edited by BYRON WEBBER. With 19

full-page and many smaller Illustrations. Cheaper Edition. Demy 8vo, cloth, 7s. 6d.

Praed (Mrs. Campbell), Novels by. Post 8vo, illust. bds., 2s. each.

The Romance of a Station. | The Soul of Countess Adrian.

Crown 8vo, cloth, 3s. 6d. each; post 8vo, boards, 2s. each.

Outlaw and Lawmaker. | Christina Chard. With Frontispiece by W. PAGET.
Mrs. Tregaskiss. With 8 Illustrations by ROBERT SAUBER.
Nulma. Crown 8vo, cloth, 3s. 6d.
Madame Izan: A Tourist Story. Crown 8vo, cloth, gilt top, 6s.

Price (E. C.), Novels by.

Crown 8vo, cloth extra, 3s. 6d. each; post 8vo, illustrated boards, 2s. each.

Valentina. | The Foreigners. | Mrs. Lancaster's Rival.
Gerald. Post 8vo, illustrated boards, 2s.

Princess Olga.—Radna: A Novel. Crown 8vo, cloth extra, 6s.

Proctor (Richard A.), Works by.

Flowers of the Sky. With 55 Illustrations. Small crown 8vo, cloth extra, 3s. 6d.
Easy Star Lessons. With Star Maps for every Night in the Year. Crown 8vo, cloth, 6s.
Familiar Science Studies. Crown 8vo, cloth extra, 6s.
Saturn and its System. With 13 Steel Plates. Demy 8vo, cloth extra, 10s. 6d.
Mysteries of Time and Space. With numerous Illustrations. Crown 8vo, cloth extra, 6s.
The Universe of Suns, &c. With numerous Illustrations. Crown 8vo, cloth extra, 6s.
Wages and Wants of Science Workers. Crown 8vo, 1s. 6d.

Pryce (Richard).—Miss Maxwell's Affections. Crown 8vo, cloth,

with Frontispiece by HAL LUDLOW, 3s. 6d.; post 8vo, illustrated boards, 2s.

Rambosson (J.).—Popular Astronomy. Translated by C. B. PITMAN.

With 10 Coloured Plates and 63 Woodcut Illustrations. Crown 8vo, cloth, 7s. 6d.

Randolph (Col. G.).—Aunt Abigail Dykes. Crown 8vo, cloth, 7s. 6d.

Read (General Meredith).—Historic Studies in Vaud, Berne,

and Savoy. With 31 full-page Illustrations. Two Vols., demy 8vo, cloth, 28s.

Reade's (Charles) Novels.

The New Collected LIBRARY EDITION, complete in Seventeen Volumes, set in new long primer type, printed on laid paper, and elegantly bound in cloth, price 3s. 6d. each.

1. **Peg Woffington;** and **Christie Johnstone.**
2. **Hard Cash.**
3. **The Cloister and the Hearth.** With a Preface by Sir WALTER BESANT.
4. **'It is Never Too Late to Mend.'**
5. **The Course of True Love Never Did Run Smooth;** and **Singleheart and Doubleface.**
6. **The Autobiography of a Thief; Jack of all Trades; A Hero and a Martyr;** and **The Wandering Heir.**
7. **Love Me Little, Love me Long.**
8. **The Double Marriage.**
9. **Griffith Gaunt.**
10. **Foul Play.**
11. **Put Yourself in His Place.**
12. **A Terrible Temptation.**
13. **A Simpleton.**
14. **A Woman-Hater.**
15. **The Jilt, and other Stories;** and **Good Stories of Man and other Animals.**
16. **A Perilous Secret.**
17. **Readiana;** and **Bible Characters.**

In Twenty-one Volumes, post 8vo, illustrated boards, 2s. each.

Peg Woffington. | **Christie Johnstone.**
'It is Never Too Late to Mend.'
The Course of True Love Never Did Run Smooth.
The Autobiography of a Thief; Jack of all Trades; and **James Lambert.**
Love Me Little, Love Me Long.
The Double Marriage.
The Cloister and the Hearth.
Hard Cash. | **Griffith Gaunt.**
Foul Play. | **Put Yourself in His Place.**
A Terrible Temptation.
A Simpleton. | **The Wandering Heir.**
Singleheart and Doubleface.
Good Stories of Man and other Animals.
The Jilt, and other Stories.
A Perilous Secret. | **Readiana.**

POPULAR EDITIONS, medium 8vo, 6d. each; cloth, 1s. each.
'It is Never Too Late to Mend.' | **The Cloister and the Hearth.**
Peg Woffington; and **Christie Johnstone.** | **Hard Cash.**

Christie Johnstone. With Frontispiece. Choicely printed in Elzevir style. Fcap. 8vo, half-Roxb. 2s. 6d.
Peg Woffington. Choicely printed in Elzevir style. Fcap. 8vo, half-Roxburghe, 2s. 6d.
The Cloister and the Hearth. In Four Vols., post 8vo, with an Introduction by Sir WALTER BESANT, and a Frontispiece to each Vol., buckram, gilt top, 6s. the set.
Bible Characters. Fcap. 8vo, leatherette, 1s.

Selections from the Works of Charles Reade. With an Introduction by Mrs. ALEX. IRELAND. Crown 8vo, buckram, with Portrait, 6s.; CHEAP EDITION, post 8vo, cloth limp, 2s. 6d.

Riddell (Mrs. J. H.), Novels by.

Weird Stories. Crown 8vo, cloth extra, 3s. 6d.; post 8vo, illustrated boards, 2s.

Post 8vo, illustrated boards, 2s. each.

The Uninhabited House.
The Prince of Wales's Garden Party.
The Mystery in Palace Gardens.
Fairy Water.
Her Mother's Darling.
The Nun's Curse. | **Idle Tales.**

Rimmer (Alfred), Works by. Large crown 8vo, cloth, 3s. 6d. each.

Our Old Country Towns. With 54 Illustrations by the Author.
Rambles Round Eton and Harrow. With 52 Illustrations by the Author.
About England with Dickens. With 58 Illustrations by C. A. VANDERHOOF and A. RIMMER.

Rives (Amelie, Author of 'The Quick or the Dead?'), Works by.

Barbara Dering. Crown 8vo, cloth, 3s. 6d.; post 8vo, picture boards, 2s.
Meriel: A Love Story. Crown 8vo, cloth, 3s. 6d.

Robinson Crusoe. By DANIEL DEFOE. With 37 Illustrations by

GEORGE CRUIKSHANK. Post 8vo, half-cloth, 2s.; cloth extra, gilt edges, 2s. 6d.

Robinson (F. W.), Novels by.

Women are Strange. Post 8vo, illustrated boards, 2s.
The Hands of Justice. Crown 8vo, cloth extra, 3s. 6d.; post 8vo, illustrated boards, 2s.
The Woman in the Dark. Crown 8vo, cloth, 3s. 6d.; post 8vo, illustrated boards, 2s.

Robinson (Phil), Works by. Crown 8vo, cloth extra, 6s. each.
The Poets' Birds. | The Poets' Beasts.
The Poets and Nature: Reptiles, Fishes, and Insects.

Rochefoucauld's Maxims and Moral Reflections. With Notes
and an Introductory Essay by SAINTE-BEUVE. Post 8vo, cloth limp, 2s.

Roll of Battle Abbey, The: A List of the Principal Warriors who
came from Normandy with William the Conqueror, 1066. Printed in Gold and Colours, 5s.

Rosengarten (A.).—A Handbook of Architectural Styles. Translated by W. COLLETT-SANDARS. With 630 Illustrations. Crown 8vo, cloth extra, 7s. 6d.

Rowley (Hon. Hugh), Works by. Post 8vo, cloth, 2s. 6d. each.
Puniana: Riddles and Jokes. With numerous Illustrations.
More Puniana. Profusely Illustrated.

Runciman (James), Stories by. Post 8vo, bds., 2s. ea.; cl., 2s. 6d. ea.
Skippers & Shellbacks. | Grace Balmaign's Sweetheart. | Schools & Scholars.

Russell (Dora), Novels by.
A Country Sweetheart. Crown 8vo, cloth, 3s. 6d.; post 8vo, picture boards, 2s.
The Drift of Fate. Crown 8vo, cloth, 3s. 6d.

Russell (Herbert).—True Blue; or, 'The Lass that Loved a Sailor.'
Crown 8vo, cloth, 3s. 6d.

Russell (W. Clark), Novels, &c., by.
Crown 8vo, cloth extra, 3s. 6d. each; post 8vo, illustrated boards, 2s. each; cloth limp, 2s. 6d. each.
Round the Galley-Fire. | An Ocean Tragedy.
In the Middle Watch. | My Shipmate Louise.
On the Fo'k'sle Head. | Alone on a Wide Wide Sea.
A Voyage to the Cape. | The Good Ship 'Mohock.'
A Book for the Hammock. | The Phantom Death.
The Mystery of the 'Ocean Star.' | Is He the Man? | The Convict Ship.
The Romance of Jenny Harlowe. | Heart of Oak. | The Last Entry.
The Tale of the Ten.

The Ship: Her Story. With about 60 Illustrations by H. C. SEPPINGS WRIGHT. Small 4to,
cloth, 6s. [Preparing.

Saint Aubyn (Alan), Novels by.
Crown 8vo, cloth extra, 3s. 6d. each; post 8vo, illustrated boards, 2s. each.
A Fellow of Trinity. With a Note by OLIVER WENDELL HOLMES and a Frontispiece.
The Junior Dean. | The Master of St. Benedict's. | To His Own Master.
Orchard Damerel. | In the Face of the World. | The Tremlett Diamonds.

Fcap. 8vo, cloth boards, 1s. 6d. each.
The Old Maid's Sweetheart. | Modest Little Sara.

Fortune's Gate. Crown 8vo, cloth, gilt top, 3s. 6d.
Mary Unwin. With 8 Illustrations by PERCY FARRANT. Crown 8vo, cloth, 6s.

Saint John (Bayle).—A Levantine Family. A New Edition.
Crown 8vo, cloth, 3s. 6d.

Sala (George A.).—Gaslight and Daylight. Post 8vo, boards, 2s.

Scotland Yard, Past and Present: Experiences of Thirty-seven Years.
By Ex-Chief-Inspector CAVANAGH. Post 8vo, illustrated boards, 2s.; cloth, 2s. 6d.

Secret Out, The: One Thousand Tricks with Cards: with Entertain-
ing Experiments in Drawing-room or 'White' Magic. By W. H. CREMER. With 300 Illustrations. Crown
8vo, cloth extra, 4s. 6d.

Seguin (L. G.), Works by.
The Country of the Passion Play (Oberammergau) and the Highlands of Bavaria. With
Map and 37 Illustrations. Crown 8vo, cloth extra, 3s. 6d.
Walks in Algiers. With Two Maps and 16 Illustrations. Crown 8vo, cloth extra, 6s.

Senior (Wm.).—By Stream and Sea. Post 8vo, cloth, 2s. 6d.

Sergeant (Adeline).—Dr. Endicott's Experiment. Cr. 8vo, 3s. 6d.

Shakespeare for Children: Lamb's Tales from Shakespeare.
With Illustrations, coloured and plain, by J. MOYR SMITH. Crown 4to, cloth gilt, 3s. 6d.

Shakespeare the Boy. With Sketches of the Home and School Life,
the Games and Sports, the Manners, Customs, and Folk-lore of the Time. By WILLIAM J. ROLFE,
Litt.D. With 42 Illustrations. Crown 8vo, cloth gilt, 3s. 6d.

Sharp (William).—Children of To-morrow. Crown 8vo, cloth, 6s.

Shelley's (Percy Bysshe) Complete Works in Verse and Prose.

Edited, Prefaced, and Annotated by R. HERNE SHEPHERD. Five Vols., crown 8vo, cloth, 3s. 6d. each.

Poetical Works, in Three Vols.:

Vol. I. Introduction by the Editor: Posthumous Fragments of Margaret Nicholson; Shelley's Correspondence with Stockdale; The Wandering Jew; Queen Mab, with the Notes; Alastor, and other Poems; Rosalind and Helen; Prometheus Unbound; Adonais, &c.

" II. Laon and Cythna; The Cenci; Julian and Maddalo; Swellfoot the Tyrant; The Witch of Atlas; Epipsychidion; Hellas.

" III. Posthumous Poems; The Masque of Anarchy; and other Pieces.

Prose Works, in Two Vols.:

Vol. I. The Two Romances of Zastrozzi and St. Irvyne; the Dublin and Marlow Pamphlets; A Refutation of Deism; Letters to Leigh Hunt, and some Minor Writings and Fragments.

II. The Essays; Letters from Abroad; Translations and Fragments, edited by Mrs. SHELLEY. With a Biography of Shelley, and an Index of the Prose Works.

⁎ Also a few copies of a LARGE-PAPER EDITION, 5 vols., cloth, £2 12s. 6d.

Sherard (R. H.).—Rogues: A Novel. Crown 8vo, cloth, 1s. 6d.

Sheridan's (Richard Brinsley) Complete Works, with Life and

Anecdotes. Including his Dramatic Writings, his Works in Prose and Poetry, Translations, Speeches, and Jokes. With 10 Illustrations. Crown 8vo, cloth, 3s. 6d.

The Rivals, The School for Scandal, and other Plays. Post 8vo, half-bound, 2s.

Sheridan's Comedies: The Rivals and **The School for Scandal.** Edited, with an Introduction and Notes to each Play, and a Biographical Sketch, by BRANDER MATTHEWS. With Illustrations. Demy 8vo, half-parchment, 12s. 6d.

Sidney's (Sir Philip) Complete Poetical Works, including all

those in 'Arcadia.' With Portrait, Memorial-Introduction, Notes, &c., by the Rev. A. B. GROSART, D.D. Three Vols., crown 8vo, cloth boards, 3s. 6d. each.

Signboards: Their History, including Anecdotes of Famous Taverns and

Remarkable Characters. By JACOB LARWOOD and JOHN CAMDEN HOTTEN. With Coloured Frontispiece and 94 Illustrations. Crown 8vo, cloth extra, 3s. 6d.

Sims (George R.), Works by.

Post 8vo, illustrated boards, 2s. each; cloth limp, 2s. 6d. each.

The Ring o' Bells.	**Dramas of Life.** With 60 Illustrations.
Mary Jane's Memoirs.	**Memoirs of a Landlady.**
Mary Jane Married.	**My Two Wives.**
Tinkletop's Crime.	**Scenes from the Show.**
Zeph: A Circus Story, &c.	**The Ten Commandments:** Stories.
Tales of To-day.	

Crown 8vo, picture cover, 1s. each; cloth, 1s. 6d. each.

The Dagonet Reciter and Reader: Being Readings and Recitations in Prose and Verse, selected from his own Works by GEORGE R. SIMS.

The Case of George Candlemas. | **Dagonet Ditties.** (From *The Referee*.)

Rogues and Vagabonds. Crown 8vo, cloth, 3s. 6d.; post 8vo, picture boards, 2s.; cloth limp, 2s. 6d.

How the Poor Live; and **Horrible London.** With a Frontispiece by F. BARNARD. Crown 8vo, leatherette, 1s.

Dagonet Abroad. Crown 8vo, cloth, 3s. 6d.; post 8vo, picture boards, 2s.; cloth limp, 2s. 6d.

Dagonet Dramas of the Day. Crown 8vo, 1s.

Once upon a Christmas Time. With 8 Illustrations by CHARLES GREEN, R.I. Crown 8vo, cloth gilt, 2s. 6d.

Sister Dora: A Biography. By MARGARET LONSDALE. With Four

Illustrations. Demy 8vo, picture cover, 4d.; cloth, 6d.

Sketchley (Arthur).—A Match in the Dark. Post 8vo, boards, 2s.

Slang Dictionary (The): Etymological, Historical, and Anecdotal.

Crown 8vo, cloth extra, 6s. 6d.

Smart (Hawley), Novels by.

Crown 8vo, cloth 3s. 6d. each; post 8vo, picture boards, 2s. each.

Beatrice and Benedick.	**Long Odds.**
Without Love or Licence.	**The Master of Rathkelly.**

Crown 8vo, cloth, 3s. 6d. each.

The Outsider.	**A Racing Rubber.**

The Plunger. Post 8vo, picture boards, 2s.

Smith (J. Moyr), Works by.

The Prince of Argolis. With 130 Illustrations. Post 8vo, cloth extra, 3s. 6d.

The Wooing of the Water Witch. With numerous Illustrations. Post 8vo, cloth, 6s.

Snazelleparilla. Decanted by G. S. EDWARDS. With Portrait of

G. H. SNAZELLE, and 65 Illustrations by C. LYALL. Crown 8vo, cloth, 3s. 6d.

Society in London. Crown 8vo, 1s.; cloth, 1s. 6d.

Society in Paris: The Upper Ten Thousand. A Series of Letters

from Count PAUL VASILI to a Young French Diplomat. Crown 8vo, cloth, 6s.

Somerset (Lord Henry).—Songs of Adieu. Small 4to, Jap. vel., 6s.

Spalding (T. A., LL.B.).—Elizabethan Demonology: An Essay
on the Belief in the Existence of Devils. Crown 8vo, cloth extra, 5s.

Speight (T. W.), Novels by.

Post 8vo, illustrated boards, 2s. each.

The Mysteries of Heron Dyke. | The Loudwater Tragedy.
My Devious Ways, &c. | Burgo's Romance.
Hoodwinked; & Sandycroft Mystery. | Quittance in Full.
The Golden Hoop. | A Husband from the Sea.
Back to Life.

Post 8vo, cloth limp, 1s. 6d. each.

A Barren Title. | Wife or No Wife?

Crown 8vo, cloth extra, 3s. 6d. each.

A Secret of the Sea. | The Grey Monk. | The Master of Trenance.
A Minion of the Moon: A Romance of the King's Highway.
The Secret of Wyvern Towers.
The Doom of Siva. *[Shortly.*

Spenser for Children. By M. H. TOWRY. With Coloured Illustrations
by WALTER J. MORGAN. Crown 4to, cloth extra, 3s. 6d.

Spettigue (H. H.).—The Heritage of Eve. Crown 8vo, cloth, 6s.

Stafford (John), Novels by.
Doris and I. Crown 8vo, cloth, 3s. 6d.
Carlton Priors. Crown 8vo, cloth, gilt top, 6s.

Starry Heavens (The): A POETICAL BIRTHDAY BOOK. Royal 16mo,
cloth extra, 2s. 6d.

Stedman (E. C.), Works by. Crown 8vo, cloth extra, 9s. each.
Victorian Poets. | The Poets of America.

Stephens (Riccardo, M.B.).—The Cruciform Mark: The Strange
Story of RICHARD TREGENNA, Bachelor of Medicine (Univ. Edinb.) Crown 8vo, cloth, 3s. 6d.

Sterndale (R. Armitage).—The Afghan Knife: A Novel. Post
8vo, cloth, 3s. 6d.; illustrated boards, 2s.

Stevenson (R. Louis), Works by.

Crown 8vo, buckram, gilt top, 6s. each; post 8vo, cloth limp, 2s. 6d. each.
Travels with a Donkey. With a Frontispiece by WALTER CRANE.
An Inland Voyage. With a Frontispiece by WALTER CRANE.

Crown 8vo, buckram, gilt top, 6s. each.

Familiar Studies of Men and Books.
The Silverado Squatters. With Frontispiece by J. D. STRONG.
The Merry Men. | Underwoods: Poems.
Memories and Portraits.
Virginibus Puerisque, and other Papers. | Ballads. | Prince Otto.
Across the Plains, with other Memories and Essays.
Weir of Hermiston.

A Lowden Sabbath Morn. With 27 Illustrations by A. S. BOYD. Fcap. 8vo, cloth, 6s.
Songs of Travel. Crown 8vo, buckram, 5s.
New Arabian Nights. Crown 8vo, buckram, gilt top, 6s.; post 8vo, illustrated boards, 2s.
The Suicide Club; and The Rajah's Diamond. (From NEW ARABIAN NIGHTS.) With
Eight Illustrations by W. J. HENNESSY. Crown 8vo, cloth, 3s. 6d.
The Stevenson Reader: Selections from the Writings of ROBERT LOUIS STEVENSON. Edited
by LLOYD OSBOURNE. Post 8vo, cloth, 2s. 6d.: buckram, gilt top, 3s. 6d.

Storey (G. A., A.R.A.).—Sketches from Memory. With 93
Illustrations by the Author. Demy 8vo, cloth, gilt top, 12s. 6d.

Stories from Foreign Novelists. With Notices by HELEN and
ALICE ZIMMERN. Crown 8vo, cloth extra, 3s. 6d.; post 8vo, illustrated boards, 2s.

Strange Manuscript (A) Found in a Copper Cylinder. Crown
8vo, cloth extra, with 19 Illustrations by GILBERT GAUL. 5s.; post 8vo, illustrated boards, 2s.

Strange Secrets. Told by PERCY FITZGERALD, CONAN DOYLE, FLOR-
ENCE MARRYAT, &c. Post 8vo, illustrated boards, 2s.

Strutt (Joseph). — The Sports and Pastimes of the People of
England; including the Rural and Domestic Recreations, May Games, Mummeries, Shows, &c., from
the Earliest Period to the Present Time. Edited by WILLIAM HONE. With 140 Illustrations. Crown
8vo, cloth extra, 3s. 6d.

Swift's (Dean) Choice Works, in Prose and Verse. With Memoir,
Portrait, and Facsimiles of the Maps in 'Gulliver's Travels.' Crown 8vo, cloth, 3s. 6d.
Gulliver's Travels, and A Tale of a Tub. Post 8vo, half-bound, 2s.
Jonathan Swift: A Study. By J. CHURTON COLLINS. Crown 8vo, cloth extra, 8s.

Swinburne (Algernon C.), Works by.

Selections from the Poetical Works of A. C. Swinburne. Fcap. 8vo, 6s.
Atalanta in Calydon. Crown 8vo, 6s.
Chastelard: A Tragedy. Crown 8vo, 7s.
Poems and Ballads. FIRST SERIES. Crown 8vo, or fcap. 8vo, 9s.
Poems and Ballads. SECOND SERIES. Crown 8vo, 9s.
Poems & Ballads. THIRD SERIES. Cr. 8vo, 7s.
Songs before Sunrise. Crown 8vo, 10s. 6d.
Bothwell: A Tragedy. Crown 8vo, 12s. 6d.
Songs of Two Nations. Crown 8vo, 6s.
George Chapman. (See Vol. II. of G. CHAPMAN'S Works.) Crown 8vo, 3s. 6d.
Essays and Studies. Crown 8vo, 12s.
Erechtheus: A Tragedy. Crown 8vo, 6s.
A Note on Charlotte Bronte. Cr. 8vo, 6s.

A Study of Shakespeare. Crown 8vo, 8s.
Songs of the Springtides. Crown 8vo, 6s.
Studies in Song. Crown 8vo, 7s.
Mary Stuart: A Tragedy. Crown 8vo, 8s.
Tristram of Lyonesse. Crown 8vo, 9s.
A Century of Roundels. Small 4to, 8s.
A Midsummer Holiday. Crown 8vo, 7s.
Marino Faliero: A Tragedy. Crown 8vo, 6s.
A Study of Victor Hugo. Crown 8vo, 6s.
Miscellanies. Crown 8vo, 12s.
Locrine: A Tragedy. Crown 8vo, 6s.
A Study of Ben Jonson. Crown 8vo, 7s.
The Sisters: A Tragedy. Crown 8vo, 6s.
Astrophel, &c. Crown 8vo, 7s.
Studies in Prose and Poetry. Cr. 8vo, 9s.
The Tale of Balen. Crown 8vo, 7s.

Syntax's (Dr.) Three Tours: In Search of the Picturesque, in Search of Consolation, and in Search of a Wife. With ROWLANDSON'S Coloured Illustrations, and Life of the Author by J. C. HOTTEN. Crown 8vo, cloth extra, 7s. 6d.

Taine's History of English Literature. Translated by HENRY VAN LAUN. Four Vols., small demy 8vo, cloth boards, 30s.—POPULAR EDITION, Two Vols., large crown 8vo, cloth extra, 15s.

Taylor (Bayard). — Diversions of the Echo Club: Burlesques of Modern Writers. Post 8vo, cloth limp, 2s.

Taylor (Tom). — Historical Dramas. Containing 'Clancarty, 'Jeanne Darc,' ''Twixt Axe and Crown,' 'The Fool's Revenge, 'Arkwright's Wife,' 'Anne Boleyn,' 'Plot and Passion.' Crown 8vo, cloth extra, 7s. 6d.
*** The Plays may also be had separately, at 1s. each.

Temple (Sir Richard, G.C.S.I.).—A Bird's-eye View of Picturesque India. With 32 Illustrations by the Author. Crown 8vo, cloth, gilt top, 6s.

Tennyson (Lord): A Biographical Sketch. By H. J. JENNINGS. Post 8vo, portrait cover, 1s.; cloth, 1s. 6d.

Thackerayana: Notes and Anecdotes. With Coloured Frontispiece and Hundreds of Sketches by WILLIAM MAKEPEACE THACKERAY. Crown 8vo, cloth extra, 3s. 6d.

Thames, A New Pictorial History of the. By A. S. KRAUSSE. With 340 Illustrations. Post 8vo, cloth, 1s. 6d.

Thiers (Adolphe). — History of the Consulate and Empire of France under Napoleon. Translated by D. FORBES CAMPBELL and JOHN STEBBING. With 36 Steel Plates. 12 Vols., demy 8vo, cloth extra, 12s. each.

Thomas (Bertha), Novels by. Cr. 8vo, cl., 3s. 6d. ea.; post 8vo, 2s. ea.
The Violin-Player. | **Proud Maisie.**
Cressida. Post 8vo, illustrated boards, 2s.

Thomson's Seasons, and The Castle of Indolence. With Introduction by ALLAN CUNNINGHAM, and 48 Illustrations. Post 8vo, half-bound, 2s.

Thornbury (Walter), Books by.

The Life and Correspondence of J. M. W. Turner. With Eight Illustrations in Colours and Two Woodcuts. New and Revised Edition. Crown 8vo, cloth, 3s. 6d.

Post 8vo, illustrated boards, 2s. each.
Old Stories Re-told. | **Tales for the Marines.**

Timbs (John), Works by. Crown 8vo, cloth, 3s. 6d. each.

Clubs and Club Life in London: Anecdotes of its Famous Coffee-houses, Hostelries, and Taverns. With 41 Illustrations.
English Eccentrics and Eccentricities: Stories of Delusions, Impostures, Sporting Scenes, Eccentric Artists, Theatrical Folk, &c. With 48 Illustrations.

Transvaal (The). By JOHN DE VILLIERS. With Map. Crown 8vo, 1s.

Trollope (Anthony), Novels by.

Crown 8vo, cloth extra, 3s. 6d. each; post 8vo, illustrated boards, 2s. each.
The Way We Live Now. | **Mr. Scarborough's Family.**
Frau Frohmann. | **The Land-Leaguers.**

Post 8vo, illustrated boards, 2s. each.
Kept in the Dark. | **The American Senator.**
The Golden Lion of Granpere. | **John Caldigate.** | **Marion Fay.**

Trollope (Frances E.), Novels by.

Crown 8vo, cloth extra, 3s. 6d. each; post 8vo, illustrated boards, 2s. each.
Like Ships Upon the Sea. | **Mabel's Progress.** | **Anne Furness.**

Trollope (T. A.).—Diamond Cut Diamond. Post 8vo, illust. bds., 2s.

Trowbridge (J. T.).—Farnell's Folly. Post 8vo, illust. boards, 2s.

Twain's (Mark) Books.
Crown 8vo, cloth extra, 3s. 6d. each.
The Choice Works of Mark Twain. Revised and Corrected throughout by the Author. With Life, Portrait, and numerous Illustrations.
Roughing It; and The Innocents at Home. With 200 Illustrations by F. A. FRASER.
The American Claimant. With 81 Illustrations by HAL HURST and others.
Tom Sawyer Abroad. With 26 Illustrations by DAN BEARD.
Tom Sawyer, Detective, &c. With Photogravure Portrait.
Pudd'nhead Wilson. With Portrait and Six Illustrations by LOUIS LOEB.
Mark Twain's Library of Humour. With 197 Illustrations by E. W. KEMBLE.
Crown 8vo, cloth extra, 3s. 6d. each ; post 8vo, picture boards, 2s. each.
A Tramp Abroad. With 314 Illustrations.
The Innocents Abroad; or, The New Pilgrim's Progress. With 234 Illustrations. (The Two Shilling Edition is entitled **Mark Twain's Pleasure Trip.**)
The Gilded Age. By MARK TWAIN and C. D. WARNER. With 212 Illustrations.
The Adventures of Tom Sawyer. With 111 Illustrations.
The Prince and the Pauper. With 100 Illustrations.
Life on the Mississippi. With 300 Illustrations.
The Adventures of Huckleberry Finn. With 174 Illustrations by E. W. KEMBLE.
A Yankee at the Court of King Arthur. With 220 Illustrations by DAN BEARD.
The Stolen White Elephant.
The £1,000,000 Bank-Note.
Mark Twain's Sketches. Post 8vo, illustrated boards, 2s.
Personal Recollections of Joan of Arc. With Twelve Illustrations by F. V. DU MOND. Crown 8vo, cloth, 6s.
More Tramps Abroad. Crown 8vo, cloth, gilt top, 6s.

Tytler (C. C. Fraser-).—Mistress Judith: A Novel. Crown 8vo, cloth extra, 3s. 6d. ; post 8vo, illustrated boards, 2s.

Tytler (Sarah), Novels by.
Crown 8vo, cloth extra, 3s. 6d. each ; post 8vo, illustrated boards, 2s. each.

Lady Bell.	Buried Diamonds.	The Blackhall Ghosts.

Post 8vo, illustrated boards, 2s. each.

What She Came Through.	The Huguenot Family.
Citoyenne Jacqueline.	Noblesse Oblige. | Disappeared.
The Bride's Pass. | Saint Mungo's City.	Beauty and the Beast.

Crown 8vo, cloth, 3s. 6d. each.

The Macdonald Lass. With Frontispiece.	Mrs. Carmichael's Goddesses.
The Witch-Wife.	Rachel Langton. | Sapphira.

Upward (Allen), Novels by.
A Crown of Straw. Crown 8vo, cloth, 6s.
Crown 8vo, cloth, 3s. 6d. each ; post 8vo, picture boards, 2s. each.

The Queen Against Owen.	The Prince of Balkistan.

'God Save the Queen!' a Tale of '37. Crown 8vo, decorated cover, 1s ; cloth, 2s.

Vashti and Esther. By 'Belle' of *The World*. Cr. 8vo, cloth, 3s. 6d.

Vizetelly (Ernest A.).—The Scorpion: A Romance of Spain. With a Frontispiece. Crown 8vo, cloth extra, 3s. 6d.

Wagner (Leopold).—How to Get on the Stage, and how to Succeed there. Crown 8vo, cloth, 2s. 6d.

Walford (Edward, M.A.), Works by.
Walford's County Families of the United Kingdom (1899). Containing the Descent, Birth, Marriage, Education, &c., of 12,000 Heads of Families, their Heirs, Offices, Addresses, Clubs, &c. Royal 8vo, cloth gilt, 50s.
Walford's Shilling Peerage (1899). Containing a List of the House of Lords, Scotch and Irish Peers, &c. 32mo, cloth, 1s.
Walford's Shilling Baronetage (1899). Containing a List of the Baronets of the United Kingdom, Biographical Notices, Addresses, &c. 32mo, cloth, 1s.
Walford's Shilling Knightage (1899). Containing a List of the Knights of the United Kingdom, Biographical Notices, Addresses, &c. 32mo, cloth, 1s.
Walford's Shilling House of Commons (1899). Containing a Complete List of Members of Parliament, their Addresses, Club, &c. 32mo, cloth, 1s.
Walford's Complete Peerage, Baronetage, Knightage, and House of Commons (1899). Royal 32mo, cloth, gilt edges, 5s.

Waller (S. E.).—Sebastiani's Secret. With 9 Illusts. Cr. 8vo, cl., 6s.

Walton and Cotton's Complete Angler; or, The Contemplative Man's Recreation, by IZAAK WALTON; and Instructions How to Angle, for a Trout or Grayling in a clear Stream, by CHARLES COTTON. With Memoirs and Notes by Sir HARRIS NICOLAS, and 61 Illustrations. Crown 8vo, cloth antique, 7s. 6d.

Walt Whitman, Poems by. Edited, with Introduction, by WILLIAM M. ROSSETTI. With Portrait. Crown 8vo, hand-made paper and buckram, 6s.

Ward (Herbert), Books by.
Five Years with the Congo Cannibals. With 92 Illustrations. Royal 8vo, cloth, 14s.
My Life with Stanley's Rear Guard. With Map. Post 8vo, 1s. ; cloth, 1s. 6d.

Warden (Florence).—Joan, the Curate.   Crown 8vo, cloth, 3s. 6d.

Warman (Cy).—The Express Messenger, and other Tales of the Rail.   Crown 8vo, cloth, 3s. 6d.

Warner (Charles Dudley).—A Roundabout Journey.   Crown 8vo, cloth extra, 6s.

Warrant to Execute Charles I.   A Facsimile, with the 59 Signatures and Seals.   Printed on paper 22 in. by 14 in.   2s.
Warrant to Execute Mary Queen of Scots.   A Facsimile, including Queen Elizabeth's Signature and the Great Seal.   2s.

Washington's (George) Rules of Civility Traced to their Sources and Restored by MONCURE D. CONWAY.   Fcap. 8vo, Japanese vellum, 2s. 6d.

Wassermann (Lillias) and Aaron Watson.—The Marquis of Carabas.   Post 8vo, illustrated boards, 2s.

Weather, How to Foretell the, with the Pocket Spectroscope. By F. W. CORY.   With Ten Illustrations.   Crown 8vo, 1s.; cloth, 1s. 6d.

Westall (William), Novels by.
Trust Money.   Crown 8vo, cloth, 3s. 6d.; post 8vo, illustrated boards, 2s.; cloth limp, 2s. 6d.

Crown 8vo, cloth, 6s. each.

As a Man Sows.	**A Woman Tempted Him.**
With the Red Eagle.	**A Red Bridal.**

Crown 8vo, cloth, 3s. 6d. each.

Her Two Millions.	**The Blind Musician.**	**The Phantom City.**
Two Pinches of Snuff.	**Strange Crimes.**	**Ralph Norbreck's Trust.**
Roy of Roy's Court.	**Ben Clough.**	**A Queer Race.**
Nigel Fortescue.	**The Old Factory.**	**Red Ryvington.**
Birch Dene.	**Sons of Belial.**	

Westbury (Atha).—The Shadow of Hilton Fernbrook: A Romance of Maoriland.   Crown 8vo, cloth, 3s. 6d.

White (Gilbert).—The Natural History of Selborne.   Post 8vo, printed on laid paper and half-bound, 2s.

Williams (W. Mattieu, F.R.A.S.), Works by.
Science in Short Chapters.   Crown 8vo, cloth extra, 7s. 6d.
A Simple Treatise on Heat.   With Illustrations.   Crown 8vo, cloth, 2s. 6d.
The Chemistry of Cookery.   Crown 8vo, cloth extra, 6s.
The Chemistry of Iron and Steel Making.   Crown 8vo, cloth extra, 9s.
A Vindication of Phrenology.   With Portrait and 43 Illusts.   Demy 8vo, cloth extra, 12s. 6d.

Williamson (Mrs. F. H.).—A Child Widow.   Post 8vo, bds., 2s.

Wills (C. J.), Novels by.
An Easy-going Fellow.   Crown 8vo, cloth, 3s. 6d. | **His Dead Past.**   Crown 8vo, cloth, 6s.

Wilson (Dr. Andrew, F.R.S.E.), Works by.
Chapters on Evolution.   With 259 Illustrations.   Crown 8vo, cloth extra, 7s. 6d.
Leaves from a Naturalist's Note-Book.   Post 8vo, cloth limp, 2s. 6d.
Leisure-Time Studies.   With Illustrations.   Crown 8vo, cloth extra, 6s.
Studies in Life and Sense.   With 36 Illustrations.   Crown 8vo, cloth, 3s. 6d.
Common Accidents: How to Treat Them.   With Illustrations.   Crown 8vo, 1s.; cloth, 1s. 6d.
Glimpses of Nature.   With 35 Illustrations.   Crown 8vo, cloth extra, 3s. 6d.

Winter (John Strange), Stories by.   Post 8vo, illustrated boards, 2s. each; cloth limp, 2s. 6d. each.
Cavalry Life. | **Regimental Legends.**
Cavalry Life and Regimental Legends.   LIBRARY EDITION, set in new type and handsomely bound.   Crown 8vo, cloth, 3s. 6d.
A Soldier's Children.   With 34 Illustrations by E. G. THOMSON and E. STUART HARDY.   Crown 8vo, cloth extra, 3s. 6d.

Wissmann (Hermann von). — My Second Journey through Equatorial Africa.   With 92 Illustrations.   Demy 8vo, cloth, 16s.

Wood (H. F.), Detective Stories by.   Post 8vo, boards, 2s. each.
The Passenger from Scotland Yard. | **The Englishman of the Rue Cain.**

Woolley (Celia Parker).—Rachel Armstrong; or, Love and Theology.   Post 8vo, illustrated boards, 2s.; cloth, 2s. 6d.

Wright (Thomas, F.S.A.), Works by.
Caricature History of the Georges; or, Annals of the House of Hanover.   Compiled from Squibs, Broadsides, Window Pictures, Lampoons, and Pictorial Caricatures of the Time.   With over 400 Illustrations.   Crown 8vo, cloth, 3s. 6d.
History of Caricature and of the Grotesque in Art, Literature, Sculpture, and Painting.   Illustrated by F. W. FAIRHOLT, F.S.A.   Crown 8vo, cloth, 7s. 6d.

Wynman (Margaret) —My Flirtations.   With 13 Illustrations by J. BERNARD PARTRIDGE.   Post 8vo, cloth limp, 2s.

Yates (Edmund), Novels by. Post 8vo, illustrated boards, 2s. each.

| Land at Last. | The Forlorn Hope. | Castaway. |

Zangwill (I.). — Ghetto Tragedies. With Three Illustrations by A. S. BOYD. Fcap. 8vo, cloth, 2s. net.

'ZZ' (Louis Zangwill).—A Nineteenth Century Miracle. Cr. 8vo, cloth, 3s. 6d.

Zola (Emile), Novels by. Crown 8vo, cloth extra, 3s. 6d. each.

The Fortune of the Rougons. Edited by ERNEST A. VIZETELLY.
The Abbe Mouret's Transgression. Edited by ERNEST A. VIZETELLY. [Shortly.
His Excellency (Eugene Rougon). With an Introduction by ERNEST A. VIZETELLY.
The Dram-Shop (L'Assommoir). With Introduction by E. A. VIZETELLY.
The Fat and the Thin. Translated by ERNEST A. VIZETELLY.
Money. Translated by ERNEST A. VIZETELLY.
The Downfall. Translated by E. A. VIZETELLY.
The Dream. Translated by ELIZA CHASE. With Eight Illustrations by JEANNIOT.
Doctor Pascal. Translated by E. A. VIZETELLY. With Portrait of the Author.
Lourdes. Translated by ERNEST A. VIZETELLY.
Rome. Translated by ERNEST A. VIZETELLY.
Paris. Translated by ERNEST A. VIZETELLY.
Fruitfulness (La Fecondite). Translated by E. A VIZETELLY. [Shortly.

SOME BOOKS CLASSIFIED IN SERIES.

** For fuller cataloguing, see alphabetical arrangement, pp. 1-26.

The Mayfair Library. Post 8vo, cloth limp, 2s. 6d. per Volume.

Quips and Quiddities. By W. D. ADAMS.
The Agony Column of 'The Times.'
Melancholy Anatomised: Abridgment of BURTON.
A Journey Round My Room. By X. DE MAISTRE. Translated by HENRY ATTWELL
Poetical Ingenuities. By W. T. DOBSON.
The Cupboard Papers. By FIN-BEC.
W. S. Gilbert's Plays. Three Series.
Songs of Irish Wit and Humour.
Animals and their Masters. By Sir A HELPS.
Social Pressure. By Sir A. HELPS.
The Autocrat of the Breakfast-Table. By OLIVER WENDELL HOLMES.
Curiosities of Criticism. By H. J. JENNINGS.
Pencil and Palette. By R. KEMPT.
Little Essays: from LAMB'S LETTERS.
Forensic Anecdotes. By JACOB LARWOOD.
Theatrical Anecdotes. By JACOB LARWOOD.
Ourselves. By E. LYNN LINTON.
Witch Stories. By E. LYNN LINTON.
Pastimes and Players. By R. MACGREGOR.
New Paul and Virginia. By W. H. MALLOCK.
The New Republic. By W. H. MALLOCK.
Muses of Mayfair. Edited by H. C. PENNELL.
Thoreau: His Life and Aims. By H. A. PAGE.
Puck on Pegasus. By H. C. PENNELL.
Pegasus Re-saddled. By H. C. PENNELL.
Puniana. By Hon. HUGH ROWLEY.
More Puniana. By Hon. HUGH ROWLEY.
The Philosophy of Handwriting.
By Stream and Sea. By WILLIAM SENIOR.
Leaves from a Naturalist's Note-Book. By Dr. ANDREW WILSON.

The Golden Library. Post 8vo, cloth limp, 2s. per Volume.

Songs for Sailors. By W. C. BENNETT.
Lives of the Necromancers. By W. GODWIN.
The Autocrat of the Breakfast Table. By OLIVER WENDELL HOLMES.
Tale for a Chimney Corner. By LEIGH HUNT.
Scenes of Country Life. By EDWARD JESSE.
La Mort d'Arthur: Selections from MALLORY.
The Poetical Works of Alexander Pope.
Maxims and Reflections of Rochefoucauld.
Diversions of the Echo Club. BAYARD TAYLOR.

Handy Novels. Fcap. 8vo, cloth boards, 1s. 6d. each.

A Lost Soul. By W. L. ALDEN.
Dr. Palliser's Patient. By GRANT ALLEN
Monte Carlo Stories. By JOAN BARRETT.
Black Spirits and White. By R. A. CRAM.
Seven Sleepers of Ephesus. M. E. COLERIDGE.
Taken from the Enemy. By H. NEWBOLT.
The Old Maid's Sweetheart. By A. ST. AUBYN.
Modest Little Sara. By ALAN ST. AUBYN.

My Library. Printed on laid paper, post 8vo, half-Roxburghe, 2s. 6d. each.

The Journal of Maurice de Guerin.
The Dramatic Essays of Charles Lamb.
Citation and Examination of William Shakspeare. By W. S. LANDOR.
Christie Johnstone. By CHARLES READE.
Peg Woffington. By CHARLES READE.

The Pocket Library. Post 8vo, printed on laid paper and hf.-bd., 2s. each.

Gastronomy. By BRILLAT-SAVARIN.
Robinson Crusoe. Illustrated by G. CRUIKSHANK
Autocrat of the Breakfast-Table and The Professor at the Breakfast-Table. By O. W. HOLMES.
Provincial Letters of Blaise Pascal.
Whims and Oddities. By THOMAS HOOD.
Leigh Hunt's Essays. Edited by E. OLLIER.
The Barber's Chair. By DOUGLAS JERROLD.
The Essays of Elia. By CHARLES LAMB.
Anecdotes of the Clergy. By JACOB LARWOOD.
The Epicurean, &c. By THOMAS MOORE.
Plays by RICHARD BRINSLEY SHERIDAN.
Gulliver's Travels, &c. By Dean SWIFT.
Thomson's Seasons. Illustrated.
White's Natural History of Selborne.

Popular Sixpenny Novels. Medium 8vo, 6d. each; cloth, 1s. each.

All Sorts and Conditions of Men. By WALTER BESANT
The Golden Butterfly. By WALTER BESANT and JAMES RICE.
The Deemster. By HALL CAINE.
The Shadow of a Crime. By HALL CAINE.
Antonina. By WILKIE COLLINS.
The Moonstone. By WILKIE COLLINS
The Woman in White. By WILKIE COLLINS.
The Dead Secret. By WILKIE COLLINS.
Moths. By OUIDA.
Under Two Flags. By OUIDA.
By Proxy. By JAMES PAYN.
Peg Woffington; and Christie Johnstone. By CHARLES READE.
The Cloister and the Hearth. By CHARLES READE.
It is Never Too Late to Mend. By CHARLES READE.
Hard Cash. By CHARLES READE.

THE PICCADILLY NOVELS.

LIBRARY EDITIONS OF NOVELS, many Illustrated, crown 8vo, cloth extra, 3s. 6d. each.

By Mrs. ALEXANDER.
A Life Interest | Mona's Choice | By Woman's Wit.

By F. M. ALLEN.—Green as Grass.

By GRANT ALLEN.
Philistia. | Babylon.
Strange Stories.
For Maimie's Sake.
In all Shades.
The Beckoning Hand.
The Devil's Die.
This Mortal Coil.
The Tents of Shem.
The Great Taboo.
Dumaresq's Daughter.
Duchess of Powysland.
Blood Royal.
I. Greet's Masterpiece.
The Scallywag.
At Market Value.
Under Sealed Orders.

By M. ANDERSON.—Othello's Occupation.

By EDWIN L. ARNOLD.
Phra the Phœnician. | Constable of St. Nicholas.

By ROBERT BARR.
In a Steamer Chair.
From Whose Bourne.
A Woman Intervenes.
Revenge !

By FRANK BARRETT.
The Woman of the Iron Bracelets.
The Harding Scandal.
Under a Strange Mask.
A Missing Witness.

By 'BELLE.'—Vashti and Esther.

By Sir W. BESANT and J. RICE.
Ready-Money Mortiboy.
My Little Girl.
With Harp and Crown.
This Son of Vulcan.
The Golden Butterfly.
The Monks of Thelema.
By Celia's Arbour.
Chaplain of the Fleet.
The Seamy Side.
The Case of Mr. Lucraft.
In Trafalgar's Bay.
The Ten Years' Tenant.

By Sir WALTER BESANT.
All Sorts & Conditions.
The Captains' Room.
All in a Garden Fair.
Dorothy Forster.
Uncle Jack.
World Went Well Then.
Children of Gibeon.
Herr Paulus.
For Faith and Freedom.
To Call Her Mine.
The Revolt of Man.
The Bell of St. Paul's.
The Holy Rose.
Armorel of Lyonesse.
S. Katherine's by Tower
Verbena Camellia, &c.
The Ivory Gate.
The Rebel Queen.
Beyond the Dreams of Avarice.
The Master Craftsman.
The City of Refuge.
A Fountain Sealed.
The Charm.

By AMBROSE BIERCE—In Midst of Life.

By PAUL BOURGET.—A Living Lie.

By J. D. BRAYSHAW.—Slum Silhouettes.

By H. A. BRYDEN.
An Exiled Scot.

By ROBERT BUCHANAN.
Shadow of the Sword.
A Child of Nature.
God and the Man.
Martyrdom of Madeline
Love Me for Ever.
Annan Water.
Foxglove Manor.
The New Abelard.
Matt. | Rachel Dene
Master of the Mine.
The Heir of Linne.
Woman and the Man.
Red and White Heather.
Lady Kilpatrick.

ROB. BUCHANAN & HY. MURRAY.
The Charlatan.

By ROBERT W. CHAMBERS.
The King in Yellow.

By J. M. CHAPPLE.—The Minor Chord.

By HALL CAINE.
Shadow of a Crime. | Deemster. | Son of Hagar.

By AUSTIN CLARE.—By Rise of River.

By ANNE COATES.—Rie's Diary.

By MACLAREN COBBAN.
The Red Sultan.
The Burden of Isabel

By MORT. & FRANCES COLLINS.
Transmigration.
Blacksmith & Scholar.
The Village Comedy.
From Midnight to Midnight.
You Play me False.

By WILKIE COLLINS.
Armadale. | After Dark.
No Name. | Antonina.
Basil. | Hide and Seek.
The Dead Secret.
Queen of Hearts.
My Miscellanies
The Woman in White.
The Moonstone.
Man and Wife.
Poor Miss Finch.
Miss or Mrs. ?
The New Magdalen.
The Frozen Deep.
The Two Destinies.

By WILKIE COLLINS—continued.
The Law and the Lady.
The Haunted Hotel.
The Fallen Leaves.
Jezebel's Daughter.
The Black Robe.
Heart and Science.
'I Say No.'
Little Novels
The Evil Genius.
The Legacy of Cain.
A Rogue's Life.
Blind Love.

By M. J. COLQUHOUN.
Every Inch a Soldier.

By E. H. COOPER.—Geoffory Hamilton

By V. C. COTES.—Two Girls on a Barge

By C. EGBERT CRADDOCK.
His Vanished Star.

By H. N. CRELLIN.
Romances of the Old Seraglio.

By MATT CRIM.
The Adventures of a Fair Rebel.

By S. R. CROCKETT and others.
Tales of Our Coast.

By B. M. CROKER.
Diana Barrington.
Proper Pride.
A Family Likeness.
Pretty Miss Neville.
A Bird of Passage.
'To Let.' | Mr. Jervis.
Village Tales.
The Real Lady Hi'da.
Married or Single ?
Two Masters.
In the Kingdom of Kerry
Interference.
A Third Person.
Beyond the Pale.

By W. CYPLES.—Hearts of Gold.

By ALPHONSE DAUDET.
The Evangelist ; or, Port Salvation.

By H. COLEMAN DAVIDSON.
Mr. Sadler's Daughters.

By ERASMUS DAWSON.
The Fountain of Youth.

By J. DE MILLE.—A Castle in Spain.

By J. LEITH DERWENT.
Our Lady of Tears. | Circe's Lovers.

By DICK DONOVAN.
Tracked to Doom.
Man from Manchester.
The Chronicles of Michael Danevitch.
The Records of Vincent Trill.
The Mystery of Jamaica.
Terrace.

By RICHARD DOWLING.
Old Corcoran's Money.

By A. CONAN DOYLE
The Firm of Girdlestone.

By S. JEANNETTE DUNCAN.
A Daughter of To-day. | Vernon's Aunt.

By A. EDWARDES.—A Plaster Saint.

By G. S. EDWARDS.—Snazelleparilla.

By G. MANVILLE FENN
Commodore Junk.
The New Mistress.
Witness to the Deed.
The Tiger Lily.
The White Virgin.
Black Blood.
Double Cunning.
A Bag of Diamonds, &c.
A Fluttered Dovecote.
King of the Castle
Master of Ceremonies.
Eve at the Wheel &c.
The Man with a Shadow
One Maid's Mischief
Story of Antony Grace.
This Man's Wife.
In Jeopardy.

By PERCY FITZGERALD.—Fatal Zero.

By R. E. FRANCILLON.
One by One.
A Dog and his Shadow.
A Real Queen.
Ropes of Sand.
Jack Doyle's Daughter.

By HAROLD FREDERIC.
Seth's Brother's Wife. | The Lawton Girl.

By PAUL GAULOT.—The Red Shirts.

By CHARLES GIBBON.
Robin Gray.
Loving a Dream.
Of High Degree.
The Golden Shaft.
The Braes of Yarrow.

THE PICCADILLY (3/6) NOVELS—*continued.*

By E. GLANVILLE.
The Lost Heiress. | The Golden Rock.
A Fair Colonist. | Tales from the Veld.
The Fossicker.

By E. J. GOODMAN.
The Fate of Herbert Wayne.

By Rev. S. BARING GOULD.
Red Spider. | Eve.

By CECIL GRIFFITH.
Corinthia Marazion.

By SYDNEY GRUNDY.
The Days of his Vanity.

By OWEN HALL.
The Track of a Storm. | Jetsam.

By COSMO HAMILTON.
The Glamour of the Impossible.

By THOMAS HARDY.
Under the Greenwood Tree.

By BRET HARTE.
A Waif of the Plains. | A Protégée of Jack
A Ward of the Golden | Hamlin's.
  Gate. [Springs. | Clarence.
A Sappho of Green | Barker's Luck.
Col. Starbottle's Client. | Devil's Ford. [celsior.'
Susy. | Sally Dows. | The Crusade of the 'Ex-
bell-Ringer of Angel's. | Three Partners.
Tales of Trail and Town.

By JULIAN HAWTHORNE.
Garth. | Dust. | Beatrix Randolph.
Ellice Quentin. | David Poindexter's Dis-
Sebastian Strome. | appearance.
Fortune's Fool. | Spectre of Camera.

By Sir A. HELPS.—Ivan de Biron.
By I. HENDERSON.—Agatha Page.
By G. A. HENTY.
Rujub the Juggler. | The Queen's Cup.
Dorothy's Double. |

By JOHN HILL. The Common Ancestor.
By TIGHE HOPKINS.
'Twixt Love and Duty. | Nugents of Carriconna.
For Freedom. | The Incomplete Adventurer.
Incomplete Adventurer.

By Mrs. HUNGERFORD.
Lady Verner's Flight. | Nora Creina.
The Red-House Mystery | An Anxious Moment.
The Three Graces. | April's Lady.
Professor's Experiment. | Peter's Wife.
A Point of Conscience. | Lovice.
The Coming of Chloe. |

By Mrs. ALFRED HUNT.
The Leaden Casket. | Self-Condemned.
That Other Person. | Mrs. Juliet.

By C. J. CUTCLIFFE HYNE.
Honour of Thieves.

By R. ASHE KING.
A Drawn Game.

By GEORGE LAMBERT.
The President of Boravia.

By EDMOND LEPELLETIER.
Madame Sans-Gene.

By ADAM LILBURN.
A Tragedy in Marble.

By HARRY LINDSAY.
Rhoda Roberts.

By HENRY W. LUCY.—Gideon Fleyce.
By E. LYNN LINTON.
Patricia Kemball. | The Atonement of Leam
Under which Lord? | Dundas.
'My Love!' | Ione. | The World Well Lost.
Paston Carew. | The One Too Many.
Sowing the Wind. | Dulcie Everton.
With a Silken Thread.

By JUSTIN McCARTHY.
A Fair Saxon. | Donna Quixote.
Linley Rochford. | Maid of Athens.
Dear Lady Disdain. | The Comet of a Season.
Camiola | The Dictator.
Waterdale Neighbours. | Red Diamonds.
My Enemy's Daughter. | The Riddle Ring.
Miss Misanthrope. | The Three Disgraces.

By JUSTIN H. McCARTHY.
A London Legend. | The Royal Christopher.

By GEORGE MACDONALD.
Heather and Snow. | Phantastes.

By PAUL & VICTOR MARGUERITTE
The Disaster

By L. T. MEADE.
A Soldier of Fortune. | The Voice of the
In an Iron Grip. | Charmer.
Dr. Rumsey's Patient. |

By LEONARD MERRICK.
This Stage of Fools. | Cynthia.

By BERTRAM MITFORD
The Gun-Runner. | The King's Assegai.
Luck of Gerard Ridgeley. | Rensh. Fanning's Quest.

By J. E. MUDDOCK.
Maid Marian and Robin Hood.
Basile the Jester. | Young Lochinvar.

By D. CHRISTIE MURRAY.
A Life's Atonement. | The Way of the World.
Joseph's Coat. | BobMartin's Little Girl.
Coals of Fire. | Time's Revenges.
Old Blazer's Hero. | A Wasted Crime.
Val Strange. | Hearts. | In Direst Peril.
A Model Father. | Mount Despair.
By the Gate of the Sea. | A Capful o' Nails
A Bit of Human Nature. | Tales in Prose & Verse.
First Person Singular. | A Race for Millions.
Cynic Fortune. | This Little World.

By MURRAY and HERMAN.
The Bishops' Bible. | Paul Jones's Alias.
One Traveller Returns. |

By HUME NISBET.
'Bail Up!'

By W. E. NORRIS.
Saint Ann's. | Billy Bellew.

By G. OHNET.
A Weird Gift.

By Mrs. OLIPHANT.
The Sorceress.

By OUIDA.
Held in Bondage. | In a Winter City.
Strathmore. | Chandos. | Friendship.
Under Two Flags. | Moths. | Ruffino.
Idalia. [Gage. | Pipistrello. | Ariadne.
Cecil Castlemaine's | A Village Commune.
Tricotrin. | Puck. | Bimbi. | Wanda.
Folle Farine. | Frescoes. | Othmar.
A Dog of Flanders. | In Maremma.
Pascarel. | Signa. | Syrlin. | Guilderoy.
Princess Napraxine. | Santa Barbara.
Two Wooden Shoes. | Two Offenders.

By MARGARET A. PAUL.
Gentle and Simple.

By JAMES PAYN.
Lost Sir Massingberd. | Under One Roof.
Less Black than We're | Glow-worm Tales
  Painted. | The Talk of the Town.
A Confidential Agent. | Holiday Tasks.
A Grape from a Thorn. | For Cash Only.
In Peril and Privation. | The Burnt Million.
The Mystery of Mir- | The Word and the Will.
By Proxy. [bridge. | Sunny Stories.
The Canon's Ward. | A Trying Patient.
Walter's Word. | A Modern Dick Whit-
High Spirits. | tington.

By WILL PAYNE.
Jerry the Dreamer.

By Mrs. CAMPBELL PRAED.
Outlaw and Lawmaker. | Mrs. Tregaskiss.
Christina Chard. | Nulma.

By E. C. PRICE.
Valentina. | Foreigners. | Mrs. Lancaster's Rival.

By RICHARD PRYCE.
Miss Maxwell's Affections.

By Mrs. J. H. RIDDELL.
Weird Stories.

By AMELIE RIVES.
Barbara Dering. | Meriel.

By F. W. ROBINSON.
The Hands of Justice. | Woman in the Dark.

By HERBERT RUSSELL.
True Blue.

Two-Shilling Novels—*continued.*

By Rev. S. BARING GOULD.
Red Spider. | Eve.

By HENRY GREVILLE.
A Noble Woman. | Nikanor.

By CECIL GRIFFITH.
Corinthia Marazion.

By SYDNEY GRUNDY.
The Days of his Vanity.

By JOHN HABBERTON.
Brueton's Bayou. | Country Luck.

By ANDREW HALLIDAY.
Every-day Papers.

By THOMAS HARDY.
Under the Greenwood Tree.

By JULIAN HAWTHORNE.
Garth. | Beatrix Randolph.
Ellice Quentin. | Love—or a Name.
Fortune's Fool. | David Poindexter's Dis-
Miss Cadogna. | appearance.
Sebastian Strome. | The Spectre of the
Dust. | Camera.

By Sir ARTHUR HELPS.
Ivan de Biron.

By G. A. HENTY.
Rujub the Juggler.

By HENRY HERMAN.
A Leading Lady.

By HEADON HILL.
Zambra the Detective.

By JOHN HILL.
Treason Felony.

By Mrs. CASHEL HOEY.
The Lover's Creed.

By Mrs. GEORGE HOOPER.
The House of Raby.

By Mrs. HUNGERFORD.
A Maiden all Forlorn. | Lady Verner's Flight.
In Durance Vile. | The Red-House Mystery
Marvel. | The Three Graces.
A Mental Struggle. | Unsatisfactory Lover.
A Modern Circe. | Lady Patty.
April's Lady. | Nora Creina.
Peter's Wife. | Professor's Experiment.

By Mrs. ALFRED HUNT.
Thornicroft's Model. | Self-Condemned.
That Other Person. | The Leaden Casket.

By WM. JAMESON.
My Dead Self.

By HARRIETT JAY.
The Dark Colleen. | Queen of Connaught.

By MARK KERSHAW.
Colonial Facts and Fictions.

By R. ASHE KING.
A Drawn Game. | Passion's Slave.
'The Wearing of the | Bell Barry.
Green.'

By EDMOND LEPELLETIER.
Madame Sans Gene.

By JOHN LEYS.
The Lindsays.

By E. LYNN LINTON.
Patricia Kemball. | The Atonement of Leam
The World Well Lost. | Dundas.
Under which Lord? | Rebel of the Family.
Paston Carew. | Sowing the Wind.
'My Love!' | The One Too Many.
Ione. | Dulcie Everton.
With a Silken Thread.

By HENRY W. LUCY.
Gideon Fleyce.

By JUSTIN McCARTHY.
Dear Lady Disdain. | Donna Quixote.
Waterdale Neighbours. | Maid of Athens.
My Enemy's Daughter | The Comet of a Season.
A Fair Saxon. | The Dictator.
Linley Rochford. | Red Diamonds.
Miss Misanthrope | The Riddle Ring.
Camiola.

By HUGH MACCOLL.
Mr. Stranger's Sealed Packet.

By GEORGE MACDONALD.
Heather and Snow.

By AGNES MACDONELL.
Quaker Cousins.

By KATHARINE S. MACQUOID.
The Evil Eye. | Lost Rose.

By W. H. MALLOCK.
A Romance of the Nine- | The New Republic.
teenth Century. |

By J. MASTERMAN.
Half-a-dozen Daughters.

By BRANDER MATTHEWS.
A Secret of the Sea.

By L. T. MEADE.
A Soldier of Fortune.

By LEONARD MERRICK.
The Man who was Good.

By JEAN MIDDLEMASS.
Touch and Go. | Mr. Dorillion.

By Mrs. MOLESWORTH.
Hathercourt Rectory.

By J. E. MUDDOCK.
Stories Weird and Won- | From the Bosom of the
derful. | Deep.
The Dead Man's Secret. |

By D. CHRISTIE MURRAY.
A Model Father. | A Bit of Human Nature
Joseph's Coat. | First Person Singular.
Coals of Fire. | Boh Martin's Little Girl
Val Strange. | Hearts. | Time's Revenges.
Old Blazer's Hero. | A Wasted Crime.
The Way of the World. | In Direst Peril.
Cynic Fortune. | Mount Despair.
A Life's Atonement. | A Capful o' Nails
By the Gate of the Sea. |

By MURRAY and HERMAN.
One Traveller Returns. | The Bishops' Bible.
Paul Jones's Alias. |

By HENRY MURRAY.
A Game of Bluff. | A Song of Sixpence.

By HUME NISBET.
'Bail Up!' | Dr. Bernard St. Vincent

By W. E. NORRIS.
Saint Ann's. | Billy Bellew

By ALICE O'HANLON.
The Unforeseen. | Chance? or Fate?

By GEORGES OHNET.
Dr. Rameau. | A Weird Gift.
A Last Love. |

By Mrs. OLIPHANT.
Whiteladies. | The Greatest Heiress in
The Primrose Path. | England.

By Mrs. ROBERT O'REILLY.
Phœbe's Fortunes.

By OUIDA.
Held in Bondage. | Two Lit. Wooden Shoes
Strathmore. | Moths.
Chandos. | Bimbi.
Idalia. | Pipistrello.
Under Two Flags. | A Village Commune.
Cecil Castlemaine's Gage | Wanda.
Tricotrin. | Othmar
Puck. | Frescoes.
Folle Farine. | In Maremma.
A Dog of Flanders. | Guilderoy.
Pascarel. | Ruffino.
Signa. | Syrlin.
Princess Napraxine. | Santa Barbara.
In a Winter City. | Two Offenders.
Ariadne. | Ouida's Wisdom, Wit
Friendship. | and Pathos.

By MARGARET AGNES PAUL.
Gentle and Simple.

By EDGAR A. POE.
The Mystery of Marie Roget.

By Mrs. CAMPBELL PRAED.
The Romance of a Station.
The Soul of Countess Adrian.
Outlaw and Lawmaker. | Mrs. Tregaskiss.
Christina Chard. |

TWO-SHILLING NOVELS—*continued.*

By E. C. PRICE.

Valentina.	Mrs. Lancaster's Rival.
The Foreigners.	Gerald.

By RICHARD PRYCE.

Miss Maxwell's Affections.

By JAMES PAYN.

Bentinck's Tutor.	The Talk of the Town.
Murphy's Master.	Holiday Tasks.
A County Family.	A Perfect Treasure.
At Her Mercy.	What He Cost Her.
Cecil's Tryst.	A Confidential Agent.
The Clyffards of Clyffe.	Glow-worm Tales.
The Foster Brothers.	The Burnt Million.
Found Dead.	Sunny Stories.
The Best of Husbands.	Lost Sir Massingberd.
Walter's Word.	A Woman's Vengeance.
Halves.	The Family Scapegrace.
Fallen Fortunes.	Gwendoline's Harvest.
Humorous Stories.	Like Father, Like Son.
£200 Reward.	Married Beneath Him.
A Marine Residence.	Not Wooed, but Won.
Mirk Abbey	Less Black than We're
By Proxy.	Painted.
Under One Roof.	Some Private Views.
High Spirits.	A Grape from a Thorn.
Carlyon's Year.	The Mystery of Mir-
From Exile.	bridge.
For Cash Only.	The Word and the Will.
Kit.	A Prince of the Blood.
The Canon's Ward.	A Trying Patient.

By CHARLES READE.

It is Never Too Late to Mend.	A Terrible Temptation.
Christie Johnstone.	Foul Play.
The Double Marriage.	The Wandering Heir.
Put Yourself in His Place	Hard Cash.
	Singleheart and Double-
Love Me Little, Love Me Long.	face.
	Good Stories of Man and
The Cloister and the Hearth.	other Animals.
	Peg Woffington.
The Course of True Love.	Griffith Gaunt.
	A Perilous Secret.
The Jilt.	A Simpleton.
The Autobiography of a Thief.	Readiana.
	A Woman-Hater.

By Mrs. J. H. RIDDELL.

Weird Stories.	The Uninhabited House.
Fairy Water.	The Mystery in Palace
Her Mother's Darling.	Gardens.
The Prince of Wales's	The Nun's Curse.
Garden Party.	Idle Tales.

By AMELIE RIVES.

Barbara Dering.

By F. W. ROBINSON.

Women are Strange.	The Woman in the Dark
The Hands of Justice.	

By JAMES RUNCIMAN.

Skippers and Shellbacks.	Schools and Scholars.
Grace Balmaign's Sweetheart.	

By W. CLARK RUSSELL.

Round the Galley Fire.	An Ocean Tragedy.
On the Fo'k'sle Head.	My Shipmate Louise.
In the Middle Watch.	Alone on Wide Wide Sea.
A Voyage to the Cape.	Good Ship 'Mohock.'
A Book for the Ham-	The Phantom Death.
mock.	Is He the Man?
The Mystery of the 'Ocean Star.'	Heart of Oak.
	The Convict Ship.
The Romance of Jenny Harlowe.	The Tale of the Ten.
	The Last Entry.

By DORA RUSSELL.

A Country Sweetheart.

By GEORGE AUGUSTUS SALA.

Gaslight and Daylight.

By GEORGE R. SIMS.

The Ring o' Bells.	Zeph.
Mary Jane's Memoirs.	Memoirs of a Landlady.
Mary Jane Married.	Scenes from the Show.
Tales of To-day.	The 10 Commandments.
Dramas of Life.	Dagonet Abroad.
Tinkletop's Crime.	Rogues and Vagabonds.
My Two Wives.	

By ARTHUR SKETCHLEY.

A Match in the Dark.

By HAWLEY SMART.

Without Love or Licence.	The Plunger.
Beatrice and Benedick.	Long Odds.
The Master of Rathkelly.	

By T. W. SPEIGHT.

The Mysteries of Heron Dyke.	Back to Life.
	The Loudwater Tragedy
The Golden Hoop.	Burgo's Romance.
Hoodwinked.	Quittance in Full.
By Devious Ways.	A Husband from the Sea

By ALAN ST. AUBYN.

A Fellow of Trinity.	Orchard Damerel.
The Junior Dean.	In the Face of the World
Master of St. Benedict's	The Tremlett Diamonds
To His Own Master.	

By R. A. STERNDALE.

The Afghan Knife.

By R. LOUIS STEVENSON.

New Arabian Nights.

By BERTHA THOMAS.

Cressida.	The Violin-Player.
Proud Maisie.	

By WALTER THORNBURY.

Tales for the Marines.	Old Stories Retold.

By T. ADOLPHUS TROLLOPE.

Diamond Cut Diamond.

By F. ELEANOR TROLLOPE.

Like Ships upon the Sea.	Anne Furness.
	Mabel's Progress.

By ANTHONY TROLLOPE.

Frau Frohmann.	The Land-Leaguers.
Marion Fay.	The American Senator
Kept in the Dark.	Mr. Scarborough's
John Caldigate.	Family.
The Way We Live Now.	Golden Lion of Granpere

By J. T. TROWBRIDGE.

Farnell's Folly.

By IVAN TURGENIEFF, &c.

Stories from Foreign Novelists.

By MARK TWAIN.

A Pleasure Trip on the Continent.	Life on the Mississippi
	The Prince and the
The Gilded Age.	Pauper.
Huckleberry Finn.	A Yankee at the Court
Mark Twain's Sketches.	of King Arthur.
Tom Sawyer.	The £1,000,000 Bank
A Tramp Abroad.	Note.
Stolen White Elephant.	

By C. C. FRASER-TYTLER.

Mistress Judith.

By SARAH TYTLER.

The Bride's Pass.	The Huguenot Family.
Buried Diamonds.	The Blackhall Ghosts.
St. Mungo's City.	What She Came Through
Lady Bell.	Beauty and the Beast.
Noblesse Oblige.	Citoyenne Jaqueline.
Disappeared.	

By ALLEN UPWARD.

The Queen against Owen.	Prince of Balkistan.
'God Save the Queen!'	

By AARON WATSON and LILLIAS WASSERMANN.

The Marquis of Carabas.

By WILLIAM WESTALL.

Trust-Money.

By Mrs. F. H. WILLIAMSON.

A Child Widow.

By J. S. WINTER.

Cavalry Life.	Regimental Legends.

By H. F. WOOD.

The Passenger from Scotland Yard.
The Englishman of the Rue Cain.

By CELIA PARKER WOOLLEY.

Rachel Armstrong; or, Love and Theology.

By EDMUND YATES.

The Forlorn Hope.	Castaway.
Land at Last.	

By I. ZANGWILL.

Ghetto Tragedies.